There's nothing
kid...

Christmas Marriages & Miracles

Three heartwarming romances from three favourite Mills & Boon authors!

Christmas Marriages & Miracles

LUCY GORDON
CAROLINE ANDERSON
ALISON ROBERTS

DID YOU PURCHASE THIS BOOK WITHOUT A COVER?
If you did, you should be aware it is **stolen property** as it was reported *unsold and destroyed* by a retailer. Neither the author nor the publisher has received any payment for this book.

All the characters in this book have no existence outside the imagination of the author, and have no relation whatsoever to anyone bearing the same name or names. They are not even distantly inspired by any individual known or unknown to the author, and all the incidents are pure invention.

All Rights Reserved including the right of reproduction in whole or in part in any form. This edition is published by arrangement with Harlequin Enterprises II B.V./S.à.r.l. The text of this publication or any part thereof may not be reproduced or transmitted in any form or by any means, electronic or mechanical, including photocopying, recording, storage in an information retrieval system, or otherwise, without the written permission of the publisher.

This book is sold subject to the condition that it shall not, by way of trade or otherwise, be lent, resold, hired out or otherwise circulated without the prior consent of the publisher in any form of binding or cover other than that in which it is published and without a similar condition including this condition being imposed on the subsequent purchaser.

® and ™ are trademarks owned and used by the trademark owner and/or its licensee. Trademarks marked with ® are registered with the United Kingdom Patent Office and/or the Office for Harmonisation in the Internal Market and in other countries.

First published in Great Britain 2011
by Mills & Boon, an imprint of Harlequin (UK) Limited,
Eton House, 18-24 Paradise Road, Richmond, Surrey TW9 1SR

CHRISTMAS MARRIAGES & MIRACLES
© by Harlequin Enterprises II B.V./S.à.r.l 2011

The Italian's Christmas Miracle, *A Mummy for Christmas* and *The Italian Surgeon's Christmas Miracle* were first published in Great Britain by Harlequin (UK) Limited in separate, single volumes.

The Italian's Christmas Miracle © Lucy Gordon 2008
A Mummy for Christmas © Caroline Anderson 2008
The Italian Surgeon's Christmas Miracle © Alison Roberts 2008

ISBN: 978 0 263 88449 4

05-1111

Printed and bound in Spain
by Blackprint CPI, Barcelona

THE ITALIAN'S CHRISTMAS MIRACLE

BY
LUCY GORDON

Dear Reader,

Being English by birth and Italian by marriage, I've experienced Christmas in both countries. Both celebrate the Nativity, but in Italy there is the extra festival of Epiphany, January 6th—the coming of the Three Kings, bearing gifts.

The great gift of Christmas is that with its promise of new beginnings it can heal wounds that had once seemed beyond hope.

Alysa approaches Christmas full of joy at the life that's opening up for her. Then a cruel act of betrayal snatches everything away, leaving a long, bitter road ahead.

She can only travel that road with the help of Drago, a man whose loss has been as terrible as her own. Two damaged people, they must stumble on together, supporting each other through pain that nobody else understands, hardly daring to believe the love growing between them, until they reach another Christmas with its promise of rebirth, new hope, and a life together.

May all your Christmases be happy.

Lucy Gordon

Lucy Gordon cut her writing teeth on magazine journalism, interviewing many of the world's most interesting men, including Warren Beatty, Richard Chamberlain, Sir Roger Moore, Sir Alec Guinness and Sir John Gielgud. She also camped out with lions in Africa, and had many other unusual experiences which have often provided the background for her books. She is married to a Venetian, whom she met while on holiday in Venice. They got engaged within two days. Two of her books have won the Romance Writers of America RITA® award, *Song of the Lorelei* in 1990, and *His Brother's Child* in 1998, in the Best Traditional Romance category.

You can visit her website at www.lucy-gordon.com

PROLOGUE

THE Christmas lights winked down from the tree, which was hung with tinsel. It was only a small tree, and made of plastic, because the modern apartment of a successful businesswoman had room for nothing larger.

Alysa had always loved her home, its elegance and costliness affirming her triumphant career. Now, for the first time, she sensed something missing. Placing her hand over her stomach, she thought, smiling, that she knew what that something was.

Not that this was a good place for a baby. James's home had more room, and when he knew he was to be a father he would want to finalise the marriage plans that had been vague until now. She would tell him tonight that she was pregnant.

There was one other thing to set out: a small nativity scene, showing Mary leaning protectively over the crib, her face glowing as she watched her child. Alysa had bought it on the way home as an expression of her joy.

Gently she laid it on a shelf, close to the tree so that the lights fell on it, illuminating the baby's face. He looked up at his mother, perhaps even smiling. Alysa tried to dismiss the thought as fanciful, but it returned, whispering of happiness to come.

Why didn't James hurry? He was an hour late, and she loved him so much, every moment in his company was precious. But he would be here soon—very soon.

For the hundredth time she checked that everything was perfect, including her appearance. For once she wore her long hair flowing freely. Usually it was pulled back and wrapped up in a chignon. She kept meaning to cut it short and adopt an austere style, suitable for her job as an accountant. But she'd always deferred the decision, possibly because she knew that her hair was her chief beauty.

She had never been pretty. Her face was attractive but, to her own critical eyes, her features were too strong for a woman.

'No feminine graces,' she'd often sighed. 'Too tall, too thin. No bosom to speak of.'

Her women friends were scandalised by this casual realism. 'What do you mean, too thin?' they'd chorused. 'You've got a figure most of us would die for. You could wear anything, just like a model.'

'That's what I said—too thin,' she'd responded, determinedly practical.

But then there was the hair—rich brown, with flashes of deep gold here and dark red there, growing abundantly, streaming over her shoulders and down to her waist, making her look like some mythical heroine.

James loved her hair, which she'd been wearing down when they'd first met.

'I couldn't take my eyes off it,' he'd told her afterwards. 'One look and I began scheming to get you to bed.'

'You mean you didn't fall in love with my upright character and solid virtue?' she'd teased.

'What do you think?'

How they had laughed together, and the laughter had ended, as it always did, in passion.

'I thought you looked like Minerva,' he'd said once. 'I've got a picture of her with flowing hair, although not as beautiful as yours.'

'But who was she?' asked Alysa, whose education had been practical rather than artistic.

'She was the ancient goddess of warriors, medicine, wisdom and poetry.'

It had become his special name for her, to be used only in the darkness.

He scowled when she dressed for work, taking up her hair and donning a severe suit.

'It's for my job,' she'd chided him fondly. 'I can't be Minerva for my clients, only for you.'

Once she'd had a couple of inches cut off, without telling him, and he'd been annoyed.

They had actually squabbled about it, she recalled now, smiling.

But tonight she'd taken care to look just as he liked—a slinky dress that took advantage of her slim figure, hair flowing down to her waist so that he could run his fingers through the cascade and bury his face in its perfumed softness. Then they would go to bed, and afterwards, as they lay in each other's arms, she would tell him her wonderful secret.

If only he would get here soon!

CHAPTER ONE

THE cold February sunlight glittered over the place where fifteen people had died in one terrible moment.

Far below, the crowd looked up to where the hanging chairs swung over the top of the waterfall. They were newly installed, replacing the ones that had broken suddenly, tossing the screaming occupants down, down to the churning water, to be smashed on the rocks.

That had been one year ago today, and the crowd of mourners was there to remember the loved ones they had lost. Out of respect for the foreign victims the service was held in both Italian and English.

'Let us remember them at their best—with pride. Let us rejoice in having known them...'

Then it was over. Some of the crowd drifted away, but others remained, still gazing up, trying to picture the tragedy.

Alysa stayed longer than the rest because she couldn't think what to do or where to go. Something inside her, that had been frozen for a long time, held her prisoner.

A young journalist approached her, microphone extended, speaking Italian.

'*Sono Inglese,*' she said quickly. '*Non parle Italiano.*'

He looked astonished at someone who could deny speaking Italian in such excellent Italian, and she added, 'Those are all the words I know.'

He switched to English.

'Can I ask why you are here? Did you lose someone?'

For a wild moment she wanted to cry out, 'I came here to mourn the man I loved, but who betrayed me, abandoned me and our unborn child, a child he never even knew about, then died with his lover. She had a husband and child, but she deserted them as he deserted me. And I don't know why I came here except that I couldn't stay away'.

But she mustn't say any of that. For a year she'd allowed nobody into her private grief, hiding behind steel doors that were bolted and barred against the world, lest anyone suspect not only her desolation but also her terrible fear that, if she let go, she might never regain control over the torrents of grief and anger.

Let us rejoice in having known them...

'No, I didn't lose anyone,' she said. 'I'm just curious.'

He was a nice lad. He gave a rueful sigh.

'So you can't point anyone out to me? Nobody wants to talk, and the only one I recognise is Drago di Luca.'

She jumped at the name. 'Is he here?'

'He's the man over there, scowling.'

She saw where he pointed. Her first impression of Drago di Luca was of darkness. His hair was dark, and so were his eyes, which mysteriously managed to be piercing at the same time. Yet it wasn't just a matter of appearance. This darkness was there inside him—in his mind, his heart, even perhaps his soul. Alysa shivered slightly.

His face seemed to be made from angles, with no roundness or softening anywhere. The nose was sharp and distinctive, the mouth and jaw firm, the eyes ferocious, even at this distance. The whole effect was one of hauteur, as though he defied anyone to dare speak to him.

'You wouldn't want to get on his wrong side, would you?' the young man said. 'Mind you, he's got a lot to scowl about. His wife died here, and the grapevine says she'd left him for another man.'

It took a moment before Alysa could answer. 'The grapevine? Doesn't anyone know for sure?'

'She was a lawyer, and the official story is that she was on a trip to see clients. If anyone dares to suggest otherwise di Luca comes down on them like a ton of his own bricks. He's a builder, you see, takes on big projects—new stuff, restoring ancient buildings, that sort of thing.'

She looked again. Di Luca was tall and powerfully built, with broad shoulders and large hands, as though he personally constructed his projects.

'I can see that people could find him scary,' she mused.

'I'll say. He's a big man in Florence. Someone suggested that he stand for the council and he laughed. He has all the influence over the council that he needs without spending time in meetings. They say he has the ear of every important person in town, and he pulls strings whenever it suits him. I tried to speak to him earlier and I thought he was going to kill me.'

She took a last look at Drago, and was disconcerted when he seemed to be looking back at her. Impossible, surely? But for a moment the surroundings faded to silence and all she could hear was a call that he seemed to be sending to her.

Stop being fanciful, she told herself.

'I must be going,' she told the journalist.

She drifted away, managing to keep Drago di Luca in her sights. She knew his face from a hundred obsessive searches of the internet. James had accidentally let slip that his new lover was called Carlotta. Then he'd clammed up.

Three weeks later the tragedy at the Pinosa Falls, near Florence, in Italy, had hit the headlines and she had learned from a newspaper that he was dead. Going through the list of names, she'd discovered Signora Carlotta di Luca, a young lawyer of great promise. Searching the internet, Alysa had discovered several articles about her, and some photographs.

They'd revealed a dark-haired, vivacious woman—not beautiful, but with a special quality. One picture had showed Carlotta with her husband and child, a little girl about four years old, who bore a strong resemblance to her mother. The man with them had been in his late thirties with a face that Alysa hadn't been able to read—strong, and blank of emotion.

Was he also a brutal husband whose unkindness had driven his wife into the arms of another man, and so to her death? Seeing him today, she could believe it.

The internet had also contained depictions of the accident that no newspaper would have dared to publish—intimate, shocking pictures taken by mercenary ghouls, showing smashed bodies in terrifying detail. One had showed Carlotta and James, lying dead on the ground. James's face had been covered with blood, but Alysa had recognised his jacket.

They'd still been in the chair, leaving no doubt that they had travelled together. She'd just been able to make out that in the last moments before death he and Carlotta had thrown themselves into each other's arms.

Now it was over, she told herself. Ended. Finished. *Forget it.*

One night, as she'd stared at the computer screen, she'd felt shafts of pain go through her like knives. What had happened then had been too fast for her even to call for help. Stumbling to the bathroom, she'd collapsed on the floor and fainted. When she'd come round, she had lost James's child.

Afterwards she'd been glad that she hadn't confided in

anybody. Now she could weep in privacy. But the tears hadn't come. Night after night she'd lain alone in the darkness, staring into nothing, while her heart had turned to stone.

After giving the matter some rational thought she'd decided it was for the best. If she couldn't cry now she would never cry again, which was surely useful. When you loved nothing, feared nothing, cared for nothing, what was there to worry about?

With that settled, she'd embarked on the transformation of her life. A shopping trip had provided her with a collection of trouser suits, all stunningly fashionable and costly. Next she'd lopped off the extravagant tresses that had marked her earlier existence. The resulting boyish crop was elegant, but she cared little. What counted was that it marked the end of her old life and the start of her new one.

Or just the end of life?

Her face too had changed, but in ways she couldn't see. It was tense, strained, so that every feature was sharpened in a way that would have been forbidding if her large eyes had not softened her appearance. They were now her main claim to beauty, and more than one man had admired them, only to find them looking right through him.

She'd thrown herself into her career with renewed fervour. Her bosses were impressed. The word 'partnership' began to be whispered. A year after James's death, she should have completely moved on. And yet...

She wandered slowly back to the water and looked up again to the place where James and Carlotta had swung up high, moments before the cable had snapped.

'Why am I here?' she asked him. 'Why haven't I managed to forget you yet?'

Because he was a ghost who haunted her even now, and in this place she'd planned to exorcise him. Foolish hope.

'Leave me alone,' she whispered desperately, closing her eyes. 'In the name of pity, leave me alone.'

Silence. He wasn't there, but even his absence had a mocking quality.

Beneath a huge tree a stone had been erected, bearing the names of the dead, with James near the bottom. She knelt and touched his name, feeling the stone cold beneath her fingers. This was as close to him as she would ever be again.

'Sapevi che lui?'

The voice, coming from behind her, made her turn and find Drago di Luca towering over her, glowering. He looked immense, blotting out the sun, forcing her to see only him.

'Sono Inglese,' she said.

'I asked if you knew the man whose name you touch.'

'Yes,' she said defiantly. 'I knew him.'

'Well?' He rapped the word out.

'Yes, well. Very well. Is that any business of yours?'

'Everything concerning that man is my business.'

She rose to face him. 'Because he ran off with your wife?'

She heard his sharp intake of breath and knew that he would have controlled it if he could. His eyes were full of murder. Much like her own, she suspected.

'If you know that—' he said slowly.

'James Franklin was my boyfriend. He left me for a woman called Carlotta.'

'What else did he tell you about her?'

'Nothing. He let her name slip, then refused to say any more. But when this happened—' She shrugged.

'Yes,' he said heavily. 'Then every detail came out for the entertainment of the world.'

The crowd jostled her slightly and she moved away. At once he took her arm, leading her in the direction he chose, as though in no doubt of her compliance.

'Are you still in love with him?' he demanded sharply.

Strangely the question didn't offend her as it would have done from anyone else. Their plight was the same.

'I don't know,' she said simply. 'How can I be? By now it should be all behind me, and yet—somehow it isn't.'

He nodded, and the sight gave her an almost eerie feeling, as though she and this stranger were linked by a total understanding that reduced everything else to irrelevance.

'Is that why you came?' she asked.

'Partly. I also came for my daughter's sake.'

He indicated the child standing a little way off with an elderly woman who was leaning down, talking to her. It was the same child who'd been in the picture, a year older.

As Alysa watched, the two moved across to where the flowers lay, so that the little girl could lay down her posy in tribute. Looking up, she saw her father, and she smiled and began to run towards him, crying, 'Poppa!' At once he reached down to pick her up.

Alysa closed her eyes and turned slightly. When she opened her eyes again the child would be out of her sight line. Something was happening inside her, and when it had finished she would be all right. It was a technique she'd perfected months ago, based on computer systems.

It started with 'power up' when she got out of bed, then a quick run-through of necessary programs and she was ready to start the day. A liberal use of the 'delete' button helped to keep things straight in her head, and if something threatened her with unwanted emotion she hit the 'standby' button. As a last resort there was always total shut-down and reboot, but that meant walking away to be completely alone, which could be inconvenient.

Luckily, standby was enough this time, and after a moment she was able to turn back and smile in a way that was almost natural. She could do this as long as she aimed her gaze slightly to the right, so that she wasn't looking directly at the child.

Drago was absorbed in the little girl, whom he was holding up in his arms. Alysa marvelled at how his face softened as he murmured to his daughter, words she could not catch.

The woman spoke in Italian. Alysa picked up *'introdurre'*, and guessed it meant 'introduction'.

'I am Signorina Alysa Dennis,' she said.

The older woman nodded and switched to English.

'I am Signora Fantoni, and this is my granddaughter, Tina.'

Tina had been watching Alysa over her father's shoulder, her eyes bright. Now Drago set her down and she immediately turned to Alysa, holding out her hand, speaking English slowly and carefully.

'How do you do, *signorina*?'

'How do you do?' Alysa returned.

'We came here because of my mother,' the child said, like a wise little old woman. 'Did you know someone who died?'

Beside her, Alysa heard Drago give a sharp intake of breath, and her heightened sensitivity told her everything.

'Yes, I did,' she said.

Incredibly she felt a little hand creep into hers, comforting her.

'Was it someone you loved very much?' Tina asked softly.

'Yes, but—forgive me if I don't tell you any more. I can't, you see.'

Without looking at Drago, she sensed him relax. He'd been afraid of what she might say in front of his little girl.

Tina nodded to show that she understood, and her hand tightened on Alysa's.

'It's time to go home,' Drago said.

'Yes, I'll be leaving too,' Alysa agreed.

'*No!*' Drago rapped out the word so sharply that they stared at him. 'I mean,' he amended quickly, 'I would like you to join us tonight, for supper.'

His mother-in-law frowned. 'Surely a family occasion—'

'We all belong to the same family of mourners,' Drago said. '*Signorina*, you will dine with us. I won't take no for an answer.'

He meant it, she could tell.

Drago stroked his daughter's hair. 'Go ahead to the car with your grandmother.'

Signora Fantoni glared, silently informing him of her disapproval, but he ignored her and she was forced to yield, taking Tina's hand and turning away.

'Poppa,' Tina said, suddenly fearful. 'You will come, won't you?'

'I promise,' he said gently.

Relieved, she trotted away with her grandmother.

'Since her mother died she's sometimes nervous in case I vanish too,' he said heavily.

'Poor little mite. How does she bear it?'

'With great pain. She adored her mother. Thank you with all my heart for guarding your words. I should have warned you, but she came to us so suddenly there was no time.'

'Of course I was careful. I guessed you hadn't told her very much.'

'Nothing. She has no idea that Carlotta had left us. She thinks her mamma had to go away to visit clients, and was on her way home when she stopped off at the waterfall. If she hadn't died, she would have been home next day. That's what Tina believes, and what I want her to believe, at least until she's older.'

'Many mothers would have taken their child with them,' Alysa mused.

'Yes, but she abandoned hers, and that's what I don't want

Tina to know. Even my mo[...]
thinks Carlotta was on a bus[...]
Why should I hurt her with the [...]

'No reason, so it's better if I d[...]

'Not at all. I trust you. You've al[...]
so. You understood everything at onc[...]

But suddenly Alysa's alarm bells w[...]
was dangerous to her precarious peace. [...] take
her consent for granted? She should run a[...]st, take the
next plane back to England and safety.

'Look, I'm sorry,' she said. 'But I never agreed to this. I have to go home.'

'Not before we've talked,' he said firmly.

Her anger rose.

'Don't try to give me orders,' she flashed. 'We've only just met, and you think you can dictate to me? Well, you can't. I'm going.'

She tried to turn away but he gripped her arm.

'How dare you?' she snapped. 'Let me go at once.'

He gave no sign of obeying her demand.

'Only just met,' he scoffed. 'You know better than that.'

She did, and it was like a blow to the heart. They had known each other only a few minutes, yet their shared knowledge gave them a painful intimacy, isolating them together, facing the whole world on the far side of a glass barrier.

'When you saw me across the water,' he grated, 'you knew who I was, didn't you?'

'Yes.'

'How?'

'I researched your wife on the internet, and you were part of what I found. Somehow I just had to find out about the woman James left me for.'

'Yes, you *had* to find out. I felt the same, but for me there

I knew nothing about the man she went away with, not his name, and that led nowhere. You've been able to answer some of your questions, but can you begin to imagine what it's like for me, never to be able to find a single answer?

'In there—' he stabbed his own forehead '—there's a black hole that I've lived with for a year. It's been like standing at the entrance to the pit of hell, but I can't see what's there.'

'Do you think I don't know what that's like?'

'No, you *don't* know what it's like,' he raged. 'Because the torment springs from ignorance, and you've managed to deal with your ignorance. But I've lived with mine for a year and it's driving me crazy.' He shuddered then seemed to control himself by force. 'You're the one person who can free me from that horror, and if you imagine that I'm going to let you go without—without—'

It was harsh, almost bullying, but beneath the surface she could feel the desperate anguish that possessed him, and her anger died. So he was ill-mannered—so what? When a man saw his last hope fading, he would do anything to prevent it.

Slowly his hold on her arm was released. 'Please,' he said. *'Please!* You and I must talk. You know that, don't you? You know that we *must*?'

She'd fought his bullying, but his plea softened her.

'Yes,' she said slowly. 'We must.'

Why should she flee? There was no safety anywhere, and in her heart she knew that this was why she had come here— to meet this man, and learn from him all the things she didn't really want to know.

'Come on, then.'

'Only if you let me go. I've said I'll come with you, and I'll keep my word, but if you continue to try to push me the deal's off.'

Reluctantly he released her, but he watched closely, as

though ready to pounce if she made a wrong move. His nervous tension reached her as nothing else could have, softening her anger. Wasn't his state as desperate as her own?

His limousine was waiting for them, chauffeur in the driving seat. But Tina and her grandmother were standing outside, watching for his return, the little girl bouncing as soon as she saw him.

'I suggest you sit in the front,' Drago told the woman, and she did as he wanted, leaving him to open the rear door for Alysa and join her with Tina.

'The drive will take about an hour,' Drago said. 'We live just outside Florence. Where are you staying?'

She named a hotel in the centre of town, and he nodded. 'I know it. I'll drive you back there later tonight.'

She spent most of the journey looking out of the window as the land flattened out and Florence came into view. Once she glanced at Drago, but he didn't see her. All his attention was for the little girl nestling contentedly against him, as though he was all her world. Which was true, Alysa thought. She wondered how he coped with the child's heartbreaking resemblance to her dead mother.

At that moment Tina opened her eyes and smiled up at her father. His answering smile made Alysa look away. She had no right to see that unguarded look. It was for his child alone.

But it was the little girl's adoring face that lingered in her mind, and instinctively she laid a hand over her stomach, thinking of what might have been.

Now they were driving through the city and out again, taking a country road leading to a village, then turning into a lane lined with poplar trees. After half a mile the house came into view, a huge, gracious three-storeyed villa stretching wide, surrounded by elegant grounds.

She knew little of Italian architecture, but even so she could tell that the building was several-hundred years old and in fine condition, as though Drago, the builder and restorer, had lavished his best gifts on his home.

The entrance to the house lay through an arched corridor where the walls were inlaid with mosaics, and the ceiling adorned with paintings. At first sight it was so impressive as to be almost forbidding, but as they went deeper inside the atmosphere became more homely, until finally they came to a large drawing-room where Alysa gasped.

Everywhere she saw Carlotta's face. On one table stood a huge picture of her alone, while on the next table another picture showed her with Tina in her arms. The next one showed mother, father and child together. Various other pictures were dotted around the room, plus souvenirs, as Tina eagerly explained to her.

'That was Mamma's medal for winning a race at school,' she said.

'My wife was a fast runner,' Drago explained. 'We always used to say that she could have been an athlete if she hadn't preferred to be a lawyer.'

'She could run faster than anyone, couldn't she, Poppa?'

Alysa saw Drago's suddenly tense face, and realised how cruelly double-edged this remark would seem to him. But he gave his child a broad smile, saying, 'That's true. Mamma was better at everything,' he said with a fair pretence of heartiness. 'Now, we must entertain our guest.'

Tina set herself to do this, the perfect little hostess. If she hadn't been functioning on automatic, Alysa knew she would have found her enchanting, for Tina was intelligent and gentle. When supper was served she conducted her guest to the table, and in her honour she spoke English, of which she had a good grasp.

'How do you speak my language so well?' Alysa asked, for something to say.

'Mamma taught me. She was bi—bi—'

'Bilingual,' Drago supplied. 'Some of her clients were English, as are some of mine. We're all bilingual in this family. Tina learned both languages side by side.'

'Do you speak Italian?' Tina asked her.

'Not really,' Alysa said, concentrating on her food so that she didn't have to meet the innocent eyes that were turned on her. 'I learned a little when I was researching someone on the internet.'

'An Italian someone?'

'Er—yes.'

'Was that someone there today?'

'No.'

'Are you going to see them tomorrow?'

Her hand tightened on her fork. 'No, I'm not.'

'Will you—?'

'Tina,' Drago broke in gently. 'Don't be nosey. It isn't polite.'

'Sorry,' Tina said with an air of meekness that didn't fool Alysa. Even hidden away inside herself as she was, Alysa could see the enchanting curiosity in the little girl's eyes, and understood why Drago was determined to protect her at any cost to himself.

That's how I would feel, she thought, *if I had a—* She blanked the rest out, and fixed her attention on drinking her coffee.

CHAPTER TWO

For the rest of the meal Alysa forced herself to act the part of the ideal guest, assuring herself that it was no different from concentrating on a client. You just had to focus, something she was good at.

She became sharply aware of tensions at the table, especially between Drago and his mother-in-law, whom he always addressed as 'Elena'. For her part she looked at him as little as possible, and talked determinedly about Carlotta, who had, apparently, been a perfect daughter, mother and wife. Drago had spoken truly when he'd said his mother-in-law had no idea of the truth—or, if she had, she'd rejected it in favour of a more bearable explanation.

'My daughter's clients had no consideration, Signorina Dennis,' she proclaimed. 'If they had not insisted on her travelling to see them, instead of coming to her as they ought to have done, then she would have been alive now.'

'Let's leave that,' Drago interrupted quickly. 'I would rather Tina forgot those thoughts tonight.'

'How can she forget them after where we have been today? And tomorrow we go to the cemetery...'

Alysa saw Tina's lips press together, as though she were trying not to cry. She put out her hand and felt it instantly enclosed in a tiny one. The little girl gave her a shaky smile, which Alysa returned—equally shakily, she suspected.

This was proving harder than she had expected, and the most difficult part was still to come.

When supper was over Elena said, 'You're looking sleepy, little one, and we have another big day tomorrow. Time for bed.'

She held out her hand and Tina took it obediently, but she turned to her father to say, 'Will you come up and kiss me goodnight, Poppa?'

'Not tonight,' her grandmother said at once. 'Your father is busy.'

'I'll come up with you now,' Drago said at once.

'There's no need,' the woman assured him loftily. 'I can take care of her, and you should attend to your guest.'

'I'll be perfectly all right here for a while,' Alysa said. 'You go with Tina.'

Drago threw her a look of gratitude, and followed the others out.

While he was gone Alysa looked around the room, going from one photograph to another, seeing Carlotta in every mood. One picture showed her with a dazzling smile, and Alysa lifted it, wondering if this was the smile James had seen and adored. Did her husband still look on this picture with love?

She heard a step, and the next moment he was in the room, his mouth twisting as he saw what she was holding.

'Let's go into my study,' he said harshly. 'Where I don't have to look at her.'

His study was a total contrast—neat, austere, functional, with not a picture in sight. After the room they had just left, it was like walking from summer into winter, a feeling Alysa recognised.

The modern steel desk held several machines, one of which was a computer, and others which were unknown to her, but she was sure they were the latest in technology.

He poured them both a glass of wine and waved her to a chair, but then said nothing. She could sense his unease.

'I'm sorry you were kept waiting,' he said at last.

'You were right to go. I get the feeling that Tina's grandmother is a little possessive about her.'

'More than a little,' he said, grimacing. 'I can't blame her. She's old and lonely. Her other daughter lives in Rome, with her husband and children, and she doesn't see them very often. Carlotta was her favourite, and her death hit Elena very hard. I suspect that she'd like to move in here, but she can't, because her husband is an invalid and needs her at home. So she makes up for it by descending on us whenever she can.'

'How would you feel about her moving in?'

'Appalled. I pity her, but I can't get on with her. She keeps trying to give my housekeeper instructions that contradict mine. Ah, well, she'll ease up after a while.'

'Will she? Are you sure?'

He shot her a sharp look. 'What do you mean by that?'

'I mean the way she tried to stop you going upstairs to kiss Tina goodnight. Tina needs *you*, and Elena wanted to keep you away. Are you sure she isn't trying to make a takeover bid?'

'You mean—?'

'Might she not try to take her away from you—for good?'

He stared. 'Surely not? Even Elena wouldn't—' He broke off, evidently shocked. 'My God!'

'Maybe I'm being overly suspicious,' Alysa said. 'But during supper I noticed several times, when you spoke to Tina, Elena rushed to answer on her behalf. But Tina doesn't need anyone to speak for her. She's a very bright little girl.'

'Yes, she is, isn't she?' he said, gratified. 'I noticed Elena's interruptions too, but I guess I didn't read enough into them.' He grimaced. 'Now I think of it, Elena keeps telling me that a child needs a woman's care. It just seemed a general remark, but maybe…'

He threw himself into a chair, frowning.

'You saw it and I didn't. Thank you.'

'Don't let her take Tina away from you.'

'Not in a million years. But it's hard for me to fight her when she's so subtle. I manage well enough with everyone else, but with her the words won't come. I'm so conscious that she's Tina's grandmother—plus the fact that she's never liked me.'

'Why?'

'I'm not good enough,' he said wryly. 'Her family have some vaguely aristocratic connections, and she always wanted Carlotta to marry a title. My father owned a builder's yard—a very prosperous one, but he was definitely a working man. So was I. So am I, still.'

'But your name—di Luca—isn't that aristocratic?'

'Not a bit. It just means "son of Luca". It was started by my great-grandfather, who seems to have thought it would take him up in the world. It didn't, of course. They say his neighbours roared with laughter. What took us up in the world was my father working night and day to build the business into a success, until he ended in an early grave.

'I took over and built it up even more, until it was making money fast, but in Elena's eyes I was still a jumped-up nobody, aspiring to a woman who was socially far above him.'

'It sounds pure nineteenth-century.'

'True. It comes from another age, but so does Elena. She actually found a man with a title and tried to get Carlotta to marry him. When that didn't work, she told me that Carlotta was engaged to the other man. I didn't believe her and told her so. She was furious.'

'So you really had to fight for Carlotta?'

'There was never any doubt about the outcome. As soon as I saw her, I knew she was mine.'

'Was', not 'would be', Alysa noted.

'How did you meet?' she asked.

'In a courtroom. She'd just qualified as a lawyer and it was her first case. I was a witness, and when she questioned me I kept "misunderstanding" the questions, so that I could keep her there as long as possible. Afterwards I waited for her outside. She was expecting me. We both knew.'

'Love at first sight?'

'Yes. It knocked me sideways. She was beautiful, funny, glowing—everything I wanted but hadn't *known* that I wanted. There had been women before, but they meant nothing beside her. I knew that at once. She knew as well. So when Elena opposed us it just drove us into an elopement.'

'Good for you!'

'Elena has never really forgiven me. It was actually Carlotta's idea, but she won't believe that. She never really understood her own daughter—how adventurous Carlotta was, how determined to do things her own way—'

He stopped. He'd gone suddenly pale.

'How did you manage the elopement?' Alysa asked, to break the silence.

'I'd bought a little villa in the mountains. We escaped there, married in the local church and spent two weeks without seeing another soul. Then we went home and told Elena we were married.'

'Hadn't she suspected anything?'

'She'd thought Carlotta was on a legal course. To stop her

getting suspicious, Carlotta called her every night, using her mobile phone, and talked for a long time.'

So Carlotta had been clever at deception, Alysa thought. She hadn't only been able to think up a lie, she'd been able to elaborate it night after night, a feat which had taken some concentration. The first hints had been there years ago. In his happiness Drago hadn't understood. She wondered if he understood now.

He'd turned his back on her to stare out of the window into the darkness.

Images were beginning to flicker through Alysa's brain. She could see the honeymooners, gloriously isolated in their mountain retreat. There was Drago as he must have been then: younger, shining with love, missing all the danger signals.

Suddenly he turned back and made a swift movement to his desk, unlocking one of the drawers and hauling out a large book, which he thrust almost violently towards her. Then he resumed his stance at the window.

It was a photo album, filled with large coloured pictures, showing a wedding at a tiny church. There was the young bride and groom, emerging from the porch hand in hand, laughing with joy because they had secured their happiness for ever.

Carlotta was dazzling. Alysa could easily believe that Drago had fallen for her in the first moment. And James? Had he too been lost in the first moment?

She closed the book and clasped it to her, arms crossed, rocking back and forth, trying to quell the storm within. She'd coped with this—defeated it, survived it. There was no way she would let it beat her now.

She felt Drago's hands on her shoulders.

'I'm sorry,' he said heavily. 'I shouldn't have done that.'

'Why not?' she said, raising her head. 'I'm over it all now.'

'You don't get over it,' he said softly. She turned away, but he shook her gently. 'Look at me.'

Reluctantly she did so, and he brushed his fingertips over her cheeks.

'It was thoughtless of me to show you this and make you cry.'

'I'm not crying,' she said firmly. 'I never cry.'

'You say that as if you were proud of it.'

'Why not? I'm getting on with my life, not living in the past. It's different for you because you have Tina, and the home you shared with your wife. You can't escape the past, but I can. And I have.'

He moved away from her.

'Maybe you have,' he agreed. 'But are you sure you took the best route out of it?'

'What the devil do you mean?'

'"Devil" is right,' he said with grim humour. 'I think it must have been the devil who told you to survive by pretending that you weren't a woman at all.'

'What?'

'You crop your hair close, dress like a man—'

She sprang to her feet and confronted him.

'And you call Elena nineteenth-century! You may not have heard of it, but women have been wearing trousers for years.'

'Sure, but you're not trying to assert your independence, you're trying to turn yourself into a neutered creature without a woman's heart or a woman's feelings.'

'How dare you?' She began to pace the room, back and forth, clenching her fists.

'Maybe it's the only way you can cope,' Drago said. 'We all have to find our own way. But have you ever wondered if you're damaging yourself inside?'

'You couldn't be more wrong. I cope by self-control,

because that's what works for me. Without it I might have cracked up, and I wouldn't let that happen. So I don't cry. So what? Do *you* cry?'

'Not as much as I used to,' he said quietly.

The answer stopped her in her tracks. It was the last thing she'd expected him to say.

'The emotions and urges are there for men as well as women,' he added.

'Maybe you can afford to give in to them,' she snapped. 'I can't. This is how I manage, and it works fine. I'm over it, it's finished, past, done with.'

'Do you know how often you say that?' he demanded, becoming angry in his turn. 'Just a little too often.'

'Meaning?'

'Meaning that I think you're trying to convince yourself— say it enough and you might start to believe it.'

'I say it because it's true.'

'Then what were you doing at the waterfall today? Don't try to fool me as you fool yourself. If it was really finished, you'd never have come here.'

'All right, I wanted to tie up a few loose ends. Maybe I needed to find out the last details, just to close the book finally. It troubles me a little, but it doesn't dominate me, and it hasn't destroyed me *because I won't let it.*'

But she heard the shrill edge to her own voice, and knew that she was merely confirming his suspicion. He was actually regarding her with pity, and that was intolerable.

'Stop pacing like that,' he said, taking hold of her with surprisingly gentle hands. 'You'll fall over something and hurt yourself.'

She stood, breathing hard, trying to regain her self-control. She wanted to push him away, but the strength seemed to have drained out of her. Besides, there was something comforting about the hands that held her: big, powerful hands that could lift a stone or console a child.

'Sit down,' he said quietly, urging her back to the chair. 'You're shaking.'

After a few deep breaths she said, 'Aren't we forgetting why I'm here? You wanted me to fill in the gaps in your knowledge, and I'll do it, but my feelings are none of your business. Off-limits. Do you understand?'

He nodded. 'Of course.' He managed a faint smile. 'I told you that Elena thinks I'm a mannerless oaf, without subtlety or finesse, going through life like a steamroller. I dare say by now you agree with her.'

She shrugged. 'Not really. You said yourself, we all find our own way of coping. Yours is different to mine, but to hell with me! To hell with the rest of the world. If it works for you…'

'My way no more works for me than yours works for you,' he said quietly. 'But with your help I might find a little peace of mind. I'm afraid my manners deserted me earlier today.'

'You're referring to the way you kidnapped me?'

'I wouldn't exactly say— Yes, I suppose I did. I apologise.'

'Now that I'm here,' she said wryly.

'Yes, it's easy to apologise when I've got my own way,' he agreed with a touch of ruefulness. 'That's how I am. Too late to change now. And if you can tell me anything…'

'Are you sure you want to know? Learning the details doesn't make it any easier. If anything it hurts more.'

He nodded as if he'd already thought of this.

'Even so, I've got to pursue it,' he said. 'You of all people should understand that.'

'You really know nothing about James?'

'Carlotta rented a small apartment in Florence, but it was in her name with no mention of him on the paperwork. I went over there and found enough to tell me that her lover was called James Franklin, but that was all.'

'No other address?'

'One in London, in Dalkirk Street, but he'd left it shortly before.'

'Yes, that was where he lived when I knew him. Did you discover when the Florence apartment was rented?'

'September.'

'So soon after they met,' she murmured.

'That was my thought too. Their affair must have started almost at once, and the first thing she did was hunt for a love nest. I found it looking oddly bare—very little personal stuff, almost like a hotel room. I suppose they spent all their time in bed.'

'Yes,' she agreed huskily. 'I suppose so. But surely he must have brought some things with him from England?'

'It's a very tiny apartment. They were probably looking for something larger.'

'And his things would be stored in England until he was ready to send for them,' Alysa said. 'Only he never had the chance. I wonder what became of them?' She gave a sigh. 'Oh well!'

'I couldn't find anything on the internet about him. What did he do for a living?'

'Nothing for the last few months. He used to work in a big city institution—that's how we met. I'm an accountant and they hired me. He hated the job—being regimented, he called it. Then he came into some money and he said he was going to fulfil his real ambition to be a photographer. He left the job, bought lots of expensive equipment and started taking pictures everywhere, including several trips abroad. He asked me to go with him, and I promised I would when I could get some time off.

'But that never seemed to happen. I should have gone with him to Florence, but at the last minute I couldn't get away. I had several new clients.'

'And they mattered more than your lover?' Drago asked curiously.

'That's what he said. He said I couldn't even spare him a few days. But I'd worked so hard to get where I was—I knew he didn't really understand, but I never imagined— I thought James and I were rock-solid, you see.'

He didn't reply, and his very silence had a tactful quality that was painful.

'I should have gone with him,' she said at last. 'Maybe no love is as solid as that. So he came to Florence without me, and that's probably when he met Carlotta.'

The picture show had started again in her head, and she watched James's return to England, herself meeting him at the airport although he'd told her there was no need.

Now she noticed things she'd missed at the time: the slight impatience in his face when he saw her, showing that he really hadn't wanted her there. Nor had he been pleased when she accompanied him to his apartment, although he'd cloaked his reluctance in concern for her.

'Shouldn't you be at work? They won't like it if you take too much time off.'

Laughing, she'd brushed this aside.

'I told them I wasn't going back today. When we get home, I'm going to cook you supper, and then... And then, anything you want, my darling.'

'So today your time's all mine?' he'd asked.

Had she been insane to have missed the note of irony?

'When we met at the airport he wasn't pleased to see me,' she murmured now, to Drago. 'Of course he wasn't. He'd met *her*, and his heart and his thoughts were full of her. The last thing he wanted was me. He tried to dissuade me from going home with him.'

'Did you go anyway?' Drago asked.

'Oh yes. I was that stupid. I tried to take him to bed, and believed him when he said he was too tired after the journey. I didn't even get the message when he wouldn't let me help him unpack.'

'We can be frighteningly blind when we don't realise that things have changed for ever,' Drago said quietly. 'And perhaps we fight against that realisation, because we're fighting for our lives.'

'Yes,' she whispered. 'Yes.'

James had put his suitcases in the wardrobe, insisting that he would unpack them later. There had been no need for her to worry herself. But he'd kept out the bag where he kept his cameras.

'I'm dying to see the pictures you've taken,' she'd said, opening the side of one of them, ready to take out the little card that fitted into the computer.

It had been gone.

'I've removed them all,' he'd said quickly. 'If anything happens to the cameras on the journey, at least I've got the cards.'

'But you always keep the cameras with you. You've never bothered taking the cards out before.'

He'd shrugged.

It was obvious now that the cards had been full of pictures of Carlotta, and he'd made sure she wouldn't see them.

Reaching into the bag, she'd found a small metal object, which she'd drawn out and studied curiously. It was a padlock, but unlike any padlock she'd ever seen, with tiny pictures on each side. One side had showed a heart, and the other side depicted two hands clasped. The shapes had been studded with tiny, gleaming stones that had looked as though they might be diamonds.

'How charming,' she'd said.

'Yes, isn't it?' he'd said heartily. 'I thought you'd like it.'

'Is it for me?'

'Of course.'

She'd felt for the key in the rucksack. Then she'd smiled at him, all fears removed.

'I shall keep you padlocked in my heart,' she'd told him. 'See?'

But the key hadn't fitted into the lock.

'Sorry,' he'd said. 'It must be the wrong one. I'll sort it out later.' He'd kissed her cheek. 'Now I'm going to collapse into bed. I'll call you in the morning.'

That memory returned to her now, but she didn't mention it to Drago, because she didn't know what it meant. James had never given her the right key, and had taken back the padlock in the end.

'When did this happen?' Drago asked.

'About September.'

He nodded. 'Yes, I remember Carlotta suddenly started spending a lot of time away from home. She was gone for a whole week in September, then she was at home for a while. There were weekends, then another week in November. I found out afterwards that she'd spent that week in England.'

'The tenth to the seventeenth?' Alysa asked, dazed.

'Was *he* away then?'

'He said he was. He said he was going to drive north and get pictures of some wild scenery, immerse himself in the landscape, talk to nobody, even me. I tried to call him once but his phone was switched off. Then someone mentioned seeing him near his home in London. I said they were mistaken, but I guess they weren't. He must have spent the week at home—with her.'

'She was more shrewd than him,' Drago said. 'She never turned her mobile phone off. She used to call me every day and talk as though all was well with us.' He drew a sudden, sharp breath.

'Just like the other time, when you eloped,' Alysa said, reading his mind.

'Yes, just like then. It's so easy to see it now.'

'Did you never suspect anything?'

'No. I trusted her totally. I went on being blind right up until the moment when she told me she was in love with someone else, and was leaving me for him. And do you want to hear something really funny? I didn't believe her. I thought it wasn't possible. Not my Carlotta, who'd been so close to me that she was like a second self. Only I'd been deluding myself. There was no second self. I'd been alone all the time and never known it.'

'You felt that too?' she asked quickly. 'That's it exactly—as though you'd imagined everything. And suddenly the whole world seems full of ghosts.'

'And you feel as though you're going mad,' he confirmed. 'In a strange way, my other self is you. I can say things to you that I could say to nobody else, and know that you'll understand them.'

'And even the words don't always have to be said,' she mused. 'It's a bit scary. To me, anyway.'

'You think I'm not scared?' he asked with grim humour. 'Do I do that good a job of hiding it?'

'Not really. Not from me.'

'Exactly,' he said in a quiet voice.

She had a fatalistic sense that she was being drawn onwards by powers too strong for her. She'd neither wanted nor sought this alliance, but there was no escaping it.

CHAPTER THREE

'How did you find out?' he asked.

'I suppose the first hint was at Christmas, although I didn't see it. We were going to spend the time together, and I got everything ready—tree, decorations, new dress.' She gave him a faint smile of complicity, as if to say, 'I do wear them sometimes'. He nodded, understanding.

'Then he rang to say he wouldn't be coming. A friend had suffered a tragedy and was suicidal. James didn't want to leave him. It sounds a weak story now, but it might have been true. At any rate, I trusted him. I suppose you think that sounds stupid.'

Drago shook his head. 'My own credulity strikes me as stupid, not yours. There's no limit to what we can believe when we *want* to believe.'

'Yes,' she sighed. 'And I wanted so much to believe.'

She still couldn't bear to speak of her dead child, but unconsciously she laid a hand over her stomach. Drago, watching her, frowned slightly, and a sudden question came into his eyes.

'How long was he away?' he asked.

'Until the first week in January. I guess he came here and spent time with Carlotta, but she couldn't have seen much of him at Christmas.'

'She was with us on Christmas Day, but the rest of the time she did a lot of coming and going. In Italy we also have another big occasion—Epiphany, January sixth, when we celebrate the coming of the three wise men. Carlotta was there for Epiphany—loving mother, loving wife—' He broke off.

After a moment he resumed. 'She played her part beautifully. When it was over Tina left with her grandmother to visit Carlotta's sister and her family. Elena wanted her to go too, but Carlotta said she wanted to stay with me, that we needed some time together. I think that was one of the happiest moments of my life. I'd seen so little of her, and I was overjoyed that she wanted to be with me.

'But as soon as we were alone she said she was leaving me for another man, and there was no point in discussing it. I'd never heard her sound so much like a lawyer.

'I reminded her that she was a mother, but it was like talking to a brick wall. She knew what she wanted, and nothing else counted. I said I wouldn't let her take my daughter. I thought that would make her stop and think. But I discovered that she'd never meant to take Tina.'

'Would you have taken her back?' Alysa asked curiously. 'Knowing that she'd been unfaithful?'

'It would never have been the same between us,' he said sombrely. 'But, for Tina's sake, I would have tried.'

After that there was silence for a while. Drago got up and poured a couple more glasses of wine, handed her one and sat down again.

'I began to realise that I'd never really known her,' he said. 'She seemed not to understand what she was doing to other people, or care. She kept saying, "We've had a lovely Epiphany. Tina will have that to remember".'

Alysa winced. 'She really thought that would be enough?'

'She seemed to. She said she'd come and see Tina sometimes, as though that settled it. Then she left. When Tina came home I told her that Mamma was away on business, because I still hoped she'd come back, and Tina need never know the truth. But then Carlotta died, and how could I tell her then?'

'You couldn't, of course. But can you keep it a secret for ever? Suppose she hears it from someone else?'

'I know. Maybe one day, when she's old enough to cope, but not yet.'

'I can't understand why she didn't want her daughter.'

'Neither can I. Carlotta kept saying we had to be realistic— Why, what's the matter?'

Alysa had turned and stared at him. 'She actually used that word—*realistic*?'

'Yes, why?'

'Because James used it too,' she said, beginning to laugh mirthlessly. 'When he came home in January he called me to meet him at a restaurant. He kept it short, just said he'd met someone else. He said it hadn't been working out for us, and we had to be "realistic". Then he called for the bill, we said goodbye and I never saw him again.'

'Like a guillotine descending,' Drago said slowly.

'Yes, that describes it perfectly,' she said, much struck. 'And when the blade had descended it stayed there, so that I couldn't look back beyond it. I knew the past had happened, but suddenly I couldn't see it any more. And when I finally did, it looked different.'

'Oh yes,' he murmured. 'It's exactly like that. And you never heard from him? Not a postcard or a phone call to see if you were all right?'

'His lawyer called me to say James had left some things with me and wanted them back. I packed them up in a box and someone from the lawyer's office collected them.'

Drago said something violent in a language she didn't understand.

'What does that mean?' she asked. 'It didn't sound like Italian.'

'It's Tuscan dialect, and I won't offend your ears by translating.'

'Sounds like some of the things I said in those days.'

'You told Tina that you'd learned a little Italian by researching online. Was that—?'

'Yes. When I was trying to find out about Carlotta I discovered a lot of stuff in Italian newspapers. The computer translated it, but very badly, so I got an Italian dictionary. I worked on it night after night and I suppose I went a bit mad.' She gave a short, harsh laugh, turning to the mirror on the wall. 'Look at me.'

In the dim light the mirror made her eyes seem larger than ever in her delicate face. They were burning and haunted.

'Those eyes belong behind bars,' she murmured.

'*Stop that!*' His voice crashed into her brooding thoughts, making her jump. 'Stop that right now!' he commanded. 'Don't put yourself down. It's the way to hell.'

'It's a bit late for that.'

'All the more need to be strong.'

'Why?' she shouted. 'Sometimes I'm tired of being strong. I've spent the last year working at that—hiding my feelings, never letting anyone suspect.'

'And what's inside you now?'

'Nothing, but that's fine. I can cope with "nothing". Don't dare to judge me. What do you think you know about me?'

'I know you're a steely accountant, but as a woman you're settling for a narrow life because you think you'll be safe. But you won't. It's just another kind of hell.'

'Look, I came here to help you—'

'But maybe you need my help too.'

'*I don't.*'

Instead of arguing, he shrugged and said, 'Let's get some coffee.'

He led her into the kitchen, a shining temple to the latest hi-tech cooking equipment, incongruous against the rest of the house. In a moment he had the coffee perking, and brought some spicy rolls out of the cupboard. He'd made the right move. Alysa felt herself growing calmer as she ate and drank.

'Thank you,' she said as he refilled her cup. 'I don't normally lose my temper.'

'Tonight's been hard on you,' he said. 'I shouldn't really have put you through it, but I'm clutching at straws.'

'We all do what we must to survive. I was never going to let this get the better of me.'

'But you've paid a price.'

'Yes, all right, I have. There's always a price to be paid, but anything's better than giving in.'

'You're a very strong person. I admire that. I've often felt it was getting the better of me.'

'Did you mean what you said about crying?' she asked.

'Yes,' he said quietly. 'I meant it. What about you? You said you never cried.'

'I can't. And, if I could, I wouldn't.'

'How did you get to be so strong?'

'Through my mother. When I was fifteen my father walked out on us, and it finished her. She never recovered. I can still hear her sobbing, night after night. Three years later she died of a heart attack. She had no strength to fight it.'

'Poor soul.'

'Yes, and you know why she went under? Because my father was all she had. She was an actress before she met him—a good one, people said. But she had to choose, and she chose him. She wouldn't take jobs that took her away from him, and in the end the offers stopped coming. She became a barmaid, a shop assistant, any number of dead-end jobs. He left her with nothing. That's where I'm different. When I lost James, I didn't lose everything.'

He gave her a quick look and seemed about to speak, but thought better of it and poured some more coffee.

'Did your father stay in touch?' he asked at last.

'He contacted me after she died, said he thought we could repair the past. I told him to get out of my sight and never come back. And he did. I'll never forgive him for what he did to my mother, and I'll never let myself go under as she did.'

He nodded slowly. 'And you have no other family?'

'My mother has a couple of sisters, but they more or less deserted her when she hit the bad times. I suppose they couldn't cope with her depression, and perhaps I ought to be understanding, but they weren't there when she needed them.'

'Maybe it would have made no difference,' he mused. 'Other people can't always help, unless it's exactly the right person. And you may never meet that person.'

'You sound as though you had a lot of experience with the wrong ones.'

'One or two. It wasn't their fault. They tried to sympathise over her death, not knowing that the real grief lay elsewhere.'

'How did you hear that Carlotta was dead?'

'From the press. Somebody recognised her body and called me. I don't recall exactly what I said, but I think I recited the line about her being away to visit clients. If I did, I was on automatic. Then there were more calls, as the press began to sniff something out.'

'How ghastly!' she said in genuine sympathy.

'I think I went off my head for a while. I was in a rage—

I can be really unpleasant.' He gave a faint, self-mocking smile. 'Though you might not believe that.'

'I'll try,' she said lightly. 'Did you actually hit anyone?'

'There was one moment with an editor—but he gave as good as he got. Then I told him if he slandered my wife I'd have his paper closed down.'

'Could you do that?' Alysa asked, remembering what the young journalist had told her.

'Who knows? I'd have had a good try. But he believed it, and that was all I needed. Are you shocked?'

'No. I've done that too. Not the punch-up, but making the other side think you're stronger than you are. It's very useful. What about the rest of the press? Did you have to get tough with them?'

'No need. The word got around, and after that nobody would challenge me.' He regarded her satirically. 'I dare say your reputation goes ahead of you as well?'

'Well, I'm in line for a partnership.' She too became self-mocking to say, 'So there are some advantages to renouncing my femininity.'

'Look, I shouldn't have said that. Will you please forget it?'

'Of course.' But it had struck home, and Alysa knew she wasn't going to forget any time soon.

'What about you?' Drago asked. 'How did you hear?'

'I got a call from Anthony Hoskins, James's lawyer. He said he'd been contacted by a man who wouldn't say who he was, but was asking about James.'

'That was me. I found a letter from Hoskins in their apartment. I didn't get anywhere talking to him, so I simply passed his name on to the undertakers.'

'They called Hoskins too, and he called me again,' Alysa remembered. 'He said they wanted burial instructions. James had no family.'

'What did you tell them to do about the burial?'

'Nothing. I was in a dreadful state, so I said I didn't know him and put the phone down. I never heard any more. I don't know what happened to his body.'

'I can tell you that. He's near the Church of All Angels, the same place where Carlotta is buried. There's going to be a ceremony there tomorrow.'

'I didn't know. I only discovered about today's gathering by accident online. There was no mention of anything else. Do you go to the cemetery often?'

'I take Tina to visit her mother, and sometimes I go to see her alone.'

'You visit her, after what she did to you?'

'I have to. Don't ask me why, because I couldn't tell you. I always look at his stone when I'm there. Then I can tell him how much I hate him. I enjoy that. I only wish I could picture him. When I went to identify Carlotta I made them show me him as well, because I wanted to see his face.'

'What did you think of it?' she asked, almost inaudibly.

'Nothing. It was badly damaged, so I still don't really know what Carlotta saw when she looked at him. But you can tell me. Would a woman think he was handsome?'

'Yes,' she said with a touch of defiance. Something about his tone was making her defensive. 'He was very handsome. Do you want to see?'

He stared. 'You've actually got his picture? You still take it everywhere?'

'No, just here. After all, I came here to remember him. I wanted him to be with me. I suppose that sounds crazy?'

He shook his head. She felt in a compartment of her bag, and offered it to him.

To her surprise he hesitated before taking it, as though at the last minute he was unwilling to face the man his wife had loved. Then he took it quickly and studied it, his mouth twisted, so that his turbulent emotions were partly concealed.

'Pretty boy,' he said contemptuously.

'I suppose he was,' Alysa said. 'I used to be proud to be seen with him, because all the other women envied me. They would try to get his attention and they never did because he always kept his eyes on me. That was part of his charm. He had beautiful manners—until the end, anyway. Maybe that's why I didn't see it coming.'

'Tomorrow I'll show you where he lies, a place where nobody is competing for him,' Drago said with grim satisfaction. 'But I dare say you don't need a grave to tell him you hate him.'

'I don't hate him any more.'

'You're fortunate, then. I don't believe you for a moment, but perhaps even the illusion is useful—until it collapses.'

Once she would have insisted that it would never collapse, but this evening had left her shaken, and suddenly she longed to bring it to an end. If anything brought about the collapse it would be Drago di Luca, with his unnerving combination of ruthlessness and vulnerability.

'It's late,' she said. 'I should be going.'

'I'll drive you. We have to be at the cemetery at noon tomorrow. My car will call for you at eleven.'

'No, please. I won't go to the cemetery. Today was enough.'

'Think about it tonight. I'll call you tomorrow.'

She made no answer and he showed her out into the hall, saying it would only take him a moment to bring the car around. She sat down to wait, so sunk in thought that at first she didn't see the little figure coming down the stairs, and jumped when Tina spoke to her, asking anxiously, 'Is Poppa all right?'

'Yes, of course,' Alysa said. 'Why do you ask?'

'He was unhappy all day.'

'Well, your mother…'

'I know. He's always unhappy about her, but today he was nervous too.' Tina lowered her voice to say, 'I think he's nervous of Nonna.'

'Nonna?'

'My grandmother. She hasn't been very nice to him today.'

There was an almost motherly note in the child's voice. Alysa realised that, while Drago was protecting her, this little creature was protecting him.

He returned at that moment.

'What are you doing out of bed?' he demanded, in a voice in which authority and tenderness were equally mixed.

'I came to see how you were,' the child explained.

'I'm going to drive the *signorina* home, but then I'm coming right back. Now, get back to bed before your grandmother finds out, or I'll be in deep trouble.'

At that moment the sound of Elena's voice upstairs made them all freeze.

Tina reacted like lightning. Reaching up to Alysa's ear, she whispered, 'Look after him,' and darted away up the stairs. Next moment they heard her saying, 'I'm here, Nonna. I had a bad dream so I went looking for you—I thought you were downstairs.'

'That's one thing she gets from her mother,' Drago said in a voice that shook slightly. 'She's never lost for words.'

'She's marvellous,' Alysa agreed.

'What did she say to you?'

'She told me to look after you, but I probably shouldn't have repeated that. Don't tell her.'

'I won't. Did she say why she thought I needed looking after?'

'She thinks Elena isn't nice to you.'

That deprived him of speech, she was interested to note. He simply ushered her outside and into the car. For some time he drove in silence, and she had the feeling that he was still disconcerted.

The city was quiet as they entered, and Alysa realised that it was nearly one in the morning. In a few hours she seemed to have lived a whole lifetime, and time had lost all meaning.

'Is this the way to the hotel?' she asked after a while. 'Surely it's on the other side of the river?'

'I'm taking a slight detour, to show you something that may interest you. It's just along this road.'

At last he stopped the car outside an apartment block with an ornately decorated exterior, that looked several-hundred years old.

'This is where they lived,' he said when they were both standing on the pavement. 'Just up there.' He indicated one floor up.

It was a charming area, perfect for a love nest. Alysa studied it for a moment, then wandered down a short, narrow alley that ran along the side of the building and found herself overlooking the River Arno. A multitude of lights was on, their reflection gleaming in the water, and in the distance she could see the Ponte Vecchio, the great, beautiful bridge for which Florence was famous.

This was what James would have seen from the apartment window, standing with his lover in his arms. Here they had held each other, kissed, teased, spoken fond words, then taken each other to bed—while she had lain tormented in England, while the life of her baby had died out of her.

'That's their window,' Drago said. 'I once saw them standing there together.'

'You came to see them?'

'Yes, but I made sure they didn't find out. I skulked here like a lovesick schoolboy, hanging about to catch a glimpse of her, and retreating into the shadows when I saw her.' He paused and added wryly, 'And if you ever repeat that I'll deny it and sue you for every penny.'

'Don't worry, I did the same. I passed James's flat when I didn't need to. But I didn't see him. I suppose he'd already left.'

'You're lucky. I couldn't stay away from this place. I pictured them walking by the river, looking at the lights in the water, saying to each other the things that lovers have always said in this spot.'

'It's perfect for it,' she agreed, looking along the river to the Ponte Vecchio. 'It's the sort of place people mean when they say that Italy is a romantic country.'

The ironic way she said 'romantic' made him look at her in appreciation.

'It can be romantic,' he said. 'It can also be prosaic, businesslike and full of the most depressing common-sense. Romance doesn't lie in the country or the setting, but in the moment your eyes meet, and you know you're living in a world where there's only the two of you and nothing else exists.'

He added heavily, 'The night I saw them at that window, I knew they had found that world, and *I* no longer existed for her.'

Just then a brilliantly lit boat came along the river, casting its glow upward to where he stood leaning forward on the low wall, illuminating his harsh features. Regarding him dispassionately, Alysa realised that, though far from handsome, he had something that many women would have found attractive.

James had been wonderfully good-looking in a boyish,

conventional way. But there was nothing boyish about Drago. He was a man—strong-willed, yielding nothing. His manners could be clumsy, and he lacked what was commonly called 'charm'.

Yet he had the mysterious something called 'presence'. In a room he would draw all eyes, not just because he was large, but because of his uncompromising air, and because he mattered.

And even Alysa, who had loved James passionately, was fleetingly puzzled that Carlotta, the adored wife of Drago di Luca, had turned away from him and settled for less.

For herself men no longer existed. Otherwise she guessed she might have found him intriguing.

Drago was looking into the distance. Suddenly he dropped his head almost down to his chest, as though the burden had become too great to be borne.

She touched him. 'I know,' she whispered. 'I know.'

A cold wind was blowing from the river, and she shivered. Drago didn't speak, but he straightened up, putting his arms tightly around her, and rested his cheek on her head. It was the embrace of a comrade, not a lover, receiving her kindness thankfully, offering the same in return, and she accepted it, glad of the warmth.

'Are you all right?' he asked at last.

'I'm fine—fine. But I don't want to stay here any more.'

He kept his arm about her on the way back to the car. On the journey back to the hotel she sat in silence, feeling hollowed out. When he drew up outside, he handed her a card.

'Here's how to contact me if you need to,' he said. 'I shall hope to see you tomorrow. If not—thank you for everything you've done for me.'

He leaned over and briefly kissed her cheek. *'Adio!'*

'Goodbye,' she said. 'I don't know if— Goodbye.'
She hurried into the hotel without looking back.

That night she dreamed of James as she hadn't done for months. The shield she'd created against him seemed to dissolve into mist, and he was there, standing at the window with Carlotta, laughing at her. She cried out for help, and for a moment seemed to sense Drago. But he vanished at once, and she knew herself to be alone again.

CHAPTER FOUR

IN THE morning she awoke unrefreshed, and the thought of going to the cemetery was suddenly more than she could bear. She would leave a day early, not risking another meeting with Drago.

But even as she thought this she was taking out clothes that might be proper for a ceremony in a graveyard. There was a severely tailored, dark-blue business suit complete with trousers. It occurred to her that she now owned very few skirts, and she'd brought none of them with her. Drago had been uncomfortably perceptive.

She donned the suit which was expensive, elegant and, above all, suitable.

This was something that had often made James tease her.

'Why does everything have to be so perfectly chosen, so *suitable*?' he'd demanded, half-fondly, half-exasperated. Strange that she'd never noticed that note in his voice until now.

'I'm a "suitable" person,' she'd teased back.

'Suitable for what?'

'Suitable for advising people on what to do with their money. I couldn't do that in a skimpy top and shorts. Hopefully I'll be suitable for a partnership in the firm.' She'd put her arms around him. 'But what I really want to be is suitable for you.'

'Ah, well, for that you need the skimpy top and shorts.'

Now, dressing to visit his grave, she tried not to remember that conversation, or the hectic hour in bed that had followed it.

She took a taxi there and arrived early, finding few other people, so that she had time to wander through the cemetery, studying the graves. Many of them were in family plots, carefully tended and adorned with flowers. One in particular held her attention because of the loving attention that had been lavished on it.

Everywhere that Alysa looked she saw red roses. They stretched up to the foot of the headstone with its ornate, carved decoration, and its two candle-holders, both with flickering candles that glowed against the picture of the woman buried beneath.

Looking closer, Alysa recognised Carlotta di Luca.

She stared. After everything that had happened the day before she'd thought nothing could surprise her again, but this lavish tribute went beyond what she had expected.

'*Ciao.*'

'*Sono Inglese,*' she said, turning to see a priest standing close by. He was elderly and had kindly eyes.

'Are you a friend of the family?' he asked.

'No,' she said quickly. 'I was just amazed to see roses at this time of year.'

'Her husband has an arrangement with a firm that imports flowers. This is an exceptional delivery for today, but there's a new bunch every week.'

Every week. After a whole year.

It might only have been for Tina, but she didn't believe it. They weren't just flowers, they were red roses, flaunted everywhere like a declaration. Drago was still passionately in love with the wife who had betrayed him.

'Do any of the others have roses?' she asked.

'Oh no, some of them are almost never visited, which is sad.'

'Just this one,' she mused.

'It's good to see a man so devoted to his wife. But I sense that he's still tormented by his memories, and has a long way to go before he finds peace.'

'Are all the victims buried here?'

'No. Some were visitors from other parts of the country, and their bodies were sent home—except for one, a man, who was a stranger. Nobody knew anything about him except his name and he was English. He didn't seem to have any family. He was buried over there.'

He indicated a far corner where several neat rows of small graves lay that were little more than slabs in the earth. The plot was neat and cared-for, but this was clearly the place for those with no relatives to pay for a fine headstone. Alysa wandered over slowly and went along the lines, seeking James. She found him at last at the very far end, near the corner.

'He looks so lonely out here,' she said.

'I know, this place is very sad. We tried to contact his family in England, but he didn't seem to have one. I believe someone spoke to a young woman who was supposed to have known him well, but she sent back a message that he was nothing to do with her.'

'She shouldn't have done that,' Alysa murmured.

'Perhaps, but we'll never know what she might have been suffering. Ah, I see people arriving.'

She hardly noticed him moving away. She was looking at James's bare little plaque, tucked away in this lonely spot.

'Where I banished you,' she whispered.

It had never occurred to her before that James should be pitied, but now she saw him again at his best: young, laughing with the joy of life. She remembered how he'd broken into her austere existence, tempting her to enjoy new delights, teasing her. And his life had been snatched from him just when he had discovered his true joy. For the first time she knew sadness for his tragedy.

Now everyone was arriving for the ceremony, and Alysa stood back among the trees as Drago appeared. He seemed to be with a large family party that consisted not only of Tina and Elena, but several other adults and two children. Alysa watched until they had gone into the church, then she followed them quietly in and sat down at the back.

The family stayed close together. Tina's hand was in her father's, and on her other side a boy of about six was patting her shoulder. Glancing around the other families, she saw the same thing repeated in several different ways. These people were here to support each other in their loss. She was the only one isolated.

When the short service was over she slipped out of the door and went to stand among the trees once more. From here she could see the second part of the ceremony as the families walked among the graves and honoured their loved ones.

But for James there was nobody except herself.

'They've shunted you away so that you don't spoil their picture of the perfect wife and mother,' she told him sadly, looking down at the little slab that seemed so paltry on the ground. 'To everyone else but me, you don't exist.'

A step nearby made her turn to see Drago, looking drawn and tired.

'I sent the car to the hotel for you,' he said. 'You'd gone, but I still hoped to find you here.'

'I couldn't keep away. You knew that would happen, didn't you?'

He nodded.

'I guess you know me better than I know myself,' she said.

'Then it's the same for both of us,' he said quietly. 'Are you all right?'

'Yes, I'm fine. But you don't look as though you slept well.'

'I didn't sleep at all.'

'Was last night worse than you thought?'

'Not really. It was thinking about today that kept me awake. Carlotta's sister is here, with her husband and children.'

'And they don't know the truth either, so you have to do the performance for them too,' she said sympathetically.

'Exactly. But they'll be going tomorrow, so perhaps we could talk again?'

For a moment she hesitated. It would be good to enjoy the consolation of speaking freely, just once more. But it was a dangerous pleasure, one that she might come to enjoy too much.

Drago di Luca disturbed her. He was an impatient, domineering man, implacable in getting his own way, and if she'd met him under other circumstances she might have disliked him. But with her he was defenceless and it touched her heart.

But that was what made her wary. She'd worked so hard at deadening her heart, and now he threatened her peace.

'I don't know,' she said. 'It might not be a good idea.'

Drago glanced down at James's grave.

'Because of him?' he demanded. 'Why do you still bother with him?'

'Because he has nobody else.'

'And who do you have? Forget him and live your life. When Carlotta betrayed me, I did what had to be done and cut her out of my heart.'

'Hence the showers of red roses?'

'That's for Tina's sake. She needs to believe that I'm grieving.'

'You're deluding yourself. You're feeding your little girl nothing but pretty lies—'

'For her sake!'

'Is it? Is it only for her sake?'

He scowled, and she knew he had no answer. After a moment he said, 'What about you? Are you managing to cope?'

'Yes, I'm doing fine.'

'We need to talk again. I'll call you as soon as I can be rid of them.'

'No, Drago, it's better if we don't. We sorted out a lot of things last night, but there has to come a time when we say no more.'

A faint cry of, 'Poppa,' from behind made him look around.

'Just a moment,' he told Alysa. 'I'll be back. Don't go, please.'

He hurried off to talk to his daughter. After a brief hesitation Alysa began to back away under the trees. Her eyes were still fixed on him, noticing how, as soon as he joined the family, he seemed to become a different person—smiling, seemingly at ease, just as they expected.

She knew what it was doing to him inside, and part of her longed to respond to his plea for help. But now her sense of self-preservation was telling her to run for safety. When she'd backed away far enough, she turned and slipped out of the cemetery.

She spent the rest of the day strolling around Florence, looking at the sights without really seeing them. After all, it was only sensible to make the most of her brief trip. Then she blamed herself for prolonging the torment by trying to imagine James and Carlotta here in this lovely place, wandering the streets together, kissing in the shadows.

Then she admitted the truth: that she was avoiding Drago di Luca.

Everywhere looked the same, with no one place mattering more than another, no destination luring her.

'Nowhere to go,' she murmured wryly. 'That just about says it all.'

Darkness came early, bringing the lights on in the mediaeval streets. Almost of their own accord her steps turned to the Ponte Vecchio, the magnificent bridge over the River Arno that she had seen at a distance the night before. It was lined with shops on both sides, mostly jewellers and goldsmiths, and she strolled past them until she reached a shop at the end that sold not jewels but padlocks.

The window was full of them, covering shelves and hanging from the ceiling. The costliest jewels in the world couldn't have been displayed more lovingly. Looking closer, Alysa saw that many of them had tiny pictures etched on the side.

Just like the one she'd seen before, she thought. And there it was, nestling among the others—a padlock with a heart daintily engraved on it, so like the one James had given her and then secretly taken back that it might have been the same.

Alysa stared and blinked, as though hoping that she would see something else next time. But it was the same padlock.

'I don't understand,' she murmured.

She didn't know she'd spoken aloud, but a middle-aged man standing beside her grinned and spoke cheerily, first in Italian, then, when she looked puzzled, in English.

'You like my padlocks? They are the best in Florence.'

'I can see that,' she said politely. 'But why so many?'

'Why, for Cellini, of course.'

'I don't understand.'

'You've never heard of Benvenuto Cellini?'

'I know he was a great Florentine goldsmith and sculptor in the sixteenth century, but that's all.'

'Come and meet him.'

Taking her arm gently, the man led her to the end of the bridge, where she found a bust of Cellini raised high on an ornate plinth. It was impressive and elegant, but what caught Alysa's attention were the railings that surrounded it, which were covered with padlocks. Hundreds of them.

'Lovers put them there,' the shop owner confided. 'It's an old tradition. They buy a padlock, lock it onto the railings and throw the key into the River Arno. That means that their love has locked them together for all time, even unto death.'

'How—how beautiful,' Alysa stammered. A terrible dread was rising in her.

'Isn't it charming? It's also good business, because when lovers come to me I usually manage to sell them three. Then they leave one with Cellini, and each gives one to the other, but they also swap keys so that only they can open each other's locks.'

'Can I see some of them?' she asked, speaking in a daze.

'Of course. It's this way back to the shop.'

Once there he spread a collection on the counter, and she picked up the one that was exactly like James's gift, the heart studded with tiny stones.

'Ah, yes, everyone likes that,' the shopkeeper said. 'They're real diamonds and it's the most expensive one I have.'

'Even unto death,' she murmured.

'That's the part that always affects them,' he said. 'They know they'll be together for eternity.'

There in her mind was the picture of James and Carlotta, lying in the smashed chair, dead in the same moment. Together for eternity.

'How much?' she asked in a bleak voice.

He told her the price and she gasped.

'Yes, you'd have to be really in love to pay so much,' he conceded. He lowered his voice conspiratorially. 'If your lover gives you this one, then you can rely on him for ever.'

'Oh yes,' she murmured. 'For ever.'

'Why don't you bring him in to see it?'

'I think we're a bit past that point,' she said wryly. 'Thank you, but I must be going.'

She fled while she still had some self-command, turning back across the bridge so that she didn't have to pass the statue again with its terrible display of lovers' vows.

James and Carlotta had been here, hung a padlock on the railings, tossed the key into the Arno and swore love unto death. Then they had exchanged padlocks, each taking the other's key. That was what she'd found in his bag, and that was why the key hadn't fitted. It was all so clear when you knew.

She'd told herself that nothing could hurt her any more, but she found she was shaking as she'd done so often in the past. But, instead of weeping, she began to laugh at this last deadly joke that had lain in wait for her. It was hilarious, the funniest thing that had ever happened.

She made her way blindly along the streets, shuddering, laughing, pressing her hand to her mouth, knowing that she was receiving strange looks, caring nothing for them, or even for the fact that she was lost.

Now she was in a quiet part of the city, within sight of the river, and went down to lean on a low wall overlooking the water. Vaguely, downstream, she thought she could see the apartment building where Drago had taken her last night—the place where James and Carlotta had been free to indulge their love.

And, to her dismay, she was swept with longing for the one person in the world who she could reach out to at this moment. If Drago were here she would run to him, blurt out her misery, knowing that he would understand everything that was too hard for her to say. And she would find his powerful arms open to her in comfort. She had no doubt of it.

He'd known that soon her brave façade would collapse, leaving her defenceless. He alone had seen the fear behind the mask, because it was so like his own.

The need for him was so strong that she took out her mobile phone and found the card with his number. But when she'd dialled two figures she stopped and hurriedly turned the phone off.

'What am I doing?' she whispered. 'I must be mad. Everything that happened last night just wasn't real. I've got to get home to England, then everything will be normal again.'

Using the river as a guide, she finally managed to make her way back to the hotel.

'There are some messages for you,' the young man at the desk told her, pushing a paper towards her. 'The gentleman sounded urgent.'

'Thank you. Please have my bill ready first thing tomorrow. I want to leave early. And, if anyone else should call, please tell them I haven't returned.'

She was booked on the two o'clock flight the next day; she would leave for the airport as early as possible. In her room she packed hurriedly, ignoring the phone when it began to ring.

She was afraid he would turn up at her hotel, but to her

relief he didn't. At last the phone stopped ringing, and she gave muttered thanks that Drago had given up.

Next morning she left quickly. Luck was with her. There was an earlier flight with vacant seats and she managed to change her ticket. After checking in, she went to wait in the departure lounge, telling herself that soon she would be free. Just a little longer...

'Excuse me, *signorina*.'

She looked up to find a man in uniform.

'Signorina Dennis?'

'Yes.'

'Will you come with me, please?'

'But I'm about to board the plane.'

'I'm afraid you can't do so until we have cleared up a small matter.'

His manner was pleasant but firm, and she yielded reluctantly.

'This way to my office,' he said.

She followed him, impatient to hear his explanation, but when they reached his office he showed her in and retreated, closing the door, leaving Alysa alone with the man who was waiting there.

'*You!*' she said angrily. 'I might have known!'

Drago didn't reply immediately, and she had time to study him. Now she wondered how she'd recognised him. If his face had been haggard the day before, it was deathly now. A man who'd seen a ghastly vision might have had his burning eyes. But she refused to feel sympathy. She couldn't afford it.

'I'm sorry,' he said at last. 'I would much rather not have had to do this, but something has happened. You can't go back to England until you know everything.'

'There you go again, telling me what I can and can't do. Who do you think you are?'

'I'm the only person in the world who can fill the gaps in

your knowledge, just as you did for me—except that there's much more than either of us dreamed.'

'I don't want to know. You must be mad to— Actually getting someone to fetch me from the departure lounge—how did you do that?'

'Pietro, the young man who brought you here, owes me a favour.'

'And what about my luggage? It's on the plane.'

'It'll be retrieved.'

'It must be a very big favour,' she said bitingly.

'I wouldn't have done it if I hadn't been at my wits' end. You ignored my messages, and when I went to your hotel this morning they said you'd left early. But I checked your flight and it was two o'clock. I thought I'd find you easily, but I discovered that you'd changed to the earlier flight. I had to do something.'

'And everyone had to simply step aside,' she seethed. 'But not me. I'm going back to get on the plane, and don't you dare to stop me. Get out of my way!'

Drago had positioned himself between her and the door, and showed no sign of moving.

'You're not leaving,' he said quietly. 'You're coming with me.'

'So now I'm a prisoner?'

'If you like to put it that way. I'm sorry. I don't like behaving like this, but I have no choice. Alysa, for pity's sake, won't you try to understand?'

'I understand that everyone has to do what you want because you don't recognise the word no. Enough! I'm not a pawn for you to move around, and I'm leaving right now.'

'This is important!'

'I don't care what it is. I'm finished. Now, for the last time, *get out of my way!*'

He didn't budge. If anything he seemed to dig himself in further, and Alysa prepared for battle. If he thought he could make her yield again, he would learn that he was mistaken.

But then something happened that caught her off-balance. Suddenly his shoulders sagged, as if a vital link had snapped inside him. Without further argument he pulled open the door and spoke heavily.

'Pietro, please escort the *signorina* back to the departure lounge.'

He moved out of Alysa's path, and she hurried to the door.

'Thank you,' she said. 'I'm sorry to disappoint you, but I really have to go.'

She could have got away then but she made the mistake of turning back and seeing something she would much rather not have seen. Drago looked defeated, as if he'd simply abandoned all hope.

'Please try to understand,' she begged.

'I do understand. You'd better go quickly.'

But instead of leaving she made her next mistake: going to look him in the eye, and saying, 'I don't want you to think— Look at me.' She put a hand on his arm and he raised his head to meet her gaze. His aggression had died, leaving only weariness behind. 'You're not being fair,' she protested desperately. 'You must realise that I can't—'

'I know,' he agreed. 'I shouldn't have done it this way. I was desperate, but you're right, it's not really your problem. You've done all you could, and I'm grateful.'

'And now I have to return to whatever I can make of my life, because I can't— *Oh, all right!*' The last words were almost a shout of exasperation.

'All right? What does that mean?'

'It means I give in. You've won. The new tactic worked. I'll come with you.'

The joy on his face was a startling revelation. The next moment she was engulfed in a bear hug. Somehow she found herself returning it, even laughing with him, because the violence of his relief was infectious.

'Just let me breathe,' she gasped.

He drew back to look at her. 'Thank you,' he said fervently.

'Just don't ever do this to me again.'

'When this is over, I swear you'll never have to see me. Let's go.'

'Yes, let's, before I change my mind. What about my bags? They'll be on the plane by now.'

'Pietro will get them off, and he knows where to send them. Come on.'

CHAPTER FIVE

OUTSIDE he showed her to his car—not the one he'd driven before, but far larger and more powerful. He swung confidently out of the airport onto the main road and drove fast for a few miles before swinging off.

'Where are you going?' she asked. 'This isn't the way to Florence.'

'We're not going to Florence, we're going to another little place I own, in the mountains. We need privacy.'

'What about Tina?'

'She and Elena are spending a few days with her aunt and uncle. You saw them at the cemetery.'

'So if they're gone why can't we have privacy in your house in Florence?'

'Because I have curious employees. I want total isolation, and we'll only get that in the mountains.'

Total isolation with this man, cut off from help if things went wrong. The thought should have made her nervous, but it didn't. She'd already been through the worst. Now they were like two comrades facing enemy fire together. To be comrades you only needed trust. And, despite his outrageous behaviour, she did trust him.

The land began to slope gently upwards; the buildings

became further apart. Sometimes the road wound its way among tall trees for miles, so that it felt as though they were the only two people in the world. Despite the time of year the weather was bright, and the sun glittered through the branches, dappling the way ahead.

Suddenly there was a gap in the trees, revealing the land sloping away. Alysa watched, fascinated, as they climbed higher and higher, seeming to leave the ground behind, soaring into a different world.

At last the road levelled out and they were driving through a small village. Drago stopped the car.

'I'm just going to buy a few things,' he said. 'Will you come with me, or wait here?'

'I'll come with you.'

At any other time she would have found the village fascinating, coming, as it seemed to, from another age. Some streets were cobbled; the buildings were large and decorative, with archways extending out over the pavement. Impossible to imagine a supermarket here. Drago went from shop to shop, buying fresh meat and vegetables with the confidence of an expert. Every shopkeeper knew him.

'Haven't seen you here for a while, *signore*,' one observed. 'Nice to have you back. I've got something in stock that I think you'll like.'

Then there was bread, cheese, milk and oil to be bought. Again the counter assistants greeted him as an old friend and produced his favourite items at once.

'Don't worry, I'm a good cook,' he told Alysa.

'Yes, I was really worried about that,' she said dryly.

He gave her a look of appreciation for this sally, and handed her a couple of bags to carry. Since he was weighed down by even more bags himself, she couldn't even protest.

She told herself that she'd been kidnapped, and it was an

outrage, but it felt more like going on a picnic. There was only one thing to do, and that was to stop fighting it and go with the flow.

'What's the matter?' Drago asked her.

'Matter?'

'You were staring into the distance.'

'Nothing's the matter,' she said robustly. 'Come on. Let's get going.'

Then they were on the road again, climbing among the trees, until he turned suddenly, and in a few moments they were drawing up before a small villa. There were no lights on and the place looked glum and chilly. She shivered as he unlocked the door.

'It'll be better when I've lit the range,' he said. 'It starts the central heating.'

'You have to do that by hand?'

'This is the mountains,' he said by way of explanation. 'It's different up here. Why don't you unpack the food in the kitchen—but don't touch anything apart from that.'

'I should be used to you ordering me about by now,' she observed.

'Yes, you should.'

He got to work on the range in the kitchen, piling logs in until the flames flickered up between them, then tossing charcoal on top. When two dials on the pipes showed the same high temperature, he switched on the central heating, and the place began to warm up quickly.

She began to wander around, somewhat surprised by the cosy informality of the place, which had none of the studied luxury to be found in the Florence villa. Here there were wooden floors with rugs tossed about, apparently casually. The furniture was old, even slightly shabby, and the place had a friendly atmosphere that appealed to her.

The villa was built on a steep slope, with the garage at the bottom. Next to it was a woodshed, and the rest of the place was built on top, so that, looking out of the window, she found she was on a level with the branches of the trees. The light was beginning to fade, so that she could see only shadows below, and the effect was like floating away from the earth.

'This is yours,' Drago said, opening a door and showing her into a room dominated by a large bed.

'How long are you planning for me to stay?' she asked.

'I think we'll be here tomorrow, and perhaps leave the day after. It depends on a lot of things.'

'Why don't you tell me why I'm here?'

'Let's eat first. Your bags should arrive soon.'

When he'd gone she took out her mobile phone and called her office. She'd booked herself a week off, but had hinted that she would return earlier—which had won the approval of her boss, Brian Hawk, who had always helped and encouraged her. Now she told him that she would take the full week.

'I wish you'd given me a bit more warning,' he grumbled. 'There's a lot happening at the moment.'

'I've been detained by something unexpected,' she said truthfully.

'Well, I hope you sort it out soon. Your prospects are bright, Alysa. Don't spoil them by being unreliable.'

When she'd hung up she sat considering these last words, wondering why she wasn't filled with alarm. Her dream was to be offered a partnership, and for this she'd worked hard and sometimes brilliantly, earning Brian's praise. In the last year she'd redoubled her efforts, staying in the office late to avoid returning to her empty apartment, and then taking work home with her.

Once Brian's warning would have alerted her to danger,

but now the words seemed to come from a distance. It was true, of course. She would have to be careful. But she could think about it later.

Looking at the double bed, she wondered if this was the room where Drago and Carlotta had slept together. A glance into the wardrobe confirmed it. Some of Carlotta's clothes were still here, suggesting that she'd abandoned them when she'd begun her new life, and Drago couldn't bring himself to dispose of them.

When she emerged a few minutes later he was already at work in the kitchen, doing something mysterious with oil and vegetables.

'The one thing I never thought of you doing was cooking,' she mused, studying him.

'We're not like the English, who think cooking's sissy unless you're a celebrity chef earning a fortune. My mother thought a man wasn't a real man unless he could cook.'

'What are you making?'

'*Pappa al pomadoro*—bread cooked with garlic, parsley, basil, salt, oil and tomatoes.'

'I'm impressed. And afterwards?'

'Just be patient.'

He was immersed in what he was doing, and seemed to have forgotten the reason he'd brought her here, although he'd claimed it was important. With another man she might have suspected a trick to lure her into a seduction, but not with Drago. He was in the grip of a purpose so inflexible that he could afford to set it aside until the right moment.

'Can I do anything to help?' she asked.

'Yes, you could watch this saucepan while I light the fire in the other room.'

'A fire as well as central heating?'

'Wait till you see it.'

A few minutes later she understood. The fire, nestled in a neat grate, was small but delightful, throwing darting lights over the room. While it offered little heat, it created an atmosphere of warmth and comfort that no central heating could match.

'My mother always lit a fire in the evenings,' Drago said. 'When I looked this place over the agent said it could all be renovated and the fireplace taken out. I told him to forget it. I wanted everything left just as it was.'

'Is this the place you told me about, where you and Carlotta came when you married?'

'Yes, it is. After she died I wanted to sell it, but Tina loves it, so I couldn't. Perhaps I shouldn't have brought you up here, but I couldn't think of anywhere else where we'd have some privacy.'

'It's all right. Is there anything more I can do?'

'You could lay the table. You'll find everything over there, including wine glasses.'

He indicated an old-fashioned dresser and she got to work, finding a table cloth and cutlery. In a few minutes Drago emerged from the kitchen to serve the first course and open a bottle of white wine.

She suddenly realised that she was ravenous. She'd left the hotel too quickly to eat very much, and had managed only a sandwich at the airport. The *pappa al pomadoro* had a delicious smell that drove everything else out of her head, and the taste was every bit as good.

'I needed this,' she said with a sigh.

'After the day I've given you, you mean?'

'Well, I admit you're making up for it.'

'One thing I've been wanting to ask you—when you agreed to come with me, you said, "the new tactic worked". What did you mean by that?'

'You know very well what I meant by that,' she said indignantly. 'When giving me orders didn't work, you backed off and played the reasonable card.'

'Is that what I did?'

'Didn't you?'

He hesitated. 'It wasn't all calculated. I could see I was doing everything wrong, driving you away. I tend to approach things with hobnailed boots, I know that. And when it doesn't work...' He made a helpless gesture. 'I sometimes don't know what to do next. And just then—I felt like such a loser. I didn't have the heart to fight any more.'

'You?' she asked with a hint of teasing. 'Stop fighting?'

He gave her a wry look. 'I guess I deserved that. It's almost funny that you accused me of playing the "reasonable card". I'm not good at being reasonable. Ask anyone who knows me.'

'I don't need to. I'm beginning to know you myself.'

'That's an unnerving thought.'

'Why? You don't try to hide it. Everything's upfront. Can I have some more of this?'

'Just a little. You've got to leave room for the steak.'

The steak was delicious, followed by a loaf made of flour, sugar, eggs and butter. With each course he changed the wine.

'I won't ask why you vanished so suddenly yesterday,' Drago said. 'I guess I asked for it. But I tried to call you for the rest of the day, and you'd switched your phone off. I wondered if you'd gone back to the waterfall so that you could see it without a crowd.'

'No, I just went walking around Florence.'

The constraint in her voice made him look at her quickly and ask, 'Did you go back to their apartment?'

'No, why should you think that?'

'Because something happened yesterday that hurt you more than you have been already.'

'Well, yes.'

'Can't you tell me?' he asked when she fell silent.

'You remember I said that when James came back from Florence in September he was a bit strange?' Drago nodded. 'But I didn't mention the padlock I found in his things. Yesterday I found out about Benvenuto Cellini.'

'You mean the statue at the end of the Ponte Vecchio?'

'And the padlocks.'

'Did he and Carlotta exchange them?'

'They must have done. He said the one I found was for me. But after we broke up I came home one day and he'd been there while I was out, fetching some personal stuff he'd left behind. The padlock was missing too. He must have gone through my things. He didn't leave a note or anything, just his key on the table.'

'I'm beginning to get a picture of this man,' Drago said slowly. 'He liked to do things in a way that was easiest on himself—going to your home when you weren't there.' His mouth twisted in contempt. 'And this is the man my Carlotta preferred.'

'I guess she hadn't discovered that side of him yet,' Alysa reflected. 'He just didn't like confrontation.'

'I wonder how he and Carlotta would have managed after a while,' Drago mused, looking into his wine glass.

'Did she like confrontation?'

'She was never backward about telling people what she thought.'

'Just like you. The two of you must have had some terrific fights.'

'Spectacular,' he confirmed. 'She once said—she once said she loved me because I was the only man she knew who could stand up to her. She'd have got bored with James in time.'

'And you'd have taken her back for Tina's sake?'

'Yes. What about you?'

'No,' she said slowly. 'I didn't know before, but I know now. I would never have taken James back in a million years.'

'Let's drink our coffee and brandy by the fire,' Drago said.

They cleared the plates into the kitchen, but he rejected her offer to wash up, steering her firmly back into the living room and towards an armchair close to the fire on one side. Another one stood on the other side, and he threw himself into this.

'That was the best meal I've ever tasted,' Alysa said sincerely.

'Thank you. I guess I owed you a decent meal.'

'I think you needed it too. You look more relaxed.'

'Cooking does that for me,' he admitted. 'Going to the cemetery with the whole family was very tough, having to watch every word in case they guessed. You can't imagine how I longed for the one person I can be honest with.' He raised his brandy glass to her.

'Yes, I can,' she murmured. 'Me too.'

He was about to answer when his mobile phone sounded. He answered and immediately his face became exasperated and horrified.

'I told Pietro to send them up here,' he barked. 'What does he think he—? How soon can you get them here? Why not tonight? All right, but first thing tomorrow.'

'Shall I guess?' Alysa asked as he hung up. 'My bags?'

'Pietro took them to the villa. I thought I made myself plain, but evidently I didn't. I'm sorry. That was my steward wanting to know what he should do. You find it funny?'

Alysa had given a little laugh. Now she said lightly, 'It does have its funny side. You were so determined to avoid the curious eyes of your employees.'

'I apologise for all this,' he growled. 'They can't get out

here tonight, not in the dark on that mountain road. Your things will be here tomorrow, but until then—'

'I'll cope.'

'Alysa, I swear I didn't plan this.'

'It's all right, I believe you,' she said through laughter. 'With another man I'd be suspicious, but you and I aren't about that.'

'Thank you.'

She had set her brandy glass down on a small fender before the fire. Now she reached forward to get it, and kept on sliding down until she was sitting on the floor, finding it surprisingly comfortable because of the thick rug that seemed to be made of fake fur. She leaned back against the chair, sipping contentedly.

She was enveloped by a sense of well-being. It had something to do with the fire and the fine brandy, but more to do with Drago. He'd said, 'the one person I can be honest with', and it was true for her too.

She thought of the journey home that she'd nearly taken: landing at the airport with nobody to meet her, queuing for a taxi, reaching her home to find it cold, dark and empty, as it had been for the past endless year. The lonely evening with only her bleak thoughts for company.

Here she was effectively a prisoner, but a well-fed prisoner, basking in the glow of a friendly fire, relaxed and almost happy. If she could have escaped she would not have done so. She sighed pleasurably, feeling her cares fade away.

Drago, happening to glance across at her, saw the brandy glass about to slip out of her hand and hastened to remove it. Her eyes were closed, and her breathing coming steadily.

He studied her, feeling guilty but unable to stop. It was unforgivable to watch her while she was unaware, but something about her face held him against his will. Now that her defences were abandoned, she'd changed in a way that made him grow still.

If asked to describe her mouth he would have said that it was too firm and precise to be attractive, but exactly right for the slightly grim female she'd been at their first meeting. No man, he thought, considering the matter impartially, would ever be tempted to kiss that mouth.

But now it was softened, her lips slightly apart, the breath whispering through them. Nature had shaped her more generously than she wanted the world to know, and sleep had revealed what she had tried to hide.

Her whole face was one that a man might contemplate with curiosity, even while he blamed himself for his impertinence.

She stirred and he backed off, rising to his feet and going to a chest of drawers where he'd deposited a canvas bag when he'd first come in. Having retrieved it he returned to his seat. For a while he remained still, until at last, with evident reluctance, he reached inside, drew out an envelope and sat turning it over between his fingers. He did this for some time, making no attempt to open it, and putting it aside quickly when Alysa stirred and yawned.

'Have I been asleep?' she demanded.

'Just dozing for a minute.'

'How rude of me. I'm sorry.' She pulled herself up and rubbed her eyes, gazing into the fire which cast a glow over her face.

'Well?' she said at last, turning to look at him.

'Well?'

'Well, why are we here? Drago, when are you going to stop putting things off? You wanted to show me something so important that you dragooned me into coming here, but then you seemed to forget all about it.'

'I've been trying not to think of it,' he admitted. 'It's something that was found in their apartment and only delivered to my house yesterday.'

'But didn't you go through the place?'

'Yes, and I thought I'd been pretty thorough, but it seems there was a secret place—a small cupboard in the wall that you'd never find unless you knew it was there. The people who rent the place now discovered it by accident and found a box inside, containing a cache of letters. From them they learned enough to get in touch with me.'

'You mean...?'

'Letters between James and Carlotta, dating from September, as soon as he went back to England after their first meeting. When he came to live here he brought her letters with him. His were sent to her work, and I suppose that's where she kept them, because I had no idea.'

She had to force herself to ask, 'What do they say?'

'I haven't read them.'

'How could you bear not to?'

He smiled faintly. 'Because you weren't there. I've always thought of myself as a brave man, but I found I can't do this alone.' His smile became self-mocking. 'I need you to hold my hand.'

'If you haven't read them, how can you be sure they're real? James wasn't a man for writing letters. He did it all by phone and email, like most people these days.'

He showed her the envelope. 'There are some things that you can't trust to email. Is this his handwriting?'

'Yes,' she said slowly, taking it from him. 'That's James.'

She pulled out the letter and looked at the date.

'September,' she murmured. 'He must have written this as soon as he came back.'

The words seemed to leap off the page.

> I'm sitting here at midnight, trying to imagine that I'm still there with you. It's only a few hours since you

kissed me goodbye at the airport, yet already it seems like a lifetime. All I can do is try to tell you what our meeting has meant to me, how you've transformed my life in only a few days.

She laid down the letter. 'I can't read any more.'
But even as she said it she began reading again. James had written these words on the night he'd returned from Florence in September. She'd met him at the airport, gone home with him, tried to make love to him and been rejected.

'Because he'd come from her bed only a few hours before,' she whispered. 'He sent me away, then sat down to write to her.'

Drago was reaching into the bag, pulling out more letters, searching through them feverishly.

'What does she say to him?' Alysa asked.

'She says here that her marriage is a sham,' Drago replied in a dazed voice. 'And she can endure it no longer. *Mio dio!*'

Alysa barely heard. She too was pulling out letters, seeking the ones from James. They were revealing. He wrote:

My darling, please don't be jealous of Alysa. She means nothing to me any more. Even at its best it was only an insipid love, nothing compared to what I feel for you.

And in another letter:

I've promised to be with you next week, and I will. Don't worry about my failing you, because I never will. I've made an excuse to Alysa and she's accepted it. Luckily she'll believe anything I tell her.

So I'll arrive on that plane, and, if you can be there to meet me, wonderful. If not, I'll just go to our little home and wait for you.

'It's true,' she said. 'I believed whatever he told me, I loved him so much.'

In answer to Drago's look she handed him the letter.

'It's dated just before my birthday,' she said. 'We had such plans. But then he said he had to go away for a few days—something to do with the prospect of a job as a photographer. When he came back he said he hadn't got the job and it had been a wasted few days.'

'You didn't check up on him?'

'I never checked up on him. I trusted him totally. I didn't know he despised me for it.'

'And now you can despise him,' Drago said fiercely. 'Let that be your revenge.'

'Yes,' she said in what she hoped was a strong voice. 'You're right, of course.'

But the words echoed bleakly through the emptiness inside her.

CHAPTER SIX

DRAGO studied the contents of the next letter with a set face that grew almost cruel as he read on.

> You say your husband is a harsh man. My love, it breaks my heart to think of you trapped there with him, the victim of his bullying. But it won't be long now before I come to rescue you.

'It's a lie!' Drago said violently. 'I never bullied her. Others maybe, but not her or Tina, I swear it.'

'You don't need to convince me,' Alysa said.

'But how could she tell such a lie?' he demanded.

'She was playing a part, saying what she thought would fire him up.'

She took the letter from him and scanned it quickly, finding it full of a tender possessiveness that she would have thought charming in any other man. James was writing to the woman he had passionately adored, and it was so different from the casual love he'd given her that her heart ached.

Or at least it would have ached, if she hadn't been safely past that stage, she reassured herself.

There was more about Drago, making it clear that Carlotta

had painted him in a tyrannical light. Alysa found herself disbelieving every word. Already she knew him well enough for that. It was he who was Carlotta's victim, raging helplessly like a baited bear.

'We were together for ten years,' he grated. 'Until she left me, I thought they were wonderful years. We loved and cared for each other.'

'And you were always faithful to her, weren't you?' It was a statement, not a question.

'Of course I was faithful,' he said scornfully. 'I was hers in every way, body and soul. There's nothing I wouldn't have done for her. *Nothing!*'

The last word was a shout of anguish. Alysa moved instinctively, taking his hand between both of hers. He gripped her so hard that she winced, but concealed it, letting him hold onto her as long as he needed.

'Sorry,' he said ruefully as he released her. 'Did I hurt you?'

'Not at all,' she lied, flexing her fingers.

'Do you want to stop?'

'No, we can't give in now. We've got to follow the path wherever it leads. After all, we already know the worst.'

She began to read aloud.

'"Talking to you last night was wonderful, but I wish it hadn't had to be the telephone. I so much wanted to tell you our wonderful secret in person, and see your dear face".'

'What secret?' Drago asked. 'Does she say?'

Alysa didn't reply. A suffocating fear was overtaking her. It was impossible. She was mad even to think of it. She told herself she must read on, and then, '"It's the most wonderful thing in the world. I thought nothing could make our love more perfect, but our baby will make us complete".'

'Baby!' Drago sat up, tense.

In a daze, Alysa read on. '"My darling, never doubt that

this child is yours. Since the day I met you I've kept my husband out of my bed, and no man but you has loved me. No man ever will again".'

'*Bastardo!*' Drago snatched the letter out of her hand and began to read it urgently. After a moment he crumpled it in his hand.

'I don't believe this,' he muttered. 'Why does she say things that can't be true?'

'Can't they?' Alysa asked, watching the fire intently. 'Did she "keep you out", as she says?'

'Yes, but—' He broke off with a groan. 'A few months earlier I'd told her I wanted another child, but she put me off. We quarrelled and she shut me out. I wanted to be reconciled, but she wouldn't— Now I see that it was more convenient to keep me away, because all the time—'

He slammed his hand down on a low table with such force that it smashed. A stream of violent Italian curses broke from him. His chest was heaving with the violence of his emotion, and for a moment he was too distracted to watch Alysa—and so didn't see that she was staring into space, her face wooden, her eyes dead.

She and Carlotta had become pregnant by James at almost exactly the same time. When she'd been waiting for him to arrive for Christmas, thinking how she would tell him of their baby, he had been on his way to Florence—to Carlotta, and the child he'd fathered with her.

Half unconsciously she laid her hand over her stomach, almost deafened by the thunderous beat of her own heart.

She'd thought there could be no more pain beyond what she had already suffered. She was wrong.

She climbed slowly to her feet and moved away from the fire's warmth to the window, where she stared out, unseeing. After a moment Drago came and stood beside her.

'I'm glad you couldn't understand what I was saying,' he said. 'I thought I was ready for anything, but that one—after all this time. I don't know what I want to do—throw something, bang my head against the wall, curse her to hell and back.'

But she astonished him by shrugging.

'Why bother? We knew they were sleeping together. This doesn't really make any difference.'

Drago stared, alerted less by her words than by a note in her voice that he'd heard before: harsh. Dead. It was how she'd sounded when they had first met at the waterfall, and it had fitted with the robotic severity of her appearance that day. Today that chilling note had briefly gone, revealing a vibrant sound that had suggested a whole new side to her, but now it was back like steel armour.

He'd criticised her for it then, but not now. He was beginning to understand.

'Does it really not make a difference?' he asked carefully.

'Why should it?' She gave a brittle laugh. 'What's one more betrayal? They've been dead a year. Good riddance!'

She leaned back against the window frame and regarded him with cool detachment as she observed, 'I told you there was a lot to be said for putting it behind you, and now you see I was right.'

'Then I envy you,' he said untruthfully.

He could hardly speak for horror at what he was witnessing. She was turning to stone before his eyes, retreating into a place where he couldn't follow. If he tried she would fight him off with deadly weapons. A sensible man would have feared her, but he could only feel a surge of pity, followed by anger at himself. What had he done to her?

His attention was caught by something floating past the window. Throwing it open, he saw a blanket of white. Thick flakes of snow poured down onto the leaves, through the branches and down to the ground far below. While they'd been unaware, the world had changed beyond recognition.

'It looks so cold out there,' Alysa whispered. 'So cold.' She turned away. 'I think I'll go to bed now.'

He wished she would meet his eyes. Her withdrawn look unsettled him.

'Are you all right?' he asked, feeling how inadequate the question was.

'Of course. I'm just tired.'

'This snow will block the roads, and delay your bags getting here. You'll find some clothes in the wardrobe, but I'm afraid they're hers.'

'Don't worry about me,' she said indifferently. 'I don't need—' she shuddered '—anything of hers. There's no need to show me the way. Goodnight.'

She walked away to the bedroom, moving carefully because she was afraid that any moment she would break in two. When she was inside she leaned back against the door and stayed there for several minutes, trying to find the strength to move.

Her mind was focussed. *Keep calm. Stay in control. Don't go mad. Above all, cling onto your sanity.*

'It doesn't really change anything,' she muttered. 'What difference can it make now?'

But even as the words came she wrapped her arms around herself and bent double, as if to protect the child who was already lost. Still doubled up, she managed to get to the bed, where she breathed deeply until she felt her strength return a little.

'Unpack,' she said as though it was only by giving herself instructions that she could function. 'I've got to make sure it's there.'

'It' was a small bag containing underwear and make-up that she always carried in her hand luggage ever since an airline had lost her bags for three days. She found it quickly, much to her relief, as no power on earth would have made her wear Carlotta's clothes.

But curiosity made her pull open drawers to see what was there. Carlotta hadn't got round to clearing out this place, and there were still traces of her in lacy bras and panties, delicately made and shaped to be sexy rather than functional. There were nightdresses too, frothy and transparent, cut low.

How could any woman bear to leave such beautiful things behind? Because she was buying a new wardrobe for a new lover, of course. Alysa regarded them with cold contempt.

She thought of Carlotta's photographs, which had emphasised intelligence over beauty, but these items told another story. This was a woman totally at ease with her own sexuality, happy to emphasise it—flaunt it, even—with more than one man.

She had shared this place with her husband, entrancing him with garments so sparely cut that they were almost non-existent. Then she had gone to James and worked her magic on him until she, Alysa, had vanished from his mind.

'It doesn't matter,' she said, repeating the mantra that sustained her. 'Nothing that happens now makes any difference.'

But the mantra was becoming meaningless. The more she tried to hold it up as a shield, the more useless it became. The strength that had kept her controlled for a year was vanishing fast so that the grief came welling up inside.

'No,' she said hoarsely. 'No, *no!* I won't let it—'

She couldn't have said what she meant. Her hands were moving independently of her mind, pulling open drawers, tossing the contents out onto the bed, the floor, reaching into the bag for scissors. She didn't know that tears were streaming down her face as she made the first slash and saw a filmy nightdress disintegrate.

Another slash, another, and now she was no longer destroying clothes but plunging a knife into the heart of the woman who'd stolen her love, killed her child and turned her life into a desert. She'd longed to do this for a year. She knew that now.

She stopped only when her strength had drained away. Sitting on the bed, she surveyed the devastation around her. None of Carlotta's clothes were intact; some had been ripped to tiny shreds. Shocked, she stared at them while her body heaved, as the dam broke and the sobs that had been repressed too long forced their way to the surface.

The scream that broke from her might have come from someone else. It went on and on, louder, more shrill, full of an agony that would never end.

The next moment the door burst open and Drago stood there.

'Alysa, what—?' He stopped as he took in the sight of the devastated room, then froze as he saw the scissors still in her hand.

Following his gaze, Alysa tossed the scissors into a corner and stood facing him, breathing heavily.

'For pity's sake, what's the matter?' he breathed. 'Come here.'

'Don't touch me!' she screamed. *'Don't touch me!'*

He reached for her but she eluded him, dodging past him, out and down the stairs to the front door.

'Alysa!' he cried vainly, trying to catch up. 'Don't go out into the snow. You'll catch your death.'

But she was gone. Drago raced down the stairs and out of the front door to find himself confronting a blizzard. The snow had whipped up to a storm into which she had vanished without trace.

'*Alysa!*' Drago shouted. 'Come back. It's dangerous out there.'

But she was gone in the whirling wall of flakes. Appalled, Drago realised that she could have taken any direction, have slipped on the steep slope, perhaps broken her neck.

'*Alysa!*' he cried again, but the only reply was the scream of the wind.

He began to stumble after her, but, without knowing which way she'd turned, he was lost. He doubled back, calling her name fruitlessly, becoming more alarmed by the minute.

He lost track of time. It might have been five minutes before the wind died, or it might have been hours, but at last the noise was replaced by an eerie silence. He called again and again, hoping to hear her call back, but all that returned was the echo.

He tried not to think of the worst that could have happened to her. Then a sound from nearby made him turn sharply, but he couldn't see her. He listened and heard it again; it was coming from the ground, like an animal whimpering in pain. He began to move around cautiously until he nearly fell over a mound at the foot of a tree. It was covered in snow and it took him a moment to realise that this was Alysa.

'*Mio dio!*' He dropped to his knees, urgently brushing snow away from her. 'What are you doing?'

She didn't seem to hear, but lay with her eyes closed, shaking violently and uttering a long, agonised moan. He said her name again and again, shaking her gently. When she didn't respond he pulled her to her feet.

'Come on,' he said, lifting her in his arms. 'The sooner I get you into the warm, the better.'

Moving as fast as he could he made it back to the villa and ran upstairs to the bathroom. To his relief her eyes were open, and she seemed a little more aware of her surroundings.

'Take off those wet clothes and get under a hot shower,' he said.

He hung a towelling robe on the door and got out, hurrying back to her room. The sight of it covered in ripped-up clothes shocked him anew, but he got to work quickly, clearing everything out of sight. He'd only just finished when Alysa came in slowly.

She was wearing the towelling robe, and walked hesitantly, as if in a daze. For a moment Drago wondered if she knew who he was.

'Warmer now?' he asked.

She nodded and he moved cautiously forward, brushing her cheeks, which were still wet.

'You haven't dried your face properly,' he said.

But he realised with a shock that she was still weeping—not in gasps and sobs, but quietly, endlessly.

He didn't waste time asking what the matter was. He guessed that this was rooted in the grim, emotionless front she'd presented when she'd learned about Carlotta's pregnancy, and in the explosion that had made her destroy Carlotta's things. He didn't understand anything, and he knew that only patience would help him now.

'Go to bed,' he said. 'And keep warm. No—' He stopped her as she turned to the bed. 'Not in that robe. It's damp.'

'I haven't got anything else.'

'Then I'll get you something.'

He returned after a moment with one of his own shirts.

'It's thick, for winter,' he said. 'I'll be back in a minute.'

She stared at the shirt while tears streamed, unheeded, down her cheeks. Her brain was moving slowly, realising at last that she was meant to take off the robe and put on the shirt. She did so, but then remembered that there was something else to be done. Yes: get into bed. She managed that, and was lying staring at the ceiling when he returned with a glass of brandy.

'Drink this,' he commanded, raising her with one arm and holding the glass to her lips with the other hand.

She obeyed without protest, which worried him more than anything. When he laid her back down, her tears were still flowing.

'Tell me about it,' he said. 'I want to know everything. It's not just the baby, is it? There's something more.'

'Baby,' she whispered. 'Baby…baby…'

'Yes, neither of us thought of her being pregnant by him,' he said gently.

'Baby—my baby,' she gasped. *'My baby!'*

At first he thought he hadn't heard properly. Then he saw her hands outside the blanket, placed flat across her stomach as though trying to protect something there—or something that was no longer there.

'Baby—baby!' she screamed. *'No, no, no!'*

'Alysa, did you have James's baby?'

'I was going to tell him just before Christmas,' she whispered, looking far beyond Drago. 'I was so happy to be carrying his child. I waited for him but he phoned to say he wasn't coming. I thought, just be patient, tell him next time. But when we met he told me about Carlotta, and I couldn't say anything then, could I?'

'You might have reminded him that he had responsibilities.'

'I didn't want his pity,' she said fiercely. 'I didn't want his duty, or to be a responsibility. If he didn't love me any more, there was nothing else.'

'You're right, I'm sorry,' Drago agreed quietly. He brushed her hair back. 'So the bastard made you both pregnant at the same time. He's lucky to be dead. If he was here now I think I'd kill him. What happened to your baby?'

'I lost it. It was just after they died, when I'd found out her full name and was looking her up on the internet. I couldn't stop—night after night—and then one night the pain started, and that was that.'

'Oh, dear lord!' He bowed his head. 'And then I made you find out about this. Perhaps someone should shoot me. I deserve it.'

'No—you didn't know. But I was all right before today. I didn't really mind very much—it was for the best.'

'You don't mean that.'

'Don't I?' she asked with a small hiccup. 'I'm not sure what I mean any more, but it was what I believed then. I thought I'd cry for ages, but then I found I couldn't cry at all. So I put it behind me.'

But she hadn't, he thought, discovering that he could see into her with shocking clarity. She'd coped by turning herself into a pillar of ice, freezing all emotion because that was the only way she'd been able to bear it. And all the time this had been lying in wait for her.

'Didn't your friends or family help you?' he asked.

'I never told anyone I was pregnant.'

'But wasn't there anybody at home to look after you? Hospitals usually ask about that before they'll discharge you.'

'I didn't go to hospital. It happened at home, on a Friday night. I stayed in bed for the weekend, and on Monday I went back to work.'

'Are you saying that you never told *anyone*?'

'You're the first,' she said simply.

He thought of her in that appalling isolation, and inwardly he shivered. His own loneliness seemed nothing in comparison. At least he'd never awoken to find himself alone in the house. In his bleakest moments he'd been able to go along the corridor, quietly open the door of Tina's room and stand listening to her breathing before retreating, at peace, even if only for a while.

But even that short-lived peace was denied Alysa. She had no child to provide a reason for living. Until this moment he hadn't known he was blessed.

Alysa had turned away from him to bury her face in the pillow, overwhelmed by choking sobs.

'Forgive me,' he said desperately. 'I should never have brought you here. I had no idea—I thought only of myself.'

He reached out to touch her trembling shoulders.

'Alysa, please, talk to me.'

'Go away,' she choked. 'I can't talk—I can't. *Please go away.*'

He could do nothing but leave, although it was the last thing he wanted. If he'd dared he would have put his arms around her and offered her all the comfort in his power, although he knew how inadequate it must be. But all she wanted from him was his absence, so he slipped away.

As he reached his own room his mobile phone was ringing. It was Tina.

'Poppa, I've been ringing and ringing.'

'I'm sorry, little one. It's snowing up here and I got lost in the woods.' It was a feeble excuse, and Tina thought so too because she cackled hilariously.

'*Poppa!* You never get lost.'

'I used to think so too,' he said wryly. 'But I was wrong. I've taken a lot of wrong turnings up here.'

Tina spoke with childish sternness. 'You're talking itty-bitty.'

It meant 'nonsense', and was their private joke.

'Don't be angry with me, *cara*. Are you enjoying yourself at Aunt Maria's?'

'Oh yes, we played hide and seek all over the house, and Nonna was cross, but Aunt Maria said...'

She babbled on innocently for a few minutes, and he sensed with relief that she would be happy for a few days.

'Are you snowed in, Poppa?'

'I'm afraid so. It may be a few days before I can get down.'

'Have you got enough to eat?' she asked like a little housewife.

'Plenty, thank you. The cupboard is full.'

'And you will be careful?'

'Stop nagging me,' he protested, grinning. 'It's time you were in bed.'

'That's what Nonna said, but Aunt Maria says I can stay up, and my uncle wants me to teach him how to play dice better, because I keep beating him, and…'

Her chatter was like balm. He bid her a cheerful goodnight, and hung up.

But his cheerfulness faded as he remembered Alysa and the state he'd reduced her to. After a moment he did as he'd often done with Tina—went to stand at her door, listening. From within came the sounds of violent distress, unabated. He leaned back against the wall, wondering if he dared go inside. She'd banished him, yet she needed him. Torn in two, he couldn't move.

Then the sobbing ceased suddenly, to be replaced by a violent coughing. That did it. He gave up struggling with himself and hurried inside.

The light was off but the curtains were drawn back, and in the moonlight he could see her outline heaving.

'Alysa, sit up,' he said, sitting on the bed and taking hold of her. 'It'll be much easier that way.'

She sat up, holding him for support, then leaned forward, seeming to be torn apart by the coughs that wracked her.

'You stupid woman!' he groaned. 'Going out in that snow. You've caught your death of cold now.'

She couldn't answer, too caught up in her distress to have any breath left.

'I've got to keep you warm,' he muttered. 'Wait here. Don't go away.'

The idiocy of the words struck him before he was out of the door, but he was moving fast, dashing to his bedroom to seize up his own thick dressing-gown, then back to her, ordering, 'Put this on. I'll be right back.'

He returned to find her wearing the dressing gown, but not exactly as he wanted.

'Pull it right across the front to protect your chest,' he commanded, demonstrating. 'Now get back into bed, and drink this.'

He produced another glass of brandy which he almost poured down her throat. She choked but finished it.

'That's better. Now lie down so that I can pull the bedclothes over you. What's that?'

She was struggling to speak, but another bout of coughing tore her. When she'd calmed down she gasped, 'Made—a mess—of everything.'

'I couldn't have made a bigger mess if I'd tried,' he said with feeling.

'Not you—me. Going out like that.'

'Shut up. The blame is mine and we both know it. What was I thinking of? I should have read those letters first instead of just dumping them on you.'

'Makes no difference,' she said in a hoarse whisper. 'You couldn't have known about my baby. Not your fault.'

'Don't be generous,' he begged. 'It makes me feel worse. I'd rather you yelled at me.'

'Can't—no breath.'

He managed a brief laugh. 'Then chuck something at my head. Shall I find you a heavy object?'

'No energy—consider it chucked.' The words ended in another coughing fit. 'Oh dear,' she said.

'I agree. Wait a minute, I've just thought of something.'

He left and returned after a few minutes with a bottle and spoon.

'We always kept medicine up here, just in case. I wasn't sure there was any left after all this time. This is good cough-mixture. Open your mouth.'

She let him coax her until she'd swallowed some, and felt it soothing her as it went down.

'Now lie down and try to get to sleep,' he said as he'd said so often to his child. Right this minute, that was how he felt about Alysa—she was his to protect.

Alysa lay back, exhausted from coughing and weeping. She no longer had the energy to do anything except sink into the warmth and let the world fade away. She was safe, as she hadn't been for a long time, and it was blissful to let go.

'I'm OK now,' she murmured. 'You don't have to mother-hen me.'

'Just go to sleep.'

She closed her eyes at once.

Hours later she awoke in the same position, feeling rested after a dreamless sleep. She stretched, and discovered that she was not alone on the bed. Drago lay just behind her, fully dressed and outside the bedclothes, evidently taking his nursing duties seriously.

'Mother hen,' she said tenderly.

Moving carefully, not wanting to disturb him, she eased herself out of the bed and made her way to the bathroom. When she returned Drago was lying in the same position, except that his arm was stretched out over the space she had occupied, as though he'd been searching for her. She contrived to slide in underneath his arm without disturbing him, and held quite still in case he should awake. He seemed dead to the world, but after a moment his arm tightened around her. She slept.

CHAPTER SEVEN

WHEN Alysa next awoke she was alone, and the sound of frying was coming from the kitchen. She made haste to get up, although she felt feverish, and another coughing fit attacked her. She took some more of the medicine, noting with dismay that the bottle was now empty.

'You sound bad,' Drago said as soon as she appeared in the kitchen.

'I'm all right, really. That medicine is good but I seem to have finished it.'

'Don't worry, there's another bottle. I'll make you some coffee. Sit down.'

He served her eggs, bacon and delicious coffee, smiling briefly when he looked at her, which wasn't often. She had the sense that he was uncomfortable in her company, and wondered if he was simply embarrassed at the position in which he found himself. He hadn't brought her here to nurse her through a childish ailment.

'I'm sorry,' she said after only a few mouthfuls. 'I can't eat very much.'

'I think you should go back to bed.' He touched her forehead with the back of his hand. 'You're feverish. Go on.'

He was right, and she was glad to lie down again. But it

was strange that he sounded almost curt, as though he couldn't get rid of her fast enough.

When she awoke the light had changed, becoming duller. She sat up, listening to the silence of the house, and feeling suddenly fearful.

Not to worry, she thought, getting out of bed. She would find Drago and all would be well. But as she moved through room after room a nameless dread began to take hold of her. He was nowhere to be found.

Keep calm, she told herself. He must be somewhere.

But every door she opened only revealed more emptiness, and the dread began to envelop her. Looking out of the window, she saw the mountains rearing up, covered in snow, a white hell into which he had disappeared.

The car; he might have taken it.

But when she descended to the garage the car was still there. Drago hadn't merely gone away. He'd vanished into thin air.

She stood, nonplussed, wondering what was going to happen now. She was alone, abandoned in a strange country, trapped by the snow, and she didn't feel up to doing anything except going back to bed. She ought to be strong-minded, but how would that help?

'Are you out of your mind?'

Drago's shout, coming out of nowhere, made her jump and turn to see him coming in through the garage door, enveloping her in an icy blast.

'What the devil are you doing out here, dressed like that?' he yelled. 'Get back inside.'

'I just—'

'Go in before you catch pneumonia.'

He took hold of her arm, hustling her inside and up the stairs, muttering furiously.

'Why do I bother looking after you if you have no common sense?'

'You vanished. It worried me.'

'I went to get you some more cough mixture. I thought we had another bottle, but I was wrong, so I went down to the village. I had to walk because the car wouldn't be safe in these conditions.'

'You walked all the way down there and back in the snow?'

'Yes, and for what? For a dimwit who hasn't the sense to keep warm when she's sick. If you die of pneumonia, I'll really lose patience with you.'

She gave a husky laugh, which brought on another fit of coughing.

'I've got you some pills as well. Have a couple now, and some cough mixture, then go back to bed while I get the place warmer and fix you something to eat. And stand away from me. I don't want your germs.'

She eyed him satirically. 'And they say chivalry is dead.'

'This isn't chivalry, it's self-protection. Just do as I say.'

She took the medicine and went thankfully back to her room. But before getting into bed she looked out of the window at the mountains, which were already becoming shadowy as the early-winter dusk began to fall. Down below she saw a door open, and Drago appear, heading for the woodshed. He emerged with his arms full of logs, which he carried into the house. A few moments later he made another journey to fetch charcoal.

Then sounds came from along the corridor, telling her that he was refilling the range, causing the house to grow warmer at once, or so it seemed to her.

But the consoling warmth had little to do with the heating. Drago had returned, and the demons that had haunted her for the last year were in retreat. Comforted, she climbed into bed and snuggled beneath the covers.

He brought her some soup, and a cup of coffee, both of which he set down at a careful distance.

'Eat that even if you aren't hungry,' he said brusquely. 'I don't want you starving to death either. You'd do it just to be awkward.'

'Then why don't you just throw me out of the window and get it over with?' she demanded huskily. 'Think of the trouble you'd save.'

He appeared to consider this before saying, 'Too difficult to explain away the body. It suits me better if you stay alive.'

'Gosh, thanks!'

He gave her a ribald grin before vanishing.

The grin faded as soon as he was out of her sight. He'd been on edge since he'd awoken that morning, to find himself lying with his arm over her. It wasn't what he'd meant to happen. He'd stayed with her the night before out of concern and a desire to be on hand if she needed him. When sleep had overcome him he'd lain down beside her, careful to stay outside the bedclothes, not touching her.

He wasn't sure exactly when he'd put his arm over her, but he must have done so, because he'd been holding her when he awoke. At all costs she mustn't find out. In their special circumstances it was a betrayal of trust. He could only be thankful that he'd awoken first, and had escaped without discovery.

Even so, he'd been on edge when she'd got up, waiting to detect any hint of suspicion in her manner, but there'd been nothing. She'd merely looked bedraggled and vulnerable, a different woman from the austere female he'd met only three days ago. But that had only increased his feeling of guilt, and he'd taken refuge in a surly manner.

It was almost a relief to discover that the medicine had run out, so that he'd had to take a long walk down to the village through the snow. He'd looked in to tell her he was going but, finding her asleep, had slipped quietly away.

He'd hoped the walk would clear his head, but his confusions merely settled into a different pattern. The discovery that his wife had been pregnant by her lover had shattered him, but he'd been prepared for new pain. What he hadn't anticipated was Alysa's agony.

If asked to describe himself he would have refused, then done it unwillingly: a straightforward man who loved his family, but without frills or fine words. That was him. Empathy was something for others, those with time to waste.

But Alysa's suffering had torn through him, so that he felt it with her. It was a new sensation, and if he was honest he didn't like it. From now on he would simply help her recover, pray for the snow to melt, and bid her goodbye with relief. Above all he'd decided he would behave with circumspection, and speak to her with the greatest care.

But that was before he'd arrived home to find her in the freezing garage, and his explosion of temper had banished good resolutions to the far ends of the earth. Having seen her safely in bed, he stormed into the kitchen and got to work in a fury. As he prepared the meal they would eat that evening, he lashed his anger to keep it alive, because that way he might avoid the thoughts and feelings lying in wait for him.

He scowled when she finally emerged into the kitchen, still in his robe.

'Are you sure you're ready to get up?' he growled.

'Yes, I feel better now. Those pills you got me are good.'

'Go and sit by the fire while I finish making supper.'

'Can't I—?'

'Do as you're told.'

'Yes, *sir*!'

Her office colleagues would laugh if they could see her

now, she thought, curling up on the rug by the fire and tossing on some more wood. She was famed for her cool head and ability to organise. But right now it was nice to be waited on.

Supper was steak and red wine, which he brought to her by the fire, and they picnicked like children. It was the best steak she'd ever tasted.

'I feel guilty that you had to go out for me,' she said.

'I'm the one who feels guilty, trapping you up here without even a change of clothes.'

'Look,' she said awkwardly. 'About what I did to Carlotta's things…'

'Did you really do all that?' he asked, fascinated.

'Every last slash.'

'Did it make you feel any better?'

'Much,' she said, with such feeling that he grinned. 'I'm sorry, Drago, I know you must have treasured them.'

'If I did I was a sentimental fool. I should have done what you did long ago. Have you kept any souvenirs of James?'

'I may have something lying around. It's a while since I looked.' She saw his wry look and said, 'All right, I still have one of his shirts. He was wearing it the day he said he loved me—at least, he didn't actually say that. Now I think of it, he phrased it very carefully, but at the time…' She sighed. 'I guess I heard what I wanted to hear.'

'Yes, we do that when we're very much in love.'

'And you were, weren't you? Very much.'

'I didn't think it was possible to love a woman as much as I loved her,' he said slowly. 'We met on every level—mentally, physically, everything. No matter how often I made love to her it wasn't enough. In bed she was never the same woman twice, and I always wanted more of her.'

'How long were you married?'

'Ten years.'

'And all that love you spoke of—it was still there, wasn't it?'

'As much as on the first day,' he said slowly. 'And she loved me the same way. I would have sworn it. Until she met him, and he changed her.'

'So you blame James?'

'I hate him,' Drago said simply. 'I don't hate him any less because he's dead. I'm glad he's dead. I hope he suffered agonies. I hate him as much as you must hate Carlotta, or you couldn't have carved up her clothes. If she'd been there herself, I dread to think what you'd have done to her.'

'Maybe. I blamed her for taking him from me, but I wonder if she could have done that if he hadn't been willing.'

He didn't answer, and she looked up to find him staring into the fire.

'It works both ways,' he said at last. 'You're saying that she must have been willing too, but I don't believe that.'

'Perhaps she was a little restless. Maybe she just meant to have a minor flirtation and it got out of hand.'

'*No*. She didn't flirt. At parties I used to watch her. She'd laugh and tease the men, but there was a line she never crossed. And nor did I. We had a wonderful marriage until she met him.'

'But did you know what she was thinking? Do we ever know, no matter how close we think we are?'

He grimaced. 'You mean I was fooling myself then, and I'm still doing it now? Maybe you're right and I just don't have your courage. I want to keep my memories. Nothing so beautiful will ever happen to me again, and I can't let it go.'

'You still love her.'

'No,' he said quickly. 'The love is dead, but it was glorious while it lasted, and I can't just consign it to the rubbish heap. If I have to live with dreams for the rest of my life, I'll do it rather than live without them.'

She regarded him in wonder. On the surface this big, powerful man was armoured against anything the world could do to him. The truth was hidden away inside his heart, in a place so secret that even he feared to visit it often.

He understood her look, and said, 'I've never told that to anyone but you.'

'And I'll never repeat it,' she promised.

'Thank you. I know I can trust you.'

As he said it he looked away from her. But then he looked back, and the trust he spoke of was there in his eyes, communicating directly without words.

He must have looked at Carlotta like that—with total, defenceless confidence. Only two people in the world had seen it. Carlotta was one, and she was the other. It felt strange to have something in common with that woman.

'I think you're right to keep your dreams of her,' she said. 'If only for Tina's sake.'

'What about you?' he asked. 'Is there anyone for whose sake you have to keep quiet?'

'Nobody.'

The word fell on him like stone, and he recalled what she'd told him of the bleakness of her life. Not that she would call it bleak. She would simply say she was organised.

He moved beside her and put his arms about her, holding her tight.

'You'll get my germs,' she protested.

'To hell with them.'

After a while she asked sleepily, 'Are there many more letters to read?'

He pulled over the bag so that several envelopes fell onto the floor. They each took some and began riffling through them. Alysa opened one in James's handwriting and read:

I never believed in the kind of love you hear about in songs, until I met you, and you showed me it could happen. Before that, I always settled for the easy version of love that I could take or leave. I never risked the kind that tears out a man's heart and tells him he'd be better dead than losing his woman. But then I met you and knew that you were that woman. You gave me courage. Bless you for that, my darling.

She stared into the fire until she saw Drago looking at her, and handed the letter to him.

'"Better dead",' Drago read aloud. 'He didn't know what he was saying.'

'He was never like that with me,' she murmured. 'He was always cheerful, funny—even when we— And it was nice sometimes.' She broke off to sneeze.

'Don't force yourself,' Drago said gently.

'I used to think it would be lovely if he was a bit more romantic, but I told myself that he just couldn't find the right words, and he loved me really. But the way he wrote to Carlotta—all passion and intensity—it's like a different man. I guess I never really knew him, because he didn't want me to.'

'I was luckier than you,' Drago admitted. 'Whatever Carlotta did at the end, I know who she was in the years before—the woman who gave me all herself. Nothing can change that.'

'Good,' she said with sudden decisiveness. 'Hold onto that thought. It'll stop you becoming a psycho like me.'

'You're not a psycho.'

'I was headed that way. I can see it now. I deadened my heart because I thought it would be easier. But it wasn't. Listen to your friend, Drago. Don't become like me.'

He grinned tenderly. 'If my daughter could hear you now. You really took her advice to heart.'

'You mean about looking after you?'

'Yes, you're doing a great job.'

'Then we're even.'

She didn't know how long they sat there on the floor, leaning against each other, but she could happily have stayed for ever. It wasn't thrilling or dramatic, or any of the things she had known with James. But every moment that passed was healing something deep inside her, bringing her back to life.

And him too. That thought made her almost happy. Let him put Carlotta on a pedestal if that was what he needed. She wouldn't spoil it for him.

'Time you were in bed,' he announced suddenly. 'I'll make you a hot chocolate and you can take your pills.'

While he was in the kitchen she took another letter. It was from Carlotta, and she read it with little more than casual interest. She was beginning to feel that nothing else could happen.

Within a few lines she discovered her mistake. Carlotta had written:

> We made a pact to be honest with each other, so I'm going to tell you the complete truth. You asked if you were my first lover since my marriage, and, though I'd love to say yes, the truth is that there have been others.

Alysa's hands tightened on the paper so that it crumpled. When she'd flattened it she read it again, wondering if she'd misunderstood. But there was no mistaking what Carlotta was saying.

> I know now that I married before I was quite ready. It was thrilling to defy my mother with an elopement, and Drago was insistent, so I yielded unwisely.
>
> I should have lived a more exciting life before I settled down. I realised soon after the wedding that domesticity bored me, so I compensated with a few little 'adventures'.

'Bitch,' Alysa muttered, barely aware that she was speaking.

> Drago never found out. I did my best to be a good wife to him in other ways, and I gave him Tina, whom he adores. So I don't really feel guilty.
>
> My love, never fear. To you I will be faithful. With you I find a completeness and a fulfilment that I never found with Drago.

Here it was, the proof that Drago was fooling himself. Far from being the woman who had given him all of herself, she'd shared herself out pretty freely, it seemed. He'd endured her betrayal and loss, but this would break his heart finally.

A sound from the kitchen made her stuff the letter back into the envelope. It was instinctive. Without thinking about it, she knew she wasn't going to show him this.

'Anything interesting?' he asked, coming in and setting down the hot chocolate.

'No, just more of the same,' she said casually. 'Oh, that looks lovely.'

He gathered up the letters and tossed them back into the bag.

'Enough of them for tonight,' he said.

He pushed the bag onto a low shelf. Alysa watched, blaming herself for not taking the letter while she'd had the chance. Now she could do nothing without arousing his suspicion.

She maintained a calm façade as she bid him goodnight and retired to bed. She even managed to sleep for a while. But then she awoke, every nerve on edge, knowing that she must secure that letter before he saw it.

She might argue with herself that it was illogical for her to protect him, but this wasn't logic. This was emotion, a luxury she hadn't allowed herself for too long. Drago had said he trusted her, and what happened to him now was in her hands.

Moving silently, she got out of bed and looked out into the corridor. The house was silent, and no light could be seen beneath Drago's door. This was her one chance. It took a few seconds to creep into the main room where there was still a faint glow from the dying fire, locate the bag on the shelf and speed back to her room.

A quick search revealed the cruel letter. She read it briefly to make sure it was the right one, then slipped it into the drawer of her bedside locker. Feverishly she began searching through the remaining letters, just in case there was another mention of Carlotta's infidelity. She found it in James's reply, and took that too. When she was sure she'd removed everything dangerous, she slipped back into the corridor and stood in the darkness, listening fearfully. But there was no sound.

Then a quick dash to replace the bag where Drago had left it. It was done. Now all she had to do was get back to her room. She was almost there when she heard his door opening, and turned, standing petrified in the light of the window.

Then she saw something that shocked her. A smile illuminated Drago's face, so that for a moment it was brilliant with joy. His hand moved as if to reach out to her, but then it fell back to his side and the smile died.

'Are you all right?' he asked politely.

'Yes—yes. I just had to—get up for a minute. Goodnight.'

She fled to her room and stood leaning against the door, trying not to believe what had happened: for a split second in the darkness Drago had thought she was Carlotta. He'd smiled, almost reaching out to her. But then the smile had died as the sad truth had overcome him again.

Now Alysa was passionately glad at what she had done. It was wrong, disgraceful. She was a thief. But she had protected him from further grief, and she wasn't sorry.

She could hear him moving about in his bedroom next door to hers, and the mysterious communication that seemed to unite them showed her his movements—from the door to the window and back again, from the door to the wall, to the window.

A pause, then the sound of the window being opened. In her mind she could see him standing there, looking out at the dark mountains with the moon rising behind them, trying to cool himself in the chill air. Vainly seeking an elusive peace.

She knew the moment when he closed the window and began to pace the room again, until he ended up by the wall that separated him from her. She held her breath, hoping he'd gone to bed.

But then came the sound of a long groan, like an animal caught in a trap. It shivered away into nothing, and after that there was silence.

CHAPTER EIGHT

For the next couple of days they continued going through the letters, but there were no more revelations, and at last they could relax. The pills worked well and her cold improved fast, until they were able to go out for a breath of fresh air. Drago acted like a nanny, making her wear his own coat, and buttoning it up to the throat, while she laughed with pleasure. It was bliss to be fussed over.

'You're twice my size,' she said, regarding herself in the mirror, almost vanishing into the huge coat, and flapping the sleeves which hung comically off the ends of her arms. 'Whatever do I look like?'

'You look like someone who needs a scarf,' he said, wrapping one around her neck several times. 'Has nobody ever taken any care of you?'

'My mother did, until she died. But after that I've been pretty independent.'

For 'independent' read 'alone', he thought.

'What about James?' he wanted to know.

She made a face. James hadn't been the protective kind, and until this moment it hadn't bothered her.

The beauty of the mountain was overwhelming as they went carefully up the slope, Alysa clinging to his arm at his insistence to avoid slipping. Overhead the trees hung heavy with snow, while in front of them the white path led up out of sight.

'I've never seen anything so lovely,' she sighed.

'Don't you have snow in England?'

'It turns to sludge very quickly. But this...'

She let go of his arm and turned round and round, looking up so that the bright morning sun fell on her face. Drago watched her, smiling at her ecstasy.

'You look like a scarecrow,' he said.

'Thank you, kind sir. Yes, I do, don't I?' She began to spin faster. *'Wheee!'*

'You're scaring the birds,' he protested as a startled flock rose from the branches above, fleeing these wild noises.

The next moment they were engulfed in snow that had been disturbed by the scattering birds. Alysa collapsed with laughter, leaning back against a tree and sliding down.

'Don't sit on the ground, you crazy woman,' Drago said, brushing snow out of his hair and taking hold of her.

He yanked her unceremoniously to her feet, so that she staggered and he had to steady her against him.

'Behave,' he told her firmly. 'Are you totally intent on getting pneumonia?'

'That would be very awkward for you,' she laughed. 'Especially if I died. You get me up here, and I vanish for ever. You could be in big trouble.'

'Nonsense, they'd give me a medal. Now, come on, I want to get you safely into the warm.'

'Suppose I want to stay?'

His answer was to pick her up and march firmly back to the villa.

'Why do some women argue about everything?' he growled.

'Some men are made to be argued with,' she said, steadying herself with both arms around his neck. 'The temptation is irresistible.'

He gave a bark of laughter, turning his head to glance at her, and immediately wished he hadn't. Her mouth was so close to his that their lips almost touched. He looked ahead quickly, shaken by the vibration that went through him, almost causing him to stumble, and feeling her arms tighten about his neck.

'Steady,' she said in a trembling voice. 'I don't want to be dumped on the ground again.'

'I'm sorry,' he said huskily.

She struggled to control her breathing, which was coming in awkward jerks, thankful that he couldn't sense the beating of her heart. Or could he? She could sense his. Unless it was merely the echo of her own.

Don't overreact. It was over a year since a man's lips had touched her own, and she'd been taken by surprise.

As he strode on she watched the side of his face. It was dark with something that she might have mistaken for fury if she hadn't known better. She had neither fear nor hope that he would follow through; not now, while she was dependent on him. It would be a betrayal of trust, and he was a man of honour. There was no justice in the world, she thought sadly.

As soon as they reached home they got to work, stoking up the fire, working in the kitchen, managing to avoid each other's eyes even when they said goodnight and retired to their rooms.

That night it rained, and by morning the worst of the snow had gone. Drago said he would arrange for her bags to be delivered. To her relief his manner was normal again, and she was able to respond in the same tone.

'I've managed well enough so far,' she said with a gleam of

humour. 'Although I suppose I should stop pinching your shirts.'

'That's the third one you're wearing. I'll be glad for you to recover your own clothes before I run out.'

Then his smile died. 'But it's not that. The truth is that these last few days have been— Didn't you feel it?'

'Oh yes,' she said in a tone of wonder. 'We laughed. Can you believe that? I don't think I've laughed in months.'

'Me neither. It was the last thing I was expecting when we came here. It's you—I've never known anyone like you. I don't want this time to end.'

'Neither do I,' she admitted.

'Just a couple more days?'

'All right.'

'I'll call home and get them to send the bags right away.'

But before he could take out his mobile phone, Alysa's own telephone shrilled, startling her. The sound seemed to come from another world, one she had left behind without regret. The caller was her boss.

'Alysa? Are you all right? I got worried when we didn't hear from you.'

'I'm fine, Brian,' she said, trying to sound bright. 'I took a little trip into the mountains and got snowed in.'

'Damn. There are big things happening here, and it would really help if you came back.'

'But I left everything in good order. I even cleared up all the problems with the Riley account.'

'I know, and he's very impressed,' Brian admitted. 'So impressed that he's introduced a new client and told him to ask for you and nobody else. But he wants an early appointment. You should be very proud.'

'Yes,' she said slowly. 'I suppose I should.'

His voice changed, became persuasive.

'Mind you, if it's really difficult, I suppose I could assign him to someone else. Frank's proving very good.'

She knew Frank, a newcomer who was straining every nerve to impress the boss, and would obliterate her if he could. Brian had known just what to say.

'How's the snow?' he asked.

'Clearing,' she admitted reluctantly. 'All right, I'll be back tomorrow.'

Drago was watching her as she hung up.

'Duty calls?' he asked wryly.

'I guess it does. Oh, if only—'

'Hey, that's enough. If there's one thing you and I have learned not to say, it's "if only".'

'I can't help it. If only—if only—'

She wondered what was happening to her. It had been on the tip of her tongue to tell Brian that she was still trapped and needed more time. But the habit of putting work first was too strong, and the words had come out of their own accord.

'There's a flight at six o'clock this evening,' Drago said. 'I'll book it for you.'

Her heart sank. She wanted to say that tomorrow would have done, and they could have spent one last comfortable evening together. Now it was too late. Unless, perhaps, there were no seats. But even that hope died.

'All fixed,' Drago said, hanging up.

'I should have put Brian off,' she said unhappily. 'I wanted those extra days.'

'So did I, but it wasn't to be, and maybe it's best. We've had something we both needed, and we're stronger for it. I shall be glad for the rest of my life that I met you, and you helped me survive.'

He reached out, enveloping her in a bear hug against the warmth of his chest. She turned her head so that it rested on his shoulder with her face turned away from him. His words reminded her of the letter she'd taken and which now, more than ever, she was determined that he must never see. She was afraid to meet his eyes lest they should somehow reveal her thoughts.

They had been granted a special time in which to heal each other's wounds. It had brought them suffering, but also a kind of healing. Now it was time to move on to a life that might be bearable again. But still her heart ached.

Drago called his home and arranged for her luggage to be delivered to the airport, while she went to pack up the few things she had with her, putting the dangerous letter firmly away in her bag.

He made her a final meal of spaghetti, and they washed up together.

'We'd better leave now,' he said. 'I'll need to drive slowly.'

They made it to the foot of the mountain without mishap, and then they were on the road to the airport. Once there he bought her a coffee and went to meet the chauffeur, returning a few minutes later with her suitcases.

'We've got a few minutes before you need to check in,' he said, sitting down with her at the table.

'Yes.'

Just a few minutes, and then she might never see him again. The speed of her departure had taken her by surprise. There were so many things she wanted to say to him, but suddenly she couldn't remember any of them, and the time was ticking past.

A waiter asked if Drago wanted anything, and he asked for coffee without taking his eyes off Alysa. When it came he didn't even notice.

'That's that, then,' he said.

'Yes.'

'It should be a calm flight. The weather's cleared nicely.'

'Yes,' she said again.

She wanted to meet his gaze, yet she feared to meet it. There was something there that she couldn't afford to see now that she was leaving. He was her friend and comfort, both of which she needed too much to risk them with any other kind of relationship. And yet—and yet…

'Call me when you get there,' he said. 'Just to let me know you've landed safely.'

'Yes,' she said for the fourth time. Inwardly she was cursing herself for being tongue-tied.

'Yes,' he echoed heavily.

She gave him a faint smile. 'I reckon we've exhausted the conversation.'

'It's not the words,' he said. 'It's the other things.'

'Yes,' she said before she could stop herself, and they both laughed awkwardly.

'Luckily the other things don't need saying,' he added.

As he spoke he reached out across the table to take her hand in his, rubbing his thumb softly across the backs of her fingers, then raising them so that he could brush them across his cheek. When he released her he put his hand to his eyes for a moment.

'Will you be all right, after everything I've put you through?' he asked.

'Don't worry, I'm tough.'

He met her eyes. His own were gentle.

'No,' he said softly. 'You're not.'

'You're not either.'

He gave the self-mocking smile that touched her heart. 'Don't tell anyone.'

'I promise. It'll be our secret. What about you? Will *you* be all right?'

'I will now, with your help. I'm only sorry it was so hard on you. I got off lightly in comparison.'

She thought of the letter that he must never see, and smiled at him.

'Drago, I'm not sorry we met. I'll never regret that, however hard it was.'

'Nor I.' He looked down and spoke awkwardly. 'In some ways I'm glad I didn't meet you earlier, when I was still married to Carlotta. There would have been...problems.'

'I know,' she whispered.

'We'd better be moving.'

He waited while she checked in, then came to the barrier with her.

'This is as far as I can go,' he said.

But that wasn't what he really meant; she knew. It was as far as they could go together.

'Goodbye, Drago.'

'Goodbye.'

For a moment she thought he would kiss her, but instead he pulled her close for a fierce embrace, which she went into willingly. Holding him, feeling him hold her, she told herself that this was the last time she would seek refuge in him, and feel him seek it in her. And a tide of regret swept over her.

'That's your flight they're calling,' he said with a sudden husky note in his voice. 'You'd better hurry.'

But he didn't release her.

'Yes, I suppose I must.'

'Hey, are you crying?'

'Yes,' she choked.

She tightened her arms again, then released him and moved away quickly. As she went through Passport Control, she wiped her tears and took a last glance back at him, blaming herself for being glad he was still there. Then the check on her hand luggage. Another few moments and he would be out of her life for ever.

One final look. Just one. And there was his hand raised in farewell, and his smile seeming to call her back.

And that was it, she thought. That was the mystery about their brief time together—every moment of it a contradiction of the moment before, each truth denying the others. She'd been drawn to him from the first, even while she'd raged at him. He'd made her stronger. She could only hope that she had done the same for him.

It was evening when the plane touched down, and the cold struck her as soon as she was outside. It was different from the cold of the mountains, which had been fresh and invigorating. This was merely depressing.

The queue for the taxi took ages, and she took the chance to call him.

'Safely down,' she said.

'Good. I'd say go home and have a good rest, but I guess there'll be a pile of messages waiting for you there.'

'I'd rather be back in the mountains.'

'So would I— One moment.'

Alysa could hear Tina calling in the background. So she was home now, and naturally wanted her father's attention after having been away from him.

'I have to go,' she said. 'Goodbye. And thank you for everything.'

'Goodbye, Alysa—and thank you.'

To her relief the taxi came, and she could force her mind back to the present and the future. Gradually the lights of London enfolded her again, and she told herself that it was good to come home. She said that several times.

Her apartment was chilly. As soon as she entered she saw

a light winking on her phone, telling her that there was a message. She picked it up and found it was Brian.

'Welcome back. I knew I could rely on you. I've made an appointment with your new client for tomorrow afternoon. That'll give me time to brief you in the morning. Frank's furious that he couldn't steal a march on you. I thought you'd enjoy that. Get a good night's sleep and be ready for action.'

She switched off and looked around the empty apartment, seeing it with new eyes. How bare it was! How long had it been like that? And she hadn't noticed. It spoke of a woman who hardly existed, inside whose heart nothing happened.

She wondered what Drago was doing now.

Next day Frank scowled to see her back, which really was satisfying. She listened to Brian's briefing, taking in every word, and when she met the client that afternoon everything went well. On the surface it was just as before.

But later, when Brian had finished praising her, he added, considering her, 'You've changed. I can't quite work out how, but it's good. I have great hopes of you, Alysa.'

As winter faded into spring, and then into summer, she took on more clients, worked hard and won approving looks from her employers. Unlike Brian, few people were perceptive enough to discern the difference. Her apartment would have given a clue, becoming less stark and functional, but the real change was in her mind and heart, both of which seemed to flower again.

One night she took home a tape-recording of a conference that had been held within the firm eight months previously, wanting to check whether she had really said what the notes stated.

The sound of her own voice made her lean back in her

chair, shocked. It might have been a machine talking, so dead and cold did she sound. Now she knew what Drago had heard, and why he had feared for her.

He was with her—unseen, unheard, but a constant presence. She had only to think of him to feel safe again, as though his arms were still holding her. With James there had been a constant yearning for a man who, she now realised, had never really been there. But she did not miss Drago, for how could you miss someone who was always with you?

At last a letter came from him.

> I wanted you to know how different things are with me since you were here. Not all the ghosts have been laid to rest, but the worst of them leave me in peace now. I sleep at night, and when I awake I confront the day ahead without despair.
>
> I once thought this could never happen, but now I know that there is one person who knows and understands, and that knowledge is enough to give me strength. Even if we never meet again, you are still here with me in spirit, and you give me the courage I need. I hope with all my heart that it is the same with you.
>
> God bless you.

She wrote back.

> You brought me back to life. I had become dead inside, and would have stayed that way always, but for you. It's a strange and confusing feeling to reawaken, and I don't yet know who this new person is. But, whoever she is, you made her free to grieve and one day, perhaps soon, she will be well again. For this you will always be dear to me.

He did not write again, nor did she expect him to. They had set each other on a new path, but it led away into the unknown, and they must travel it separately. Sometimes she remembered his words—that he was glad they had not met before because she would have threatened his loyalty to his wife. Who knew where that road might have led? But not yet. Perhaps not ever.

Her sleep, once so blank, had begun to be troubled with dreams. James seemed to haunt her as he'd never done before. She would see his face in that last meeting, but when she approached him he always vanished.

'Where are you?' she cried. 'Where are you?'

But when she awoke to find herself sitting up in bed she knew that she hadn't been calling to James, but to someone else, and that he was already with her. Then she would lie down and sleep again in peace.

She began studying him again on the internet, and soon managed to access Italian newspapers, including one that was local to Florence. It was a ready source of information, as excitement was rising about a mediaeval church that Drago was restoring. Work had slowed the previous year owing to many unexpected problems, but now things were moving again, as Drago seemed infused with new inspiration. It had caused him to insist on changing things that had previously seemed settled, replacing them with better ideas.

There were pictures, showing her the building before Drago had started work—tired-looking and down-at-heel. Now as it neared completion she could see its magnificence restored through his genius, and she felt a sudden happiness, for she thought she knew the source of his new life.

An increase of work left her no time to follow his progress for a while, and it was almost a week before she was able to seek him out on-line. Then she saw something that almost made her heart stop:

Di Luca critical after near-death plunge.

Struggling through the Italian prose, Alysa managed to understand that Drago had climbed high on some scaffolding, intent on examining a carved stone to make sure that it was perfect, had missed his footing and had plunged down to the ground.

It was dated five days ago. He could be dead by now.

Frantically she searched through the following days, terrified lest she find the fatal announcement. There was nothing, but she searched again, and this time she spotted a small item saying that he'd regained consciousness and seemed better. She read it over and over, terrified that she'd misread it.

To her relief there had been no mistake, but she couldn't rest until she knew more. After a few minutes, summoning up her courage, she lifted the phone and dialled his home.

Who would answer? she wondered. The housekeeper? Or perhaps Elena was there again? She was still running through the possibilities when Drago's voice said, *'Pronto.'*

At first she was too startled to speak and he had to say it again before she answered.

'It's me.'

She wondered if she should identify herself properly, but he recognised 'me' at once.

'Ciao, Alysa. How nice to hear from you.'

Trying to pull herself together, she blurted out, 'What are you doing there? You're supposed to be at death's door.'

'Is that disappointment I hear in your voice?' He sounded amused.

'Of course not. They said you'd had a terrible fall and took days to regain consciousness.'

'As usual, the press exaggerates. My fall was broken by

a ledge. I had a slight concussion and a couple of cracked ribs, but that's all. I left hospital yesterday. Tomorrow I'll go back to work.'

'With cracked ribs?' she echoed, aghast.

'Why not? They're painful, but I can still bark orders and be generally overbearing.'

'And climb scaffolding?'

'No, not that. I'll be careful, but I have to be there to make sure that everything is done the way I want.'

'That sounds like you,' she said, feeling her heart slow to a more normal rhythm.

'Slave-driver?'

'Perfectionist. Everyone says you're doing a wonderful job on that church.'

'I hope so. It must be finished soon. I've made so many changes recently that it held things up, but we're nearly there. Tell me, how did you know what had happened?'

'The internet. I can access the local Florence paper, and it was all there.'

She paused, embarrassed by what she had just revealed.

For a few moments there was silence from the other end. Then he said, 'You're not so easy to trace. There's your firm's website, which has just a little about you. And a picture of you at some official dinner last week. That's all.'

So he'd been watching her from a distance too. She smiled.

'What kind of a function was it?' he asked casually.

'Like you said, official. Accountants, lawyers, businessmen, a few politicians, lots of boring speeches.'

'You didn't seem bored by the man sitting next to you. You were sharing a laugh.'

'That's my boss, Brian. He thinks he's a wit, so I guess I play up.'

'Ah, the one who can make you a partner?'

'That's right.'

'Then you were right to laugh. Was the joke any good?'

'I can't remember.'

'That's handy. You'll be able to laugh again next time he tells it.'

His voice was warm, turning the remark into a friendly joke, so that she could say, 'I might just do that.'

'You've grown your hair. It's nicer this way.'

'I wonder why I did,' she said lightly. 'Someone may have suggested it, but I can't remember who.'

He laughed but stopped at once.

'Don't make me laugh. It hurts.'

'Please, Drago, I wish you wouldn't go back to work yet. Give yourself a few more days.'

'All right. Just a couple more days. Because you say so.'

'Thank you.'

Then his voice changed, becoming gentler. 'Alysa—how are things with you?'

'I'm managing better now.'

'So am I. Thank you.'

Silence. She felt awkward, and she could sense that he did too.

'Am I forgiven?' he asked at last.

'There's nothing to forgive. You know that.'

'I didn't. But I hoped.'

'Goodbye, Drago.'

'Goodbye.'

The line went dead. Alysa hung up and sat looking at the phone, wondering at the strange feeling that had overtaken her. It was disturbingly like happiness.

So he'd seen her with Brian, and had wondered. But there was nothing romantic in their association, even though he was an outrageously handsome man. A well-preserved fifty-three, he'd been married three times and now determinedly 'avoided shackles'.

He both worked and played hard, but the pleasure was strictly out of office hours. None of his female employees had anything to fear from him, which had caused one of them to mutter that this was because 'the old goat' preferred women who were too stupid to spell, never mind add.

He'd invited Alysa to the dinner as a professional courtesy, introducing her to a lot of influential people, congratulating her on her networking skills, showing the road that led to a partnership. Afterwards he'd taken her home, kissed her on the cheek, and had gone to spend the rest of the night with a lady whose talents were as legendary as her prices.

She wondered if Drago would call her back, or write, but a month passed with no word from him. Then a large gold envelope came through her door. Opening it, she found an invitation to the ceremonies that would accompany the reopening of the church he'd been restoring.

The card was practically a work of art in itself, elaborately embossed, the wording formal with nothing personal about it. He'd included a brief note, saying he would book a hotel for her, and inviting her to join him and his other guests at his home the night before the dedication, and again the following evening. It could have been written to almost any guest, but she knew better than to attach importance to its formality.

The true message was that, like her, he longed for another meeting but, also like her, he was cautious. Across the miles his heart and mind reached out to her, as perfectly in harmony as before.

CHAPTER NINE

SHE went to see Brian to ask for a week off.

'I know I've already had a week this year—' she began.

'Hey, don't make me sound like a slave-driver. A week is nothing, and you're due for some time off. Planning anything special?' He looked suddenly alarmed. 'I need you in the firm. You haven't got a lover trying to take you away from us, have you?'

'No, I leave that kind of thing to you,' she teased. 'I'm pursuing business. I met a well-known architect in Italy, and he's invited me to the opening of a church he's just finished restoring.'

'Drago di Luca,' Brian mused, looking at the card. 'I've heard of him. Even in this country he's beginning to be talked about. Well done. If he accepts commissions over here, his business could be valuable.'

She murmured a reply and escaped. He could think she was making a cool move, but the truth was she felt anything but cool.

Drago's chauffeur was waiting to help her at the airport, smiling as he recognised her and took her bags, and handing her an envelope as she got into the car. As he drove her to the same hotel where she'd stayed last time, she opened it and read:

> I would have liked to meet you myself but I'm drowning in formalities. You will wish some time alone this afternoon to rest, and a car will collect you at six o'clock and bring you to my home for dinner. Tina is very much looking forward to seeing you again. And so am I.

Once at the hotel, a shower refreshed her so that she had no need of rest. She wanted to go out and see Florence in the sunshine. It was high summer and everything was different, bathed in sunlight. It was hard to believe that this was the same place she'd seen in February, when the cold and damp had seemed to seep into her bones, and become one with her sadness.

Walking down by the river, she watched the light glinting on the water, and was suddenly assailed by a feeling of irrational joy. She tried to be rational. After all, it was only sun. But she didn't want to be rational. She wanted to rejoice in the light and let her steps take her where they would.

At first she thought she was wandering aimlessly, but then she admitted the truth—that she was heading for the apartment where James and Carlotta had briefly lived. She found it easily, and it was looking more cheerful now than it had done in winter. From inside came the sound of laughter, a man's voice, then a woman's, sounding young and happy.

The man might have been James if fate had been kinder to him. But it had not been kind, she thought, from the depths of her new-found peace.

Turning away, she walked on along the river until she

came to the Ponte Vecchio, and went to stand before the statue of Cellini, where James and Carlotta had pledged their love with padlocks along with many others. But there were no padlocks there today. The railings that had once been covered with love tokens were stark and bare.

She heard a sigh and turned to see the proprietor of the shop who'd told her the significance of the padlocks, way back in February—a lifetime ago.

'What's happened to them all?' she asked him. 'Don't lovers come here any more?'

'They do when they dare,' he said. 'But the council has ruled against them. If you get caught hanging a padlock there's a fine, and every now and then they clear them all away.'

'That's terrible!'

'Yes, isn't it? Ah well, it all brings me new business.'

'But do people still buy padlocks if they can't hang them?'

'Who says they can't? You don't think lovers let a few fines put them off, do you? Every single one of them who hung a token there before will be back to hang another one. Good day.'

When he'd bustled away, Alysa stood looking at the bare railings.

'Not every single one,' she whispered. 'I lost a great deal, but I didn't lose everything. *You* lost everything, and I didn't see it until now.'

Again she felt the stirring of pity, and suddenly she knew that there was another place she must see.

A few minutes in a taxi brought her to the Church of All Angels. Like everywhere else it was transformed by the sun, making even the graves look somehow cheerful, especially the monument to Carlotta di Luca, which glowed with a fresh delivery of flowers.

Red roses, Alysa noted: a silent message from Drago that she was still in his heart. She had often wondered if she'd done the right thing in taking the letter, sparing him that pain. Now she thought she had her answer.

At last she wandered over to the far corner where the unimportant graves lay, and there the illusion of cheer was dispelled.

The little slabs had received minimum care. Someone had cut the grass, but casually, so that a fringe of long grass surrounded every slab. Here there were no flowers or tributes. Only the bleakness of indifference. Suddenly James's lonely end seemed intolerable.

It was very quiet in this corner. She stood looking up at the beauty of the sky, feeling the sun bless her as she had never thought to be blessed again. Overhead a bird began to sing.

'I don't hate you,' she told him sadly. 'How can I, when it all ended so sadly for you? I wish there was something I could— But perhaps there is. If only I knew how to go about it.'

Then a memory returned to her from the day she'd first come here in February—the young journalist talking about Drago, saying, 'They say he has the ear of every important person in town, and he pulls strings whenever it suits him.'

Drago, the dear friend whose support had saved her: she could turn to him again. Suddenly decisive, she left the cemetery and hailed a taxi.

For a party in the elegant surroundings of the villa, she guessed that only grandeur would do, and accordingly chose a long dress of dark-blue satin. The neckline was modest for an evening gown, but the narrow waist hugged her figure, and the mirror showed an elegant woman.

A hairdresser from the hotel came to whip her newly

grown locks into a confection on her head. A moment to fix the dainty diamond necklace about her neck, adjust a velvet wrap about her shoulders, a last check in the mirror, and it was time to go.

The car was there for her ten minutes early, and to make friendly conversation she congratulated the driver on his punctuality.

'Signor di Luca came looking for me and demanded to know why I hadn't gone yet,' he said with a grin. 'I told him I still have plenty of time, but he said, *go now!* So I did. It doesn't do to argue with the boss.'

'I gather he can be a real slave-driver,' she laughed.

'He's been worse recently. It's like the devil has got into him. Maybe it's because he had to waste time in hospital. He hated that.'

It might be no more than that, Alysa thought. But she couldn't help wondering if there might be something else. She would know when she saw him.

Elena was waiting for her on the step as the car drew up.

'How charming to see you again,' she said. 'Drago is detained for the moment, but he'll be down soon. Let me introduce you to Signorina Leona Alecco. Our families have been friends for years.'

Leona was in her late thirties, slightly heavily built, not pretty, but with an intelligent face that would have been better with less make-up. Her neckline was just too low for her build, and made Alysa glad that she had opted for caution in her own dress.

The same idea might have occurred to Leona, for she gave Alysa a shrewd look, taking in every detail of her glamorous appearance before becoming carefully blank-faced.

'It's just a small gathering tonight,' Elena continued, ushering her inside. 'Only family and friends. Tomorrow we'll be inundated with businessmen and really important people.'

Just in case I delude myself that I'm important, Alysa thought wryly.

She took a glass of wine from the proffered tray and sipped it, looking around at the little gathering. Carlotta's sister was there again, with her husband and children. Leona seemed practically one of the family. She herself was the only outsider.

But not for long. Tina had spotted her and came scurrying across the floor to seize her hands, beaming upwards as if Alysa was a dear friend.

'Poppa said you were coming,' she confided.

Alysa was touched. At their previous meeting she'd still been tormented by her own dead child, and had been unable to be at ease with the little girl. Yet Tina had seemed oblivious, offering her friendship then, and even more now. Alysa felt shamed by such open-hearted generosity. The smile she gave Tina was warm.

'Who's your friend?' she asked, indicating a doll in an elaborate dress that Tina was carrying.

'Aunt Leona gave it to me.'

'She's very pretty,' Alysa said politely, but Tina pulled a face.

'She's too *frilly*,' she complained. 'I don't like being frilly.'

'I know what you mean,' Alysa said at once. 'I've never been frilly myself. I used to prefer making mud pies.'

They nodded in perfect empathy.

A noise made her turn around to see Drago just coming into the room. The others seized on him at once, giving her a moment to look without being seen in return.

For the first time she saw him dressed formally in a dinner jacket and black bow-tie, whose elegance had the perverse effect of making him seem taller and more powerful than she remembered. Now she could perceive him as other women did—a deeply attractive man, made even more attractive by a touch of harshness—except that she had seen past that veneer and knew how thin it was.

At last Drago looked up and saw her, and a slow smile spread over his face. There was a look of satisfaction in his eyes, as though his best hopes had come true, but there was also an astonished question: *this is* her?

Seeing that surprised admiration, she knew she'd been secretly hoping for just this. The months apart vanished. He was the same man who had supported her and leaned on her at the same time, and when he came across the floor with his hands outstretched she reached out to him.

'I was afraid you wouldn't come,' he said softly.

'And miss your moment of glory?' she teased. 'Never.'

He didn't speak, but the pressure on her hands increased slightly.

'At last you're here,' Elena's voice broke in. 'I thought you'd never join us.'

Drago released Alysa and turned to smile politely at Elena.

'A potential client turned up without warning. I had to see him briefly, but I've put him off for a few days, so now we can have dinner. Shall we go in?'

'Of course. You're sitting next to Leona, and Tina is sitting next to me.'

'I want to sit next to Alysa,' Tina said at once, adding in a confiding voice, 'She's a guest.'

'And you are her hostess,' Drago said at once. 'So of course you must sit beside her and look after her for me.'

Elena looked displeased but was unable to protest. Tina took Alysa's hand and led her into the dining room, while Drago went unprotesting with Leona.

A suspicion was growing in Alysa's mind, which was increased as she saw Leona seated firmly on Drago's right. Elena regarded them both with the complacency of a matchmaker who saw things working out.

She was deluding herself, Alysa thought. There was no sign of the lover in Drago's manner to Leona. He was charming, considerate, but slightly detached. If Leona claimed his attention, he turned to her with a smile, but he seldom made the first move.

And yet, perhaps Elena knew what she was doing. Drago wasn't in love, but he wouldn't have been the first widower to marry a sensible woman to give his child a mother. An old family friend would be a logical choice, and help to keep Tina close to her grandmother.

But not this woman, Alysa mused. For reasons she couldn't explain, she wasn't sure that Leona was what he needed.

When the meal was under way, Tina confided, 'I wanted to ask you about Poppa. You did look after him, didn't you?'

'I think I did. I tried. He looked after me too.'

'Because you both had someone who died?'

'Yes, just so.'

By the time the meal ended, Tina's eyes were drooping, and Drago gently suggested that it was time for all the children to go to bed.

'Leona and I will take care of that,' Elena said at once. 'Come, children, upstairs.'

Alysa leaned down so that Tina could give her a peck on the cheek. Then the child was whisked away by Elena.

'Come with me,' Drago said, taking Alysa's arm.

He led her out onto a terrace at the back of the house, overlooking the moonlit garden.

'Let me look at you,' he said.

He held her away from him, surveying her, while she did

the same—both silently asking how their previous encounter had changed them. Alysa held her breath, wondering what he would say. At last he spoke.

'You've put on weight.'

'What?'

'Good. I like it. You were far too skinny before.'

Alysa burst out laughing. Trust him to say something no other man would have said.

'All right,' he said hastily. 'I'm not known for my tact.'

'You amaze me.'

'But I mean what I say. You were like a ghost before. Now you're alive again.'

'And what about you? Are you alive again?'

'In some ways, not in all. I have so much to tell you, my dear friend.'

'And I have things to tell you,' she said eagerly. 'You said I looked alive again, and I'm almost there, but there's still something I need badly and you're the only person who can help me.'

His eyes grew warmer and he seized her hands.

'But of course I'll help you—anything you ask. Who knows you better than I? Tell me now, what it is that you need?'

But before she could speak there was a call of, 'Drago,' and they looked back at the house to see Leona waving to him.

'Elena wants to talk to you,' she said.

'Will you be kind enough to tell her that I'll return in a moment?' he said.

'I think she wants you now. She says you're neglecting your guests.'

Drago groaned softly.

'You'd better go,' Alysa said.

'Yes, I suppose I must, but we must talk before you leave.'

He drew her hand through his arm and they went in together, Leona watching them like a hawk.

For the rest of the evening Alysa stayed in the background. Her moment would come later. At last she murmured to him, 'I should be going.'

'Fine, I'll drive you home,' Drago said.

Elena started to protest that that was the chauffeur's job, but Drago silenced her with a deadly smile.

'I know I can rely on you to be the perfect hostess while I'm gone. Alysa, are you ready?'

When they were on the road, safely away from the house, he said through gritted teeth, 'My mother-in-law!' Then, when Alysa gave a soft chuckle, 'Yes, I suppose you find it funny.'

'Well, she's so blatant about it. She's very determined to marry you to Leona, isn't she?'

'You saw that too? I hoped it was just my imagination.'

'It's obvious. She's like a general going into battle, with everything worked out.'

'How dreadfully true. When I invited her for tomorrow's ceremony, she somehow turned it into an invitation for Leona too.'

As they reached the outskirts of Florence, he said, 'Let's find somewhere to sit down and talk.'

He chose a small café in a side street and settled her in a corner where the light was poor and few people would notice them.

'Is that why you invited me here?' she asked. 'To protect you from Leona?'

'Not really, I just needed to see you. What happened seems so unreal. I wanted to be sure you really existed. But now you're here I'm glad, because of Leona too. I don't know what's got into Elena.'

'I suppose for her Leona would be the ideal choice

because she wouldn't try to separate her from Tina as another woman might.'

'I gather they've got it all sorted. Don't I get a say in this arrangement?'

'Not much. After all, you might well decide to remarry for Tina's sake.'

'Never,' he said fiercely. 'Not just for Tina's sake, and not— Well, anyway.' He sighed. 'I don't want them choosing a wife for me. I rely on you to shield me from their intrigues.'

'Don't worry,' she assured him. 'I'm your best friend, and when the time comes I'll take a hand in choosing your wife. Tina and I will line up the candidates, put them through a series of tests and mark them one to ten.'

He laughed. 'Between you and her watching over me like a pair of guardian angels, I know I'll be safe. As for you being my best friend...'

'After all we went through together, don't you think I am?'

'I think—' He paused, as if undecided what to say next. 'I think we have a bond that will never be broken, and I want— Well, let's leave that for later. I only wish I could spend more time with you during the celebrations.'

'You have your duty to do, I know that.'

'But, afterwards, will you come to the mountains with me?'

Her heart leapt. 'I hoped you'd ask that.'

'But don't mention it to anyone else. As far as anyone knows, you're going back to England.'

'What do you take me for? I wasn't going to confide in Elena, was I?'

He grinned. 'No, I reckon you're a match for her. By the way, what was it you wanted to talk to me about?'

'It can wait. I'll tell you when we're in the mountains.'

'Now I'd better get back home, heaven help me. The car will come for you tomorrow.'

Next day a convoy drove the ten miles to the church, where it disgorged a seemingly endless line of distinguished Florentines. Drago escorted them around the building, describing everything that had been done, and received their congratulations with calm pleasure, not seeming to be overwhelmed by them.

He was his own man, Alysa thought. He knew he'd done a fine job, and he needed nobody else to tell him so.

Tina slipped away from her grandmother and attached herself to Alysa, explaining everything like an expert. Elena tried to draw her back to the family group, but the little girl had her father's stubbornness.

'I have to look after Alysa,' she explained firmly. 'She has nobody of her own.'

She clung to Alysa's hand until they were apart from the others.

'You see up there?' she said, pointing. 'That's where Poppa fell. He was terribly angry. He shouted at everyone.'

'Even you?'

'No, not me. Just everyone else. But he was better after you called. He told me about it.'

The ceremony was long and impressive. Several people rose to heap praise on Drago, which he received with a blank face that told her he was embarrassed.

Then it was time to return to the hotel so that she could prepare for the grand banquet that night. She had not managed to have a single word with Drago.

As she got into the car, Tina hugged her and asked anxiously, 'You will come tonight, won't you?'

Once the feel of those childish arms about her neck would have made her flinch. Now she hugged Tina back warmly.

'Promise,' she said.

In a sudden impulse she spent the afternoon shopping for a dress that was more daring than before, a soft-ivory chiffon that clung to her and emphasised her movements.

The villa was ablaze with lights as she joined the crowd streaming in later that evening. Drago stood there, greeting his guests with Elena on one side, and Leona on the other, as though her place in the villa was already assured. She greeted Alysa with lofty assurance, as did Elena, both women studying her attire suspiciously.

Drago studied it too, with a gleam in his eyes that won an answering smile.

Tina too was part of the reception line-up, but she slipped away to join Alysa, which won Drago's look of warm approval.

'Look what Poppa bought me,' she said, showing Alysa a locket around her neck. Inside was a picture of Carlotta.

'He said it was specially for today, because Mamma would have enjoyed this so much, and we must think of her.'

'Does he speak of her much?' Alysa asked.

'Oh yes, especially when it's her birthday—that was last week—and on my birthday, because she sends me presents. Well, it's Poppa really, but he says it's her, and I pretend to believe him 'cos otherwise he might be hurt.'

'And you don't want to hurt him, no matter what you have to do?'

Tina beamed at this understanding. 'He pretends to be a bully, but he isn't really. Just a big softy.'

'And nobody knows him better than you, so I guess you're right.'

'Tina!' It was Leona's voice. 'We are sitting down for dinner now. Come along.'

'But I've got lots of things to show Alysa.'

'Later,' Alysa said. 'Never keep your host waiting.'

'Very true,' Drago said from somewhere behind Leona, who turned to him.

As soon as her back was turned Tina seized the chance to stick her tongue out at her. Alysa hastily covered the child's mouth, but not before Drago saw and gave a wide grin.

It was all over in seconds, and then they were marching sedately to the banqueting hall. But it left Alysa feeling exhilarated. Leona might have been seated in the place of honour by Drago, but it was with her that he had the shared understanding.

She saw another side of him that night—assured and businesslike. He even managed to be charming, although she guessed he was carefully negotiating three moves ahead in such unfamiliar territory.

After dinner there was dancing to the accompaniment of an orchestra. Drago danced with Leona, then with a series of wives, mostly indistinguishable from each other, while Alysa entertained herself with several gentlemen who all spoke perfect English and had commercial interests in England. She could therefore assure herself, with a clear conscience, that she was touting for business.

She would have liked to dance with Drago. Something told her that it would be very interesting. But her time would come.

As the evening drew to a close Elena spoke to her from lofty heights.

'I hope you have really enjoyed your time here, *signorina*, and that you will return home with happy memories.'

Alysa made the polite response, and Elena immediately followed up with, 'When exactly do you leave?'

'I'll be going tomorrow.'

'How sad. We're going to stay here for a few more days. It's so seldom we can get the whole family together, and we simply must make the most of it.'

'I'm afraid the family gathering will be without me,' Drago put in. 'The man I told you about—the one who turned up last night—wants me to look over a building to see if it's worth renovating. I have to leave first thing tomorrow morning, and I'll be gone for several days.'

Elena began to protest, but his smile was implacable.

'Signora Dennis, let me escort you to the car,' he said. 'I only regret I am unable to drive you home myself.'

As she got into the waiting car, she said casually, 'I wonder where this building is?'

'You know quite well where it is,' Drago replied. 'Or have you forgotten what we agreed?'

'Not a word. I'll be waiting for you tomorrow. Now I'd better go quickly, before Elena does something desperate.'

CHAPTER TEN

'IT's a pity you only saw the mountains under snow,' Drago said as they headed out of Florence next morning. 'I've wanted you to see them now, when everywhere is at its best.'

The journey was magical. Their last trip had been made in the chill of winter. Now they climbed higher into the sunlight, the trees glowing around them in the green of summer.

Again they stopped at the village to stock up on groceries, but slowly this time, while he asked her preferences and promised her a whole series of dishes to make her rejoice.

'Does this mean I can help with the cooking?' she asked as they got back into the car.

'Not at all. Stay out of my kitchen. A woman's place is laying the table.'

When they had driven on a little way, she said, 'Stop the car. I want to look.'

He pulled in just off the road, and they left the car behind to wander among the trees.

'You'd hardly know it was the same place,' Alysa said in wonder.

'Thank you for coming,' he said quietly. 'I've thought of you all the time. Say it was the same with you.'

'Oh yes. You were always with me.'

He took her hand and they wandered higher. The trees grew more luxuriantly here, blocking out much of the light so that the sunbeams slanted down like arrows piercing the shadows.

'Do you recognise this place?' he asked, stopping suddenly by a tree.

'I don't think so.'

'I guess you wouldn't. The last time you were here it was dark and snowing.'

'Is this where you found me that night?'

'That's right. You were curled up under this very tree.'

'I can hardly believe it. It's so beautiful now, and then it was—'

'Another world,' he said.

Leaning against the tree, he raised her hand so that he could brush the back of it against his cheek, hold it there for a moment, then press his lips against it.

'I've been back here often since you went away,' he said. 'It's where I come for peace, and even happiness.'

'Can there be happiness?' she asked wistfully.

'There might be.'

'It takes time.'

'Do you know the first lesson a builder has to learn?' he asked. 'Not to go too fast. Let things happen in their own time, or you'll make a mess of the whole project.'

'And we mustn't make a mess of the project,' she agreed.

His smile was fond and warm.

'Some projects are more important than others,' he said. 'Right, let's go. I'm getting hungry.'

She nodded at his abrupt change of tone. Having moved cautiously to the edge of the precipice, he'd backed off before asking her to look over. And he was right, of course, she thought as they hurried down to the car hand in hand. They had all the time in the world to find out what lay past the precipice.

The sun was setting on the little villa as they drew close, turning the roof to red. Drago parked his car in the garage where he'd once found her standing in the cold and lost his temper. Together they went upstairs to where a fire was already laid in the grate, waiting to be lit.

'Even in summer it gets a bit chilly when the light goes,' he said. 'So I came here a few days ago and got everything ready for you.'

Despite what he'd said, he allowed her to help with the meal that evening. They ate it in virtual silence, but it was silence with a special quality. She could see ahead now, just a little way, but it was enough for this evening. After that, who could tell?

This visit had already shown her that there was more to Drago than she had discovered last time, inspiring her with a passionate desire to explore him further—heart, mind and body.

When the meal was over, by mutual consent they settled down on the thick rug before the fire, leaning against each other.

'You're so different,' he said. 'You've flowered.'

'Yes, you told me I'd got fat, you cheeky so-and-so,' she murmured contentedly.

'I didn't say that and you know it. When we were here before you were on the same slippery slope that I was. Do you remember that day at the waterfall? If anyone had told me then what you would become to me I wouldn't have believed them.'

'Nor me. I just wanted to fight you, and then when you turned up at the airport and tricked me into coming up here—'

'I never tricked you.'

'May you be forgiven! That defeated air!'

'I was frightened. You were a very scary lady.'

'I scared myself sometimes. It scares me even more to look back at what I was becoming. I put you through it too, I remember—getting lost in the snow and you had to nurse me.'

'I didn't mind nursing you.'

'You did. You suddenly became very bad-tempered,' she remembered. 'You kept barking at me.'

'After finding you in that garage—'

'No, it was before that.'

'Oh yes, I remember.'

'What do you remember? Go on, tell me.'

He hesitated, then said wryly, 'All right, I'll confess. When you got that heavy cold I was worried, so I stayed with you.'

'That's right.'

'I actually slept on the bed.'

'Outside the bedclothes, of course.'

'Of course!'

Alysa chuckled. 'How charming and old-fashioned. Positively nineteenth-century.'

'It's all very well to laugh, but you were ill, you were trapped with me, relying on me to look after you. Of course I was old-fashioned. At least, I meant to be, but I awoke to find that somehow I'd put my arm over you.'

She gasped. 'Shocking! How could you?'

'I was asleep, I didn't know—are you making fun of me?'

'Do you think I am?'

'I'm not sure,' he said cautiously. 'I don't have much sense of humour, but I think perhaps you are laughing.'

'It took you long enough to realise that,' she said gently, touched by the humility in his voice. 'Shall I promise not to laugh at you?'

'No, I don't mind if it's you. Make fun of me if you like. I might even come to understand.'

'Yes, I guess you might,' she said.

'It's just that I felt awkward next day, which is why I was a bit offhand. Anything was better than have you suspect. What is it?' Alysa had begun to laugh helplessly.

'You never guessed?' she crowed. 'Oh, I can't believe this.'

'What's so funny?'

'It was me. I slipped out to the bathroom, and when I came back you'd stretched your arm across the empty space. I eased myself in under it, being very careful not to disturb you, so that you didn't take it away.'

'You—?'

'I made it happen. It wasn't you, it was me.'

'But I felt so guilty because— And you let me suffer.'

'I didn't know you were suffering,' she chuckled. 'But I wish I had.'

'Yes, you'd have enjoyed it,' he said, chagrined. 'You—you—'

'Come on, you were going to develop a sense of humour.'

'I guess I'll need a little time for that. I can't take this in. I was feeling ashamed all that time and I didn't need to?' His tone was outraged.

'Something like that.'

'Well, I'll be—'

There was a light in his eyes that she was beginning to know. She'd seen it across the room on the night she'd arrived, and wanted to know more. Since then her curiosity had grown, and now she urgently needed to pursue it to the end. So when the words failed him, and he jerked her towards him with a grunt of frustration, she went into his arms willingly, and sighed with pleasure as his mouth touched hers.

It was he who was tentative, caressing her lightly with his lips, waiting for her response, then embracing her eagerly as he sensed the desire that she had no wish to hide. He'd been almost afraid of taking her by surprise, but now he knew that she'd been waiting for him, ready for this moment.

She was returning his kiss, her lips moving slowly but with determination, teasing and testing him, asking a question which he answered readily. Lightning seemed to streak through her. It was so long since she'd known the physical yearning for release that now it had the delight of the unexpected, as well as the pleasure of anticipation.

Now she knew that the flash of desire—so briefly sensed, so swiftly controlled, that she'd felt on the day months ago when he'd carried her home and their mouths had almost touched—had been no illusion. It had been both a promise and a warning: think carefully before going beyond this point.

She'd had months to think carefully, becoming more confused all the time. But suddenly everything was clear, and from now on there would be no more thinking.

Drago felt her reaching towards him, not just with her mouth but her whole being. He lacked the words to tell her how the hope of this moment had lured and tantalised him through the weary time apart, but movements, tender and urgent together, were saying everything for him.

Then he was laying her gently back against the thick carpet, opening her buttons, pulling her clothes away, dumbstruck as he discovered that she was already naked underneath. His astonishment delighted her, and she gave a slow smile that told him everything, relishing the dawning look of complicity in his eyes.

'You're a wicked woman,' he whispered.

'Have you only just learned that?'

'I never know what to think with you.'

'I could help you find out.'

After that nothing could have held him back. He touched her face with reverent fingers, then let them trail down her neck and onwards between her breasts while she lay trembling with the sensation, so sweet and so long-forgotten.

No, not forgotten: never known. James's love-making hadn't been like this. He'd known that she adored him and had accepted it as a right, never looking at her with the feeling bordering on awe that she saw now in Drago's eyes.

Her nights with James had been physically thrilling, but always with some element missing, because the emotion had been largely on her side. But Drago's heart was open to her own, filling her with joy, so that she lay back, her arms above her head, luxuriously spreading herself for his delight.

He moved his hands outwards, cupping her breasts in a gesture of tender possessiveness, then lay down so that his face was between them, his lips continuing the work of his fingers while she clasped her hands behind his head and arched up against him.

When he raised his head she began to open his shirt, and he helped her, moving feverishly, as though responding to a signal for which he'd been waiting too long.

When he too was naked, she had one moment of doubt. This was the first man for a year and a half. But, looking into his face, she saw the understanding that had never yet failed her.

'Me too,' he said softly. There was no need to say more.

His movements became more urgent. Request became demand. Plea shaded into insistence. His hands explored further, tracing a path on the inside of her thighs, until he reached the heart of her sensation and felt her tremble. In a moment he was over her, seeking, finding. Then he was inside, inviting her to enclose him.

She received him happily, knowing now that this was right in every way, feeling their bodies move together as though they had been made for each other. They were both so eager that their moment came quickly, almost taking them by surprise, before they had time to enjoy the pleasure to the full.

His skill and urgency were driving her on until she arched against him with a cry, and pulled him hard against her while his own release took hold of him. In the last seconds her movements were almost as wild as his own.

Afterwards she held him tightly, feeling him tremble, then grow calmer as the storm passed. He lay against her for a long time before raising himself to look down on her. He looked shaken.

'Are you all right?' he whispered.

'Mmm,' she murmured contentedly.

'I didn't mean to be so—so—'

He fell silent, so clearly embarrassed that she wanted to hug him. He was saying that he hadn't meant to be so fierce and nearly out of control. But that was what had pleased her most.

'It's just fine,' she assured him. 'I liked it that you were so—*so*—'

'You're on the floor, and it must be a bit hard.'

'Not with this lovely thick rug. Still, there are other places—more comfortable.'

He rose, drawing her with him, and they made their way to his room, almost running in their eagerness to throw themselves onto the bed and revel in each other.

It was only a few minutes ago that they had made love, yet the desire was there again, eager and vibrant, so that they laughed with triumph and the joy of being alive and together. This time he cast aside restraint from the first moment, and she gave him a response that was almost violent in its lack of inhibition.

'What happened to the light?' she asked as they lay together afterwards. 'I don't remember it getting dark.'

'We were thinking of something else,' he said.

'I guess we were. Something much more important.'

'I wanted you so badly,' he murmured. 'But I was afraid in case I spoilt things.'

'I know,' she said lazily. 'We had something so good, I didn't want to risk it either. But I guess we couldn't stand still. Maybe this was always waiting for us.'

'How wise you are!'

He buried his face against her neck, relishing the scent of her.

'Sweetness and spice,' he murmured. 'Adventure and peace. How do you manage to be everything at once?'

'You're a poet!'

'Good grief, no!' he said, shocked. 'Oh, I see, you're laughing at me again.'

'Just a little,' she said tenderly. 'Don't worry about it.'

'I don't, not any more.'

They lay for a while, half-waking, half-dozing, until he said, 'Do you remember what I said when we parted at the airport, about being glad we hadn't met earlier?'

'Yes, I thought about it a lot, and in the end I knew you were right.'

'In the end?'

'I wasn't quite ready at first. I think I began to see it when you had that accident, and I was so afraid that you might be dead.'

'I was a bit ahead of you. I felt so close to you that it scared me. The first time I came back to this place, I left at once; it was so empty without you. I meant never to return, but then I found I had to write to you, just to keep some sort of contact. When you replied I came up here again. And you were here too. You've been here ever since.'

'I know,' she said. 'I always knew I was in this place with you.'

'Did you suffer much when you returned home?'

'At first, yes. I cried a lot, but even then I knew that it was good to cry. Everything had been trapped inside me for a year, and it was destroying me. Very soon it would have been too late. When I stopped crying I knew that I'd come through it, and since then I've got stronger. The world doesn't frighten me any more.'

'I don't believe the world ever frightened you,' he said wryly. 'More like the other way around.'

'That was just the surface. I kept my armour in place to hide my fear. I don't have to do that any more. What about you? Has anything been better?'

'I haven't your courage. I still feel easier wearing the armour, except with you. But, like I told you, I sleep better. Tina is happier.'

In the poor light she could just make out the scar on his forehead, and she reached up to touch it.

'Is that where you got hit?'

'Yes, it's fading now.'

'I thought you were dead. Everything went dark. The thought of you not being there any more—even if I didn't see you, I knew you were there, and if suddenly you weren't—I didn't know how I'd manage without you.'

'I can remember lying in the hospital and thinking about you, wishing you were with me. And then you called. I think that was when I began plotting to get you out here again. I had to see you, to reassure myself that it hadn't been a dream.'

'Well, I'm here now, but it does feel like dreaming. I don't know what's real any more. Was this always going to happen?'

'Don't you know the answer to that?' he asked seriously.

The question pulled her up short. Hadn't she always known that they would end up embracing, exploring each other on the only level they hadn't yet discovered?

'I guess, if you'd just let me go home, I wouldn't have liked it. I wouldn't have liked it at all. It would have meant that something had gone wrong.'

'Me too. And I wasn't going to let it go wrong.'

'So you had this planned from the first moment?'

'Not planned. Hoped. I didn't know how it was going to work out until the other night at the villa, when I looked up and saw you standing there—so beautiful, so changed in the way I'd been hoping for. And then I knew.'

'Yes,' she said, remembering the moment when she'd seen him again, the king in his own domain. 'That was when I knew too.'

'Hmm,' he said, leaning his head on her.

'Hey, you're nearly asleep.'

'No, not really.'

'Just the same,' she said with a little chuckle, 'you are. So I may as well join you. Goodnight.'

At breakfast he said, 'I thought today we'd go out, and I'll show you how lovely this place can be. Then we'll eat in a tiny restaurant in the village.'

'Wouldn't it be nicer to eat here? Just the two of us?'

'You're right. We'll come straight back.'

The walk up the mountain was magic. As they climbed the gentle slope the sun glinted through the trees, so that they passed from shadow to sunlight to shadow again. Now and then he would take her into his arms and they would stand locked together in silence.

It seemed that there was nobody else for miles, as though they were alone in all the world, with nothing to think of but each other. When there was a gap in the trees they stood looking up at the birds flying overhead, transfixed by the beauty.

'I love you,' he said.

Alysa turned her head slowly, wondering if she'd imagined it. He looked back at her, answering her thought.

'Yes, I love you. Why do you look surprised? You shouldn't be.'

'I suppose you're right,' she said, dazed.

'You said you could see where we were heading,' he reminded her.

'Yes, but—I guess I only saw a little way ahead.'

As she said it she couldn't help smiling as she thought of their time in bed.

'I know,' he said. 'There was a time when I too only saw that much. But it's not enough. Without love it's nothing.'

'But you're going too fast for me. I think I've lost faith.'

'In me?' he asked quietly.

'No, in me. Love costs so much, and I can't pay that price any more. I guess that makes me a coward.'

'You? Not in a million years.'

'Yes, me. When I think of how I loved before, throwing myself into it heedlessly, I know I can't be like that again.'

'Of course not. No two loves are the same any more than people are the same. I love you differently from Carlotta, but not less. Or is this your way of saying that I'm fooling myself and you don't love me?'

She took so long answering that his brow darkened. 'Is it that?'

'I don't know. How can I tell? You're dearer to me than anyone else on earth, but— How can I explain? Part of me doesn't want you to be.'

'So you're going to fight me until you've driven me out? I'm stubborn, Alysa. I won't go easily. I'll haunt your mind and heart until you turn to face me. Night and day I'll be with you every moment.'

'Yes—yes,' she whispered.

'Stay with me. Marry me. Love me.'

'You make it sound so easy,' she said with a touch of anger.

'It isn't. Love's more dangerous than you know.'

'You really believe I haven't learned that?'

'You think you have, but you don't know—'

She stopped, horrified at what she'd nearly revealed. She'd been on the verge of telling him about the letter, the one thing she must never do. Too late she saw the trap she'd laid for herself.

'What don't I know?' he asked, looking at her keenly.

'You don't know anything,' she improvised hastily. 'We think we know, but we never really do.'

'What don't I know, Alysa?'

'Stop pressurising me,' she flashed. 'I only meant that nothing is how we think it is, and that's why nobody ever learns from experience. They never recognise the experience when it comes around the second time.'

He was giving her a curious look.

'I wonder what you really meant to say,' he mused. 'You're doing what my daughter calls talking "itty-bitty". It means floundering for words just to change the subject.'

'It's only that we're going too fast,' she pleaded.

'How can you say that after last night? We made love.' He eyed her uncertainly. 'Didn't we?'

'I don't know what we did. It was beautiful, but—'

'Yes, it was beautiful. You're not trying to say that it was only sex, are you?'

'No, but—'

'We've wanted each other. Don't tell me it was all on my side. Not after the way you came to life in my arms, and the things you whispered to me.'

'I've wanted you as well, but it doesn't have to be love. I won't go through that again.'

'Alysa, listen,' he said seriously. 'I don't want to love you any more than you want to love me. Do you think I haven't fought this? I have, day and night. But we may have no choice.'

'We're free beings. We make our own choices.'

'Nobody is as free as that. I thought I'd always be hounded by Carlotta, and everything that happened. But *you* set me free. Now it's you that I need.'

'Drago, please, don't rush me.'

'You mean I should stand back while you return to that life you've made a refuge because you think it's safer than love?' His voice became grimly ironic. 'A partnership in a firm of accountants! How can I compete with that?'

'You're not being fair.'

'Maybe not, but that's another thing about love—it isn't fair. Or is there something else that you're hiding?'

'Stop trying to steamroller me,' she cried. 'Give me a chance to think.'

'I didn't mean—' He checked himself with a groan. 'I'm doing it again, aren't I? Coming on strong, trying to pressurise you.'

'Does it work well with business negotiations?' she asked wryly.

He nodded. 'I've bullied people before,' he sighed. 'But I should have remembered that it doesn't work with you.'

'No, I bully back too well,' she said, trying to lighten the atmosphere. 'Why don't we go back now?'

CHAPTER ELEVEN

As they walked back to the villa Drago smiled and talked pleasantly, but Alysa felt with a heavy heart that the sun had gone in for them. He was no longer at ease with her, and she couldn't blame him. She wasn't at ease with herself. She didn't even begin to understand herself.

She had thought of him ceaselessly, had felt close enough to be his other self, despite the miles apart. Yet when the moment had come she'd backed off, driven away from him by a force too strong for her to resist.

Am I crazy? she thought. *Or just reasonable? We've only spent a little time together. It's an illusion that we know each other—a beautiful illusion, but the risk is too great. Why can't I take risks any more?*

As they were drinking wine after dinner that evening, Drago said, 'The day you arrived you said there was something you wanted to say to me. We never did get round to discussing that.'

For a moment she couldn't think what he meant. The events of the last few days had blotted out everything but him. Then it came back to her.

'Oh yes. Something happened that day—I suddenly knew what I want to do most. If only I could make you understand…'

'Try me,' he said gently.

She was too distracted to look at him closely, or she might have seen the renewed hope in his eyes.

'It's about James,' she said. 'I want to make my peace with him.'

He frowned and drew back a little. 'But how can you do that?'

'I went to the cemetery again. He looked so lonely among the rejects, and I was the person who put him there.'

'Nonsense. He put himself there.'

'In a sense, yes, but when I denied all knowledge of him just after he died I banished him. Now I'd like to take him home.'

His head shot up. *'What?'*

'I want to have him returned to England and buried there. It's terrible to see him in that corner when Carlotta is still honoured. At least he should have a little kindness. What are you staring at?'

'I think you must have taken leave of your senses.'

The light had died out of his eyes and a kind of ferocity had taken its place.

'After all this time,' he said, 'everything that's happened— you still haven't freed yourself from him. Have you learned nothing?'

'Yes, I've learned that I have to forgive him before I can find peace.'

'You don't owe him anything.'

'You don't owe Carlotta anything, but you still cover her with flowers. I know it's partly for Tina, but there's more to it. You've forgiven her, and this is my way of forgiving James. But I need you to help me.'

'How?'

'You know people, you can use your influence to get me the necessary permissions.'

'Not in a million years,' he said flatly.

'But why?'

'Have you any idea what you're asking? Do you think it's easy to raise a coffin and send it to another country? I thought you'd got beyond this point and put him behind you,' he said angrily.

'He *is* behind me.'

'I don't think so. Not if you'll go to all this trouble to keep him with you.'

'It's not like that.'

'Isn't it? Are you sure?'

She could see that he was really angry, and disappointment swept her. She'd been so certain she could rely on him, and now he was letting her down. Something stubborn rose within her. If that was how it was, she wouldn't beg.

'Fine. I'll manage this on my own. That's what I should have done from the start.'

'Then maybe that's it—the thing that was keeping you away from me. The truth is you still love him.'

'No! I don't love him, but I'm still not free of him, any more than you're free of Carlotta.'

'Don't try to pretend it's the same thing,' he growled. 'We were married for ten years. She gave me the child I love. She was a good wife, except for the end.'

He was looking at her with hard, challenging eyes. Remembering what she knew, Alysa felt her temper flare.

'That's just it,' she raged. 'She was "a good wife" because she had a family who wanted to think of her that way, but James had no family, nobody to defend him except me.'

'He rejected you.'

'And *she* rejected *you*, but you haven't faced it. That's why her grave is still covered in red roses, because you have to cling to your image of her.'

'Then how come I told you I love *you*?' he shouted.

'Maybe you do, but I'm second best, and I always will be as long as you have this fantasy picture of her as the perfect wife—except for the fact that she left you.'

'Suppose I do think of her like that. Give me one good reason why I shouldn't.'

The challenge took her breath away. She could do exactly what he suggested, if only he knew. One sight of that letter and his illusions would vanish. For a moment she hovered on the verge of temptation.

'Well?' Drago persisted. 'You think you know her better than I did. Why don't you tell me why?'

Alysa let out her breath slowly.

'I'm not saying that. All I know of her is what happened at the end.'

'You mean when she took James from you. I understand why you hate her, but don't expect me to hate her as well.'

The air seemed to be singing in her ears. She had only to tell him the brutal truth, and back it up by fetching the letter from its hiding place in England. It would be so easy to do.

'No,' she said at last with a sigh. 'It wouldn't be right to hate her.'

The moment had passed. She wouldn't tell him now.

His phone rang. It was Tina. Alysa went into the kitchen and began washing up. She was just finishing when he came in.

'Tina seems to be finding Elena rather hard-going,' he said.

'Then you should get back to her as soon as possible,' Alysa advised at once. 'She comes first. And I have to be going home.'

'Ah yes, Brian and the partnership. I'm surprised he could let you go.'

'I told him I was touting for business.' With a little laugh she showed she wasn't troubled. 'In a sense it was true. There were a lot of amazing people in your house, some with business interests in England, so I may do very well out of this visit.'

'I'm glad it wasn't a complete waste,' he said stiffly.

'Nothing's ever wasted with me. I can always turn things to good account.'

He took a step forward and seized her shoulders.

'*Stop it!* Don't talk like that. Who do you think you're dealing with?'

'I'm trying to make this easier for both of us.'

'Like hell you are. You're turning yourself back into *her*, aren't you?'

She didn't need to ask who he meant by 'her': that other self who'd lived behind a wall of ice, and who might still tempt her when things became painful.

'I'm being sensible. You have to leave, I have to leave,' she said. 'Would you rather I threw a hissy fit and begged you to put me first and your little girl second? That would be selfish and disgusting, and you know it.'

He groaned, running his hand through his hair.

'Yes, it would. But it worries me when you talk of being sensible. It's dangerous.'

'It's my natural state,' she said in a rallying tone.

'In that case, let's be sensible, and get ready to leave early tomorrow,' he said, scowling.

'Fine. I'll get packed.'

Suddenly she was glad to be leaving. The hope that had vibrated so thrillingly between them was dead, and there was no reason to stay.

Nothing was said, but they both knew they would sleep apart that night, and after their meal they retired to different rooms. Now she was in the same room where she'd slept when she'd first come here, listening for sounds coming from next door. But there was nothing, only silence, like the silence between them.

Next day he drove her to the airport.

How different this was from last time, she thought sadly. Then the atmosphere between them had been charged with hopes unfulfilled and hopes for the future that might yet be fulfilled. Their parting had been yearning and bittersweet. Now it was only resigned and slightly despairing.

At the barrier they paused and regarded each other.

'I guess we only managed to get part-way down the road,' he told her.

'We asked for too much,' she said sadly.

'I don't believe it was too much. I told you that I love you. That won't change. When you've decided what you want, I'll still be here.'

'You'd better forget about me. My head's too mixed up.'

'And so is your heart,' he said. 'But when you're ready to move on you'll find me here, however long it takes. When you come back— No, don't shake your head. You will come back.'

'Because that's what you've decided?' she asked with a faint smile.

'If you want to put it that way. I won't take no for an answer. I'm a tyrant, remember? An awkward, overbearing lout who demands his own way in everything.'

Her eyes were suddenly misty as she reached out to touch his cheek. He might bad-mouth himself as much as he liked, this great, gentle man with the tender eyes and the fierce armour that kept slipping, leaving him defenceless. She knew the truth, and her heart broke because she couldn't cast aside caution and throw herself into his arms for ever.

'No, that's not what you are,' she said. 'Tina was right.'

'What did Tina say about me?'

'Ask her. If you play your cards right, she might tell you.'

'If you're playing mind games with me,' he said, 'then we're not finished.'

He held her eyes with his own.

'I'll see you,' he said. 'I don't know when, but I will.'

Then he walked away.

Alysa landed in England at midday and behaved like a perfect, responsible businesswoman, going straight into work and conferring with her colleagues. After four hours she departed with an arm full of files and spent the evening on the phone to clients.

Finally, at one in the morning, she faced the thing she'd been avoiding, and unlocked the safe where she kept Carlotta's letter.

She read it through once more, thinking of how it would destroy Drago's illusions if he saw it, castigating herself as a fool who didn't know where her own best interests lay.

Tell him, urged her common sense. *It'll hurt him for a while, but it'll clear the way for you. You'll have all his heart then, and perhaps that will conquer your fear and free you to turn to him.*

But she knew she wasn't going to do it. It wasn't about common sense. It was about the love she felt even while she tried to deny it. It scared her that she'd come so close to telling him the forbidden secret.

She took out the letter from James that she'd also stolen, and read them both one last time. Then she tore them into little pieces, put a match to them and watched as they turned to ashes.

As the months passed she found herself doing again what she'd done before, throwing herself into the job to dull emotions that she didn't want to have. But it was harder now. Then she hadn't fully understood what she was doing. This time she knew exactly.

She'd survived once by murdering all feeling and functioning like an automaton, but Drago had destroyed that defence. Now her heart was alive again, and it yearned for him. He'd shown her a new way, and she'd rejected it.

But I can't face it going wrong again, she mourned. *Not just for me, but for him. This is my life now.*

As the time passed into November, then December, the weather grew cold—not the bright, edgy cold of approaching Christmas, but a dreary chill. Decorations went up in the office; lists were made of clients who must be sent cards.

More as a personal gesture than anything, Alysa put a few modest decorations up in her home. It wasn't the joyful display of the Christmas before last, when she'd been full of ill-fated happiness over James. But nor was it the bleak nothingness of last year, when she'd hurried past shop windows containing nativity scenes, eyes averted. She'd come to terms with what her life was turning into. Or so she told herself.

If she'd felt like weakening fate took a hand just then to stiffen her resolve, Brian chose that moment to tell her that her partnership was settled.

'We're going to make an occasion of it,' he said. 'Dinner at the Ritz, with everyone there—all the partners and their wives—just to welcome you. I'll be your escort, so take tomorrow off to buy a new dress. Go on. I don't want to see you in the office until you've bought something eye-catching.'

Next morning she got up early to head for the West End, but she soon realised that it was going to be one of those awkward days. As she was heading for the lift, she heard the phone begin to ring in her apartment, dashed back, dropped her keys and managed to get the front door open just as the ringing stopped.

She punched in the keys to find out where the call had come from, but there was nothing to tell her.

Which means it's probably a foreign number, she thought. *Drago?*

It wasn't wise to call him, but she found herself dialling his number. But all she got was the engaged signal. She held on, hoping it would stop. When it didn't she hung up and dialled again. Still engaged.

Not Drago, then. Probably a wrong number.

But it happened again, just as she reached the front door. This time she ran back fast, but the ringing stopped just as she reached out her hand.

'Well, you're not Drago,' she told the phone when she'd slammed it down. 'He'd never dither like that. Now, I'm going.'

The streets were full of Christmas. Neon angels floated overhead, their lights flickering on and off even at this early hour. Music played, notices announced, 'this way to Santa Claus'. Alysa entered one of London's exclusive department-stores and found herself almost caught up in the queue for Santa.

She could see him in the distance, sitting at the entrance to his grotto, talking earnestly with a little boy, apparently asking what he wanted for Christmas.

The impossible question, Alysa thought. *Two years ago I'd have said that I already had everything I could want—James and our baby. Last year I'd have said I was all right then, that I'd put the past behind me, never dreaming that Drago lay in the future.*

But what would I say now—that a few weeks ago I stood at a crossroads and made the wrong choice? That it's too late to go back? That my future is now my past, and my heart aches for the love I wasn't brave enough to fight for?

While she mused her feet took her to the entrance to the fashion department, and she forced herself back to the present. Her big moment had come and she was here to celebrate. She repeated that to herself again and again, hoping that it would become real. Or would, at least, start to matter.

The dress she finally chose was dark red, dramatic and magnificent, hugging her waist and hips, and low-cut—just the right side of decency. To go with it she chose a pair of golden sandals with suicidally high heels. The whole outfit was unlike anything she'd worn before, and that was fine. This was her flag of triumph.

On her return to the office she was besieged by her secretary and two others, demanding a display, so she dressed up and paraded before them. For this she'd sacrificed everything, and she was going to enjoy it. Their cries of delight attracted the others in the office. Brian appeared, adding his admiration, and soon everyone was applauding as she paraded up and down. They all knew that she was the victor about to come into her kingdom.

'Make way for the queen!' one of them cried.

'Is this vision the lady I'm to have the honour of escorting?' Brian asked.

Laughing, she turned to him and curtseyed, which made everyone cheer.

But the cheering died abruptly into silence. And Alysa turned to find Drago standing there, watching her, tension in every line of his body.

He looked as if he hadn't slept for a week. His eyes were haggard and desperate, and he reminded her of the man she'd first seen months ago at the waterfall. He carried the same aura that he'd had then, as though he was being devoured inside.

'I must speak with you,' he said harshly. 'Now.'

He looked around at the others, silently ordering them away. They were inclined to protest at this high-handedness, but Alysa said, 'Please leave us.'

They trickled away. Brian regarded her with raised eyebrows, but at last he too departed. As soon as they were alone she went to Drago.

'What's happened? Whatever is the matter?'

'I've come because I must take you back with me. It's vital.'

'But why? I can't leave now—'

'You *must*! No—no, I don't mean that. But I can't tell you how important it is. Help me, Alysa, I beg you. You're the only person who can.'

'What's happened?'

'I was going to call you,' he said distractedly. 'But when I picked the phone up I knew I couldn't say it like that.'

'Drago, was that you on the phone this morning?'

'Yes, I called, then lost my nerve and hung up. Then I did it again.'

'But I thought it was you, and I called you back. It was engaged.'

'I was sitting there with the receiver in my hand, trying to make up my mind. Just an indecisive idiot. You'd have laughed if you'd seen me.'

'No, I wouldn't,' she said gently. 'Drago, please try to tell me what's happened. I've never seen you in such a state.'

He closed his eyes.

'Tina knows,' he said simply.

'What?'

'She knows that Carlotta had left for good. She knows her mother abandoned her.'

'But how?'

'She found out at school. One of the teachers is a client of

Carlotta's law firm, and of course the people there know the truth and talk about it. Tina overheard the teachers saying how Carlotta had just walked out on her, without caring if she never saw her again.'

He broke into a stream of curses. Alysa listened in horror, not following the words, but understanding the meaning, which perfectly expressed the violence of her own feelings.

'Oh God!' she whispered. 'What happened?'

'Tina came home sobbing her heart out. I've tried to comfort her, told her it's a misunderstanding, that her mother would never leave her.'

'Good, you stick to that,' Alysa said robustly. 'Is Elena any help?'

'She's denying it too, which helps a little, but she blames me for everything.'

'But how can it be your fault if people gossip in the law firm?'

'It can't, but Elena's seen her chance to get Tina away from me. She says I must have told her. I've denied it over and over, but she just calls me a liar. She says I'm a wicked influence, and she's going to "save" Tina from me. She wants to take her for good.'

'You mustn't let her,' Alysa said at once.

'I don't mean to, but I can't fight her alone. I told you about her family with its grand connections. It also contains two lawyers and a politician, and their influence is immense. They might just manage it.'

'But don't you have a lot of influence too?'

'Yes, I can afford good lawyers. But Elena can present herself so well, and I present badly, especially if I lose my temper. You're the only one who can help me,' he said. 'Tina likes you, and you can talk to her—explain, comfort her.'

'But explain what? What do you want me to say?'

'That's up to you. Whatever it is you'll manage better than me. I love that little girl, but I don't know what to say. I've tried and tried, but my words don't comfort her. She needs something more. You can give her that something, and make all those people see that they mustn't take her away from me.

'Please, Alysa, come back with me now. Tina and I need you more than you'll ever know.'

'Come back?' she echoed.

'There's a flight in three hours. We can just catch it if we hurry. I promised Tina I'd be home tonight.'

'You've left her alone?'

'No, of course not. She's with a friend of mine and his wife. She knows them, and they can be trusted, but I have to return when I promised. Please, Alysa.'

She looked down at herself. Drago did the same, and for the first time he seemed to become aware of what she was wearing.

'What did I interrupt?' he asked.

'I just bought this for a dinner party.'

'And wore it in the office to show off to your escort. He's the guy I saw you with before, isn't he?'

'Yes,' came Brian's voice from the door. 'And the party is to celebrate her partnership.'

'Congratulations,' Drago said heavily. 'You got what you wanted.'

'Drago—'

'All I ask is that you help me out in this matter, and then I'll never trouble you again.' He lowered his voice. 'Please, Alysa, just come with me tonight.'

'Come where?' Brian asked.

'Florence,' Alysa said.

'Florence, Italy?' Brian sounded aghast.

'It would only be for a day,' Alysa pleaded. 'I'd rush back.'

'Alysa, this is Wednesday. The dinner is on Friday. You can't be sure you'll be back in time, and if you're not there when I've laid it all on...' He left the implication hanging in the air.

'I will be, I promise.'

'And what about tomorrow? Don't you have appointments?'

'My secretary will reschedule them. It'll be all right, but I have to go.'

'I'm surprised at you, Alysa,' Brian said. 'You've worked hard for this. I watched you with admiration, and I can't believe that you'd risk everything at the last minute.'

'You mean you'd take it all away from her because she missed one dinner party?' Drago demanded.

'We prefer our partners to be reliable,' Brian explained. 'And,' he added with a significant glance at Alysa, 'I'd rather not be made to look foolish. Don't disappoint me at this late date.'

'I won't. I'll be back, I swear it. But I must go, Brian.'

Brian looked at her for a moment, then gave a shrug that clearly meant, 'on your own head be it', and disappeared.

'Give me a moment to get changed,' Alysa said.

She did it in double-quick time, instructed her secretary, then hurried out with Drago. They didn't speak on the short journey to her home. She was trying to take in the enormity of what she'd done, aware of Drago watching her with a slightly baffled expression, as though he too had been taken by surprise.

They kept the taxi while she packed hurriedly, and then they were on their way to the airport.

'Suppose I can't get a ticket for this flight?' she asked.

'I took the liberty of buying you one.'

'Why didn't I think of that?' she asked with a little smile.

'Yes, you might have expected it by now. Will he really make you suffer for this?'

'I'll be back by Friday evening, so he'll have nothing to complain about. Don't worry.'

She wished she felt as confident as she sounded, but she could see the threat looming before her. Elena's takeover bid for Tina had assumed manic proportions. She'd thought to control Drago by marrying him off to her friend, but that had failed, and now she was clutching at straws.

The idea that she could steal the little girl from her father might sound paranoid, but that didn't mean it shouldn't be taken seriously. Alysa pitied the old woman's suffering, but she wasn't going to see Drago devastated. Only she really understood what he'd lost, and while she had breath in her body he wasn't going to lose any more.

And if that meant that she was the loser, that she'd pay the price by throwing away everything she'd worked for, what then?

She glanced at Drago in the corner of the taxi, his eyes closed, light and darkness chasing each other across his face, and she reached out to touch him. At once he gripped her hand painfully tight. She returned it just as hard, and they sat like that for the rest of the journey.

CHAPTER TWELVE

DRAGO hardly spoke on the plane, and Alysa didn't offer words of consolation that would have been useless. His face was drawn and haggard. Sometimes he made the effort to smile at her, but she could see the truth beneath it. He was in a hell of fear. She smiled back, telling him she was there for him.

It was snowing at the airport, where his car was waiting to take them to the home of the friends who were caring for Tina. Florence itself was bright and cheerful, the streets full of decorations, the lights gleaming against the darkness of the sky and the white of the snow.

'We'll be there in a minute,' Drago said at last. 'It's getting late. She'll think I'm not coming—'

'Stop it,' Alysa said firmly. 'It's going to be all right. When you see her you'll smile, she'll throw herself into your arms and we'll take it from there.'

But she spoke with more confidence than she felt. Elena wasn't going to see her best chance slip away without a fight, and as the house came into view she sensed that her worst fears were being realised. All the lights were on, the front door was open, and a woman was standing outside looking frantically along the road.

'That's Signora Lenotti,' Drago said. 'I left Tina with her and her husband.' As the car stopped he leapt out. 'It's all right, we're here.'

But the woman burst into tears at the sight of him.

'What's happened?' Drago demanded.

'The *signora* was here. She demanded that I hand Tina over to her.'

'But you didn't,' Drago snapped. 'Tell me that you didn't.'

'What else could I do?' Maria wailed. 'She said she was her legal guardian, and she threatened me with the law.'

Drago swore violently.

'She just marched in and walked through the house,' Maria said. 'When she found Tina she—she acted as though we'd kidnapped her, telling her everything would be all right now that she'd been "rescued".'

'That poor little mite,' Alysa said. 'What must she be imagining now?'

'How did she even know she was here?' Drago raged.

'I think someone in your house told her,' Maria said.

'I gave them strict instructions not to.'

'But are they all loyal to you?' Alysa put in. 'I'll bet she's got at least one of them on her side.'

'My God, she'll stop at nothing,' Drago muttered. 'I never knew until this moment what I was dealing with.'

'Where does Elena live?' Alysa asked. 'We've got to go on there.'

'She's in Bologna,' Drago said. 'That's about sixty kilometres north of here.'

'Then let's go.'

It was dark and the road was winding, but Drago's driver was the best, and he had them there in an hour, finally drawing up outside a splendid villa.

'There are no lights on,' Alysa said, fearing the worst. 'But why? They must be expecting you. Maybe they've just gone to bed,' she said, but she guessed they were both clutching at straws.

She knew the worst a moment later when the housekeeper came to the door and declared that the mistress had been away for two days, and she didn't know where she was or when she was coming back.

'My God, she could have taken Tina anywhere,' Drago groaned.

'Her other daughter,' Alysa said. 'Where does she live?'

'No, that family is in America at the moment, attending a wedding.'

'What about Leona? Where does she live?'

'Florence,' he said desperately.

'Fine. Let's get going.'

The driver had the engine running as they approached the car, and in a moment they were heading back the way they had come.

All the time Alysa was praying that Leona's house would be the end of the journey, and that this wouldn't turn into a hideous search for a child who'd completely disappeared.

When at last they saw the house she was fearful, for again the lights were off. But it was Leona herself who came to the door, and Alysa could see at once that she was uncomfortable.

'Is my daughter here?' Drago demanded.

She nodded and stood aside to let him in, looking anxiously at his face.

'Elena just turned up here without warning,' she said in a placating voice. 'She had Tina with her—'

'And so you couldn't turn them away,' Alysa said at once. 'You had to keep Tina safe until her father came for her. That was very kind.'

Leona smiled at this understanding and hurried away.

'Why are you sympathising with her?' Drago demanded, outraged.

'Because it's not her fault, and she hates the situation,' Alysa said hurriedly. 'Don't you see? She's already half on your side. Let's keep her there and get her the rest of the way. If you come on strong you'll alienate her and this will be harder.'

When he hesitated, unconvinced, she said, 'Drago, why did you bring me here? Because you knew I could deal with this better than you can. So let me get on with it and don't interfere.'

After a moment he nodded, and she saw something she recognised. He had the same weary, defeated look that she'd seen at the airport in February. He was out of his depth, and he knew it.

'Thank you,' he whispered.

She touched his face and turned back to the stairs, where Leona had just appeared at the top of it.

'I've knocked on her door but she won't come out,' she said frantically. 'She's locked it on the inside.'

'Where's Tina?' Alysa asked.

'In there with her.'

Beside her Alysa felt Drago stiffen, about to launch a thunderbolt, but her grip on his hand stayed him.

'Please take me up to them,' she said.

They went up the stairs, along a corridor, with Drago determinedly following them, but keeping a cautious distance. At last they stopped outside a door. Alysa tried it but it didn't give. From inside she could hear the sound of Elena sobbing.

'Hello?' she called.

'Go away,' Elena screamed.

'Elena, please let me in.'

'Go away! You tell lies, all of you. I won't let you lie about her.'

'Tina,' Alysa said. 'Are you there? It's Alysa.'

Then came Tina's voice by the door. 'I'm here.'

'Can you open the door for me?'

A pause, then a click as the bolt was shot back. But then there was a scream of, *'No!'* from inside, and the sound of a scuffle. As Alysa entered she saw that Elena had managed to seize Tina and drag her to the other side of the room. Now she was sitting on the bed with the little girl in her arms.

For a moment Alysa felt a spurt of temper. How dared this woman subject a child to such pressure? But then she saw Elena's face streaming with tears, her eyes crazed with misery, her chest heaving with sobs.

Through finding each other, she and Drago had come to terms with their own grief, but Elena's loss could never be healed in the same way. She knew it, and the knowledge had driven her to desperation.

'You're all liars,' Elena choked. 'You say wicked things about my daughter, but they're not true, *they're not true.*'

Alysa had a split second to make her decision, or rather to recognise that the decision had already been made. As the words came out of her mouth, she knew that she could have said nothing else.

'No, they're not true,' she said. 'But nobody has been telling lies. It's a simple misunderstanding, and I'm here to put it right.'

She reached out to Tina, but Elena tightened her arms and drew the child away towards the head of the bed.

'Don't come any nearer,' she said hoarsely.

'Just this far,' Alysa said, and sat down on the bed, close enough to Tina to reach out for her hand and feel the little girl grip her hard.

'They said Mamma wasn't coming back,' she whispered. 'They said she didn't love me any more, and she just left me.'

'That is nonsense,' Alysa said firmly. 'Listen, darling, I'm going to tell you something. I met your mother on the day she died, at the waterfall. I'd gone there with James, a friend, meaning to go up in one of those chairs. While we were waiting for the next ride we went to a little coffee shop nearby. Your mamma was there, also waiting, and we started to chat.

'She told us about her husband and her little girl, and how she was looking forward to getting back to them. She'd been away on business, and her route back lay past the waterfall, so she'd stopped off for a ride because she loved the excitement. "Then I'm going home to my darlings", she said.'

Tina's gaze was fixed on her. Alysa drew a long breath, knowing that she must tell the next bit carefully.

'I enjoyed listening to her,' she said. 'Because I was in love, and I wanted to get married and have children that I would love as much as she loved you. She made it sound so wonderful.'

'Truly?' Tina whispered.

'Truly. She loved you more than anyone in the world.'

'What about Poppa?'

'Yes, she loved him too, but you most of all.'

'And she wasn't going to leave me?'

'No, she wasn't, or she couldn't have spoken as she did that day. She was full of plans about all the things you were going to do together.'

Vaguely she was aware that Elena had grown still. Her grip on Tina had relaxed, and her gaze was fixed on Alysa as if she too was hanging on every word.

'Then we walked out to the waterfall,' Alysa went on, 'to get into the rides, but at the last minute I lost my nerve and stayed on the ground. I never had much head for heights. It was really James who wanted to go.'

Somewhere behind her she heard Drago draw in a sharp breath, but she couldn't let herself be distracted now.

'Was James your friend who died?' Tina asked softly.

'Yes. I backed out at the last minute, so he and your mother went up together, and then— Well, they died together. He was the man in the chair with her. That's why I was there at the memorial, the day we met. I couldn't tell you before. I couldn't bear to speak of it.'

She held her breath, wondering if she'd done enough to ease the little girl's heart. She had her answer a moment later when Tina pulled herself free of Elena and threw herself into Alysa's arms.

'Did you love him terribly?' she whispered.

'Yes,' Alysa said quietly. 'I loved him terribly.'

'And do you love Poppa now?'

Alysa turned her head to where she could see Drago, watching her in the doorway, his eyes full of fear and hope.

'Yes,' Alysa said. 'I love Poppa now.'

'Does Poppa love you?'

'Yes,' Drago said. 'He does.'

Tina struggled free and ran across the room to be seized up in his arms. Alysa watched them a moment before looking back at Elena, who'd folded her arms across her body, shaking.

'So you've got what you wanted,' she moaned. 'But I've lost everything.' Her wail filled the room.

'Alysa, let's get out of here,' Drago urged.

'Not yet. I still have something to do.'

She moved along the bed to where Elena was huddled, and put her arms around her.

'You haven't lost everything,' she said. 'Tina is still your granddaughter. She still loves you and she always will.'

'But *he* won't let me see her, not after this.'

'Drago won't part you from Tina,' Alysa assured her. 'He knows she needs you too, because you knew Carlotta longer than anyone.'

Elena turned suspicious eyes on Drago. 'Does she speak for you?' she demanded.

'She does,' he said gravely. 'Whatever she agrees to, I will honour.'

'You say that while she's here, but—'

'I'm going to be here for a long time,' Alysa said. 'You have nothing to fear.'

Elena looked at Drago. 'Don't hate me,' she pleaded.

'I'll never hate you,' he told her. 'You are still Tina's grandmother.' He glanced at Alysa. 'It is just as *she* says. It always will be.'

'But you'll forget Carlotta.'

'No, he won't,' Alysa said quickly. 'Carlotta will always be his real love.'

'*You* say that?'

'I'm just second best. That won't change.'

She was watching Elena, so didn't see Drago staring at her just before he carried Tina out of the room. Alysa, her heart torn with pity, gave Elena a final hug then went out to speak to Leona.

'I think she really needs to see a doctor,' she suggested.

'I know,' Leona said. 'Don't worry, she can stay with me a while, and I'll make sure she gets help.'

She looked at Alysa and Drago standing together, and gave a little nod of sad acceptance.

In the car the three of them sat together in the back seat. Tina was in her father's lap, clinging to him, eyes closed. Alysa glanced over, taking in the sight of them, contented in each other's arms, then she turned away to stare unseeingly out of the window. She needed a little time to take in what she'd done.

She had told Elena that she was coming to Italy for good, speaking on impulse with no time to consider all the implications. But they were huge. In one moment she'd tossed aside the partnership she'd striven so hard to win, and possibly her whole career. Who knew what use her qualifications would be in this country?

And she, a woman who'd always prided herself on thinking every problem through, had done it without a moment's thought. Was she mad?

Turning slightly, she looked again at Tina and Drago, both with their eyes closed, Tina with her head against her father's chest, Drago with his head resting on his child's hair. And she knew the answer to her question.

Yes, she was mad.

Wonderfully, gloriously mad. Mad in the way only the most fortunate on earth were mad. Heroically, blissfully mad, with the madness that lay at the heart of creation.

If her qualifications were useless here, then she would learn Italian properly and start all over from the beginning. She would do anything rather than say goodbye to Drago. No effort was beyond her, no task too great, as long as she was with him.

When had it all been decided? Long ago? Or tonight, when Drago had looked at her, imploring, putting his whole life at her mercy?

And did it matter when the decision had been made, as long as it was the right one?

As they entered Florence Tina awoke and began to look out at the streets, where the Christmas lights were still on.

'We've got lots of decorations up in the villa,' she confided to Alysa. 'And a crib. You'll like it.'

She closed her eyes again, but her hand was clutching Alysa's as though she feared to let her go.

As they reached the villa Tina opened her eyes again, looking quickly at Alysa, checking to make sure she was there.

They put her to bed together and kissed her goodnight. She was already asleep as they crept out of the room.

'What will Brian do when you don't come back?' Drago asked quietly.

'Aren't I going back?'

'You'd never have said those things to Tina if you hadn't meant them.'

'That's true.'

He led her into his own room and took her into his arms. Despite everything that had gone before, she knew that this was the first kiss of their love, the first time everything had been clear between them.

Except for one thing, her mind nudged her. But he must never know about the letter. She would keep that secret all her days, and if that meant being second best she would live with that rather than let him be hurt.

But she was strong. She would make him so happy that he would forget Carlotta. If she had still wanted revenge, that would have been the perfect way. But revenge was far from her heart now.

'Thank you for making Tina happy,' he said softly.

'Did I do the right thing?'

'You did the only thing possible to stop her heart breaking. She may have to know the truth one day, but by then she'll be strong enough to bear it.'

'I hope so,' she murmured.

'I think I knew something like this would happen, that's why I wanted you and nobody else. You see, I'd already discovered how good you were at protecting people from truths they couldn't bear.'

'What do you mean?'

'Did you think I didn't know that you did the same for me?'

She stared at him.

'The letter,' he said. 'The one in which Carlotta admitted she'd been unfaithful often before, a letter that mysteriously vanished.'

'But you—how did you—?'

'I looked in while you were reading it. I saw your face, and I saw how quickly you shoved it away to avoid showing it to me. When you'd gone to bed, I found it and I read it. Next morning it had vanished. I guessed that you'd taken it to protect me.'

'You've known since February?'

'I think in my heart I always knew about Carlotta before that, but I wouldn't admit it. I was hiding from the truth, and when I had to face it, it was almost as though something inside me grew quiet. I'd tormented myself with wondering. Now I didn't have to wonder any more, and there was a kind of peace in that.'

'I thought it would break your heart,' she said.

'And you tried to protect me, which was more than I deserved. All this time I've wondered if you'd change your mind and would tell me everything, but you never did. Last time you were here I tried to provoke you into an admission, but you held firm. I hadn't known such generosity existed. It gave me hope of winning your love.'

'How could I have let you see that letter, after what you said about clinging to your memories? It would have hurt you unbearably.'

'But you never understood my love for you, or you wouldn't have spoken of being second best. You could never be second best, don't you realise that?'

'Maybe I do now,' she whispered.

A great load had gone from her heart, leaving her free to love him totally without the slightest fear or reservation. Joy possessed her whole being.

'Could you really have gone through our life thinking of yourself as second best?' Drago asked.

Her smile was a mysterious enticement.

'If I had to,' she said. 'But there are ways to make you completely mine. I have my plans. You'll find out in time.'

'What better time than now?' he said, drawing her to the bed.

They made love drowsily, not frantic with urgency, but with the leisurely pleasure of people who knew they had all their lives. They were both tired after the long, dramatic night, but they needed this union to reaffirm that they belonged to each other heart, body and soul.

Dawn was beginning to creep around the blinds when he said, 'I need you as much as I love you. You're stronger than I am.'

'I'm stronger in some ways,' she murmured. 'You're stronger in others. It works out just fine.'

'Only if you stay with me.'

'Always—always.'

Later he said, 'When did you decide to stay?'

'When I knew that if I went back I'd have abandoned you to whatever life did to you. I couldn't do that. Would you have let me go?'

'Not for long. If this hadn't happened, I was going to call you anyway, about James. I've been doing some investigating for you. We can have him sent to England, but it would be a lot simpler to have him reburied here in a larger plot in the same cemetery. In fact...'

He seemed to become awkward and a suspicion rose in her.

'What have you done, Drago?'

'Well, you know me—the way I arrange things first and consult people afterwards, like a bulldozer. I made a few preliminary arrangements, just to get things started, and will continue only if they meet with your approval,' he finished hastily.

'What kind of preliminary arrangements?'

'I've found a good plot. He'll have a proper stone with all his details, and you can put James's photograph on it. You see, I thought—' He stopped, tongue-tied.

'Go on,' Alysa said with a little smile.

'I thought, if he was there, you'd want to visit him so you'd keep coming back. The plot isn't far from Carlotta, so even if you didn't tell me you'd arrived I could visit her at the same time and we'd bump into each other.'

'But how would you know what the right time was? Oh, of course. Silly question. You've got them all in your pocket, and there'd be a call to you as soon as I arrived. Someone would find out my hotel, and persuade me to return next day—'

'I had to find a way to lure you here if you didn't return willingly, and then— Well, it might have taken some time, but in the end you'd have realised that I was right and you belonged with me.'

'You don't even see obstacles, do you?' she demanded. 'Can I work in this country? Do my qualifications count?'

'Actually, I've been investigating that too. It's a bit complicated, but it can be done, and I know someone who'll help.'

'You're such a schemer,' she said tenderly.

'Nonsense, I just like my own way—about everything— all the time. What's wrong with that?'

She leaned close so that her hair fell on his face. 'Did you just make a joke?'

'I don't know. Did I?'

'It had better have been a joke.'

'Don't pretend to be alarmed. You do what you like with me, and you know it.'

She laughed and kissed him.

'I guess Tina was right about you.'

'She told you I was a softy, didn't she? I got it out of her in the end. It cost me a few cream buns—and a new doll, and some shoes, and books about her favourite cartoon character, and I forget the rest, but she drove a hard bargain.'

'Her father's daughter,' Alysa mused.

They laughed and embraced, but after a moment she said, 'I'll have to go back to England and work out my notice. I can't just let them down.'

'I know you won't do that.'

'I'll be here for Christmas, and every weekend until my notice is over.'

'Just promise to return here finally, and become my wife. I'm a patient man, beloved. I've waited for you this long. I can wait a little longer, if I know that you'll be mine in the end. As you were always meant to be.'

Two days before Christmas Eve the weather turned nasty. Planes were delayed, and those waiting for loved ones lingered anxiously at airports.

'She should be here by now, Poppa,' Tina said anxiously, staring out of the window into the black sky.

'The board says the plane will be late, *cara*. We just have to be patient.'

'But she will come, won't she?'

And just for a moment the little girl was back in time, waiting for her mother's return, waiting, waiting...

Drago heard the echo and quickly dropped down beside her.

'Of course she's coming, darling. It's only the weather.'

'But there could be an accident?'

'No, look up there.' He pointed up to the sky where lights

had just appeared in the distance. 'There's a plane coming in now.'

Let it be Alysa's, he prayed silently. Beside him he could feel that Tina was tense as both of them kept their eyes on the incoming lights.

Down they came, lower and lower, until the plane touched the ground, screaming away down the runway, out of sight until it could turn and taxi back.

Let it be hers—let it be hers.

'Poppa, look!'

Tina was pointing up at the board where against the London flight the red 'delayed' had changed to the green of 'landed'.

'She's here, she's here!' Tina was dancing with excitement.

Drago grinned broadly, wishing he could join her.

They hurried to the barrier to greet her, and at the first glimpse Tina rushed away, hauling her father after her.

'You're home, you're home!' she squealed.

'Yes,' she said softly, her eyes on Drago. 'I'm home.'

Drago's driver had almost gone to sleep waiting, but he roused and greeted her with a wave as they exited the airport hand in hand.

They all sat in the back of the car. Alysa took Tina onto her lap, wrapping her in her arms while the little girl babbled happily on their way to the villa.

'Look, it's snowing really hard.'

'So I see,' Alysa said, gazing out of the window to where the white flakes filled the air. 'I'm glad that waited until I landed.'

'Was it a bumpy flight?' Drago asked.

'A bit, and I'm not a good flyer. But I just kept thinking about what was waiting for me here—both of you, and the future we'll all have.' She met Drago's eyes again. 'The journey can be easy if you know what journey's end will be.'

She knew, because Drago had told her in a phone call two days ago, that this journey's end would include a meeting with the head of a local accountancy firm who had 'matters to discuss' with her. She was looking forward to that. Brian had been more reasonable than she'd dared to hope, and her release might be in as soon as six weeks. For this the ambitious Frank could take some credit, having avidly scooped up her clients in a way that had reminded Alysa of herself as she had once been.

The other person who would be waiting for her in the villa was Elena.

'I promised her that she wouldn't be shut out,' Drago had explained on the phone.

'And this is the perfect time to prove it,' she'd agreed.

'The thing is, she doesn't seem able to accept reassurance from me. It has to be you.'

'How is Tina with her? Does she seem frightened after what happened?'

'Strangely enough, no. I explained to her that Nonna wasn't well because she was so unhappy about Carlotta, and Tina understood at once. Now, as well as mothering me, she mothers Elena. Give her half a chance, she'll start mothering you.'

Now, as they drove up to the villa, Alysa could see Elena's pale, anxious face looking through a window, and she knew what she had to do—not only for Elena, but for Tina, who was watching closely.

So she burst into the house with a happy smile on her face, her arms thrown wide in greeting, and had her reward in Elena's look of passionate relief as they hugged each other. There was no more to be said.

'Now it's time you were in bed,' Drago told Tina.

'Please, Poppa, let me show Alysa the crib first?'

'I'd like to see it,' she said.

It was there, dominating the hall. Unlike the one she'd had two years ago, it was an expensive creation, but there at its heart was the same beauty and simplicity. Mary sat by the crib, her face radiant and tender as she watched over her child, while Joseph stood just behind, never taking his eyes from the two creatures that were his to love and protect.

'He's just been born,' Tina explained. 'And Mary is so happy that she has him.' She added confidingly, 'Mamma told me that.'

'And he's happy too,' Alysa said softly. 'Because he has his mother, and they make a family, even though—' she spoke carefully '—he has another family as well. Because you can love more than one person, even more than one mother.'

'Yes,' Tina said firmly.

'Now it's time for you to go to bed,' Drago said. 'We've got a big day tomorrow, with lots of shopping to do.'

'Why don't you ask Nonna to take you up?' Alysa said, indicating Elena.

They watched the old woman and the child climbing the stairs together, contented again in each other's company.

'I was afraid Tina might not be able to accept me,' Alysa said in wonder. 'But she did, from the first moment.'

'She looked at you and just knew that we all belong together,' Drago agreed. 'A family. The kind of family I never dared to hope for again. Alysa, my love, my dearest, my future. Do you believe in miracles?'

'I believe in this one,' she answered at once in a voice so fervent that it was almost a prayer. 'And I believe in all the others that we're going to make together. I love you, and I believe you love me. I believe that your love will be with me for all eternity. And that is the greatest miracle of all.'

A MUMMY FOR CHRISTMAS

BY
CAROLINE ANDERSON

Caroline Anderson has the mind of a butterfly. She's been a nurse, a secretary, a teacher, run her own soft-furnishing business, and now she's settled on writing. She says, 'I was looking for that elusive something. I finally realised it was variety, and now I have it in abundance. Every book brings new horizons and new friends, and in between books I have learned to be a juggler. My teacher husband John and I have two beautiful and talented daughters, Sarah and Hannah, umpteen pets, and several acres of Suffolk that nature tries to reclaim every time we turn our backs!' Caroline writes for the Mills & Boon® Cherish™ and Medical series.

CHAPTER ONE

'AH. MR MCEWAN. Good of you to join us.'

James stifled a growl of frustration and nailed a smile firmly on his face. 'Sorry I'm late. I was held up in HR—some technical hitch with my registration.'

'So I gather. Sorted now?'

'It is.' And it wouldn't have arisen if he'd remembered to post the damn form back to the hospital once he'd completed it, but hey-ho. And now this dark-haired dynamo with eyes the colour of toffee was gunning for him. His boss.

He swallowed his pride and joined the group gathered round the nursing station. A doctor, two nurses—and the woman. Kate Burgess, consultant general surgeon and his reluctant boss. Well, she wasn't the only one who was reluctant. He managed a more genuine smile for the others. 'Hi—I'm James. Good to meet you all. So—what are we doing?'

The dynamo arched one of those elegant, fine brows and speared him with a look. 'We? Well, *I'm* about to take a patient to Theatre.'

'Then I would imagine I'm assisting you? They said you were expecting me.'

'I was. An hour ago. As it is, I've taken Jo away from her job to do yours.'

He forced a smile. Actually it wasn't hard. What was hard was making sure it didn't look like a smile of relief, because he wouldn't be trapped in Theatre with her in this clearly combative mood. 'Why don't I do Jo's job, then, since I have nothing else that I'm expecting to do and it's fairly pointless for me to join you in Theatre without some kind of introduction to the patient—'

'Which you would have had if you'd been here on time.'

'Well, you need to talk to HR about that,' he said a little tightly, conscious of the interested and speculative looks they were attracting from the rest of the team. Damn her, how dare she give him a public dressing down?

'I did—a form you failed to return,' she said, her voice softer but nevertheless as sharp as a razor. 'Not a good start, McEwan. Paperwork is important.'

He hung on to his temper with difficulty. 'I am aware of that.'

'Good—so I won't need to labour the point. Right, Jo, since Mr McEwan is now here, perhaps you'd like to carry on with what you were supposed to be doing while I fill him in, and then he can assist me in Theatre, as he seems to be so keen.'

'Sure.' Jo smiled at him, pocketed her pen and headed for the door, winking at him as she shouldered it open. He chuckled under his breath. Oh, well, at least he had one ally in the department.

'Right,' she said, and fixed him with those toffee-coloured eyes. The sort of toffee you broke your teeth on. Or maybe your career.

'I'm about to do a hemicolectomy on a patient with a primary tumour in the terminal ileum,' she said, and he felt cold sweat break out all over his body. Oh, God. No. Stick to the plot, he told himself as she went on, 'Stephen Symes, aged fifty-four, been experiencing abdo pain, alternate bouts of diarrhoea and constipation, he's been fast-tracked but was admitted yesterday with vomiting and rectal bleeding.'

He didn't need to hear the list. He knew it by heart.

No! Stop thinking about it. Focus. Focus.

'Scan shows a mass which is almost totally obstructing the terminal ileum and attaching to the peritoneum over the femoral artery—hence the emergency surgery—but we won't really know exactly the extent of it until we open him up, or even if we can do anything at all. It could be tricky, which is why he's our only patient this morning.' She smiled challengingly. 'I tell you what, I'll be generous and let you lead.'

Something clenched in his gut. Did it show on his face? She looked at him keenly.

'Well?'

'I haven't seen the scans,' he said.

'No problem. I'll brief you now. Scans are up there,' she told him, nodding her head at the light box behind him. He turned, and his heart sank. Poor bastard.

'We can't hope to get it all,' he said.

'Almost certainly not. Besides, he's also a little jaundiced, so it's quite likely it's metastasised to his liver already.' She filled him in further on the man's history, his symptoms and probable prognosis, which, even before they got inside him, he knew was appalling. And once in there, might prove to be even worse. The oncology team would obviously be involved, but there was a limit to what they would be able to do if it was as bad as it looked from the scan.

'So—there you are, McEwan. Let's go get some answers—and we can see how good you are, now you're finally here.'

* * *

'Ready when you are,' he heard the anaesthetist say, and Kate—*Ms Burgess*—said something pithy on the lines of being there just as soon as the team had finished organising itself.

Stifling a sigh, he finished scrubbing, dried his hands and gowned up. He'd met women like her before—tough, uncompromising, hard as nails, trying to prove themselves as better than the men they worked with, clawing their way up over the backs of anyone who dared to stand between them and their ultimate goal. Well, tough. He could be uncompromising with the best of them, but that wasn't what he was here for. He was here to test the water, to see if this time he could make it work.

And he could. He could grit his teeth and put up with her nasty sense of humour and her evil little digs about his lack of organisation, and make it work.

He had to. He had a living to earn, a career to reconstruct, and a family to hold together.

And Kate Burgess wasn't about to be given the chance to sabotage that.

He was even better looking than she'd remembered.

Not that she'd been exactly studying him at his interview, but she had noticed, and now, in his scrubs—well, they did things for that solid, muscular frame that should have been illegal.

Not overly tall but too tall for her to look him in the eye without tipping her head back, strongly built, with floppy, tawny brown hair that had a tendency to fall down over his forehead—or did, until he'd scraped it back with those long, powerful-looking fingers and tucked it into a theatre cap—

and curious pale blue eyes that seemed to look right through her and find her wanting.

She felt a twinge of guilt, but it wasn't her fault he'd been late, and she'd hung on as long as possible before removing Jo from her duties when her uncomplaining young SHO already had more than enough to do. And she hadn't really been unkind, she thought, trying to justify her behaviour to herself and knowing that she couldn't. She shouldn't have criticised him like that in public, it was unfair and unethical. Damn. She'd have to apologise, but she'd seen the scans and knew what lay ahead, and she hadn't needed a slack member of the team to deal with at the same time.

Especially not a member she hadn't wanted in the first place, even if he was supposedly a fantastic surgeon.

He had an odd history. He'd been a consultant in a London hospital—only for a year—but then he'd left abruptly and hadn't worked since, apart from a few—a very few—highly temporary locum jobs. And it was now well over eighteen months since he'd given up his consultant's post, but he'd applied for the locum job to cover her registrar's maternity leave here at the Audley Memorial in mid-Suffolk, and the hospital board had welcomed him with open arms.

Not her, though. There were too many unanswered questions, too many potential complications, but there wasn't another candidate to come within miles of him. There was just something about him she didn't trust, something she didn't want in a colleague. He was too guarded, too unforthcoming, and he'd refused to be drawn on his career break, deflecting their questions gently but firmly, and citing personal commitments when they had asked why he wasn't going for a permanent post.

'Maybe one day,' he'd said, and that was that. Current employment law precluded any more searching questions, so they were stuck with what he volunteered. Which was next to zilch.

It was odd, though. Odd that a man whose rise through the ranks had been by all accounts meteoric, and whose disappearance from those ranks had been even faster, should emerge only to take a short-term post. Because her registrar *was* coming back, just the moment she'd had her baby and got her child care sorted.

And the previous hospital had spoken incredibly highly of him without telling her anything in the least revealing. So what was the story?

She didn't know, but she was damned if she was going to ask him again, when he couldn't even get himself organised enough to turn up on time with his ducks in a row for his first day at work. The only thing she was sure of was that she wasn't cutting him any slack. He did his job properly to her satisfaction, or he was out. She had a busy surgical team to run, and she didn't carry passengers, no matter what their personal commitments.

She didn't suffer fools gladly, either, and she wasn't starting with this one, no matter how beautifully put together he might be.

She was finished with all that. So finished that she couldn't imagine why she was even thinking about it.

'In your own time, McEwan,' she snapped. Heading for the table, she picked up the iodine swab and sloshed it liberally over the man's abdomen. Then she looked up and met those disturbing pale blue eyes over the body of Mr Symes.

'Your patient, Mr McEwan.'

Meeting the challenge in her eyes with a quirk of his brow, he stepped up to the table and held out his hand.

'Knife, please.'

He ripped off his gloves, peeled off his gown and ditched it in the bin with his hat, and headed for the changing room, Kate hard on his heels.

Of all the cases to start with, of all the evil twists of fate—

'Have you got a problem?'

As if she cared. He turned his head slowly and met her eyes, too raw to be diplomatic. 'Not as far as I'm aware, but you clearly have. Want to get the assassination over now?'

She frowned, propping up the doorframe and managing to look genuinely puzzled. 'Assassination?'

'You've had nothing good to say to me or about me yet today, and I know you didn't want the board to appoint me, so I don't imagine it's going to be pretty. So, do you want to do this now, or would you rather wait until you have an audience before you give me a blow-by-blow of my inadequacies?'

She coloured interestingly, but she held his gaze, to her credit.

'I'm sorry. I shouldn't have said what I did in public like that, but I was…'

'Angry?'

'Frustrated. I wanted to meet you, introduce you to Steve Symes and his wife, go through the case.'

'Instead of which you gave me a scant glance at the scans and hurled me in at the deep end. Why?'

'Because if you were only half as good as everyone said, I knew you could do it, and I wanted to see for myself how good you really were.'

'Or watch me fail.'

She shook her head. 'Not at all. And I was right to trust you. You did a very good job. I couldn't have done it better myself. Possibly not as well. The graft on his femoral artery was a superb piece of surgery, and I'm glad you were able to do a bowel resection so he doesn't have a stoma, so at least he'll have his leg and his dignity if nothing else. It's just a shame it won't save him.'

'We don't know that. It's only just gone off to Histology for grading,' he said. He wasn't falling for her flattery, and he was more concerned about their patient than scoring points, but she shook her head.

'Come on, James, you're good. You saw that mass, and you felt his liver. You know as well as I do what's going on.'

He swallowed and opened his locker door. 'Yes.' He stripped off his top, pulled on his shirt and waited for her to turn away. Apparently she wasn't going to, so with a slight shrug he dropped his scrub bottoms, kicked them off and reached into his locker for his trousers.

She moved then, he noticed wryly, soft colour flooding her cheeks for the second time as she took a step back and then turned on her heel and squeaked across the corridor in her rubber boots to the female changing room as if the floor was on fire.

Dear God, he was gorgeous.

Seriously hot, she thought as she stripped off her own theatre blues and reached for her clothes. And she was his boss, the woman who was going to have to put up with his weak excuses and his evident lack of organisation for the duration.

Fabulous.

Oh, well, at least he was an excellent surgeon, and anyway, she wasn't about to be distracted by his physical charms. She was immune. Utterly immune. She glanced over her shoulder and got a perfect view through the two open doors as he hauled his trousers up over that taut, muscular bottom in its snug jersey boxers, and she stifled a moan.

Maybe she needed a booster vaccine.

She kept her eyes firmly to herself after that, but it didn't help. She'd seen him now, and it wasn't an image she was likely to forget in a hurry. It didn't help, either, that they then went to the ward and she had to watch everyone falling over themselves to find an excuse to talk to him. Well, the women, anyway. The men were giving him wary looks and reassessing their chances with the nurses they'd been hoping to get lucky with, if she knew anything about ward dynamics.

And he was charm itself, but she noticed with interest that he kept a slight distance without being unfriendly, and she also noticed the reappearance of a wedding ring since they'd finished surgery. They'd be disappointed, she thought, and wondered if that curious twinge she'd felt when she'd seen the ring could possibly be put down to it.

Ridiculous. Of course not. She wasn't interested. She didn't do relationships with work colleagues. With men, full stop. Not any more.

'Right, time for a quick check of yesterday's post-ops and we can go and have some lunch before my clinic this afternoon. It'll give me a chance to fill you in on our schedule,' she said, and took him away from his fan club.

And she wasn't sure if that quiet sigh that eased from his throat as they turned and walked down the ward was one of relief or disappointment.

* * *

'So how was your day, Rory?'

''K, I s'pose.'

'Do anything interesting at school?'

'No. Can I watch cartoons?'

'Sure, but just for a little while, then you need a bath and bed.' James stifled a sigh and gave his son a quick one-armed hug. 'Are you hungry? What did you have to eat?'

Rory shook his head, heading for the sitting room. 'We had fish fingers and chips.'

James frowned. Fish fingers and chips? OK occasionally, and goodness knows he'd resorted to that on numerous occasions over the past eighteen months, but if this was what the childminder was going to give the kids every day for supper he was going to have to say something, and he dreaded it. It had been hard enough to find anyone with space who could take Freya all day and pick Rory up from school and keep him till he finished. The last thing he needed to do was make waves.

'Was Freya all right?'

Rory shrugged uncommunicatively. 'S'pose,' he mumbled, dropping down onto the floor and turning on the television, his back to his father.

James put the kettle on, went back into the sitting room and stared broodingly down at his sleeping daughter, still lying where he'd put her when they'd got in a minute ago, out for the count. She was oblivious to the noise of the cartoon, but she'd been up in the night and she was exhausted—and there were tear stains on her downy cheeks.

Oh, damn. Why? Why him? Why Beth? Why any of them?

He wanted to throw back his head and howl at the moon, but it wouldn't get them anywhere and the kids had enough to deal with without their father going off the rails, so he scooped Freya gently into his arms, carried her up to her bedroom and undressed her, changed her nappy and slid her into her cot without waking her.

He'd bath her in the morning. For now she needed sleep more than anything, and he needed to spend some time with Rory and brush up on a few things for work, then phone the childminder and talk to her about their diet.

And then he could go to bed.

'So how was your new registrar?'

Kate gave her father a fleeting smile. 'Oh, very good—if you don't count the fact that he was an hour late because he'd failed to send a vital form back to HR.'

'Oops,' her mother said softly from the Aga. She stirred the gravy thoughtfully and cast her daughter a searching look. 'Will you forgive him?'

'Not if it happens again,' she retorted, and then sighed. And of course her parents both noticed.

'So what's the problem with him?'

'I have no idea,' she said quietly, her thoughts troubled. 'Family problems, I think. Personal commitments, he described them as at his interview, but he looked tired today as if he'd been up all night.' As well as drop-dead gorgeous.

'Married?'

'I don't know. We can't ask that sort of thing any longer, but…he has a ring,' she said slowly, for some reason holding back on saying yes because she just felt, somehow, that he wasn't married. Not any more. So—what, then? Divorced? Widowed? Divorced, most likely. Sharing custody. A messy divorce, then—the sort of divorce that had led children to this house and her parents over and over again, to be loved and cared for and put back together again until things were a little straighter at home.

If they ever were. Sometimes it just didn't happen.

'Sounds as if there's a story there,' her father said, handing her a plate laden with tender slices of roast chicken and crunchy golden roasties. He pushed the bowl of steaming Brussels sprouts towards her and stuck a spoon in it.

'Oh, I'm sure there is,' she said, toughening up. 'There's always a story, but I don't want to hear it. He shouldn't have taken the job if he couldn't hold it down. His personal life is nothing to do with me, and I don't want it affecting his work. If he can't keep it sorted, he shouldn't be there.'

'I think that sounds a little harsh,' her mother said, sitting down at the other end of the battered old farmhouse table and setting the gravy jug down in the middle. 'I know you don't want to get involved, and I realise he has to do his job, but surely, if there was some mix-up?'

'He didn't send in the right forms. If he does that with a patient, fails to get the paperwork in order, then tests could get missed and results disappear and people could die.'

'I'm sure he'll be aware of that,' her father put in, which earned him a look that he returned evenly until finally she sighed and smiled and gave a tiny nod of concession.

'Yes. Yes, of course he's aware of it. And he's a brilliant surgeon—fantastic. Neat, quick, decisive—he'll be a real asset. I'm not surprised he was a consultant. God only knows what he's doing as a locum registrar.'

'Holding his family together, perhaps?' her mother suggested softly, and Kate felt a stab of guilt.

Was that what James was doing? Holding his family together?

'Then why not say so?'

'Maybe he's a very private man. Maybe he doesn't want to talk about it. Maybe it's messy and embarrassing or just too hurtful to talk about.'

Like her own divorce.

'Maybe,' she conceded, wondering.

'Cut him a little slack, Kate,' her mother advised. 'Give him time—for the children.'

'We don't even know if there are any children,' she pointed out, but she had to bear it in mind, just in case. She couldn't do anything else, because without her parents, who weren't her parents at all, her life would have been very, very different.

'OK, enough about work. How are you guys? Good day?' she said, handing over the conversation to them. Piling the hot, steaming sprouts onto her plate, she poured over the gravy, picked up her knife and fork and started eating as she listened.

He couldn't sleep.

Apart from the fact that he was kicking himself about the bloody form he'd failed to send in, and the heart-rending interview he'd had with Amanda Symes at her sleeping husband's bedside in the high-dependency unit, there was an image of Kate Burgess in her underwear burned onto his retinas, and every time he closed his eyes he could see it, the smooth skin, the sleek curves—and the ugly, wicked scar that snaked over her ribs.

Surgery. Emergency surgery. A thoracotomy?

Looked like it. He'd dragged his eyes away and finished dressing, and then for the rest of the day he'd felt as if his eyes were burning through her clothes. It was a wonder they hadn't caught fire, and he was stunned at himself.

He hadn't looked at another woman since he'd met Beth eight years ago, and he sure as hell didn't need to be fantasising about a woman who wouldn't be out of place in *The Taming of the Shrew*!

No. That was unfair. She'd been right, he should have been there on time with all his boxes ticked. It had been unprofessional, and all the excuses in the world wouldn't make it right.

He swallowed the disappointment that he'd let himself down at the first hurdle. Stupid, stupid oversight. And now, of course, she'd be worried that his paperwork wouldn't be up to scratch.

Well, he'd just have to prove her wrong.

He rolled to his side, punched his pillow and rammed it into the side of his neck, then closed his eyes and saw her again. Naked, except for a few scraps of outrageous underwear and a scar that raised more questions than he wanted answers for.

He was on time the next day, but he looked exhausted.

'How's Stephen Symes?' he asked without preamble, and Kate gave him a searching look and smiled pointedly. 'Good morning.'

'Morning. Sorry,' he mumbled. 'So—Mr Symes?'

'He's back on the ward. He spent the night in HDU but he's OK. The histology's back.'

'Bad?' he asked, and she nodded.

'As it can be,' she told him, and the muscle in his jaw tensed. 'It's a grade three, dirty margins—but we knew that at the time, knew we hadn't got all of it. And the histology indicates that it's aggressive, which is borne out by the liver involvement. So it's Stage IV, as we suspected, and we're talking palliative care. Oncology is onto it.'

'Have you spoken to him, or have they? Told him the news?'

'I thought I might let you do that, as you were the one who operated, and as you spoke to his wife yesterday afternoon. I gather from what she said over the weekend that he was the sort of man who wanted all the answers, and when I spoke to her yesterday after you'd discussed the operation with her she told me he'd want to know the truth.'

'How much of it?'

'Not enough to terrify him,' she said, and something flickered in his eyes. 'Just give him the bare bones, and let the oncologist and onco nurse fill him in on the treatment plan and likely course of events. It's their department, not ours.'

'Is his wife here?'

'Not at the moment. She's gone home—she's coming back shortly.'

'Right. Where is he?'

'Bay two, bed four.'

'Notes?'

She arched a brow and handed him the notes, and he took them and glanced at the results, then shut the file and walked away, pausing to wash his hands and rub them with alcohol gel. He took his ring off to wash it before putting it back on, and she was relieved to see that he was fastidious and she didn't need to keep an eye on that, at least.

But she couldn't stop herself keeping an eye on that ring, and she found herself wondering about him again as he replaced it and twisted it round, just once, thoughtfully, before squaring his shoulders and heading towards their patient.

Crazy. She was wondering altogether too much. She watched him walk up to Mr Symes and pull the curtain a little to screen him from his neighbour, then shake his hand, his face serious. He didn't let go of his hand, though, didn't distance himself as he delivered the news, and she stood there and watched the man's face through the gap in the curtain as it all sank in, and wished it could have been different.

He spent several minutes with him, and then came back to the nursing station, his eyes bleak.

'OK?' she asked, and he nodded.

'It wasn't exactly unexpected. He said he'd had an idea that was what it was, so he wasn't expecting a miracle, but that sort of news is always a shock. I think he just needs time for it to sink in before we tell him much more, or it'll go straight over his head.'

'We can go through it again. I'm sure we'll have to, to answer all his questions.' She sighed. 'It's such a waste. If only he'd reported his symptoms sooner, before it'd had time to metastasise.'

'But you don't, do you?' he said flatly. 'Even if you know—even if you're a doctor—you just assume it's IBS or something you ate and it becomes part of life to have an irregular bowel pattern, because nobody wants to believe that it can be anything sinister.'

There was something odd about his voice, and that bleak look in his eyes was even bleaker. He sucked in a breath and straightened up, his eyes going blank. 'So—we need to contact the onco nurse and the oncologist, get some treatment set up for him asap.'

'I've done it,' she told him. 'The oncologist is on his way down. I'd like you to speak to him and tell him exactly what you've told Mr Symes, and I'd like you to be there when he talks to them. His wife's on her way. I've asked her to join us, so she can be involved in the discussion.'

He nodded. 'Good. Thanks.'

He was about to say something when she caught sight of the oncologist striding down the ward towards them, and she opened her mouth to greet him and was cut off by his exclamation.

'James? What the hell are you doing here?' he asked, shaking his hand warmly.

It was the first time she'd seen James smile with his eyes, and the change was astonishing. 'Working—locuming, as of yesterday. How are you? I'd forgotten you'd moved up here. How's it going?'

'Fine, great. What about you? I haven't seen you for ages, not since—well, last September, I suppose. I didn't realise you'd left London now as well.'

'No,' he said, the smile fading. 'We're OK, Guy. We're getting there. We've moved to be closer to my mother and my in-laws.'

'And Freya?'

The smile was back, softer this time. 'Freya's fine. Doing well, and Rory's started school. We ought to meet up.'

'That would be good. Come over some time. Sarah would love to see them again. So—what have you got for me, Kate?' he asked, getting back to business, and Kate saw James's smile retreat once more as she spoke.

'CA bowel—terminal ileum, caecum and attachment to the rear wall over the right femoral artery. We did a hemicolectomy to remove the obstruction and James dissected out what he could, but it's only a short-term fix to give him some symptomatic relief. He's almost certainly got liver mets. We're waiting for some blood results to confirm that but he's jaundiced and there are small but palpable masses in the liver.'

Guy winced and gave James a keen look. 'Ouch.'

James shrugged, and Kate picked up swirling undercurrents. She'd known there was something, but now Guy was watching James closely and those curious blue eyes were flat and shuttered. 'It was a bit tricky, but he's come through it well, considering,' he said gruffly. 'I've told him what to expect within reason and without putting the fear of God into him, but you'll need to go over it and dot the Is and cross the Ts.'

'Shall we go and talk to him, then, in a few minutes? I'd like to see the notes first.'

'Of course. I'll be back in a minute.' James handed over the notes and excused himself, and Guy flicked through them and sighed.

'Tough one, this, for him to start with.'

'So it seems,' she said, fishing, but before he could say any more they were interrupted by a soft voice.

'Dr Burgess?'

She turned and saw Amanda Symes standing at her side, her eyes strained and red-rimmed and her face pale. 'Mrs Symes—thank you for joining us. This is Dr Croft. He's the oncologist who's going to be taking over your husband's care. He's going to go through things with you both.'

'Oh. Right. Um—and the other doctor? James—Dr McEwan, was it? I'd like him there, he was so kind to me yesterday.'

'I'm right here,' James said, appearing again from nowhere and smiling gently at her. 'Hello again, Amanda. Shall we go into the office?'

It wouldn't have been so bad if he hadn't known exactly what was in store for them.

As it was, he was only too painfully aware of every twist

and turn in the road ahead, but Guy led the discussion and he really didn't need to have anything to do with it.

Except, of course, he felt involved for all manner of unsound and unprofessional reasons. He put them on one side and forced himself to concentrate on this case, this man, this spouse whose life was about to be turned upside down, this family that was going to be torn apart by fate.

But not his. Not this time.

CHAPTER TWO

THE next few days were tough.

Rory was OK-ish and coped with the change of routine just like he'd coped with everything the last year and a half had thrown at him, with quiet stoicism, but Freya was slower to settle. She'd spent time with the childminder before he'd started the job, to give her time to get used to her, but the new regime of long days and early starts was making her tired and grizzly.

At least the food issue wasn't an issue, really. Helen had given them fish fingers and chips at Rory's suggestion because they'd gone home via the park to feed the ducks and had needed something quick, and she'd been meaning to ask him for a list of things the children liked. And the next night they'd had roast chicken with lots of veg, which he was more than happy about.

But on Wednesday night, as they'd arranged, his mother picked them up from the childminder straight after school and took them home with her to her little flat because he was on call, and that unsettled Freya even more.

'She just wouldn't go to bed,' his mother told him unhappily on the phone the next day. 'I know it's difficult, but I think it would be better if I came to you in future—familiar territory and all that. It makes the bedtime routine more normal and I can't bear it when she's so unhappy.'

All of which made absolute sense—except his spare bedroom was a storeroom at the moment, and it would take a mammoth effort to clear it.

An effort he didn't have the time or inclination to make, but he knew he had to stop stalling and get to grips with the house, so he ordered a little skip on Friday and in the evening systematically went through all the stuff in the room—old paperwork, things from his student days, some of Beth's things that he'd kept—nothing important, nothing sentimental or relevant or remotely useful, just things he hadn't got round to dealing with before the move—and first thing in the morning, he carted them downstairs and threw them all out.

He was heading towards the skip with the last armful when Kate walked up the drive towards him.

Hell. He stopped, horribly conscious of the state of the house, the task he was undertaking and the mess he was in, but she just smiled and waggled his mobile phone at him.

'You left this on my desk. I found it this morning when I popped in to check up on something. It's got several missed calls, so I thought you might want it. I would have called you, but HR said it was the only number registered to you, and I didn't want to call your mother and worry her. They gave me your address.'

I'll just bet they did, he thought, wondering how she'd sweet-talked that out of them, and what else she'd managed to get them to yield up. Not that it mattered.

'Thanks.' He dropped the last of Beth's possessions into the skip with a quiet sigh and took the phone from her, then added, 'Want a cup of tea?'

He didn't know why he was asking, except she'd gone out

of her way to return his phone, he was dying of thirst and he'd decided he didn't actually care whether she was impressed or not by where he lived. It was none of her damn business.

'That would be lovely,' she said, looking slightly surprised. 'Thank you.'

He ran a mental eye over the inside of the fridge and wondered if he had milk. Probably. And maybe even teabags. And perhaps at a pinch he might even find a biscuit...

He led her through to the kitchen and put the kettle on, wincing at the dishes piled in the sink, but she stood in front of them, looking out of the window, and totally ignored the mess.

'What a lovely garden.'

'It is—or it will be when I get round to doing anything with it. That's one of the reasons I bought the house. Well, that and the fact that it's got four bedrooms, so my mother can come and stay when I get the spare room straight—if I ever get round to that, either. I have a hell of a to-do list!' he added wryly.

She turned and studied him. 'Is that what you're doing with the skip?' she asked, and he busied himself with the mugs so he didn't have to meet her eye.

'Yes. I've been lazy—used the spare room as a glory hole. Thought it was time for a sort out.'

She didn't need to know what he'd been sorting out, and he didn't volunteer anything further. He carefully avoided telling her why his mother needed to stay as well, or anything else about his child-care arrangements. It was none of her business, and if he possibly could, he'd like to keep it that way. Keep all of it that way, except of course she couldn't fail to notice the absence of a woman's touch. He'd never been good at the stage-setting part of houses, unlike Beth, who'd been fantastic at it and would have had the place licked into shape in no time.

And she certainly wouldn't have had dishes stacked in the sink! Oh, well, he'd get a dishwasher just as soon as the kitchen was refitted, but one thing at a time, and washing up never hurt anyone.

The kettle boiled and he poured the water onto the last two teabags in their mugs, poked them with a spoon and lifted them out. 'Milk?'

'Yes, please.'

'I might even have some biscuits,' he said, rummaging in the cupboard, but she shook her head, and her hair, long and loose today so it hung down round her shoulders, swung and bounced and gleamed in the sunshine and did something odd to his gut.

'I don't need a biscuit, thanks. The tea's fine.'

'OK.' He straightened up, and suddenly there was a curious tension in the air between them, a strange electric current that drew his eyes to hers and made his heart beat just a little harder. He needed space—more than an arm's length between them—so he didn't feel tempted to reach out and see if that hair felt as soft and smooth and heavy as it looked.

'Um, come through to the sitting room,' he said, holding the door for her, and led her to yet another scene of chaos.

Rory was lying on his stomach in front of the television, watching cartoons again, Freya was sitting in a pool of Lego bricks and constructing a rather wobbly tower, and the cushions were all pulled off the sofa and propped up against it to make tunnels and hidey-holes. And there was an ominous smell.

He closed his eyes and sighed.

'Have you guys trashed this place enough?' he asked

mildly, putting his cup down and picking up two of the cushions. and Freya ran over to him and pulled them back off the sofa.

'Daddy, no!' she wailed, even though she hadn't been playing with them at the time. 'House!'

He stopped and sat down, scooping her onto his lap. 'I'm sorry, sweetheart. It's just we need to sit down. Look, this is Kate—she's a friend of mine,' he said, wondering if that was pushing it too far, but Freya looked up at Kate and studied her dubiously, Rory swivelled round and sat up and stared, and Kate, to her credit, ignored the cushions, sat on the floor in front of the sofa and stared right back, a smile playing round her lips.

'Hi, guys,' she said softly. 'Did you make a den? I used to do that.'

'Did you get into trouble?' Rory asked soberly.

The smile became rueful. 'I don't remember, so probably not very much. So—who are you guys?'

'I'm Rory,' Rory said, 'and she's Freya. Dad, she needs her nappy changed.'

'I know,' he said, wrinkling his nose and smiling at Kate, a little bemused by the change in her. 'Sorry. Will you excuse us for a minute?'

'Go right ahead,' she said.

He took Freya out and dealt with the nappy and found her and Rory a cracker, which was the closest thing he could get to a biscuit, and some juice, then went back in to find Kate sitting cross-legged on the floor next to Rory in the midst of all the toys, watching cartoons with every appearance of enjoyment. Bizarre.

He raised a brow, and she laughed a little self-consciously and got up and perched on the edge of the sofa.

'Sorry. I like cartoons,' she confessed, and he rolled his eyes and handed her her tea with a reluctant smile, trying not to think about how that laugh and the faint touch of colour accompanying it had softened her features and brought warmth and something else to those surprisingly lovely caramel eyes.

Something that made him think of things he'd put out of his mind a lifetime ago.

'I should drink it fairly fast, it's getting cold,' he said hastily, and dropped into the other corner of the sofa, wincing as he hit the unprotected springs. 'Sweetheart, can we please have the cushions back for a bit?' he asked Freya, and she nodded absently, her attention drawn by the television.

He sorted them out before she changed her mind, and Kate settled back into the cushions and smiled at him. 'This is a lovely house.'

He gave a stunned laugh. 'Well, it probably will be, but it's a bit of a project. I wanted something we could make ours and, let's face it, there's plenty of potential here. Not much else, though.'

'Oh, it'll be beautiful. It's got fabulous high ceilings. I love Edwardian houses.'

'I've never had one before. I'm beginning to think it might have been a mistake.'

'Really?'

He laughed. 'No, not really. I'm sure it'll be lovely eventually.'

She tipped her head on one side and regarded him thoughtfully. 'It must be a bit of handful having two very young children and a new job and trying to do the house up all at once,' she said softly.

And he thought, She doesn't know the half of it, and I'm damned if I'm telling her.

'It's OK,' he said, reluctant to suggest for a moment that it was anything other than plain sailing. She didn't need to know the number of times this last week he'd come *that* close to throwing in the towel. Except, of course, he couldn't afford to. Eighteen months out of work had left him sailing pretty close to the wind. His investments had buffered them, and he was careful, but the house was going to take a substantial sum to fix it up and, besides, it was time to get their lives back on track.

And if they were really lucky, they'd all survive the experience...

He hadn't said 'we'.

Not once, unless he'd been referring to the children as well. 'I bought the house—when I get it straight—if I ever get round to it. I've been lazy.'

As if there wasn't a Mrs McEwan.

There was certainly no evidence of a woman's touch in the rundown and desperately outdated house, although the furniture obviously came from better times and there was no lack of homeliness or warmth. And the children were lovely once they opened up, especially Rory. Funny and charming and sweetly innocent, and the spitting image of his father. Freya had been just as charming, but more wary of her.

James had been a little wary, too, she thought as she drove home. As if he hadn't really wanted to invite her in, but hadn't felt there was a choice. He'd almost been defiant about it—*this is me, take it or leave it.*

And his blunt honesty had sneaked under her guard.

Her mother was just unloading shopping from the car when she turned into the drive, so instead of going into her own home in part of the converted barn on the other side of the farmyard, she went over and helped her mother carry the food into the big farmhouse kitchen, the dogs trailing hopefully at their heels.

'Been at work?' her mother asked, and she gave a little smile as she put the bags down on the table and patted the dogs.

'Sort of. Earlier. I've just been to see James—he left his phone behind last night and I dropped it in to him.'

Her mother straightened up from the fridge. 'And?' she asked, getting straight to the point.

'He's got two little children—Rory, who's about five, I suppose, and Freya, who must be coming up for eighteen months or so. Toddling about and starting to talk, and definitely got a personality.'

'Don't sound so surprised. Babies are born with personality.'

And she knew that, of course, and over the years she'd seen enough small children in her mother's care to be well aware, but somehow Freya's personality had taken her by surprise. She was so *stubborn*, such a determined little thing, and very much her daddy's girl.

But, then, that wouldn't be surprising, would it, if she didn't *have* a mother in her life?

'And the mum?' her mother asked, as if reading her mind, and Kate shrugged thoughtfully.

'I don't know if there is one.'

She tutted softly, her face pleating in a sad frown. 'Poor little mites.'

'Mmm.'

She thought of the dishes in the sink, the chaos in the sitting room, the garden that still, even in December, had garden furniture and toys lying out in it, and she thought of the dark shadows round his eyes and the weary grey pallor of his skin, as if all the sun had gone out of his life.

And then she thought of the way she'd greeted him on his first morning, less than a week ago, and felt a wash of guilt.

'Don't beat yourself up,' her mother advised, reading her mind again. 'You didn't know, and if he chose not to tell you...'

'But he still hasn't, so I still don't really know. She might just have been out shopping. They might be bone idle and useless at housework.'

But she knew that wasn't the answer.

Fortunately, because he had the rest of the weekend off, James was able to get the bedroom sorted out so his mother could come and stay when he was next on call.

Well, sorted was perhaps a little generous, he thought, staring gloomily at it late on Sunday night. He'd given it a quick coat of paint over the top of the existing wallpaper just to freshen it up, but apart from that he hadn't had time to do more than wipe down the woodwork with a damp cloth, vacuum the elderly carpet and make the bed.

Oh, well, he thought tiredly, at least the bed was a comfortable one. They'd had it in London, bought it so their friends and relations could come to stay at a time when things had been looking good.

He switched off the light, walked out and closed the door.

He'd done all he could for now. It needed some serious attention in the future, but it would do for the short term and get over the problem of unsettling the children.

He dropped them off with the childminder on Monday morning, and walked into the ward to discover that Stephen Symes had started to feel pins and needles in his right hand and was feeling dizzy.

It could have been anything—maybe a few tiny clots from the femoral artery repair he'd had to do—but he had a hideous sinking feeling that it was more metastases, this time in his brain.

Well, at least it would be quick, he thought heavily as they did the ward round and checked their post-ops who'd been in over the weekend. They were all doing well, and while he was waiting for Mr Symes to come back from the scanner, he discharged two of the patients and filled out the paperwork. By the time he'd finished, Mr Symes was back, so he went to talk to him.

'Is there any news?' he asked James instantly, and he shook his head.

'Not that I know. They'll contact us later. You got missed in the ward round so I thought I'd come and check up on you—how's the tummy?' he asked.

'A bit tender, but much better than it was. I've stopped feeling sick and things are starting to go through me again, so I suppose I should look on the bright side, but it's a bit hard with everything else caving in all around me.'

'I'm sure. I'm glad it's made you more comfortable, though. That's good. Mind if I have a look?'

He shook his head, so James turned back the bedclothes and examined the wound. Neat, clean, healing well, and looking on the bright side, as he'd said, his bowel symptoms were relieved for now. Not so the liver. The yellowish tinge to his skin was a little worse, and the whites of his eyes were also starting to show the effects of the bilirubin in his system.

And then there were the neurological symptoms...

'Will Dr Croft be coming to give me the results of the scan, do you know?' the man asked as James covered him again.

'I expect so. I'll ask him to keep me informed.' He paused

and met his eyes. 'It may be nothing, you know. Don't borrow trouble.'

He smiled wearily. 'No. I've been feeling a little light-headed and woozy off and on for weeks. I thought it was because I wasn't keeping much down or eating very much, but I doubt it. Is there any way I can get the results before my wife gets here for visiting at three?'

'I'll chase it up,' James promised, and, leaving him, he went back to the nursing station and got the switchboard to page Guy.

'Any news on Symes?'

'Yes—I was just coming up. Not good, I'm afraid.'

James sighed. He'd thought as much. 'OK. I'll be on the ward.'

'I'll come and find you before I tell him, show you the photos.'

'Cheers.'

Guy took a few minutes, and in that time James chased up some lab results for another patient and requested a nasogastric tube to aspirate a nauseous patient in under observation for query appendix with a very atypical presentation.

He'd just finished writing up the notes when Guy arrived at his elbow and snapped the film onto the light box. 'There you go. Three of the little bastards,' he said softly, pointing out the small white blobs on the plate.

'Will you do anything?'

He shrugged. 'We could give him radiotherapy, but it needs a head mask to hold him in the same position every time and he struggled with the scanner, apparently. A bit claustrophobic—and the mask is worse, as you know. I'll talk to him, see how he feels. He might think it's not worth the hassle, given the odds. I don't need to elaborate, I take it?'

James shook his head and took a nice, slow breath. 'No. It's all utterly familiar.'

Guy cocked his head on one side and studied him searchingly, so that he felt like a bug under a microscope. 'Are you OK with this? Do you want me to handle it alone?'

'No, and no,' James said frankly, and Guy gave a wry, understanding smile and laughed without humour.

'Let's go and tell him, then.'

'I gather Stephen Symes has got brain mets.'

'Yup.'

Kate studied him for anything further, but there wasn't a flicker. He could have been utterly indifferent, but she just knew he wasn't. 'How sad,' she prompted.

There was a flicker then, a tiny one, gone before she could analyse it. 'You think? In his shoes I'd welcome it. At least it'll get it over with.'

Kate sighed inwardly. She'd have to see if she could get some information out of Guy. So far he'd been disappointingly unforthcoming, but she didn't want to come right out and ask James where his wife was and what had happened to her. She had a horrible feeling she knew the answer.

'Clinic this afternoon,' she said, changing the subject. 'There's a teenage girl with vomiting, weight loss and a small mass in the upper abdomen. I was going to see her, but I'm busy with follow-ups on patients I really want to see, and I'm feeling generous, so I'll let you have her—see what you make of it. You might want to do a gastroscopy. And if you have any difficulties—if you feel I need to see her…'

'Is that likely?' he asked, and she had to convince herself to let go. She liked to see the kids herself.

'Probably not. But just in case. There's also a patient

with Crohn's who might need surgery tomorrow, and I'll give you a few others. I know you're more than capable. Have you had lunch?'

He shook his head.

'Neither have I. Why don't we go down now and grab something on our way to the clinic?'

For a moment she thought he was going to refuse, but then he shrugged. 'Sure,' he said, and scrubbed his hand through his hair. It fell straight back down again, and she had a sudden urge to lift it out of the way, to run her fingers through it and see if it felt as soft and silky as it looked.

Crazy. He was a colleague. Her locum registrar—which made her his boss, for goodness' sake! She couldn't go fantasising about running her fingers through his hair.

Or kissing that firm, unsmiling mouth, or any of the hundred and one other inappropriate things she'd been thinking about ever since Saturday morning when she'd seen him in his lovely, rundown house in those washed-out charcoal jeans and a pale blue jumper that had matched his eyes and looked soft enough to stroke.

She glanced again at his hair as they sat down with their sandwiches and coffee, and smiled.

'Is the job getting to you, or were you painting over the weekend?'

He frowned, then before she could stop herself she lifted a hand to his hair and tested the offending lock between finger and thumb. Oh, yes. Soft. So soft, except for the crisp little strands of white.

'Ah. Painting,' he said with a crooked grin, making her heart lurch, and she snatched her hand back.

No! She couldn't let him get to her. She didn't do relationships, and she certainly didn't do casual sex, so there was no point torturing herself with the thought. No matter how suddenly appealing...

'I needed to get the spare room sorted so my mother can stay when I'm on call,' he went on, fingering the strand she'd touched. 'Hence the skip, as you so rightly surmised, and the paint—which I seem to be wearing. I'm not exactly gifted in the DIY department. Well, the house department generally,' he qualified, torturing her again with that reluctant grin. 'Give me a nice messy RTA victim with massive internal injuries over decorating any day.'

She chuckled. 'I love decorating,' she confessed. 'I find it relaxing and therapeutic.'

One eyebrow quirked sceptically. 'Probably because you're better at it than I am. I get paint everywhere except where I'm meant to, and I always get the ceiling colour on the walls and the walls on the ceiling.'

'Remind me not to let you loose on my barn, then,' she said with a laugh. 'I don't need paint splodged on my beams.'

'You've got a barn?'

She nodded. 'Well, part of one. On my parents' farm,' she added, wondering why she was revealing things about herself that she wouldn't normally discuss at work, but for some reason her tongue kept on rolling. 'We converted it and split it into two units, and I've got one half and the other half is a holiday cottage-cum-guest accommodation.'

He cocked his head on one side. 'Do you know, I would have put you in a modern penthouse flat,' he said thoughtfully, and she found a smile from somewhere.

'Been there, done that,' she said lightly, trying not think about it, but while they were on the subject, she wondered yet again why he was in a house that needed so much work when she would have expected him to own something much better.

Something, for instance, that went with the furniture in his house and the BMW on the drive.

Unless his wife had left him and taken him to the cleaners? She pushed a bit.

'I would have put you in a rather smart executive house in a quiet leafy avenue,' she returned, testing him out, and his face went carefully blank.

'Been there, done that,' he said in an echo of her words, and she decided not to push any more for now. There'd be plenty of time to find out more about him—and, anyway, it was irrelevant. On a need-to-know basis, she didn't.

So she'd keep her nose out, and so long as he turned up and did his job, his private life was none of her business.

Just like hers was none of his.

Tracy Farthing, the fifteen-year-old with the vomiting and weight loss, was interesting. His first reaction had been, Oh, no, not another one. But once he'd looked at her, his gut instinct made him consider less obvious possibilities.

He examined her, and could feel a diffuse but very definite mass in her abdomen, just where her stomach would be. He helped her up off the examination couch and sat down again opposite her and her mother, running the various possibilities through his head.

'So—what do you think, Doctor?' her mother asked, looking worried.

As well she might.

'I'm not sure. I want to run some tests, take some bloods and see if anything significant emerges from the results. We know from the urine sample you brought in that you're not pregnant.'

'Well, of course she's not pregnant!' her mother said indignantly, but he noticed that Tracy's shoulders dropped a fraction, as if she was relieved, and he just smiled.

'Mrs Farthing, it's in no way a value judgement—a pregnancy test is routine in any woman between puberty and the menopause to eliminate the possibility,' he explained, and watched her subside, mollified. 'Having done that, we can then proceed to all the other possibilities.'

And then he noticed the girl's hair. It might have been the way she'd slept on it, or dried it, but it seemed thinner on the left side, more sparse. That wouldn't fit, though, unless—and as he glanced down at the notes, he noticed out of the corner of his eye that her hand had crept up and she was fiddling with it. Her left hand.

'Do you do that a lot?' he asked, and she nodded, looking embarrassed and lowering her hand quickly.

'Oh, she's always fiddling with her hair,' her mother said a little impatiently. 'She's done it for years. Why?'

'Just curious. Tracy, I think I'd like to have a look into your stomach,' he told her. 'There's a very simple procedure called a gastroscopy, where we numb the back of your throat and ask you to swallow a tube that's connected to a special camera, so we can see inside without having to give you an operation. It's painless, a little bit unpleasant and takes about five minutes, but there are no side-effects and it'll give us answers very quickly. I'd like to do it now, if you're willing? It could save an awful lot of time.'

She gave her mother a worried look. 'Mum?'

Her mother shrugged. 'Tracy, it's not my body, I can't tell you what to do.'

'That's rubbish, you tell me all the time!'

'But not about something like this.'

'Well, what would you do?'

She smiled worriedly. 'I'd listen to the doctor,' she replied. 'If he thinks it's a good idea, I'd believe him. Besides, you want to know what's going on, don't you?'

She hesitated another moment, then nodded. 'All right, then,' she agreed. 'If you're sure you need to do it?'

'I need to—and it's really not that bad.'

'How do you know? Have you ever had it done?'

He shook his head and smiled. 'No, but I've done it to lots of people and, believe me, they'd tell me if it was too dreadful. They don't usually hold back.'

She gave a faint smile and nodded. 'OK. But can you stop if I really don't like it?'

'Yes, of course I can, but it's very quick. Probably less than five minutes. Two?'

'Promise?'

He gave a little chuckle and shook his head. 'No, I can't promise, but I wouldn't lie to you.'

'Would you have it done?'

'Oh, yes. No hesitation. It's very straightforward, and it doesn't hurt. It just feels a bit odd and makes you retch a bit. If you could go back to the waiting room, I'll make the necessary arrangements and then let you know if we'll be able to do it today.'

She hesitated again, then nodded, and he gave a silent sigh of relief as they left and reached for the phone. 'Kate, I've just seen Tracy Farthing. Can I have a word about her?'

'Sure. I'm free for a second. Come on in.'

He went next door to her consulting room and perched on the desk. 'I'm guessing wildly, but her hair's a bit sparse and she fiddles with it. Her mother says she's done it for years.'

Kate frowned curiously. 'A trichobezoar? I don't think

I've ever seen one—unless you count the hairballs my mother's cat used to bring up!'

He chuckled. 'No, I haven't either. Certainly I've never seen one large enough to cause this kind of obstruction. I'd like to do a gastroscopy—what are the chances this afternoon?'

'Ring Endoscopy and tell them you're bringing her up—unless you want me to do it?'

He laughed softly. 'You really don't trust me with her, do you?' he murmured, and was fascinated to see a little brush of colour on her cheeks.

'Of course I trust you. I'm just not used to being able to delegate to such an extent,' she said, trying to talk her way out of it. 'Are you going to sedate her or use the anaesthetic spray?'

'Spray,' he said firmly, having done both and having assessed that Tracy was basically calm, reasonable and likely to be compliant. He much preferred working with an alert, co-operative patient so he could explain things as he went along.

'In which case there shouldn't be a problem,' Kate said. 'Ring them now. I'll carry on working through the clinic patients—but feel free to call me if you want a second opinion.'

'Kate, I'm fine,' he said firmly, and he took Tracy and her mother up to the endoscopy suite, talked them through the procedure and showed Mrs Farthing out, then sprayed the back of Tracy's throat and quickly and easily passed the tube down into her stomach.

Her full, distended, hair-filled stomach.

'Well, I've got your answer,' he told her when he'd removed the tube and called her mother into the room, showing them the tiny bit of hair he'd teased off.

'What is it?'

'Hair,' he said. 'You've probably been pulling it out and swallowing it in your sleep. The trouble is the hair gets in a knot, then it can't move on, and it just gets bigger and bigger—'

'Oh, gross,' Tracy said, wiping her mouth on a tissue and gagging slightly. 'That's disgusting.'

'It's one of those strange things that people do for no very good or known reason. It's called trichophagia, which means literally hair-eating, and it often starts in childhood and can persist into adulthood totally subconsciously—you probably do it in your sleep.'

She pulled a horrified face and looked near to tears. 'I want it out.'

'That's the plan, because it's not doing you any good at all. You need to stay here in the waiting area until your throat's feeling normal again and you can swallow properly, Tracy, then come back to the clinic and see me and I'll run through what we're going to do.'

He left them with the endoscopy nursing staff and went back to the clinic, tapping on Kate's door. She looked up and smiled.

'Perfect timing, I was just about to call my next patient. So—what do you know?'

'Spot on. It's massive. I want to admit her as a matter of urgency and remove it before she starts to suffer with gastric bleeding from the abrasion.'

'I agree. We're operating tomorrow. I've got a couple of patients I've seen today who are much more urgent than their referrals suggest, one of them the Crohn's case I was telling you about, so stick her on the list with them and we'll just have to hope we aren't too busy overnight.'

'I'll tell her to come in later today, then,' he said. 'What do you want me to do now? More outpatients?'

She frowned. 'Actually, no, I'd like you to talk to Mrs Symes. She's waiting for you.'

He felt his heart sink, and swallowed. 'OK. I'll talk to her now, and then see Tracy when she's back down.'

He walked along the corridor to the waiting area, saw Amanda Symes staring out of the window blankly and went over to her.

'Amanda?'

She turned, her hand on her chest, and gave him a very half-hearted smile. 'You made me jump, I was miles away.'

In hell, he thought, judging by the look of her. 'I'm sorry. Come on, let's go and have a chat. Fancy a cup of tea?'

'Have you got time, James? I don't want to be a bother.'

'It's no bother, I could murder for one. I haven't had time to stop yet this afternoon.'

He paused by the reception desk. 'Any chance of two cups of tea in my consulting room?' he asked, and the receptionist nodded.

'I'll get them brought through to you,' she said, reaching for the phone, and he took Amanda to his room and sat her down.

'So—how can I help?' he asked gently.

'I don't know that you can. I don't know that anyone can, but— Oh, James, I don't want him to die,' she said, and started to cry.

CHAPTER THREE

THERE was nothing he could do except let her talk, and he did that, for as long as he felt it was productive, but when they started going round in circles he stopped her.

'You really need to talk to the oncology nurse. She's trained to deal with this situation, and she has lots of practical things she can offer to help you both. I'm not trying to get rid of you, but I'm not really the best person to help you now. I've done all I can to make things better for him, unless he needs further bowel surgery in the future, but the onco nurse has an amazing range of things she can offer to make things easier. Talk to her. Make friends with her, and with the Macmillan or Marie Curie nurses. They'll look after you, Amanda. They won't let you deal with this alone.'

Her face crumpled again, and she made a valiant effort to control the threatening tears. 'I am, though. I feel so alone. It's crazy. It's as if in a way he's already gone, and I feel so *angry* with him for leaving me.'

He nodded, aching for her, knowing that distancing himself was impossible because he was with her every step of the way. 'That's the start of the grieving process,' he explained, his voice a little gruff. 'Accept it for what it is, and just remember that, however hard it gets, it's not going to go on for ever, and you can get through it, and you're not alone. And although I can't really help you, if you want to talk to me again, at any time, I'll always find time to see you.'

He showed her out, a little surprised when she hugged him, and then shut the door and leaned on it.

I feel so alone. It's crazy. It's as if in a way he's already gone.

He swallowed hard, trying not to get sucked in by the memories, and after a moment he eased himself away from the door and sat down again.

Poor woman. Poor man. Poor all of them. He hauled in a steadying breath, closed his eyes for a moment and then picked up the receiver.

'Is Tracy Farthing back in the clinic?'

'How did the Farthings react?'

James ran his hand round the back of his neck and frowned. 'OK. She's gone home to get some things and she's coming back in this evening.'

'Have you set up a psych referral?'

He shook his head. 'I was going to ask you about that. I don't know what your protocols are here, but she'll need counselling and psychotherapy or she'll just do it again. I think there's a lot going on in her life that her mother doesn't know about.'

Kate laughed. 'She's a teenager. Of course there is. I'll sort Psych out. What about Amanda Symes?' she added, and watched a shadow pass over his face.

'I've referred her to the onco nurse and the Macmillan or Marie Curie people and given her a couple of websites to look up.'

'Good. Thank you. Right, we're on call tonight. I'm just

going to shoot up to the ward and check things are OK for tomorrow, then I'm going home to read up on the hairball op. Can you give me a ring if anything comes in that I need to know about? Jo's here—she'll help you.'

He nodded, and she thought she could see tension around his eyes. 'Will do,' he said, and, picking up the notes for Tracy Farthing, he headed out of the door.

She followed slowly, contemplated staying around, and told herself not to be ridiculous. He was paid to do a job. Let him do it—he was more than capable. And if he couldn't manage it because of his family commitments, then he'd have to go, kids or no kids. She couldn't carry him.

James headed up to the paediatric ward, wondering what the night would bring and if he'd manage to get through it without his children waking and refusing to let him out of the door if his pager went.

Hopefully not.

He introduced himself to the charge nurse, then told her, 'I've got a fifteen-year-old coming in for tomorrow's list. She's got a trichobezoar—a hairball in her stomach—and we're going to remove it in the morning.'

She blinked and widened her already wide eyes. 'Wow. That's unusual.'

'Absolutely. I've never done one and neither has Kate. Hopefully she'll be fine and won't need to go to ITU, but she'll need careful monitoring in case she gets gastric bleeding because of the abrasion of the hair on her stomach lining.'

The charge nurse nodded. 'We'll make sure she's got qualified cover for the first twenty-four hours. What about a psychiatric referral?'

'Kate was contacting them.'

'OK. I'll follow it up. They can come and chat to her this evening, reassure her about the surgery.'

'Thanks. She's called Tracy Farthing—oh, and mum's a bit unaware of her social life, I think. She looked relieved about the negative pregnancy test, but the mother was indignant.'

She laughed. 'They always are. Don't worry, we'll look after her. I'll put her with a girl who's having a knee op tomorrow. They can keep each other company in our teenagers' section.'

'Thanks. Jo's around overnight, and I'm on call so I'll be in and out. Page us if you need to, and I'll pop in and make sure she's OK at some point.'

'Cheers. I'm Trina, by the way. I'll be on again tomorrow morning so, if I don't see you later, I'll see you then.'

'Great. Cheers, Trina.'

He walked away, wondering if that had really been an invitation in her wide and welcoming eyes, and if so how he felt about it.

Stunned, he decided. It was so long since he'd been in the marketplace he'd forgotten what it was like. Horrible, from what he could remember, but then for some reason an image of Kate flashed into his mind and took him by surprise.

No fluttering lashes there, no wide-open soft baby blues, just sharp shards of toffee slicing through him assessingly.

Not always, though. Sometimes—like when she'd been in his house, watching cartoons with Rory, or after he'd painted the room and she'd lifted her hand and touched his hair—then her eyes had been soft and warm and—

No. She was his boss, and he'd do well to remember it. And, please, God, nothing would happen tonight to shake her faith in his ability or make her question giving him the job...

* * *

'Freya, I have to go, darling.'

'No!'

'Yes. I'm sorry, sweetheart. We'll do something lovely at the weekend.'

'Not go!' she sobbed, clinging to him, and he handed her, screaming, to his mother, ran down the stairs and walked out of the door, blinking back the tears that had come from nowhere.

Her wails followed him out to the car, and he shut the door and started the engine to drown out the heart-rending sound. She'd get used to it. The trouble was they'd had too much time together, and she wasn't used to him leaving her. She'd stop crying soon. She'd probably stopped already.

'Penny for them.'

He scrubbed a hand through his hair and sighed. 'Oh, nothing, Jo. Freya was a bit miserable when I left her,' he confessed.

'Freya?'

'My daughter.'

'Can't your wife comfort her?'

He looked at the SHO, her eyes red with exhaustion as they snatched a much-needed coffee in a quiet moment, and for some reason—tiredness, probably—he told her about Beth. Nothing much. Very little, really. The bare bones, but it was enough.

'That's such a shame. I'm really sorry.'

'Yeah. Thanks. My mother's with them, so it's not like leaving them with a stranger.'

'But kids are funny. She'll get used to it, though.'

His pager sounded, then Jo's, and he sighed and glanced at the little screen. 'Finish your coffee. I'll go down to A and E and see what we've got. I'll page you if we need Theatre.'

He made his way to A and E, and found Tom Whittaker, the consultant on duty, in majors. He was working on a young man, inserting a second IV line, and James glanced at the monitor and frowned at the blood pressure.

'Blunt abdominal trauma—we haven't done a DPL but he's hypovolaemic. I think you've got time to get him upstairs, but not much else. He's crashing. Apparently he's been kicked.'

'Charming. Right, let's get him stabilised and we'll take him into Theatre. I'll page Jo and get her primed.'

'The police'll want to talk to him.'

'Well, we'll have to make sure we keep him alive, then,' he said drily.

They set up fluids and then sent him off on his way to Theatre. Following the trolley, James paused at the door and turned to Tom.

'Are you OK?' he asked, looking at him keenly, and Tom gave a wry smile.

'Ah, I just hate violence. Bit too close to home.'

James tilted his head questioningly, and Tom went on, 'I was stabbed here by a patient last year—in April. I nearly bled out. It's still a little fresh in the mind.'

A year ago last April. The month his own life had fallen apart. It was, as Tom said, still a little fresh in the mind.

'I can understand that,' he said. 'Thanks for your help. I'll keep you posted on this one.'

'Do that.'

It was touch and go, once they'd opened him up, but there was no point in calling Kate. She wouldn't have got there in time, and anyway he and Jo could manage.

Just about.

Jo's surgical skills were slight, but she was a fast learner and she did as she was told without question, which meant he could rely on her. Always an asset in a crisis.

He removed the man's spleen, stitched the tear in his liver and put him back together again. And then, once their patient was stable and everything was back under control, he phoned Tom and told him, then went home, crept in through the door and fell into bed, exhausted.

Three hours. That was all. Three hours, before he had to be up again and on the way out. At least his mother was here, so he didn't have to get the children ready first.

Three and a half, then.

Oh, joy.

'Kate, I'm sorry, I'm going to be late. Can you start without me and I'll get in as soon as possible?'

She swung round and propped her feet on her desk, rolled her eyes and thought, *Here we go.* 'Do I have a choice?'

She heard him sigh. 'Yes, you have a choice. If you can't cope without me, I'll come in now. But I'd rather not. It would be...difficult,' he said after a pause.

Difficult? 'Oh, I can *cope*, McEwan,' she said, wondering if her voice sounded as bitter as she thought it did. 'I just don't see why I should be expected to without any kind of explanation. Is it a problem with the children?' she added, softening her voice, and he sighed.

'Yes, and no. It's...complicated. Don't worry, I'll deal with it. I shouldn't be too late.'

'James, it's always complicated,' she said, exasperated by his refusal to open up. 'We've got a busy morning—Tracy Farthing, for starters. Your patient. I need you here doing your job. Whatever's wrong, if it's not a matter of life or death, just sort it and get here asap.'

She hung up the phone with a bang and turned, to find Jo standing right behind her.

'He's going to be late. I'll need you to help me.'

'Oh. I wondered. His daughter was playing up in the night. It's such a shame about his wife. He's a lovely guy.'

'Jo, don't gossip,' she said, sounding like a shrew again for the second time in as many minutes, but Jo was used to her, she could cope, and Kate swung her feet to the floor and stood up, putting James and his wife—whatever had happened to her—right out of her mind. 'Right, let's have a look at what came in last night. Were you busy? I was half expecting a call.'

'Oh, no, we coped fine. It was quite quiet in a frantic sort of way. James was amazing—well, apart from being hassled. He's a brilliant surgeon.'

Kate said nothing, not really caring how amazing and brilliant he was if he couldn't manage to get here, still irritated by his refusal to tell her what was going on, and Jo went on, 'There was a straightforward appendix, and a couple of admissions for observation and assessment—oh, and we had to open up Mr Reason again. His drain had dislodged—he'd pulled on it by accident a couple of days ago, he said, and he'd developed an abscess. And then there was a ruptured spleen and liver laceration from a fight. He'd been kicked in the abdomen and it was a bit tricky, but James was fantastic. He's fine, doing well, but the police want to talk to him once he's up to it, to see if he can identify his attacker.'

Oh, Lord. She felt a surge of adrenaline but pulled her mind back into focus. 'Good. Right. We'll start with a look round them, then the pre-ops, and then if James still hasn't turned up, I'll go and talk to Tracy Farthing in Paeds.'

She didn't want to hear that James had been amazing and brilliant and fantastic, she was feeling antsy about the police and the fight victim, and generally she was irritated. Whatever had happened to her nice, orderly existence? It was all so messy and complicated now, and until her registrar had gone off on maternity leave, it had all been going so well.

Trust a man to come in and throw a spanner in the works, she thought crossly, and stalked off down the ward, leaving Jo and Liz, the staff nurse, to follow with the notes.

She didn't want to think about the fight, so she thought about James, instead, and how he'd talked to Jo. *Such a shame about his wife.* That was another annoying thing. How could he? How could he just open up and talk to her SHO when she'd been deliberately kept in ignorance?

'Morning, Mr Reason. I'm sorry to hear you had to go back to Theatre in the night. How are you feeling now?'

Tracy Farthing's operation went smoothly, no thanks to the start of his day, with Freya clinging to him like a limpet and his mother's rather tepid attempts at removing her.

Saying things like, 'Oh, poor little thing, she doesn't want you to go, James. You can't do this to her, she needs you, she's lost her mummy,' really didn't help. At all. Any of them.

Particularly not Rory, who was the only one of the two to remember his mother and even he didn't talk about her any more.

'This is nothing to do with Beth,' he said firmly. 'This is about a little girl who doesn't want her father to leave her, but she needs to learn that I have to go to work, and that I come back at the end of the day. I'm hardly the world's first lone parent. Millions of people do it. It's simple.'

But it didn't feel simple, and in the end his mother had refused to be left with her while she was so upset, in case she couldn't get her to stay with the childminder.

'You know I'm supposed to be going to see my sister, James—she's expecting me. She's seeing the consultant today, and she wants me there. Please, don't leave me with them,' she pleaded, and so he took the children to the childminder himself, prised Freya off him again and handed her to Helen, took Rory straight to school since it was now so late, gave him a brief, hard hug at the gates and arrived at the hospital just before nine.

In time to start the list with Kate, in a taut silence broken only by terse remarks relating to Tracy's operation. Then, once they'd finished and he'd closed, he straightened up and met her eyes and knew he was in trouble again.

Deep, deep trouble—and he really didn't give a damn.

They walked out of Theatre, leaving the team to clean and restock it ready for the Crohn's patient, and he watched as she dropped into one of the plastic chairs in the lounge area and fixed him with a look that could have melted a hole in the wall.

Tough. He walked over to the coffee-machine, poured two cups and went back, handing her one and lowering himself into a seat at right angles to her.

'Come on, then, spit it out.'

'I don't think I've got anything to say,' she told him bluntly. 'I think you have, though—starting with an apology, and following up with an explanation, because I don't think you can expect me to support you when things go wrong if I'm kept in the dark like a bloody mushroom! What's going on, James? I need to know.'

He ran a hand round the back of his neck and sighed, conceding her point. 'Fair enough,' he said tiredly. 'But not here. Not now.'

'Why not?'

He met her eyes defiantly, his impotence at the situation

turning suddenly to anger, boiling up inside him like lava and threatening to spill over and destroy everything it touched. He clamped it back under control and bit out, 'Because if you're going to want me to spill my guts, I'm doing it on my turf, on my terms.'

'Tonight, then? At yours?'

'Won't your husband mind?'

She looked startled for a second. 'I don't have a husband,' she retorted after a breathless pause. 'My time's my own.'

He nodded curtly, storing that bit of information. 'All right, then, tonight, if you insist. Come about eight. No. Make that eight-thirty—let the kids get off to sleep.'

'Fine. Will you have eaten?'

'What's that got to do with anything?'

She shrugged. 'I probably won't have done. I can bring something—Chinese? Indian?'

Oh, Lord. A curry. He hadn't had a curry in ages. He so nearly said no, anger getting the better of him, because he knew perfectly well that she was just doing it to soften him up and make it harder for him to kick her out before she was ready, but then he thought of the pitiful contents of his fridge and his self-control went belly up. So what if he went a little over budget? It was damn well about time. 'Indian,' he said decisively, and let his taste buds decide. 'Lamb balti, Bombay potatoes, pilau rice and a peshwari naan. And beer. I'll order it in,' he added, trying to repossess the moral high ground, but she wasn't having any.

'No,' she said, holding up her hand. 'I'll bring the food. This meeting's my idea. And in return I want my questions answered. Properly. The truth, the whole truth, et cetera. You owe me that.'

She drained her coffee and stood up, walked out to the

sinks and started scrubbing for the next case, leaving him to follow in his own time, his anger tempered by the curiously interesting fact that there was no Mr Burgess...

Oh, God, he was turning her into a dragon.

She wasn't a dragon. She was usually reasonable, caring, accommodating—it was only James who did this to her, and it was driving her nuts.

Was that why she was dithering and vacillating over her wardrobe? For a *meeting*?

'Oh, good grief, you are ridiculous!' she told herself. Pulling on a clean pair of jeans and a pretty V-necked jumper over a little vest top, she gave herself a last look in the mirror, ran her fingers through her hair and decided to leave it down and headed for the door.

She looked fine. It wasn't a date.

It wasn't.

Freya was in bed and asleep by seven. She'd obviously worn herself out the night before, and the childminder had taken her and her own child to feed the ducks in the afternoon on the way to pick Rory up from school, so she'd been out in the fresh air and been running around.

Thank heavens, because frankly he'd had enough emotional turmoil with his tiny daughter for today and he could have done without Kate coming round and giving him the third degree tonight.

Curry or no curry.

He went into the kitchen and found it spotless. His mother had obviously cleared everything away before she'd left, and the sitting room, similarly, was tidy, except for a little random chaos generated before bedtime. He breathed a sigh of relief, because he really didn't have the energy to get a duster out, never mind the vacuum.

He glanced in the mirror and wondered if he should change, then gave a soft grunt of derision.

Into what? A power suit?

This was his house, his territory—his home, for goodness' sake. What he wore in it was his own affair, and he was perfectly certain that Kate would have her say no matter what he had on.

And, anyway, it was too late. His jeans would have to do. Her headlights swept across the front of the house, then cut out, and taking a deep breath, he ran downstairs and opened the front door as she got out of the car. Keep it civil, he told himself, but he couldn't quite get himself to dredge up a smile.

'Hi.'

'Hi.' She looked up and smiled tentatively, brown paper carrier in hand, and he held open the door and beckoned her in, mesmerised by the waterfall of dark, glossy hair that tumbled down her back and jerked him suddenly and comprehensively out of the sexual coma he'd been in since Beth's diagnosis.

'I couldn't remember what you said—lamb balti and some kind of naan bread and rice, so I just got that and a few other bits and pieces, and a chicken passanda.'

He forced himself to concentrate on her words, and unglued his tongue from the roof of his mouth. 'Fantastic. It smells amazing. I haven't had a curry for ages. Come on in, let me take your coat.'

She slid it off and handed it to him, and then he nearly dropped the curry because she was wearing snug jeans that cuddled her lush little bottom like a lover and a pretty, pale pink jumper with a low V-neck, and if it hadn't been for the little frill of white lace across it he would have had a perfect view down her cleavage.

Thank heavens for vest tops, he thought fervently, and went into the kitchen with the carrier bag and pulled the containers out. Several of them. Wow! 'Table or knees?' he asked.

'Table, I think,' she said with a slightly embarrassed smile. 'There's quite a lot. I got a bit carried away.'

He chuckled, but it sounded a bit rusty. All he could think about was her getting carried away, and his mind was going into meltdown. He plonked the things onto a tray and led her through to the dining room.

She'd probably over-ordered by about fifty per cent, she thought, going back to the passanda and rice for another helping and ripping a bit off the peshwari naan just for good measure.

Still, he was diving into it as if he hadn't eaten in ages, and maybe he hadn't. But they hadn't talked yet, and possibly he was stalling. She let him eat, though, until even he was slowing down, and then she decided to call a halt.

Putting her fork down, she pushed her plate away and met his eyes across the mess of containers and spilt rice and scraps of naan.

'Talk to me,' she said softly. 'I don't bite.'

'Like hell,' he muttered, but he put his own fork down and reached for his beer, turning the glass round while he studied it thoughtfully, a frown pleating his brow.

Then he looked straight at her. 'OK, what do you want to know?'

'I have no idea, since I have no idea what it is I don't know. I know you have children, I know you've spent a long time away from work, I know that at interview you were cagey in the extreme about your domestic situation, but I have no idea what that situation really is. I don't even know,' she went on evenly, 'if your wife is still alive.'

He put the glass down very carefully and met her eyes again, his breath easing out in a shaky sigh. 'No. She died last year, in August. She had cancer.'

Oh, God. She'd thought as much, but hearing it...

She didn't bother with platitudes. Her regrets or otherwise were irrelevant. So she waited, and after a moment, he went on.

'It all started in April. Beth was six months pregnant with Freya, and she wasn't feeling great. She'd been suffering from constipation, and thought it was the iron tablets. She hadn't told me anything, but then one morning she vomited and started passing blood. She got a taxi to the hospital, got herself admitted and by the time I knew about it she'd had a load of tests and was waiting for the results.'

'She didn't tell you?'

'No. Because she knew—she was a doctor, and she wasn't stupid—and she didn't know where to start. Anyway, the results came back. She had a tumour in her ascending colon, but because she'd ignored her symptoms for months—possibly even years—it had spread to her liver. By the end she had mets in her spine and ribs, and finally her brain.'

Like Steve Symes, she thought, and wondered if that explained his terse and rather crabby behaviour on the first day. Of all the dreadful coincidences...

'She died at the end of August, three months after Freya was born.'

He lifted the glass and drained it, then sat forward, picking up his fork and prodding the food on his plate, his expression bleak. 'It was tough. I was angry with her, because she'd ignored her symptoms until it was too late to do anything about the pregnancy, but even if she'd had it terminated, she wouldn't have survived. She might have had longer with Rory, but Freya would have been dead and that would have destroyed her. As it was they had a few good weeks together before she started to really go downhill.'

He put the fork down and stood up abruptly.

'Coffee?'

'Thank you, that would be lovely,' she said, feeling a little surreal, and when he headed out of the door towards the kitchen, she sat there for a few seconds, gathering her thoughts. He'd said his wife had been a doctor, and she remembered something else he'd said to her, after he'd told Steve Symes the news. *Even if you know—even if you're a doctor—you just assume it's IBS or something you ate, because nobody wants to believe that it can be anything sinister.*

His remark made sense now, she thought, and suddenly the way he'd dealt so sensitively and sympathetically with the whole family made absolute sense as well. He'd been great with them. As if he had known exactly what they were going through. Which, of course, he did. And by making him the lead on the operation, she'd hurled him in at the deep end of his worst nightmare.

Oh, if only she'd known...

With a soft sigh, she got to her feet and started to clear the table.

It was a mess—bits of this and that—but enough to make another meal. She took the tray of containers through to the kitchen and put it down. 'Shall I put these onto a plate for you to have tomorrow?' she suggested, and then she looked up and realised he was standing motionless, staring out of the window into the black night.

She could see his face reflected in the glass, drawn and expressionless, and she shrugged and left him to it, finding a plate in a cupboard, piling the remains of the food onto it and covering it with a bowl.

It was ridiculously easy to find space for it in the fridge. It was all but empty, and she wondered when he found time to shop for food.

Not your problem, she told herself, and scraped the plates into an empty container before putting them by the sink.

'Dishwasher?' she said, but he didn't move.

'James? Do you want me to go? Or just go to hell?'

He made a strangled sound that could have been a laugh, and turned towards her. 'Now, there's an idea,' he said, and then smiled a little crookedly. 'However, since I need your goodwill—just leave them there, I'll do them later. We haven't got a dishwasher yet. It's on the list, like everything else. Do you mind instant? I think the real coffee's probably on its last legs. I forgot to put it back in the freezer.'

'Instant's fine,' she agreed. 'Where's your bin?'

'Under the sink,' he said, taking the empty containers and ditching them. 'You don't have to do that.'

'Well, someone does, and you're making coffee. Have you got a cloth? The table looks as if we've had a food fight.'

His mouth kicked up at one side, and he wrung a cloth out under the hot tap and handed it to her. 'You can't hurt the table, it's sealed,' he said, and turned back to the kettle, dismissing her—but not for long. She hadn't had all her answers yet, not by a long way, and she wasn't going until she had...

CHAPTER FOUR

IT WASN'T over, of course. She'd barely started. He knew that, and they went through to the sitting room with their coffee, settled down at opposite ends of the sofa and he waited for her to get back into her stride.

It didn't take many seconds.

'Talk to me about your child-care arrangements,' she said bluntly, and he felt his right eyebrow climb, but of course she didn't back down, just fixed him with that implacable gaze and waded on in.

'Yes, I know, I shouldn't ask, but since I had to cover for you this morning, and as I'm sure it won't be the last time, I need to know that you're doing everything you can and that there's nothing else that could be done to make things smoother.'

'You have shares in child care?' he said, with only a trace of sarcasm, but she caught it, of course, and gave him one of her patented looks with those toffee-shard eyes.

'You want my help? Work with me here, McEwan,' she said firmly, and he gave up. At least talking about his problems kept his mind off his libido.

'I have a childminder. I drop the children off on my way to work, she takes Rory to school, keeps Freya all day, fetches

Rory from school and I pick them up from her at the end of my day. When I'm on call, my mother stays here and does it for me.'

At the moment, but he wasn't sure what the hell he was going to do after the fiasco this morning.

'So what went wrong today?'

'Freya,' he said reluctantly. 'She didn't want to me to go to work in the night—the pager woke her. We sleep with the doors open, and she heard it go off, heard me talking and getting dressed, and kicked off. And then this morning she wouldn't let me go, my mother said she was too upset to go to the childminder and she couldn't look after her—her sister's not well and she had to go to visit her in hospital in Cambridge—and, well, she wouldn't back me up. Said Freya didn't want me to go, poor little thing, she'd lost her mummy—well, I do know that, I have noticed,' he said, unable to kept the sarcasm out of his voice, 'but in fact she hasn't lost her mother, she's never really had one, she just didn't want me to leave. We've had a couple of bad experiences—an au pair who was a living nightmare, and a crèche that she hated. I thought the childminder might be the answer, once she got used to the idea.'

'Hence taking a locum job?'

He nodded. 'A short-term contract, just to see if I can make the arrangements work this time. I thought I could, with my mother to rely on as back-up, but...' He broke off with a short sigh, staring down into his coffee, but there were no answers in the bottom of the mug, just the dregs of an indifferent brew that frankly he couldn't be bothered with.

He put the mug down on the coffee-table and sat back, searching her eyes for clues to her reaction, but there were none.

'So that's my sorry, pathetic little tale. Does it answer all your questions?'

God, he sounded so bitter, but he couldn't deal with this. He had so much on his plate that Kate analysing his childcare arrangements was just the last straw. He knew they were inadequate. He knew it wasn't ideal, but what the hell else was he supposed to do?

'It sounds as if you've done everything you can to smooth the way for them. I'm sorry I was hard on you, but—'

'The patients have to come first? I know that.'

'Actually, no. Without a doctor to treat them, the patients don't get better, so the doctor has to come first. Which is why I wanted to know if there was anything that could be improved, to make your arrangements more robust.'

'Short of fostering them out or giving them up for adoption, probably not,' he said with an attempt at humour, but her face paled and she drew back.

He frowned at her thoughtfully. 'Did I say something?'

She looked away, shook her head and put her cup down with a clatter on the table, her usually rock-steady composure obviously unsettled. 'No. No, of course not. It's late, I'd better go. Um—thank you for telling me all of this. I realise it can't have been easy.'

'Kate? I was joking. There's no way on God's earth I'd give my kids up. Although it has been suggested.'

Her eyes flew back to his, wide with shock. 'Why? Who by?'

He shrugged. 'Friends? My mother, even, at one point. I think she still believes it would be better for them in some ways.'

'No!'

So much emphasis on such a tiny little word, scarcely audible over the indrawn breath, and yet...

'No?'

'Not unless…'

'Unless?'

She gave a tiny shrug. 'Unless there's no choice. Adoption isn't always bad. Sometimes it can be a miracle. But—not just because you don't want them.'

'But I do want them,' he assured her, 'so it won't ever happen. Not while there's breath in my body. I love my kids to bits, and I'd go to the ends of the earth before I'd give them up or let anything bad happen to them.'

Her shoulders dropped, and she smiled and stood up, tugging her jumper down unconsciously, still ill at ease. 'Good. Right, now I have to go—things to do before tomorrow. And I'm sorry I was so hard on you. If there's anything I can do—you know, if you have a problem, if things don't go right…'

'I thought I had to sort it unless it was a matter of life or death?' he said wryly, and he saw something very human and rather desperate going on in her eyes. As if she was torn between her role as his boss and the warm and caring woman he was beginning to realise she hid under that crisp exterior.

'It's only an offer of help in an emergency, so don't push it,' she said, dragging back control of the situation, and he smiled and held her coat for her.

'Thank you—and thank you for the curry,' he said quietly. 'It was a good idea, and I really enjoyed it.'

She looked up, her eyes soft, and her lips curved up in a warm, genuine smile. 'My pleasure. Your turn next time.'

There was going to be one?

'Done,' he said quickly before she changed her mind.

'And next time I promise I won't bully you.'

He grinned and reached for the doorknob. 'I'll hold you to

that,' he said, and for a second he found himself contemplating kissing her goodnight.

Not a proper kiss. Just a peck on the cheek, a brush of his lips against that soft, baby-smooth skin.

He yanked the door open, held it until she'd started her car, then shut it firmly. It was cold out there, a definite nip in the breeze, but inside him a fire was starting to smoulder, and it was the last thing he needed.

He cleared up the kitchen, washed up the dishes and went to bed.

There was ice on the windscreen the following morning, and he had to scrape it off before he could take the kids to the childminder, and then he got caught in the traffic and so, of course, he was late.

Kate was going to skin him, and all the ground he'd made up the night before would be down the pan.

Oh, well, he thought, at least he'd find out how sincere she'd been about helping him through this, but when he arrived on the ward he found her talking to the police, and she turned to him with relief in her eyes, his lateness apparently not the first thing on her mind.

'Ah, Mr McEwan. The police would like to talk to you about Peter Graham, the man in the fight.'

'Oh, right. Sure.'

'If you're happy without me?' she said, and left them as if she couldn't get away quick enough. Things to do?

Or something else?

He spoke to the police, told them what little he knew, accompanied them while they spoke to the patient and then sent them away when the patient became distressed.

'Did they get what they needed?' Kate asked, her eyes not

nearly as casual as her voice, and he looked at her keenly. She looked away. Interesting.

'Not really. He says he doesn't know the man.'

She lifted her head and met his eyes again briefly. 'Well, maybe he doesn't.'

'I think he does. I think we should keep a close eye on his visitors. One of them might be trying to stop him talking.'

She stood up abruptly. 'Well, you do whatever you feel is necessary. Would you go and check on Tracy Farthing, please? I've got a meeting,' she said, and walked away, leaving him even more convinced there was something going on.

He could always suggest a curry at her place and grill her like a kipper until he found out the truth. He had a feeling it was something to do with the scar on her ribs, but short of coming out and asking her, which would mean admitting he'd looked across into the female changing room on the first day and spied on her, there was no way he was going to find out until she was ready to tell him.

He had a feeling hell would freeze first.

And talking of freezing, he ought to buy some de-icer on the way home, ready for the morning. Tomorrow, if he was late, he might not get off so lightly.

It was bitterly cold.

She drove home at the end of the day, wishing Peter Graham had never come onto their ward, wishing it had happened when someone else had been on take so she didn't have to be reminded, and she looked at the dark windows of her little home and felt a shiver of something cold run over her.

The lights were on in the farmhouse. She could go in there,

sit down with them, spend the evening with them. Her father would walk her back later and stay while she put the lights on without needing to be asked, but she couldn't keep relying on them. She had to deal with this on her own. It had been years. It was time she got over it.

She got out of the car and the security lights on her barn came on, flooding the yard with light.

There. She could see the door, she didn't need her parents to hold her hand. She let herself in, turned on all the lights and went up to her bedroom, changed into jeans and a jumper and went back down. Her fridge, although better filled than James's, was still a little on the scanty side and nothing much appealed to her.

She poured herself a glass of wine, sat down and flicked on the television, then her mobile phone rang. She glanced at the screen and saw James's name. 'What's the problem?' she said without preamble, and she heard him sigh.

'Kate, I'm sorry to trouble you but my boiler doesn't seem to be working. I thought it was a bit cold this morning, but tonight it's just plain off and there's a smell of gas in the kitchen.'

'Turn the gas off!' she said quickly, and he gave a weary chuckle.

'Don't panic, Kate, I'm not a total dunce. Can you give me the name of a plumber?'

'No, but I know someone who can,' she said with a smile, ridiculously pleased that he'd phoned her, stupidly happy to hear his voice again after—oh, an hour? 'You need Fliss Whittaker, Tom's wife. You know, from A and E?'

'I know Tom. His wife's a plumber?'

His voice sounded incredulous, and she laughed. 'No. Well, she's all sorts. She's a nurse, but she's done property developing and she knows everyone in the trade. She'll sort you out if anyone can. I'll text you their number.'

'They won't mind you giving it to me?'

'Of course not. They're lovely. If they don't answer, leave a message and they'll ring you back. They'll be putting the kids to bed. They have a lot. I forget how many, but six or seven.'

'Good grief,' he said faintly, and she laughed.

'Quite. The only person who thinks it's reasonable is my mother. Let me know how you get on. And if they can't help you, if you need anything else, ring me back. It doesn't matter how late it is.'

'I will. Thanks.'

She returned the phone carefully to its cradle, then stared at it for a moment before she realised she had a silly smile on her face.

Stupid. And, anyway, it was nothing to smile about. He had two small children in a house without heating, the weather had taken a turn for the worse and the forecast was awful, and this close to Christmas she doubted he'd get anything done unless it was a very simple repair.

Oh, well. He could always go and stay with his mother, she thought, and then remembered the trouble they were having over the business of Freya going to the childminder, and realised that that was unlikely to work.

Not your worry, she reminded herself fiercely, and turned her attention back to the television.

'Sorry, mate, it's shot. You need a new boiler, and half of your radiators are on the point of giving up. You need a complete new system to bring it up to scratch, and there's no way I can get to you now until after Christmas, and that means putting someone else off.'

James stared at the plumber in disbelief, then stabbed his

fingers through his hair and let out a huff of desperation. 'Um—what about a temporary fix?' he asked, clutching at straws, but Joe shook his head.

'Sorry. Can't do it. The burner's gone and it's such an old boiler it's a miracle it's still going. I wouldn't fix it even if I could. It's a miracle it hasn't blown up.'

James felt sick. Sick with the thought of what could have happened, sick with the fact that yet again he was going to have to fall back on his mother's rapidly diminishing goodwill—and even if they went to hers, it could only be for one night. There was no way they could stay there for weeks.

'Can I light the gas fire in the sitting room?' he asked, clutching at straws. 'Or use the cooker?'

'Yeah, sure. I'll cap the supply to the boiler so you'll still have gas, but what about hot water?'

'Um—there's an immersion heater.'

'Is it working?'

He shrugged. 'Probably not, knowing my luck. I've never tried it.'

The plumber smiled. 'Let's have a look.'

He opened the door and pulled out a pile of towels and sheets, and Joe stuck his head in and turned on the switch. 'Let's have a cup of tea while that heats up and I cap the boiler, and then I can tell you if it's OK,' he said, so James obediently put the kettle on, watched him sort out the gas before they had a crisis. No sooner had he made the tea than Freya started to cry, and he went and lifted her out of her cot and brought her down to the kitchen to meet the plumber.

'This is Joe,' he said, and Joe grinned at her.

'Hello, love. You look about the same age as my youngest. What's your name?'

'F'eya,' she said, and then suddenly became overwhelmed

and burrowed into her father's neck. He hugged her gently, then met the plumber's eyes.

'Shall we find out the verdict on the immersion heater?' he asked, and they trooped up to the landing and Joe reached his hand in and felt the top of the tank under the old jacket that barely covered it, and shook his head.

'Dead as a dodo. Sorry, James. You haven't got any hot water.'

'Can you change it?'

'I don't know. It's been there so long it might be seized in. I'll try for you, I've got a spare on the van. Give me a minute.'

But it was hopeless. He couldn't free it without risking twisting the fitting out of the thin copper wall of the cylinder, which meant no hot water.

Joy. No heat, no water.

And no home.

He swallowed hard as he shut the door behind the plumber. He'd refused to charge him, which might have been something to do with Rory coming out of his bedroom and telling him he was cold and asking Joe if he could fix it, the hopeful look in his eyes dashed by Joe's reply.

'I'm cold, Daddy,' Rory said now, shivering in his little pyjamas with one foot crossed over the other for warmth as he stood in the chilly hall, and James gathered him into his side and hugged him.

'I know. I'm cold, too. Let's go in the sitting room and light the fire,' he said, and he got their bedding and snuggled them down in the room, then when they were settled he went out to the kitchen and phoned Kate to give her the news.

She was mad.

She had to be mad. They weren't her problem, she kept telling herself crossly as she trekked across the farmyard to the house and let herself in.

Not in any way her problem.

'What's the matter?' her mother asked, shooting her a keen look as she went into the drawing room, and she sat down next to the fire and sighed.

'James,' she said. 'His boiler's broken, the plumber says he needs a new heating system, he's got no hot water and they're huddled round a little fire in the sitting room, freezing. And his mother's got a tiny flat with a very small second bedroom, a four-foot sofa and a very low opinion of his ability to cope.'

'And we've got the barn,' her father added softly.

She sighed. 'Have you got any bookings for it?'

'Only the family coming for Christmas, but that's not for two weeks, and even then I'm sure we can squeeze everyone in. We always do. Why don't you give him a ring?'

'He'll refuse.'

'No, he won't,' her mother said firmly. 'He'll think of the children. I'll go and make the beds up. Andrew, give me a hand. Kate, ring him.'

So they went back to the barn, Kate to her side to ring him, her parents to the other side to turn the heating up from frost protection to full blast and make the beds.

She dialled James's number and he answered on the first ring.

'Hi, Kate. Have you found a boiler fairy in the *Yellow Pages*? I hope so. We're freezing.'

She laughed. 'No. I haven't found a boiler fairy, I've found you a warm house. I want you to come here. You and the children. You know I told you the barn's got a holiday cottage as well as my house? Well, it's empty, and my mother says you're to come.'

'Kate, I can't,' he said with only the slightest hesitation, but he sounded tempted. Very tempted.

'I said you'd say that, and she said you wouldn't, you'd think of the children.'

There was a silence, then a ragged, untidy sigh. 'Kate, I—'

'Don't argue, James,' she told him, softening her voice. 'Pack some clothes, get the children in the car and come over. It's sitting here going begging. It would be ludicrous not to use it.'

'They'll have to let me pay,' he said, and she stifled a smile.

'Whatever,' she said, knowing there wasn't a prayer her parents would take a brass farthing off him. 'Just get here.'

She gave him directions, went next door to help them finish off and her mother looked up from the cot and met her eyes and said, 'Well?'

'He's coming,' she said, and her mother smiled.

'I said he would.'

'He said no. He's talking about paying you.'

'Fiddlesticks!'

'Don't tell him that until the children are safely asleep,' she advised drily, and her father laughed.

'Like that, is he? We'll sort him out. I'm sure he's a sensible man and won't let macho pride get in the way of his children's wellbeing.'

'I don't think he'll let anything get in the way of his children's wellbeing,' she said softly, remembering their conversation about adoption. Grabbing the quilt, she stuffed it into the cover, gave it a hearty flap and tucked it into the cot.

'I've switched on the electric blanket on the double bed, but I'll get hot-water bottles for the children,' her mother said, looking around. 'Oh, and I'll bring over some milk and bread and butter so they can have breakfast. I might even have a box or two of cereal tucked away.'

'I'll go and give her a hand,' her father said, leaving Kate there checking the toiletries in the bathroom and running a duster over the sitting room. Then the lights of James's car swept across the farmyard and she went out and opened his car door and smiled at him.

'OK?'

He nodded, his face defeated. 'Kate, this is so good of you. I feel so guilty, I can't even manage to house my family properly.'

'Don't. Save it, James. You're a good man. You're just in a bad place at the moment. Come on inside and let's get the children tucked up in bed.'

She looked into the back of the car and met the children's eyes, confused and unhappy, and her heart ached for them.

'Come on, kids,' James said softly, and helped Rory out. He reached back in for Freya, and Kate held her hand out to Rory, touched when he put his trustingly into it and leaned against her side.

'Our boiler's broken,' he told her solemnly, and she nodded.

'I know. This one isn't, though. Come on inside, it's lovely and warm. Do you want a nice hot drink?'

'They've had two already to keep them warm. They'll be up and down all night,' James said, emerging from the car with Freya in his arms. Ruffling Rory's hair, he grabbed the bag he'd slung on the floor behind his seat and met her eyes. 'Could you manage this? I've got another one with all our clothes—that's just Freya's emergency bag.'

'Sure.'

She took it and watched him as he lifted another bag out of the boot, locked the car and then turned to her. 'Right. All set?'

'Have you got Mummy's teddy?' Rory asked, and Kate's heart hiccuped.

'It's in the case,' James promised, and then they were ready and she led them inside.

He couldn't believe it.

It was warm. Not just warm, but cosy, and welcoming, and beautifully decorated and furnished in lovely soft neutrals and earth colours, with lots of brick and wood and great thick beams.

It made his house look like—well, like what it was, he thought wretchedly. Shabby and rundown and sad. And cold.

Rory was wide-eyed. 'Wow,' he said softly, looking all around. 'It's huge, Dad!'

'It's only because it's all one room,' Kate said with a smile for his son. 'The kitchen's in here,' she told them, and led them through an open studwork wall into a room the size of his sitting room, with solid wood cabinets and granite worktops and every possible appliance.

Not that you'd know. She had to open the doors to show him where the fridge and freezer and dishwasher were, and it brought it home to him yet again just how far he had to go to sort his house out.

'Ah—here are my parents,' she said, and he turned to see a smiling woman armed with a basket of food. Without hesitation she plonked it down on the worktop and reached for him.

'James, welcome,' she said, enveloping him in a brief, hard hug, patted Freya on the shoulder and said hello, then smiled at his little son, who was stroking the worktop in awe, as well he might. 'You must be Rory. You've had a bit of an adventure, haven't you?' she said calmly, and filled the kettle.

'Our boiler's broken,' he said again. 'Daddy says it's screwed and so are we. What's screwed?'

James nearly choked, but Kate's mother took it in her stride.

'Well—imagine you've got a bit of paper and you twist it up until it's all crumpled. But you can straighten it out again,' she said. She met James's appalled gaze, laughter dancing in the blue depths of her eyes. 'Can't you, James?'

'Absolutely,' he said, his voice sounding strangled.

She straightened up from the fridge. 'There you are—I've put a few essentials in there to start you off, so you can get sorted out in your own time. Kate'll show you where everything is, I just wanted to say hello. I'm Sue, by the way, and this is Andrew—Andrew?'

'I'm here, I was just putting some wood on the fire,' he said, coming through and dusting off his hand before extending it. 'Welcome, James,' he said, and James felt his throat starting to close up.

'Thank you,' he said, his voice suddenly gruff, and he pressed his lips together and eased in a long, slow breath. They were such good people, and without them he didn't know what would have happened to them.

'Right, we'll leave you in peace. There are hot-water bottles in the children's beds, and your electric blanket's on. Kate'll sort you out. We'll see you tomorrow.'

'Let me show you where the bedrooms are so you can get the children off to sleep,' she said as soon as they'd gone, and headed for the stairs, Rory at her side chattering nineteen to the dozen and pretending not to yawn.

'Stay and have a drink with me.'

She looked up into his eyes, on the point of refusing, and saw despair and pride and above all loneliness in them.

'I tell you what, I was just having a glass of wine,' she told him. 'Why don't I go and bring the bottle?'

'My boss, a wino?' he said softly, and she smiled back.

'You don't have to join me if it's against your principles. You can have tea if you like.'

'No way. Go and fetch it. I'll see if your mother's put anything like bread in there. I seem to have forgotten to eat and I could kill for a piece of toast.'

'Me, too. Make lots.'

She went back to her house and retrieved the bottle, then swung back the bookcase and knocked on the communicating door that led from her hall through into the lobby behind the stairs. 'James? Unlock the door!'

She heard the scrape of the key, then he opened the door. 'It's connected,' he said, pointing out the obvious, and she grinned mischievously.

'Ten out of ten. I'll have to get you a pay rise,' she said, pushing past him and heading for the kitchen. 'It was done so that when the family all come down they can take over the barn, but it's usually locked on both sides. Yum, the toast smells good. Here, find a couple of glasses and pour the wine and I'll butter the toast.'

'The family?' he said, clinking glasses. 'You make it sound like there are thousands of them.'

'Oh, there are. Well, not thousands, but lots. My parents foster children. Not so much now, but they have done, for years, and they've grown up and got married and had children and they all come back—and then there are their own children, of course, three of them, and me and my brother.'

He stood and looked at her, and she realised what she'd said and coloured. 'Um—I'm adopted,' she said, and after a long moment he nodded slowly.

'That explains it—your reaction when I said what I did about giving up the children.'

'Oh. Yes. Sorry. I overreacted a bit.'

'No. You were absolutely right. They're my children—my babies. You can't overreact to the idea of losing them—and for the record, I wouldn't ever do it. Here—your wine.'

'Swap,' she said, handing him a plate of hot buttered toast, and they took their little feast through to the sitting room, sat down in front of the glowing woodburner and ate in a silence broken only by the crackle of logs and the distant barking of a dog.

'It's so peaceful here,' he murmured, putting his plate down and settling back into the sofa with a sigh. 'I can't believe I'm sitting here, drinking your wine, eating your food…'

'Not my food,' she corrected with a smile, and he grinned crookedly and stared into the flames.

'Thank you, Kate,' he said softly. 'I don't know what we would have done without you. I can't tell you how grateful I am.'

'Don't be grateful. Just look after your children, get your boiler fixed when you can, and life will sort itself out. It always does, one way or another. You know the saying, when one door closes, another…'

'Slams in your face,' he finished, and gave a quiet snort. 'Or in mine, anyway,' he added.

'James, give it time,' she advised, not really knowing what to say to him but worried that he was expecting too much, too soon. 'You'll get there.'

'I wish I could believe you.' He rested his head back, closed his eyes and sighed. 'It's so nice here. Like a real home. I had one, once. A real home—with love and laughter and the promise of so much still to come. One minute we were sailing along in smug suburban satisfaction, the next it was all gone—like a tatty old jigsaw in a charity shop, with a bit missing.'

Oh, God, she thought, what do I say? What *can* I say? Nothing. So she said nothing, and just waited, giving him time and trying not to cry for him.

'It's not even Beth,' he went on after a long pause. 'It's all the other things. Company. Someone to go to dinner with, or a film or just a walk in the country. Someone to talk to after the kids go to bed, so I don't just go stir crazy and surf the net or go to bed at nine because there's nothing else to do and then lie there alone wondering if I'll ever have a sex life again…'

Oh, yes. She could easily identify with all of that.

Especially, since he'd come into her life, the lying alone and wondering bit.

'I need to go,' she said, getting to her feet and scooping up the dirty plates and her glass. 'Keep the wine, there's only a dribble left. You may as well finish it. Give me a yell if you need anything. I'll leave the door open my side.'

And dumping everything in the kitchen, she headed back next door before she said or did anything stupid.

CHAPTER FIVE

'You're in early.'

His mouth twisted. 'You mean I'm not late,' he said wryly, and she smiled back, unable to resist his rather rumpled charm.

'Whatever. How are the kids? Did they sleep well?'

'Like logs. They're so confused, they don't know whether they're coming or going, and I think they've just given up trying to make sense of it. Freya didn't make a sound when I handed her over to Helen this morning.'

'She was probably too tired.'

'Probably.' He chuckled and scrubbed a hand round the back of his neck, looking a little awkward suddenly. 'Look, about last night—I'm sorry about the self-pity thing. I didn't mean to wallow all over you like that. I was just at the end of my tether, and you threw me a lifeline and all I could talk about was my tragic and barren existence, so I'm sorry if I came over as ungrateful, because I'm not. I owe you. Big time.'

'It's a pleasure. Right, getting down to business, if you haven't got anything else urgent, could you take a look at Tracy Farthing? I was just about to go up there and check on her. Trina called. She's looking a bit peaky, and complaining of epigastric pain. You might want to have a look at her stomach aspirate and see if there's anything to worry about. Trina said she thought there was evidence of a slight gastric bleed, but that might just be post-op.'

'I'll have a look,' he said, and headed towards the doors, leaving her to do the ward round without him. That was fine, she thought. He could catch up later.

Steve Symes had been discharged to Oncology now, old Mr Reason was doing fine now his abscess had been drained and the only patient apart from Tracy causing them the slightest concern was Peter Graham, the man who'd been kicked in the gut.

He was making slow but good progress, his bowel sounds were returning and they were starting him on free fluids today. Kate normally spent as little time as possible with him, but this morning, for some reason, she hesitated before she walked away.

'This guy who kicked you, Peter,' she said softly. 'Does he bear you a grudge?'

'Nah. Wrong place, wrong time,' he said, but his eyes were shifty and she found herself agreeing with James.

'Well, that's good, because I don't want to send you out there and find you end up in the wrong place at the wrong time again. You might not be so lucky next time.'

Did she imagine it, or did he swallow a little nervously? She left him to it and made her way back to the nursing station with the notes. The senior sister, Ali, was there, and Kate put the notes down and said, 'Can I have a word, Ali?'

'Sure. What's the problem?'

'Peter Graham.'

She frowned. 'What's wrong with him? He was fine earlier.'

'I think he knows the guy.'

'Ah.' Her face cleared. 'So do I. Do you want me to have a word with the police if they come in again?'

'If you catch them. And in the meantime, can you keep an eye out for his visitors in case any of them are dodgy or threatening, or he looks worried while they're here?'

'Of course. I'll give you a head's up if anything odd happens.'

'Tell James,' she said, the fingers of dread plucking at her again. 'He's bigger than me.'

Ali laughed. 'Sure thing. Oh, he rang. He thinks Tracy's got a little gastric bleed. He said, do you want him to do an endoscopy and fix it?'

'That would be a good idea, if he thinks it's bad enough. We don't want to go in again unnecessarily. I'll ring him.'

'Ring who?'

Kate turned round, her hand on her chest, and gave James a mock scowl. 'You made me jump. I was going to call you about Tracy.'

'I've booked a slot in the endoscopy suite for ten to fix it. I'm pretty sure we can do it that way, it's only slight. Want to join me?'

'Could do. I've got a meeting but I know what I'd rather be doing! I'll send my apologies.'

'And we might even get time for coffee,' he murmured. 'I've just realised I didn't manage to get any breakfast.'

She frowned at him. 'And you didn't have supper. You need to eat, James. You'll fade away.'

'Hardly,' he snorted, then cocked his head on one side. 'So—if I need to eat, and you need to eat, is it my turn for the take-away tonight?'

She felt her heart kick up a little speed, and tried for a casual smile. She should say no. She should say—

'Your place or mine?'

He chuckled. 'Rather one and the same, isn't it? Perhaps we'd better make it mine—just in case the kids call out.'

She nodded. 'Whatever. Right, I have to get on. I've got letters to dictate and a whole pile of forms to fill in before I can sneak out and see you do Tracy's gastroscopy.'

'I'm doing it?'

'Sure. Your patient, James, and I'm sure you're quite big enough to do it yourself.'

He tipped his head slightly. 'You're not in the least bit territorial, are you?'

'Not if it means someone else gets to do my work,' she said with a cheeky smile, and, waggling her fingers at him, she headed to her office to wrestle with the hated paperwork.

He got a page that afternoon in his clinic from Ali, and rang her.

'There's a man with Pete Graham and I don't like the look of him,' the ward sister said. 'Nasty—you know what I mean? I don't really want to start anything with him, but Kate said to call you.'

'I'll come. Alert Security, just in case. I don't want him trying anything.'

'Oh. James, he's starting to shout—'

'Call Security. I'm coming,' he said, and ran up to the ward. If the man hit Pete again, so soon after his surgery...

'Get off me!'

'Not a chance,' James said, joining in the fray and pressing the man firmly down onto the end of Pete's bed so the security guard could cuff him. 'Call the police.'

'They're on their way,' Ali said, but he hardly heard her, because Pete was looking pale and shaken, holding his side and—

'Damn, he's going off. He must have hit him. Pete, stay with me. What happened, mate?'

'Hit me,' he whispered threadily.

'Is this the man who hit you before?'

'Brother,' he mumbled, and slid into unconsciousness.

'You're his brother?' he said in disbelief to the man the security guard had wrestled upright.

'He took my girl, all right?'

'I don't care what he did, you don't kick him and nearly kill him and then come in here and have another go! Get him out of the way, please, we're going to Theatre. Ali, let's move!'

They moved. They moved like the wind, wheeling the bed down to Theatre. Someone must have phoned ahead because the doors were standing open and Kate was changed and scrubbing.

'I'll start, you scrub,' she snapped, and took over. By the time he was gowning up, Pete was under and she was ripping opening up the careful layers of sutures that James had put in on Monday night. It hadn't healed much in three days, but by the time she was in, the blood was welling in his abdomen.

'Have we got any blood on order?' he asked, and she nodded.

'Six units on the way up. Ah, it's here. Can you get it in fast, please, someone? Suction, James. I can't see a bloody thing. Thanks.'

'There—the liver, just where I repaired it.' He swore viciously. 'I'd left that lobe, I thought it would heal, but that's gone out the window now, hasn't it? Damn.'

'I might be able to save it. Let me try.'

She did it. To his amazement, she did it, suturing the tear so carefully that he could scarcely see the stitches, and the bleeding stopped.

'Very beautiful. Your great-grandmother would be proud of you,' he said, and she grinned behind her mask, her eyes crinkling up and sending heat shooting through him.

'My great-grandmother would have a fit to think of a girl doing this,' she said. 'But my mother would be proud of me, and that's good enough for me.'

And then he realised her eyes were sparkling, and she blinked and looked away, and he took the instruments out of her hands and took over, closing the wound and replacing all his careful stitches before straightening up and standing back.

'Thank you,' he said to the anaesthetist. Stripping off his gloves, he followed her out and found her slumped in the staffroom, coffee in hand, reading the paper. She put it down when he came in and met his eyes.

'All right?' she said.

'I am. Pete is. What about you?'

She smiled softly. 'I'm fine, but I suppose we should go back to our clinic. They'll be wondering what's going on and Jo will be sinking without trace. I tell you what, I'll be ready for that take-away tonight. I don't know what happened to lunch.'

'You need to eat, Kate, you'll fade away,' he mimicked, and she threw the paper at him, stood up and walked out, a smile she tried to hide peeking out around the edges of her façade. He put the paper back on the table and followed her, whistling softly under his breath.

Life was suddenly looking a whole lot better...

It was funny how quickly something could become a habit.

He brought supper round to hers in the end that night because the children had settled without a murmur—a lovely Thai curry which he had delivered, much healthier than the

Indian cholesterol-fest she'd taken to his place, in deference to their livers, he said—and they ate it in the kitchen, with the communicating door open so they could listen. Then the following night, because there was a bit left in the bottle of wine he'd brought round, she took it back and they sat and watched the television for an hour and argued about a documentary and she went to bed with a smile on her face.

They weren't on call that weekend, blissfully, and she decided to give herself the luxury of a lie-in on Saturday morning.

She reckoned without the sound of James's children, though, all the little shrieks and squeals and the sound of running feet on the landing. And his deep, gruff voice shushing them, then the giggles because he must have caught them and picked them up, because the shrieks got louder and the running feet stopped.

She realised she was smiling. Nuts. She should be cross at losing her lie-in, but she found she wasn't. Far from it. It was lovely to hear the sound of happy children.

Especially James's happy children, after all they'd had to endure recently.

She got up, showered quickly and went downstairs in her scruffy old robe, her hair twisted up in a towel, and put the kettle on to boil while she got dressed. Then she heard a crash and a scream, and without even thinking about it she whipped the door open and ran through, to find James sitting at the bottom of the stairs with Rory on his lap, rubbing his knee and hugging him, while Freya hovered on the top step with her eyes like saucers.

'Freya, sweetheart, come here, he's all right,' she said softly, running up the stairs to her and scooping her up. She carried her back down and sat on the bottom step next to them with the toddler snuggled on her lap. 'Are you OK, Rory?'

'I fell downstairs,' he said, hiccuping, and James pulled his head in hard against his chest and rubbed it lovingly.

'You're all right, darling. It's OK. Let's just put some ice on it.'

'It's OK now,' he said. Wriggling off his father's lap, he got to his feet and limped through to the kitchen. 'Can I still have the last cake?' he asked, and James rolled his eyes and grinned at her.

'Is that what this is about? The last cake?' she asked, and he chuckled.

'Yeah. I thought he'd get dressed, but he just ran and opened the stairgate and slipped on his pyjamas. They always fall down, he's got such a skinny little bottom. He's OK.'

He'd said that so many times she wondered who he was trying to convince, but, following Rory into the kitchen, it seemed that he was probably right, because the boy was sitting at the table with his legs swinging, munching happily on a muffin and looking victorious.

'F'eya muffin!' Freya said, holding out her hand and opening and shutting it like a little starfish, but Rory wasn't giving up his muffin for anyone, and James was starting to look desperate, so she intervened.

'I tell you what, I've got some lovely chocolate biscuits next door,' she told them, and Rory stopped eating and Freya stopped crying and swivelled her head round and looked up at her hopefully. James just shrugged.

'Whatever,' he said, and she carried Freya through, Rory limping behind them, and they had tea and biscuits in her sitting room in front of cartoons, and it was just like having one of her brothers there with his kids.

Except for one very glaring difference. None of her brothers, whether blood, adoptive or foster, had ever made her feel the way James did. Good job, too, she thought, because her thoughts were seriously X-rated, but he just looked so good in those lovely washed-out old jeans with the top button undone and a T-shirt dragged on hastily and those somehow curiously sexy bare feet propped up on her coffee-table as if he belonged there.

'There's an icepack in my freezer if you think he needs it,' she told James, and he went and investigated and came back with it a moment later, wrapped in a tea-towel, and laid it over Rory's knee.

'I think it's fine,' he said, peering at it as he covered it, 'but it won't hurt to be careful. And as for you, young lady, I think you've had enough biscuits.'

'I think we all have, probably,' Kate said with a laugh, and offloading his daughter onto his lap, she put them back in the kitchen and came back, removing the towel as she did so and shaking out her hair. It tumbled over her shoulders like wet rope, and she sighed. 'I'll never get a comb through it,' she said, and looked up to find him watching her oddly.

Very oddly, as if he, too, was having X-rated thoughts, and the breath jammed in her throat.

Oh, help. If this wasn't one-sided, if they were going to become crazily aware of each other all the time, it was going to make working with him a nightmare.

She looked away hastily, scooped up their cups and turned off the television. 'Sorry, guys, I have to get dressed and sort my hair out. You'll have to go home.'

'What—properly home?' Rory said, looking aghast, and James, catching his expression, looked gutted.

'Next door, silly,' she said with a grin. 'Go on. Off you go. I won't be long.'

'Then can we come back?'

'Rory,' James said firmly, steering him towards the door with a hand on his shoulder and propelling him through it. 'Thanks for the tea and biscuits.'

'My pleasure,' she said, blowing a kiss to Freya, and he shut the door and left her in peace.

Except it didn't feel like peace, it felt curiously empty and lonely...

James heard the door open and saw Kate come out of her house. Opening his door, he hailed her.

'Kate! I need to speak to your parents.'

'Why?' she asked, turned back and coming towards him. 'Is there a problem?'

'No, not at all. I just need to sort out something about rent.'

'James, they won't take anything.'

'Then we'll move out.' He was adamant about it. 'They must have a tariff—some kind of letting fee.'

'No, they don't,' she said a little too quickly. 'It's only used for the family. We call it a holiday cottage, but it's really just a guest annexe. And you're my guest, so that's fine.'

Was she lying? Impossible to know, but there were all sorts of overheads. 'I need to pay the running costs, at least,' he protested. 'I need to speak to them, Kate. Today.'

'Well, come with me, then, I'm going over there now.'

So he rounded up the children from in front of the television and they all trailed across the farmyard and into the lovely old Tudor house that was her family home.

Sue was in the kitchen, up to her elbows in flour. 'Dan's coming for lunch tomorrow, so I thought I'd get ahead a bit,' she told Kate. 'He's got a new girlfriend.'

'Oh. Good. About time. Dan's one of my foster-brothers,' she explained to James. 'He's been a bit of a nightmare, but he's lovely now and things are really starting to work out for him.'

Andrew came in then, and before James could say a word, she greeted him with, 'Hi, Dad, James has some notion about paying the overheads on the barn—he seems to have some fixation about rent, but I explained that we don't rent it out. I told him you'd sort out the meter readings and things.'

'Of course. I'll see to it. Don't worry about it, James, it's all very straightforward.'

'Can't I just rent it from you?'

'Oh, no. That would cause havoc with the tax man. No, we'll just read the meter. That'll be the easiest thing.'

Her father didn't miss a beat, so if they were lying to him, they were doing it very proficiently, he thought, and gave up arguing. He'd buy them something as a thank-you when they were finally able to go home again. Whenever that might be...

'On the subject of the barn, Kate said something about the family using it over Christmas. Is that right? Because if it is, we can move back to our house for a while. We can always wash at my mother's, but I don't want to be in the way. It sounds like you'll have quite a crowd.'

'You won't be in the way, and of course you won't take the children back to that cold place over Christmas and unsettle them even more,' Sue said adamantly. 'In fact, what are you doing for Christmas?' she asked, and he realised he hadn't even considered it.

'No plans,' he said. 'My mother's spending it with her sister. My aunt was recently widowed and she hasn't been well. That's been arranged for ages. As for me and the kids, well, we haven't really thought about it, have we, kids?'

'I've thought about it,' Rory said, running his finger

through the dusting of flour on the kitchen table that Sue was rolling the pastry out in. 'I want a big tree, and a stocking, and I'm going to write a letter to Father Christmas. Kate, will you help me write it?'

'What about me?' he asked, but Rory shook his head.

'I want Kate to help me,' he said stubbornly.

James couldn't argue any more. It might never happen, but anyway he had better things to worry about, because Freya had seen a dog come in and was trying to wriggle out of his arms.

'Doggy!' she was saying insistently, and he looked down a little uncertainly at the black Labrador sniffing at her toes.

'Is it OK with children?' he asked, and Sue chuckled.

'If you don't mind them being washed. Mungo's a sweetie. She'll be fine with him.'

She was more than fine. She was in love. She stroked and patted and giggled, and he wagged and slurped until she was washed from end to end, and they ended up curled up together in a heap on an old blanket beside the Aga while she pulled his ears gently.

'Children need germs,' Andrew said, reading his mind, and James just laughed and let them get on with it. Frankly, to see them both so happy, Rory helping Sue put dollops of mincemeat into the little pies while Freya stroked Mungo's ears and crooned to him, was such a relief after the last year and a half that he didn't care if they caught something dreadful.

It would almost be worth it just for this one morning.

'There, all done. Now I'm going to put them in the oven and clear up. Kate, if you're not doing anything, why don't you and James and the children take the dogs for a walk down by the river? There might be some ducks.'

'Can we feed them?' Rory asked excitedly, running over to Kate and looking hopefully up into her eyes.

As if she could resist that, even if she'd wanted to. She smiled at him and got up. 'Sure. Mum, got any bread?'

'In the breadbin—there's a bit of corn bread that's past its sell-by date. James, have you got boots?'

'Ah. No.'

'That's fine,' Kate said. 'We have boots here in every conceivable size from tiny tots up to something huge. What size are your feet?'

'Ten.'

'Easy. Come on, then, lazybones, up you get,' she said to him. 'Freya? Coming to feed the ducks with Mungo?'

'Doggy coming?' she asked, and Kate nodded. 'He's coming. So's Badger.'

'Have you got a badger?' Rory asked, and she thought if his eyes got any bigger they'd fall out of his head.

'No. Just a dog called Badger. We've got badgers on the farm, though—and foxes and rabbits and squirrels and pheasants and—oh, all sorts.'

'Good grief,' James said faintly. 'It sounds like a wildlife park.'

'It is a bit. Then there are the farm animals. I'll show you those, if you like, kids. They belong to my uncle. He's got sheep and goats and cows.'

'Wow!'

She was wrong about the eyes. They could get bigger without falling out.

'Right, boots. James, try these. Rory, what size are your feet?'

It took a few minutes to sort them all out, then they needed thick coats and scarves and gloves, and then they were ready, the dogs bouncing and wagging their tails at the door. She took them down the lane to the ford so the kids could splash in the river, and they shrieked and giggled and everything was going fine until Freya fell over and got her mittens muddy.

Then James scooped her up, cleaned her off and sat her on his shoulders, and they walked back up round behind the farm to see the animals, and Rory climbed on a gate and scratched a goat's ears and Kate thought she'd never seen such a transformation from the children she'd first met.

'They seem to be having fun,' she said to James when he put Freya down and let her feed the ducks on the pond.

'They are. There hasn't been enough of that in the last few months. We had a good time in the summer, but that seems ages ago, and since Rory started school and I've been trying to find a job and a childminder, it's all been a bit more fraught. And as for the boiler…'

He rolled his eyes, and she smiled ruefully. 'I had a car like your life once. Every time I started it, something else fell off or went wrong.' She felt her smile fade. 'Still, at least I could sell the car.' Unlike his life, or her marriage.

He gave her a wry grin. 'Hey, it's not all bad. We're getting there—particularly, this week, thanks to you. I don't know what we would have done without the barn.'

'You would have found a way. Tom and Fliss have got a flat. They could have put you up. There are lots of options.'

'I'm more than happy with this one,' he said softly, and she followed his gaze to the children who were standing on the path by the pond, the dogs lined up in front of them sitting at attention, eyes fixed hopefully on their hands while they fed the ducks and the dogs in turn. And then he shifted his gaze to her, those strangely piercing blue eyes staring right down into her soul.

'More than happy. I owe you, Kate. Big time.'

She tried to smile, but her lips wouldn't really co-operate, and her lungs had forgotten how to work. 'I'll bear it in mind—I'm sure there'll come a time when I need a favour.'

'Make sure you ask me.'

'I will.'

It was one of those odd, timeless moments when the world seems to come to a halt. Their eyes locked, and she could feel herself swaying towards him, drawn in by his warmth and sincerity and downright sex appeal, and then suddenly there was a shriek and a splash and the children were laughing, and as if the spell had been broken he stepped back, dragged his eyes away from hers and turned towards them, and the mood was gone.

Thank goodness. The last thing she needed was to get sucked in by him and his children. No matter how much she adored them.

Any of them.

Oh, no, no, no! Stop it!

She called the dogs, and James gathered up the children and the bread bag and they headed back to the house.

'Perfect timing,' her mother said as they went back into a kitchen that smelt comforting and homely. 'I've made a big pot of Saturday soup, and the bread's cooling on the rack. Wash your hands, all of you, and come and sit down.'

That was it?

She didn't even bother to ask if they had plans, just laid the table and settled them all down like a mother hen with her chicks under her wings while Andrew carved up the loaf, and James felt the lump in his throat growing ever bigger.

'I don't like soup,' Rory told Kate doubtfully, but she just laughed and leant over, her dark head next to his.

'You'll like my mother's Saturday soup. It's got bacon and beans and all sorts of stuff. Everybody likes Saturday soup,' she told him confidently, and, sure enough, he did. Not only liked it, he went back for more.

Twice.

So did James, and even Freya had a respectable helping. Then Sue put an apple pie down in the middle of the table, and a steaming jug of custard, and it just got better.

'So what are you wearing for the wedding party tonight?' Sue asked Kate as she passed her a bowl, and for a second James thought she was going to drop it. And the look in her eyes was—

'Oh, damn. I'd forgotten. Is it really tonight?'

'Yes—oh, Kate, you can't have forgotten! You bought the present weeks ago.'

'I know. Um—the red dress, I suppose? It's sort of Christmassy and dressy enough. Fiddle. I'd really forgotten about it.'

Her mother gave her a keen look. 'Will you be all right?' she asked softly, and Kate lifted her shoulders a fraction.

'I suppose so. I'll have to be, won't I? I just—'

'Hate going alone?'

Her smile was wry. 'Absolutely.' And then she turned to James and said, 'My brother's brother-in-law is getting married to my ex's sister. And he'll be there.'

'Ouch.'

'What's an ex?'

'A has-been,' she said to Rory without looking at him.

'What's a has-been?'

'Someone who was a friend a long time ago,' James said,

modifying the truth just a little and watching Kate out of the corner of his eye. 'Somebody who's not a friend any more.'

'Why? Did you do something wrong so he doesn't like you?'

'Rory, stop asking questions and eat your apple pie,' he said, watching Kate carefully, then, before he had time to think about it too much, he said very softly, 'Would it help if you weren't alone?'

Her eyes flew to his, and her lips parted in surprise, then soft colour warmed her cheeks and she looked away, pressing her lips together.

'You don't need to do that.'

'Would you like me to?'

'It's an imposition.'

'Kate, yes or no?'

She looked across at her mother. 'Are you free to babysit?'

Sue didn't hesitate. In fact, if anything she looked quite enthusiastic. 'Of course,' she said.

'Then—yes, please. If you really don't mind, I'd be very grateful.'

'Of course I don't mind.'

'It's black tie—is that a problem?'

He shook his head. 'No. No problem.' Or he didn't think it was. He just had to find his suit.

'And that'll make us quits.'

'Quits?'

'On the favour front.'

She must be mad if she thought that taking her out for the evening could in any way be counted as a favour, but he let it go. For now.

When he finally got the children away from the table, he took them back to the house and dug out a few more changes of clothes for them, then took out his DJ and dress shirt. Goodness knows if it needed a clean. He couldn't even remember the last time he'd worn it. Two years ago? The Christmas ball, when Rory had been two and a half and Beth hadn't even realised she was pregnant.

Ah, hell.

He chucked it in the car, remembered his black dress shoes at the last minute and went and found them, too, then loaded up the children, locked the house and headed back. She was there outside the barn, tidying up a tub of pansies by her front door, and as they drove in she straightened up, lifting her hair back out of her eyes and smiling at them all, and he felt a tug of something long forgotten and probably totally inappropriate deep in his gut.

'Got everything you need?'

'Even the shoes,' he said wryly. 'What time's kick-off?'

'Seven for seven-thirty. We need to leave about a quarter to. Is that all right?'

'Sure. Knock on the door when you're ready.'

He took the children inside, found an iron in the kitchen and pressed his shirt, checked his suit and cleaned his shoes. Thankfully, there was some universal shoe cream stashed under the sink. He bathed the children, gave them scrambled eggs on toast and sat them down in front of the television while he showered.

Then at six-thirty, after he'd tucked the children up in bed and read them a story, he put the suit on. It was a lot looser on him, to his surprise, and he had to tighten the tabs on the waistband of the trousers, but he decided on balance it fitted better. He checked the pockets and found a handkerchief and a pair of tickets. Tickets for the hospital Christmas ball, his last Christmas with Beth.

He sat down on the edge of the bed and stared at the tickets for a moment. He could remember the event, but he could hardly remember Beth. What had she been wearing? Black, probably. She always wore black. He couldn't remember.

With a sigh he stood up and dropped the tickets into the waste-paper basket, and before he had time to think about it any more, he slipped off his wedding ring and put it in the bedside table drawer.

It was time to move on. Time to start living again, not only for him, but for Kate, too.

CHAPTER SIX

'Wow. Smart place.'

'Smart people,' she said flatly. 'I never really fitted.'

'So why are you here?'

Her laugh felt a little hollow. 'My brother's brother-in-law Adam is a lovely guy. And I got on really well with Jenny, my sister-in-law. And it's not really her fault her brother's a cold-hearted, self-centred bastard.'

'Ouch.'

'Oh, ignore me, I'm just bitter. But he's not a nice man. Pity I didn't work that out before I married him.'

'So why didn't you?'

She shrugged. 'I don't really know. He can be very charming, but he didn't want me to be a doctor, and I think he always imagined I'd give it all up to have his babies and settle down. He was a bit shocked when I refused, but I really wasn't ready. There were things I needed to do first.'

'I'm surprised,' he said quietly. 'I would have thought you'd have jumped at the chance of having children. You're wonderful with them, and they adore you. Well, mine do, anyway. They're wearing your name out talking about you.'

She gave a guilty little laugh. 'I'm sorry about that. They're lovely. I have to admit I adore them, too.'

'So how come you didn't want children when you were married?' he asked, and she shrugged.

'I did, in a way, but apart from the fact that I didn't think he'd make much of a father, like I said, I had things to do first.'

'And have you done them yet?'

'Some of them. Not all.' And not all of them mattered, of course. Some were just things to fill the future she could see stretching out ahead of her like a long, empty road.

'So what's his name?'

She dragged herself back to the present. 'Jon—short for Jonathan.'

'Right. Is there anything else I need to know about him?'

'Apart from the fact that the last time I saw him I was recovering from surgery? Not really.'

She didn't look at him, but she heard his indrawn breath, and after a moment he moved on.

'So—will there be anyone from work here?'

'Good grief, no,' she said, laughter bubbling up at the very thought. 'Two totally different worlds.'

'And ne'er the twain shall meet?'

She flashed him a smile. 'Something like that. Right, shall we?'

'I'm ready when you are.'

'I'm ready as I'll ever be.'

He was there by the time she'd worked out where the doorhandle was and picked the present up off the floor, and he extended her a firm, warm hand and helped her out, then closed the door and offered her his elbow.

'Such a gentleman,' she teased, and he smiled.

'I can be—when my boss isn't giving me strain.'

'I'll have to bear that in mind,' she said. Straightening her shoulders and pulling her wrap a little tighter, she dredged up her most brilliant smile.

'Before we go in,' he said, pausing on the steps, his hand over hers in the crook of his elbow, and she turned and looked up at him questioningly. 'You look beautiful tonight,' he said, his voice a little gruff, and she felt a warm glow sweep over her.

'Thank you, James,' she said, a tiny tremor in her voice, and she ran her eyes over him and smiled. 'I have to say you don't look so bad yourself.'

'It's amazing what you can do with a bar of soap and a well-cut suit.' He grinned and inclined his head towards the doors. 'Shall we?'

She was fabulous.

Taut as a bowstring, but composed, dignified and very, very close to him.

He was introduced to her brother Michael, very like her, with the same warm brown eyes, and his pretty pregnant wife, Louise, who was the sister of the groom. They were lovely people, and very interested in him, he could tell, although they tried to be discreet.

'Don't get excited, he's a colleague and he's only here as a smokescreen,' she told them drily, but they didn't look any less interested or at all convinced, and he wondered what he was giving away, or if it was that Kate absolutely never went out with a man? And if so, why? Because it would get in the way of her achieving all her goals?

Something about that didn't fit, because she'd admitted she wanted children.

Which was a thought worthy of considerably more attention later, he decided, and filed it.

They chatted for a few minutes, but they were in demand and so he and Kate moved on. She introduced him to the blissfully happy bride and groom, Jenny and Adam, and a couple of other people, and all the time he was aware of the curious glances that followed them around the room.

Maybe she really never did go out with a man—in which case, thank goodness there was nobody from the hospital there, or the gossipmongers would be having a field day.

There was a finger buffet served by a diligent army of waiters, but he wasn't interested in food, or the free-flowing champagne that was circulating. The only thing that held his attention was Kate, and he was riveted.

Especially when she introduced him to Jon.

The dreaded ex.

She was brilliant—and James loathed him on sight.

'Katherine—how nice to see you!' he said, hardly sparing James a glance. 'You're looking well.'

Better than she had when she was recovering from surgery? That was when Kate had said she'd last seen him, and James had to stifle the urge to knock the self-satisfied smile down his throat. He remembered the wicked scar around her ribs and his jaw clenched. Had this man been in any way responsible for that?

'Thank you, Jon.' Nobody else would have realised how false her sparkling smile was, but he knew the effort it must have cost her, and his hand settled on the hollow of her back in support, and he felt her lean back into him.

'It's lovely to see you, too,' she said brightly. 'You're looking well.' And then she added innocently, 'The extra weight suits you.'

He nearly choked at the man's expression, but managed to contain the laugh.

'Ever the wit,' Jon said a little crisply, his smile slipping a little, and then assessing eyes swivelled James's way. 'I hadn't realised you weren't alone tonight. Aren't you going to introduce me?'

'Of course. Jon, this is James McEwan. He's—'

'Good to put a face to a name,' James interrupted, cutting her off and taking charge of this one as he shook the man's hand. 'I've heard a lot about you. Kate and I are very...' He paused. '*Good* friends.' The emphasis wasn't lost, and Jon's eyebrows rose fractionally.

'Well, I hope she doesn't bore you to death,' he replied with a slightly mocking laugh. 'She's got a morbid obsession with cutting people up. Never could understand it. So what do you do?'

Oh, he was enjoying this. 'I cut people up,' he said deadpan.

'Oh, I might have known it, you're another bloody doctor,' Jon said with undisguised disgust, and then laughed again dismissively. 'Oh, well, Kate, you'll be all right with this one. He won't even notice when you work ludicrous hours.'

'Actually, he does notice, and he works even more ludicrous hours than I do, so, as you were kind enough to point out, we're well suited.'

And sliding an arm round his waist, she leant up against James and smiled like the cat that had got the cream.

'Pompous ass. I hope he never needs my attention,' James growled as Jon walked away to more interesting pastures, and she chuckled.

'Not a chance. He only goes private. That should have told me something. I still haven't worked out if I'm a lousy judge of character or if he's got worse as he's got older.'

'Both, probably. You're a bit inclined to see the good in people. Well, except me.'

'I see the good in you!' she protested, turning to face him, and his lips twitched.

'Not on my first day.'

'You were late because you'd been incompetent!'

He grinned. 'Fair cop. Fancy a dance?'

'Do you know, I think I do?'

She smiled at him, relaxing now the dreaded meeting was over, and he led her to the dance floor, just as the song finished and the music slowed, so he slid his arms round her and eased her up against him.

Oh, hell. Big mistake. Huge, massive mistake, because the feel of her body, soft and warm and very feminine against him, was enough to send him into meltdown.

He moved away a fraction, and the moment the beat speeded up he let her go and created a little space between them. Not too much. Just enough, so that he didn't have to feel her thighs brushing against his, her breasts pressing into his chest, her hands warm and light against his waist.

But he could still smell that intoxicating fragrance and in many ways it was worse because now he could watch her, and the sight of her body moving sinuously in time to the music was going to do his head in.

'I need a drink,' he said a trifle desperately, and led her away from the dance floor before he disgraced himself completely.

'Do you really need a drink? Or do you need to get out of here?'

'Can we? Before the bride and groom leave?'

'I'm sure we can. Knowing them, they'll be partying until three o'clock.' And then she added with a little grin, 'I've got a nice bottle of Merlot in my kitchen.'

Was he dreaming, or was that a very definite invitation in her eyes? He wasn't taking any chances.

'Give me a minute,' he said. Diving into the gents', he raided the conveniently full dispensing machine in the corner next to the hand-dryer. He could hardly get the coins into it his hands were shaking so badly. It was ridiculous. She probably didn't intend anything of the sort, but there was no way he was going back there unprepared.

Finally he managed the simple task, pulled open the drawer, slid the packet into his trouser pocket and turned round, just as Jon walked in.

'Ah, McEwan. Wondered where you were. Kate was looking lost. I think she suspects you've slipped off without her.'

'I doubt it,' he said drily. 'She knows I wouldn't do that. I keep my promises. You know—in sickness and in health, and all that...'

And without another word, he brushed past him and went out into the foyer.

'Did you see Jon?'

'I did. He said you were looking lost.'

'Liar. I was saying goodbye to my brother. Are you all set?'

'Yes. Let's go before we run into him again and I feel obliged to feed him his teeth.'

She gave a surprised little chuckle, and the sound of it warmed him to the soles of his shoes.

'Mum? We're back.'

'Oh, hello, darling, you're early,' her mother said, turning off the television and getting to her feet. 'Hello, James. So did you both have a good time?'

Kate just laughed. 'Hardly. Well, the party was fine, but Jon was as obnoxious as usual.'

'I think you got your own back,' James replied, and her

mother raised a questioning eyebrow. 'She told him the extra weight suited him.'

Her mother's eyes widened and filled with laughter. 'Oh, Kate, you are naughty.'

'I know. It was great. He had the nerve to tell me I was looking better!'

'Oh, stupid man. Still, you got through it.'

'She more than got through it, she was fabulous, and we did have a good time,' James said beside her, and her mother looked from him to Kate and back again, and a tiny, knowing smile flickered around the corners of her mouth.

'Good. Well, I'm glad you enjoyed it. I haven't heard a sound out of the children, by the way. They must have worn themselves out this morning on your walk.'

'Probably. Thank you so much for looking after them.'

'Any time. It's good to see Kate getting out. She should do it more.'

Just go, Mum, she thought, wondering what she was going to say next, but she just kissed her on the cheek and went out. 'Don't forget Dan's coming for lunch tomorrow. You're all invited, if you'd like to come. It's open house.'

'It's always open house,' she said ruefully as her mother closed the door. 'I've never known it be anything else. It's a wonder she doesn't drag the postman in and give him breakfast.'

'She's wonderful,' James said, and she smiled.

'I know, and I love her to bits. She's a brilliant mother. Right, I'm going to get out of this dress.'

'That's a shame. You look lovely in it.'

She hesitated. It itched, and the bra was too tight over her ribs, but the look in his eyes…

'OK, then. Just give me a minute.'

And she went through into her half of the barn, ran upstairs and wriggled out of the hard, uncomfortable strapless bra that pressed on her ribs, and went back down, hoping that the boning in the dress was adequate and that she wouldn't fall out of it and embarrass herself to bits.

He was standing in her kitchen. He'd shed the jacket and left the bow-tie dangling when he'd undone the first three buttons of his shirt, so she could just see a tantalising glimpse of his broad, muscular chest, and he looked amazing.

Warm and relaxed and just so damn sexy she was going to make a fool of herself.

'Is this the wine you were talking about?'

'Do you see another one?'

He grinned. 'I didn't know if you had a secret stash.'

'No secret stash. I know I seem to have done nothing else since you moved in, but I don't really drink. Occasionally I like a glass after a particularly long day, so I keep a bottle in stock. You've obviously just caught me in a weak moment.' Why was she justifying herself? 'Here, you can earn your keep and open it.'

She passed him two wineglasses and rummaged in a cupboard for crisps.

'Sour cream and spring onion or sea salt and cracked pepper?' she asked, waggling the packets at him.

'Whatever. You choose.'

'Well, I like both, that's why I bought them.'

'Sea salt.'

'Right.'

They headed through to the sitting room, and she put on some soft bluesy music, turned the lights down low and sat beside him on her sofa, the crisps between them and their feet propped side by side on the coffee-table.

'Tell me about Dan,' he said, munching the crisps, and she rolled her head towards him and smiled.

'Dan's lovely. He's been a bit of a wild child—he's mixed race, and his father didn't want to know and his teenage mother's family were horrified to have a coloured child thrust into their white middle-England midst and kicked them out, so he didn't really belong, and he went off the rails a bit— stealing cars, joy-riding, that sort of thing. Mum and Dad sorted him out, though, and he's been to uni and he's a motoring journalist now. He's doing well, but his self-esteem is still a bit shaky and so he doesn't expect his relationships to work. He's always surprised when people like him.'

James frowned. 'That's tough. I really would have thought in this day and age it wouldn't make any difference what your ethnic background was.'

'And you think I'm naïve?' she teased, and pushed the crisps towards him. 'Come on, eat up or I'm going to have to finish them and then I'll be like a house.'

'Yeah, right. I can see that happening.' He shifted a little so he was facing her, and she could feel his eyes on her like lasers. She felt instantly self-conscious, and had to stop herself forcibly from tugging at the top of her dress.

'Don't.'

'What?'

'Look at me like that.'

'Like what?' He sounded surprised.

'Like—I don't know. Like you're studying an insect.'

He laughed. 'Actually, I was just looking at you. I find it's easier to talk to people when I can see them. And, anyway, I like looking at you. You're beautiful.'

She felt herself colour. That was the second time he'd said it tonight, and it made her feel vaguely uncomfortable.

'Hardly,' she replied. 'I mean, I know the dress is lovely, but it's just me.' She shrugged, and he just shook his head slowly.

'What's wrong? Why can't you take a compliment, Kate?'

She forced herself to meet his eyes. 'I can—when it isn't a blatant lie.'

'It's not a lie.'

'James, I'm not beautiful. I may be reasonably attractive, but—'

'Kate, you're beautiful. Believe me.'

Could she? He sounded sincere enough, but he hadn't seen—

'Do you know why I was in hospital?' she said abruptly.

'No, but I'm guessing it was something to do with the scar on your ribs?'

She sucked in her breath and met his eyes, shocked. 'How do you know?'

He looked a little awkward. 'The changing-room door was open. I glanced up. I wasn't spying, I just...saw you.'

'Oh, God.' She closed her eyes and turned her head away, colour flooding her cheeks. She felt a flicker of guilt, because she'd sneaked another peek at him, but it had never occurred to her that he'd do the same. 'I didn't realize...'

'Tell me about it,' he prompted gently. 'What happened? Was it something to do with Jon?'

'Jon? Good grief, no. He's a pompous ass but he's not violent. No, a patient lashed out at me and kicked me in the ribs. One of them punctured my lung and nicked the pulmonary vein. It was pretty exciting for a while, I gather.'

'For heaven's sake! How hard did he kick you?'

'Hard. He had steel toecaps on. I was called down to A and E to examine him because he'd got a query appendix. I poked him, and he didn't like it—especially when I told him there was nothing wrong with him.'

'Idiot.'

'Oh, absolutely. I should have been more careful.'

'Not you! Him!'

'Oh.' Funny, she'd got so used to thinking it was her fault—and was that Jon's fault?—that she'd lost sight of the simple truth. 'Yes, I suppose he was an idiot. But it scared me. And I hate the dark now.'

'What's the dark got to do with it?'

'Well, that's where it happened—in the car park. He followed me when I left work.'

'You weren't still examining him?'

'No, there was nothing wrong with him so I'd got rid of him ages before. He was just trying to skive off work, and I made him look a fool. So he hung around waiting for me and left me lying on the ground in the car park. Luckily someone came along shortly afterwards, otherwise I would have died. And all Jon could say was that it was my own fault, he'd told me I worked stupid hours and if I'd been at home where I belonged it wouldn't have happened. He'd had to cancel an important dinner and it had cost him thousands in lost contracts.'

'All this, while you were lying in bed in hospital?'

She nodded. 'I told him to go away—told him if his stupid contracts were more important than me then I didn't want to see him again. He took all my things round to my parents' and left them there on the porch, and that was it. Finish. The end of my marriage.'

'You're better off without him.'

'Oh, tell me about it. It's not all bad, though. He's paid for this.' She waved a hand at the room and dredged up a smile. 'The conversion work, anyway. Both sides. I had it done for the family, as a thank you, and at the moment I'm living here. I've got another house, but...'

'But?'

She sighed. 'I just don't like going back there in the dark, so I rent it out. And I've been fine here, mostly, but—well, Pete Graham brought it all back a bit.'

'I'm sure. You should have said something. I would have made sure you didn't have to deal with him.'

'James, it's not a problem, I can handle it.'

'Of course you can, but if you don't have to, why should you? And, anyway, what's all this got to do with whether or not you can take a compliment?'

She looked away. 'Well—you've seen the scar. It doesn't exactly enhance me.'

'I disagree,' he said softly. 'It adds another layer to the complex person I'm getting to know—and it certainly doesn't detract from you.'

'Doesn't it?'

'Of course not. Why should it? Has it put anybody else off?'

She couldn't look at him. 'I wouldn't know. I haven't been in a situation where the subject might arise.'

He stared at her. 'What? But—that's not a recent scar.'

'Three years old—nearly four.'

'And...' He frowned, then shook his head. 'You're unreal.'

The music came to an end, and he stood up and went and rummaged through her CDs. 'Choose what you like,' she told him, wondering what he'd go for, and to her surprise he put on an album of love songs that she'd bought in a lonely moment, and came back to her and held out his hand, his eyes unreadable in the soft lighting.

'Dance with me,' he murmured.

Her heart lurched. 'Really? Here?'

'Why not?' he asked softly. 'It's better here. Nobody can see us.'

Because it was crazy, and silly, and so, so dangerous. If she touched him, she'd be lost. But she'd been dying to dance with him again, and he was just there, looking so damn sexy she couldn't resist him. And he didn't care about her scar...

She took his hand, let him pull her to her feet and moved into his arms, resting her head on his shoulder and feeling the fine, soft cotton of his shirt under her cheek. Her nose was close to his throat, and she could smell the clean citrus tang of his aftershave and the undercurrent of his own personal scent, warm and intoxicating. She rested her hands against his sides, her fingers splayed against his ribs, and she felt his breath ease out, teasing her hair, warm against her ear.

'You smell wonderful,' he murmured, nuzzling her cheek, his voice low and gruff and incredibly sexy.

She felt the brush of his thighs, the shift of his ribcage under her fingers, the heat of his hands against her waist, and then they slid down, cupping her bottom and easing her closer, and she felt heat pool low down in her body at the intimate contact.

'Kate?'

She lifted her head a fraction and his jaw grazed her forehead, the stubble just rough enough to excite. The touch of his lips was warm and gentle, coaxing as they glided over her skin, down her nose, across her cheek, then back again, drifting over her mouth, backwards and forwards, until finally they settled.

Her lips parted, and with a muffled sigh he lifted his hands and tunnelled his fingers through her hair, holding her steady as he deepened the kiss and took her mouth with a hunger that both terrified and excited her.

She'd *never* been kissed like this, as if he'd die without her, and it was shocking and wonderful and incredibly potent. She lifted a hand to his jaw, loving the feel of it, smooth and yet rough against her palm, driving her higher. She needed more than this, needed to kiss him back, needed...

Sliding her hand around the back of his neck, she pulled him down harder against her, opening her mouth to the full onslaught of his.

It was like putting a match to tinder. One of his hands slid down, cupping her bottom and lifting her hard against him, and she gasped at the shockingly intimate contact of her body with his. She could feel his response, knew what it was doing to him, what it was doing to her, also, and her resistance crumbled.

What resistance? She didn't *want* to resist. She wanted James—here, now, no questions asked. She needed him.

She'd die without him.

He drew away, lifting his head a fraction and resting his forehead against hers while his chest rose and fell against hers and his breath was hot against her face.

'Kate, this is getting out of hand,' he said raggedly.

'Yes.'

'You'd better stop me now.'

'No.'

He groaned softly, then lifted his head a little more and stared down into her eyes. 'Are you sure? We can't undo this later.'

'Do you want to?'

'No. Hell, no. I want to take you upstairs to your room and make love to every single square inch of you.'

Delicious promise shivered over her, leaving her strung tight with anticipation, and she stared up into his eyes, his pupils black, rimmed with blue fire. His lips were parted, his face taut, and she could feel his self-control making his body tremble under her hands.

She slid her hand down his arm, threaded her fingers through his and led him up the stairs to her room.

She didn't turn on the light, but the moon was full and the light poured through the roof window and streamed across the bed, silvering everything it touched.

She turned to him, freeing the buttons of his shirt one by one, taking out the cufflinks and throwing them aside, then running her hands slowly over his chest, his shoulders, his arms, back down to the bottom of his ribcage, turning her hands over so her knuckles grazed his skin and made him suck in his breath.

'Kate...'

'Shh.'

Suddenly brave, her eyes locked with his and she let her fingers explore him, finding the catch on his trousers and freeing it, sliding the zip down slowly, so slowly, while he held his breath and stared back at her with those mesmerising, fiery eyes.

The backs of her fingers brushed the thick, solid ridge of his erection, and he exhaled sharply and took her hands and lifted them away.

'Enough,' he grated. 'Please. I need to see you.'

His arms went round her, his fingers searching while she waited impatiently, unable to think about anything except being close to him. 'How the hell do I get into this?' he growled, and she remembered.

'Side,' she said, lifting her arm, and he found the tab and unzipped it, then grasping the fabric, he tugged her dress down. For a moment it resisted, then slid away and puddled at her feet, and he sucked in his breath, his eyes fixed on her.

Oh, Lord. Her scar. She'd forgotten...

He reached out a hand and touched not the scar but one

breast, his thumb skimming lightly over the tip, making the air lodge in her throat.

'James...'

'I want you so much,' he muttered unevenly.

His head bent, and she felt the warmth of his breath on her skin just moments before his tongue brushed her nipple, circling it, teasing it as his thumb had done. Then he drew it into his mouth and suckled it, while his other hand cupped and kneaded the other one, rolling her nipple between finger and thumb until she thought the sensation would push her right over the edge.

Her legs buckled, and he caught her and lifted her, putting her down in the middle of the bed and carrying right on exploring her with his mouth. His lips moved on, over her ribs, feathering a gentle, healing kiss along the scar before moving down, his breath hot across her abdomen. His fingers traced the edge of the audacious red French knickers she'd been wearing under the dress.

'You wicked woman,' he murmured, running his finger round the loose leg, grazing her most sensitive spot with the back of his knuckle, making her gasp. 'Oh, yes,' he whispered. Bending his head, he laid his mouth over the aching mound and blew hot breath on her, so that she cried out, bucking under his hands.

'James, please...'

'I thought you'd never ask,' he teased, but his voice was tight with control, and as he shucked off his trousers and reached for the pocket, she felt her heart nearly stop.

Oh, it had been so long. What if she disappointed him? What if—

His hand slid over her, curling around her breast, down over her ribs, across the flat plane of her abdomen, then on, catching the lacy knickers and peeling them away as he ran his hand slowly, firmly down her legs and over her feet, then drew his hand back up, his fingertips skimming the spot behind her knee that seemed to link with every erogenous zone she had and set them all on fire.

Then he parted her legs, kneeling between them and staring down at her, his breath coming hard and fast. She couldn't see his eyes, but she could feel the burning intensity of them as he lowered himself down and touched her, his hand testing her, parting her, making way for the long, slow thrust of his body entering hers.

'Kate...'

Her name was a breath on his lips, and she wrapped herself around him and drew him in, her heart opening to him as surely as her body, and then he started to move, slowly at first, then faster, harder, carrying her along until she felt the first tightening of her orgasm claiming her.

'James!' she sobbed, and then he was with her, driving her over the edge, his body shuddering against her in release, until at last he rolled to his side, drawing her with him. Pressing his lips to hers, he cradled her close against his chest until their breathing slowed and their hearts settled and the silence of the night enfolded them...

CHAPTER SEVEN

HE DUCKED out of lunch with Dan and his girlfriend, taking the children over to the house instead to check that everything was all right, and then doing some work in the garden.

It was a lovely day, and he felt full of energy and life and hope.

Not that he thought anything would come of his relationship with Kate. She'd made it clear that she wasn't ready yet to settle down and have a family, and the one thing he could be sure of was that he had a family!

But their love-making had been spectacular, and he wasn't sure he could sit at her parents' table and have a civilised conversation with the frantic, desperate sounds she'd made last night still echoing in his ears. So he dressed the children up warmly, and they ran about in the garden and dug in the sandpit and Freya went on the swing and Rory pushed her, and he cleared the dead leaves and stems from the perennials and cut back some of the shrubs and started a bonfire, and then they went and bought burgers and shoestring fries for lunch and watched the fire burn down.

Then, when the sun started to get low in the sky, he took them back to Kate's. There was a sports car on the drive when they pulled in, and Andrew was at the woodpile with a huge log basket. He straightened up and waved as they got out of the car.

'James! We missed you at lunch. Have you had a good time?'

'Wonderful, thank you. We've been in the garden.'

'Well, come on in, we're in the drawing room—Sue's just made a pot of tea and there's cake and all sorts, not that anybody'll be able to eat another thing, but you know how she is. Come and join us and warm up.'

He glanced down at their clothes and shook his head ruefully.

'We're not really dressed for it, Andrew.'

'Nonsense! You're fine. Come on in. Dan's girlfriend's got a little boy just Rory's age. They'll have fun together.'

It was impossible to refuse without sounding rude, but he at least had to stall.

'I need to change Freya's nappy, and we really are grubby. Can you give us five minutes?'

'Of course. Take as long as you like, and let yourselves in—just follow the noise.'

He looked gorgeous—windswept and ruddy and full of the outdoors, and it suited him.

Kate smiled at him as he came in, and patted the sofa beside her, and after he'd greeted everyone and been introduced to Dan and Rachel and her little boy Sean, he sat down beside her with a muffled groan.

'Hi, there.'

'Hello again. Are you all right? I gather you've been gardening.'

'I have—and I haven't done it for years, so just about everything hurts!'

She chuckled. 'But you had a good day?'

'Great. We've cleared up a lot of the garden, and we had a fire.'

'I know, I can smell the woodsmoke on you, and you've got some colour in your cheeks, all of you. It sounds like you've had fun,' she said wistfully.

'We have. I'll probably regret it for a few days, but we had a good time.'

She hesitated. 'I don't like to spoil it, but I had a phone call from the hospital.'

He frowned and went still. 'About?'

'Tracy Farthing—her boyfriend was so grossed out by the idea of the hairball that he dumped her, so she tried to hang herself in the bathroom from her IV line.'

He dropped his head back and closed his eyes. 'Oh, my God. Poor little kid. Are Psych on it?'

'Oh, yes, but she's very distressed.'

'I'm sure she is, and it won't help her at all.'

'No, it won't,' she agreed. 'What an idiot.'

'Her or the boyfriend?'

'Both, but I meant him. What is wrong with people that they have to hurt each other all the time?'

'He probably just needs some counselling himself. I think it was quite a serious relationship. I had a chat with her. You know they were sleeping together?'

'That doesn't necessarily mean it's serious,' she said. Why should it? James had slept with her last night, but she was under no illusions about the long-term nature of their relationship. After all, he'd run a mile that morning rather than have lunch with her family.

'I think she was serious,' he said thoughtfully. 'Maybe more than him, I don't know. Kids are complicated, and hormones are dreadful things.'

'Not always,' she murmured, and she saw his eyes flare.

'No, not always,' he agreed with a lazy smile. Turning his attention back to the children, he drank his tea and made polite conversation with her family while all she could think about was getting him away from them, settling the children for the night and taking him back to bed.

He went and saw Tracy on Monday morning, and found her subdued and miserable.

'Hiya,' he said, and perched on the edge of her bed. 'You've had a bit of an eventful weekend, I hear. I'm sorry about your boyfriend.'

She turned her head away. 'He said I'm disgusting.'

'You're not disgusting, Tracy. You didn't even know you were doing it and, anyway, it's not so much disgusting as worrying, because it can make you ill. Do you think it would help if I talked to him?'

'The shrink was going to do that, but he wouldn't see him. Anyway, it's over. I'm dumped, and that's that.'

Her voice broke, and she started to cry, but then pulled herself together and sat up carefully. 'I'm all right, Mr McEwan. I'll be OK. I'm not going to try anything silly like that again.'

He wasn't in the least bit sure she was OK, but he left her, promising to have a word with her boyfriend if he wanted to talk about it, and he went back down to the main surgical unit to catch up with Kate.

'So how is she?' she asked.

He shrugged. 'Pretty down. I said I'd try to have a word with the boyfriend if he comes in—maybe ring him if he doesn't. I might be able to get through to him.'

'When the others haven't?' she asked, looking doubtful.

'Well, it's worth a try. The whole mental health team seems to be female, so are most of the ward staff—I just thought maybe, being a man, he might be more likely to listen to me and I might be able to bring a different perspective to it.'

'Well, as you say, it's worth a try.'

'If he even agrees to speak to me, which is a bit of a shot in the dark. So, how is it down here? Anything I should know about?'

'Pete Graham—he's looking good. I was hoping we could discharge him now the brother's out of the way. His mother said he can go home and she'll look after him. He lives in a bedsit or something, so as long as he does go home to her, that's fine with me. Do you agree?'

He felt his eyebrow climb. 'You're asking my opinion?'

She smiled wryly. 'Only for a male perspective, since we're on the subject. So—do you think he's ready?'

'I think he's ready to be discharged, but only if the brother really is out of the way. We don't want him getting bail and going back for another go.'

'No, we don't, but we can't babysit the man, he's twenty-four and it's up to the police to make sure he's safe, not us. If you think he's fit, then he goes. We need the bed.'

'We always need the beds,' he pointed out, and wondered if she really thought Peter was ready or just wanted him out of the way, because of the uncomfortable reminders. No. He was ready. And they couldn't babysit him, she was right. 'OK, let's send him home and clear the bed. Did they have a busy weekend?'

'Looks like it. Let's hope tonight isn't busy, because we're on. Will your mother be able to look after the children?'

He shrugged. 'I don't know. I haven't spoken to her for a

day or two. To be honest I'm so frustrated with her I don't know what to think. Is it all right if she stays at the barn? Assuming I can get her to do it.'

'Of course it is! Don't be silly. Ring her and sort it out, James, and if she can't do it, bribe your childminder, because if we're busy, I'm going to need you.'

He gave her a keen look, then nodded and walked away, and she sighed. She couldn't stop being his boss just because they were sleeping together.

Or had done for two nights.

Not even slept, because of the children. Each time he'd gone back to his room afterwards and stayed there in case they woke, and she'd missed him.

Stupid. Stupid, stupid woman. Fancy letting him get so deeply under her skin so quickly. It didn't help that he was so damned good at it. No other man had ever made her feel the way he did, as if she'd die if he didn't touch her, and it wasn't even just that. There were the kids, as well, and she could so easily imagine them all together.

She picked up a pile of notes, glanced through them and made her way to her office. She'd catch up on some paperwork before her clinic started. If she didn't do it now, she'd never get it done.

And it would take her mind off James and his all too enchanting family.

'Mum, of course I'm speaking to you.'

'But only because you need me.'

He sighed. 'That's rubbish and you know it. We went into this knowing it was going to be hard, and you agreed to be there for them when I'm on call. If I'd known you were going to…' He broke off, and mentally changed 'be' to 'find it'. 'Find it so difficult, I would have made other arrangements in advance, or not taken the job. It's only for four months. Please, don't let me down.'

'It's not a case of letting you down.'

'Well, what the hell would you call it?' he said, hanging on to his temper with difficulty. 'If you really don't want to help us, then I'll see what I can set up for the New Year, but until then, I don't really see what else I can do. Kate's giving me grief as it is, and I don't want to annoy her any more than I have to. But I need to do this, and you need to help me, and accept that it won't be easy, that I'm a lone parent and there will be compromises. It can't be helped.'

'James, I find it so hard,' she said, sounding even more distressed. 'If only you hadn't let Beth die—if you'd made her have the treatment—'

He sighed shortly and rammed his hand through his hair. 'I didn't let Beth die, Mum, you know that. You know how much I loved her. It just happened. I had no say in it.'

'You could have made her get rid of Freya.'

'No. No, I couldn't have made her get rid of Freya, and I wouldn't have done. Anyway, it was too late, you know that. If she'd wanted a termination, I would have supported her, but she didn't. And it wasn't easy for any of us, and it won't be, ever, but it's the way it is and we have to move on. And I'm moving on. We've got a new house, I'm getting back to work, I'm making a new life for us all. And we need your help. Please. I can't do this without you, and you promised. God knows, I haven't asked you for much.'

His mother was silent for a moment, then she sighed. 'All right. I'll do it for now, but I'm really very uncomfortable about it, James. Freya's so unhappy.'

'No. She's not unhappy. She's fine. She's just a bit clingy, and she's getting better every day. Just see it through, Mum, please. Don't make it any harder. I'll pick them up from the childminder tonight and come round to you, then take you back to the barn and show you where everything is. If you could be ready at six, that would be good. I'll see you later.'

He hung up, let his breath out on a growl of frustration and slouched back in the chair.

'That sounded like a prelude to World War Three,' Kate said from behind him, and he spun the chair round and stared at her in horror, scrolling back through the conversation and groaning mentally.

'How long have you been there?'

'Long enough. She's giving you a hard time.'

'Yeah. She is, and there's nothing I can do about it. She's got this bee in her bonnet about me not being able to look after them, and every time she gets like this, it makes it true. So you're right. My child care is precarious.'

'Perhaps you need a nanny,' she suggested, settling on the edge of the desk, too close for his peace of mind. He made himself concentrate.

'No. Too much power. It was a disaster before—and, anyway, our house isn't fit for a nanny to live in. I can see me interviewing them in it. They'd run a mile.'

She laughed. 'It's not for long, and it's going to be lovely. Any idea when the plumber can do your boiler?'

'And the rest,' he said morosely. 'It should be finished some time in January, hopefully. Why? Is there a problem with the barn?'

'No, not at all. I was going to suggest that you move into my side for Christmas, and the gang can have your side, unless you think the children would be very disrupted by that, in which case I can come to you and we'll all share, but it will be a bit of a squash.'

'I can take them home...'

'Don't be silly, you'll freeze. Anyway, you're with us for Christmas so you may as well be staying there.'

'Are we?' He knew Sue had said something about it, but he wasn't aware of having accepted. 'Is your mother expecting us?'

'I thought so, and if your mother's elsewhere and you've got nothing better planned, you may as well join us. You're all more than welcome, and the kids'll love it, James. There'll be so many little ones for them to play with, and they'll all adore Freya. She'll be the baby of the family and she'll be spoiled to death.'

The baby of the family? Was that how she saw them? As part of the family?

He felt a longing so great it was almost a pain, and the idea of spending another lonely Christmas was just too much to contemplate.

'If you're sure.'

'Of course I'm sure. Mum would skin me if you didn't join us. And now, if you've finished with my desk, I've got letters to write. In fact, you could do some of them, they're your patients.'

And she handed him a sheaf of notes, shooed him out of her chair and settled down to dictate into a little hand-held recorder.

'Have you got another one of those?'

She opened the drawer, pulled out a second one and lobbed it at him. He caught it one-handed, tested it and, dropping into the chair on the other side of the desk, he flicked open the notes, refreshed his memory and started to dictate.

A few minutes later he realised she'd stopped talking and was watching him thoughtfully.

'What?'

'There's a job coming up.'

He frowned. 'Really?'

'Really. They're looking for a new consultant general surgeon, and they've asked me what I think about you.'

He put the recorder down slowly. 'And?'

She met his eyes frankly. 'I told them I had reservations about your child-care arrangements, but that in principle I thought you'd be an excellent choice.'

He sighed and ran a hand over his face. And she'd had to come in and hear him rowing with his mother over that very subject. Damn.

'What? Did you expect me to lie to them, James, just because we're sleeping together?'

He dropped his hand and stared at her. 'No. Not at all. I'd rather you didn't. It's only the truth. In fact, if us having a relationship outside work is going to make things awkward for you, then perhaps I should find alternative accommodation and we'll cool it off. I don't want you feeling compromised.'

Her eyes widened slightly, then she looked away. 'It's entirely up to you what you do about your accommodation, but you're more than welcome to stay. I've told you that over and over again.'

'And the rest?' he asked softly.

She swallowed. 'Again, that's up to you. If you decide you'd rather not go on, then just say so. And don't worry about me. It's separate, and I'm capable of keeping it that way. It's just a question of whether you are.'

'But what do you want?'

She met his eyes, but hers were so guarded he couldn't tell

what she was thinking. 'What do I want? I want you to do whatever you feel is right.'

'Then we keep it separate, and we carry on,' he told her, because the alternative, to lose that amazing vibrant warmth from his life, was too hard to contemplate.

She heard his pager bleeping at one twenty-five.

His bedroom was next to hers, just through the wall, and she could hear the soft murmur of his voice, then the sounds of him moving around.

And then she heard Freya cry, and his footsteps on the landing, and then his mother's voice remonstrating with him.

'I have to go!' he said, raising his voice so she could hear him clearly, then his mother replied, her voice tearful.

'James, I can't do this! She's getting so upset.'

'Mum, we've talked about this over and over again. I have to go to work.'

'James, please.'

Kate pulled on her dressing-gown and tapped on the communicating door. 'James? Let me in.'

It swung open, and he stood there, his eyes tormented, Freya in his arms, an older woman hovering in the background, twisting her hands.

'Give her to me,' Kate said, taking the baby from him. 'Now go. I'll join you later.'

'But—'

'No buts. Go.'

'I owe you.'

'I know.'

He sighed sharply, kissed Freya on the cheek and ran down the stairs. Seconds later the door banged behind him, and his car drove away, leaving them in silence.

'Right, sweetheart, let's get you back to bed,' she said to the gently grizzling Freya, and, kissing her soft, downy cheek, she tucked her back into her cot, covered her up and left her.

There was a little wail of protest, but nothing untoward, and she stood on the landing outside the partially open door and met James's mother's anguished eyes.

'You probably think I'm dreadful,' Mrs McEwan said unhappily.

'No. I think you're not very supportive of your son, but you obviously have your reasons for that, and they're none of my business. What is my business is getting him to work when he's meant to, so he can fulfil his contract, and I understood you had an agreement, so if you suddenly find you can't stick to that and you're going to let him down and make it even more difficult for him to keep his family intact, then I think that's somewhat unfair.'

'But I can't,' she said, and to Kate's complete astonishment, she started to cry.

'Come on, let's go and put the kettle on. You need to talk about this.' She put a hand on her shoulder and steered her towards the stairs, and once they were down in the kitchen she put the kettle on and settled back against the worktop while Mrs McEwan blew her nose and pulled herself together.

'Beth was so lovely. They were such a wonderful family,' she said unsteadily, 'and then this dreadful disease got hold of her and he just let her carry on with the baby, and if he hadn't, if he'd saved her—but they didn't even try, and now he wants me to support him, and I can't do it. I'm worried about my sister, and she wants me to spend time with her, and James needs me, and I can't deal with it on my own at night when he has to go. The responsibility just terrifies me, and I'm so afraid something dreadful will happen to one of them and it'll be my fault.'

'Right, let's take this one at a time,' Kate said gently but firmly, sitting her down at the kitchen table with a cup of tea.

'One, as I understand it, the cancer had already spread by the time Beth realised, and it was too late to save her, so whatever they'd done, it wouldn't have changed the outcome, it just would have given her more time. Probably only weeks, maybe months at best. And doing nothing, for the sake of Freya, was a very brave thing to do, and it must have torn James apart to sit there and watch it happen, knowing he was just going to lose her even sooner, but it was what she wanted, what she felt was right, and he supported her decision. I think that shows immense courage and fortitude, and you should be very proud of him.'

His mother stared at her, and then her eyes filled again. 'I am proud of him, but I can't be Beth.'

'He doesn't want you to be Beth. He wants you to be his mother, and you can do that. You can look after the children—you just need to be firmer. Freya doesn't miss her mother, she never knew her, and Rory's as good as gold. He sleeps through the night, he's happy and well adjusted—they really aren't a problem. They're a good family unit, and you really shouldn't try to undermine that because you haven't got the confidence to do what James is asking of you.'

'But I can't do it!'

'Then you need to tell him why. You need to tell him that you're afraid, and not tell him that he isn't in a position to keep his children, because losing them would destroy him, you know. He loves them so much, he's absolutely devoted to them, and he's only trying to do his job and maintain their quality of life. He's not trying to be unreasonable, but if you really are afraid to help him or too worried about your sister to feel able to give him the time he needs, then you need to explain that. I'm sure he'll understand, and he can make other arrangements, but it might take time. As long as he's here my parents are just over there in the farmhouse, and if you really couldn't cope, they'd give you a hand, but—Mrs McEwan, there's a permanent job coming up, and I think he should have it, but while there's this uncertainty hanging over him, I can't recommend him without reservation.'

Mrs McEwan stared at Kate for an age, then shook her head. 'I don't know what to do. I just know I can't.'

'What exactly are you afraid of?'

She huddled her arms around herself miserably. 'I don't know. What if the baby was sick and choked? Or got meningitis and I didn't realise? And what if Rory did something dangerous and fell or burnt himself or something? It's so silly,' she said, wringing her hands, 'but I feel like a new mother—that I don't know what to do, and I get so tired, but I don't know how to settle them if they wake.'

'Just be firm. Listen—what can you hear?'

There was absolute silence, apart from the ticking of the clock on the wall, and she stared at Kate.

'She's gone back to sleep!' she said, looking stunned.

'Of course she has. She had a busy day. She needs her sleep, and so do you. Don't pander to her, and she won't expect it.'

'That's what James always says.'

'Then maybe he has a point,' she said with a wry smile. 'She's his daughter, he's looked after her from day one. I think perhaps he knows her.' She lifted her head. 'That's my pager. It must be a big one. I'm going to have to go—will you be all right, Mrs McEwan, or do you want me to ring my mother? My parents are just over there, they won't mind.'

'No. No—I'll manage.'

'Look, I'll leave you the number so you can ring them if there's a problem, but I really don't think there will be,' she said, scribbling it on the back of an envelope. 'There. Call them if you need them.'

She nodded. 'Thank you, Kate. I'm sorry I've been such a nuisance. I really don't want to spoil his chances of a job, but—'

'Just talk to him. I have to go. Go back to bed and get some rest.'

She ran upstairs and through to her side, looked at her pager and dressed quickly. She was needed in Theatre, two victims of an RTA with internal injuries needing surgery, one of them pregnant, and James's mother would just have to cope.

He felt sick.

His mother was bottling out on him, he'd had to call Kate in because Jo didn't have enough experience to deal with the emergencies, and all he could see was Kate's implacable eyes when she'd taken Freya from him. If it hadn't been for her, he'd still be standing on the landing, arguing with his mother, and he just couldn't do it any more.

There was no way he could struggle through to the end of this contract, far less take the consultancy if he was offered it, and he felt gutted. He loved his work, he needed it. It was the only thing that kept him sane—apart from Kate—and after the fiasco on the landing that was no doubt all about to come to a crashing halt.

'What have we got?'

He gave a sigh of relief at the sound of her voice, calm and businesslike and in control. He met her eyes, and saw just cool caramel, and knew that it was all right. For now.

'Twenty-five-year-old male driver with ruptured diaphragm

and lacerated liver, and a twenty-six-year-old pregnant female passenger who's nearing term. I don't like the look of her at all, but there's nothing obvious and the ultrasound wasn't showing anything serious like a placental abruption. Yet. She's under observation and I've called for an obstetrician and got six units cross-matched to be on the safe side, but she might have splenic injuries. I'm not sure, but she's all right for now and the driver isn't, which is why I started on him—and he's got a fractured right radius and ulna as well that the orthos are going to deal with shortly.'

'OK. Can we have some music on, please? A nice bit of rock, I think.'

He met her calm, clear eyes. 'Rock?'

'Is that OK?'

He could have kissed her. 'That's fine.'

'Right, how far have you got?'

'I've clamped the liver to stop it bleeding. I'm just about to repair the diaphragm and then I'll go back to the liver and suture it properly.'

'OK, you lead, I'll assist, and when you're OK I'll go and see your pregnant lady.'

He nodded, put his child-care issues and the future of his career out his mind and concentrated on saving a young man's life.

'I don't like the look of her.'

'No. I agree. But is it abdominal or obstetric?'

He shrugged. 'I don't know. Where the hell is the obstetrician?'

'Pressure's dropping.'

'Kate, we've got to open her up and find out,' James said decisively, and she nodded.

'Want me to lead?'

'If you like.'

She didn't. Not really. It was the sort of situation where things could go wrong very fast, and although the baby's heartbeat was fine at the moment, she was very wary. Where *was* the obstetrician? 'We'd better call Obs again, and get a neonatal team standing by just in case. Are there any SCBU beds available?'

'I have no idea,' he muttered, scrubbing fast. 'This is ridiculous. Where are they?'

'I'll chase them up,' one of the theatre nurses said. Kate nodded. She was the only person who wasn't scrubbing or busy, and they didn't have time to waste. She was going downhill fast.

Faster than they'd realised, and when Kate opened her abdomen, there was nothing to indicate such a sudden deterioration.

'OK, she's got a ruptured spleen, but it's encapsulated, and there's no free blood in the abdomen. It must be obstetric,' she muttered.

'She's crashing,' the anaesthetist warned simultaneously, and James frowned, whipped back the drapes and swore.

'She's bleeding. She must have a placental abruption. We can't wait, I'll have to do a C-section. Can you stall the spleen?'

'Sure. Someone chase Obs and SCBU, please!' she snapped, and then a paediatrician came in, followed by a neonatal nurse pushing a crib.

'Thank God for small mercies. Suction!' James said, and Kate desperately tried to deal with the flood of blood and amniotic fluid as he opened the uterus and wriggled the baby free, passing it to the waiting paediatrician.

'Syntocinon!' he snapped. 'We're going to lose her if we can't get this bleeding stopped! Kate, deal with this.' And he handed her the placenta, grabbed a large pack and pressed it hard down on the inside of the uterine wall over the haemorrhage while the anaesthetist injected Syntocinon into her thigh to make her uterus contract.

Then a thin wail pierced the air, and he closed his eyes and laughed softly under his breath. 'Now, that's music to my ears,' he murmured, and, looking up, he met her eyes and smiled. 'So. That's one of them safe. Now, what's happening under here?'

He lifted the pack cautiously, and to their relief the site was just welling gently. As they watched, the uterus started contracting and the flow stopped completely. His shoulders dropped.

'OK. I think we're out of the woods, but I'll let the obstetrician check the placenta and close the uterus. Does anyone know where he is?'

'Delivering triplets, but he's nearly done. They're all out and fine. I'm in two places at once,' the paediatrician said with a wry grin. 'Still, this little chap looks good and he won't need me. We'll get him shipped up to SCBU and check him over thoroughly. Well done, guys. Not bad for a GS team.'

James snorted, but Kate couldn't keep the grin off her face.

There was no way she could have done that—well, not with his confidence. She hadn't done a C-section for years, and then only a few. He'd been fantastic—calm, decisive, confident.

He deserved that job—and if it was anything to do with her, she'd make sure he got it...

CHAPTER EIGHT

IT WAS like waiting for the other shoe to drop.

For three hours, she'd said nothing that wasn't directly connected to what they were doing, but now it was over, and he straightened up, walked away from the table and stripped off his gloves and gown and hat, chucking them in the bin as he passed.

He'd finished the driver alone while Kate checked the pregnant woman, then they'd left the driver with the orthopaedic surgeon and moved with the pregnant woman to the theatre next door, because there hadn't been time to wait.

And thank God they'd had that other theatre available.

She'd left him and the obstetrician closing and gone to check the driver in Recovery, and now everything was under control.

Except his private life.

'Good work, McEwan. That was...amazing.'

She was sitting in the staffroom, fingers curled around a mug of coffee, and he helped himself to one and sat down beside her, his head tipped back against the wall and his eyes closed, drained now that the adrenaline rush was over.

'I only did what anybody else would have done.'

'No. I couldn't have done it. I don't think I could have

remembered where to start—James, you were fantastic. You saved that baby's life—and the mother's.'

He turned his head and looked at her in astonishment, then smiled wryly. 'I've probably seen a C-section more recently than you, don't forget. Freya's only eighteen months old. And don't run away with the idea that I wasn't scared to death, because I was. Well, sort of. There wasn't a lot of time for that. Still, it worked, thankfully, and everything seems fine now. And I couldn't have done it alone, so thanks for coming in.'

She smiled, her eyes warm and approving. 'My pleasure. I haven't had so much excitement in years, and I wouldn't have missed it for the world.'

He grunted and sat up, taking a long slug of coffee and sighing before meeting her eyes again. 'Look—I'm sorry about earlier. I'm going to have to do something about this.'

Her smiled faded and she pressed her lips together and nodded. 'You are. You need to talk to your mother. She's scared of the responsibility, you know.'

He stared at her incredulously, unable to believe his ears. 'What?'

'You heard. She's worried there'll be an emergency and she won't know what to do, and she's frightened she won't cope alone.'

He closed his eyes and dragged his free hand over his face. 'Oh, that's crazy. She can't be serious.'

'She is—deadly serious. It's not you she thinks can't look after the children, it's her, and she doesn't know how to tell you.'

'Is that what this is all about? Good grief. So how was she when you handed Freya back to her and went out?'

'Fine—and I didn't hand Freya back to her, I put her back

to bed and she went straight to sleep. She whinged for about a minute, tops, and your mother was amazed.'

He laughed, unable to believe it. 'Just like that? How did you know that? I mean, I know that, but she's my daughter. You don't do kids. You're too busy ticking your boxes.'

She gave a wry laugh. 'That's what you think. I've been brought up with random children arriving in the house from who knows what kind of circumstances for almost my entire life, and getting kids back to sleep when they wake in the night is second nature to me. And the only thing wrong with Freya was that she'd been disturbed and wanted to go back to sleep.'

He shook his head in disbelief. 'You're a marvel. I leave you alone with my family for five minutes and you've got them all sorted out. I should hire you.'

'In your dreams, McEwan,' she said drily, and he snorted.

She was in his dreams, all right. In his dreams, in his thoughts, in his arms. She was so deeply enmeshed in his life he couldn't imagine what he'd do without her. He put that out of his mind and turned towards her. 'So—what do I do about my mother, oh wise one?'

'Well, I left her with my parents' phone number in case of emergencies, but she really isn't confident. Which is silly, because I'm sure she's perfectly capable. She brought you up, didn't she, and you survived.'

'Mmm. Maybe that's the trouble,' he murmured. 'I was a horror. Rory's a total angel compared to me. If there was something to climb, I was up it, and if there was something dirty or muddy, I was in it. By the time I was five I'd broken both arms, been in hospital with concussion and nearly killed myself falling down a cliff. And I took everything to bits. I took the iron to bits when I was six and turned it on to see how it worked, and set fire to the ironing board. It's a miracle no one was killed. They got me a really complicated construction set after that to keep my fingers out of mischief, and enrolled me in the Cubs. At least it gave them one night a week when they didn't have to worry.'

'Poor woman,' she said, smiling sympathetically. 'No wonder she's so stressed. You've damaged her for life.'

'I'd better ring her—apologise for yelling at her.'

'It might be an idea. And you need to sit down and have a nice long chat and see where you go from here, because I really think she'll struggle to have them for a whole weekend—and we're on this weekend. And, no, I can't manage without you. You've seen the sort of thing that can go wrong, and Jo just hasn't got the experience to handle it.'

His relief evaporated, and with a heavy sigh he got to his feet. 'I hadn't forgotten. Don't worry, Kate, I'll sort something out—get some back-up of some sort. Maybe Helen can have them. And in the New Year I'll get a nanny. I want that job—and I intend to get it, if there's the slightest chance. So I will get it sorted. Properly.'

She studied him in silence for a moment, then gave him an enigmatic smile. 'I know you will. Now, go and ring her, and I'll check the post-ops again, and then we'd better go and get ready for the day.'

After the events of the night, the day was relatively peaceful.

Their two RTA victims were doing well and had met their new baby, and when he went up to check on them, they were both highly emotional and almost embarrassingly grateful.

'Thank you so much. I don't know what I would have done if I'd lost them both,' the driver whispered unsteadily.

'My pleasure. You just concentrate on getting better and enjoying the baby.'

He left them to it and went to see Tracy, and found her sitting up in her chair looking hugely better.

'Hey! Nice haircut. You look fabulous,' he said, sitting down on the edge of her bed and admiring the short, choppy style—a much safer choice for someone with trichophagia, and the first line of defence, usually, so he wasn't surprised to see it.

She touched it self-consciously, but she looked pleased. 'I'm going to have it coloured. Mum said I can have highlights, but I want to do it purple.'

He laughed. 'Well, it's your hair, but are you sure purple would suit you? You're quite pale. The highlights might look more sophisticated, but you've got to do what makes you feel best.'

'You think highlights?'

'Whatever. It's not my hair, but the good thing about it is, whatever you do, it'll grow out. How are you otherwise?'

'Better. My stomach's stopped hurting, and I can eat now, just sloppy stuff, but I'm so hungry. I haven't really been eating for ages, and Mum says I need to catch up.'

'You do, but take it easy and don't have too much at once for a while. Let your stomach heal, and you need to keep taking the pills to stop your stomach acid from damaging the wall until it's healed properly. The dietician will give you a list of things to avoid for a while, but you need to play it by ear and only eat the things that don't upset you. Apart from that, as far as I'm concerned you're doing really well, and the mental health team are happy to treat you as an outpatient, so you could go home today or tomorrow if you feel ready.' He hesitated, then said, 'Any word from your boyfriend?'

She shook her head. 'My friend said he's really sad.'

'Then maybe you need to ring him—or give me his number. Let me talk to him.'

She scribbled it on a piece of paper, and he put it in his pocket and stood up. 'You take care—and I want to see the hair when you come back to Outpatients for a check-up.'

He went back to Kate's office and rang the number, but it went straight to the answering machine. Lessons, he thought, realising that the lad was still at school. He'd try him later. He couldn't get his mother, either, so she'd probably gone to Cambridge to visit her sister.

Which meant there was nothing for it but paperwork—starting with Tracy's discharge.

'Kate?'

'James, hi. Are you OK?'

His laugh sounded a little off-kilter, and she sat up straighter. 'What's happened?'

'Um—you know that car you had, that was like my life? Well, another bit just fell off it. Are you busy?'

'No-o,' she said cautiously. 'Why?'

'Because I've been a complete idiot, and I'm stuck. I put petrol in my car.'

'So?'

'It's a diesel car.'

'Ah.'

'So it has to go to the garage and be pumped out and rinsed through and decontaminated and filters and fuel lines and stuff changed, and it's going to cost a fortune, and I really don't need it right now, and I'm sitting in it with the kids waiting for the recovery truck to come and get me, and

Freya's crying and Rory's hungry and this is going to take ages and I just want to *scream*, really. And I hate to ask, but…'

She laughed, even though it wasn't funny. 'OK, where are you?' she asked, standing up and wriggling her feet into her shoes.

'On the road out to you, just off the bypass. You can't miss us.'

'Give me five minutes.'

She was there in four, and, sure enough, he was standing by the car waiting for her, arms folded over his chest and looking thoroughly disgusted.

'You're a star. I can't believe I was such an idiot.'

'I'm sure it's easily done,' she said. 'Right, kids, come on, let's go home and have some tea while your daddy sorts out his muddle, shall we?'

And scooping up the baby's bag and Rory's booster seat, she installed him in her car while James sorted out Freya and her seat, then she looked at him over the roof. 'I'll see you at home whenever. Don't worry about them, I'll get them into bed if you're still not back—and I'll cook for you.'

His shoulders drooped with relief. 'Thanks. I owe you.'

'Again?' she teased, and, getting into her car, she drove home.

'So what were you doing at school today?' she asked Rory while she loaded the dishwasher.

'Christmas stuff,' he said, little legs swinging under the kitchen table. 'We made cards and angels and things and hung them on the tree.' He put his head on one side and rested it on his hand, studying her earnestly. 'Will you help me write a letter to Father Christmas? You said you would.'

'Yes, sure. It sounds as if Freya's asleep, so we can do it now. Stay here, I'll get some paper.'

She slipped through to her side of the house and went back armed with a sheaf of coloured paper and some pencils, and settled herself down beside him.

'You'd better kneel up so you can reach,' she said, and put some paper in front of him. 'Right, what do you want to say?'

'Dear Father Christmas.'

Well, that was easy. 'Dear Father Christmas,' she repeated slowly as she wrote it out nice and clearly on a separate sheet. 'Right, you copy that, and we'll do the next bit.'

She watched him, his tongue sticking out of the side of his mouth in concentration, and she was sure if she could see behind James's mask when he was operating, he'd be doing the same. It made her smile, and Rory looked up at her and grinned.

'There. Done it. Now "I want".'

'Don't you think it should be, "Please may I have"?' she suggested, and he nodded.

'OK,' she said, and wrote 'Please may I have' on the sheet he was copying from, then turned to him. 'Have what? What do you want to say now?'

'A mummy for Christmas.'

Her heart jammed in her throat, and she felt her eyes fill. 'Oh, Rory, sweetheart—I don't think Father Christmas does mummies,' she said gently, her heart breaking. 'I think he only does toys and stuff like that.'

His face fell, that wonderful sparkle in his eyes dying right away and taking her heart with it. 'But I don't want toys,' he said, sounding bewildered and unbearably disappointed. 'I've got toys. I want a mummy. Grandma always says Freya misses her mummy, and I thought, if we had a mummy, then Freya wouldn't cry when Daddy goes to work and Grandma wouldn't get upset and cry, too, and everybody would be happy, and Daddy wouldn't cry any more. I hear him at night, sometimes, when he thinks we're sleeping, and I hate it.'

'Oh, darling.' She wrapped her arms round him and gave him a hug, and he snuggled into her and stayed there for ages, his face buried in her chest, his little knees pushed up against the sides of her thighs while she rested her cheek against his hair and rubbed his back gently and thought of James crying in the night, and she had to blink the tears away.

She could be his mummy, she thought longingly. She'd love to be his mummy, and Freya's, and live with them and James, and be happy ever after...

She heard a car pull up, and lifted her head. 'That sounds like your daddy now,' she said, and he sat up away from her and stared at the paper.

'I don't want to write to Father Christmas any more,' he said, getting down and screwing up the letter and throwing it at the bin. 'He's rubbish.'

And without another word, he ran away upstairs and went into his room, banging the door shut.

'Hi. I'm sorry I've been so long, but I had to sort out a hire car. Everything all right?'

Kate was sitting at his kitchen table smoothing out a sheet of paper, her eyes anguished, and he felt a sudden flicker of dread.

'What? What is it?'

'We were writing to Father Christmas,' she said, her voice hollow.

He glanced down at the table. 'Dear Father Christmas, please may I have,' he read in Rory's shaky script, the paper crumpled and torn. He looked up at Kate. 'Have what?'

'A mummy for Christmas,' she said, and closed her eyes. A tear slid down her cheek, and he sighed sharply and rammed his hands through his hair.

Whatever next?

'I can't give him a mummy,' he said desperately, his voice cracking. 'They don't just grow on trees. What does he want me to do, get a mail-order bride?' His voice cracked again, and he slammed his fist down on the worktop. Damn. Damn, damn, damn.

'So what did you say to him?'

'I told him Father Christmas only does toys, so he said he's rubbish and ran up to bed. James, I'm so sorry. I didn't know what to say to him.' She scrubbed away the tear with her fingertips, but it was joined by another one and he went over to her and rested his hand on her shoulder.

'Don't cry,' he said gruffly. 'It isn't your fault. I'll go and talk to him.' He dragged in a breath. 'Where's Freya?'

'Asleep.'

Thank God for small mercies, he thought. Leaving Kate there, he ran upstairs and went into Rory's room and found him in a huddle in his bed, Beth's teddy clutched against his chest, sobbing his heart out. 'Hey, come on, where's my brave boy gone?' he asked softly, gathering him into his arms.

'I just wanted a mummy,' he said, and James felt his heart break all over again.

'I know, but we can't always have what we want, and we've got each other and Freya, and we can be happy, Rory. We can. We don't need Father Christmas for that.'

He wasn't sure if he was saying it to his son or to himself, but if saying it could make it true, he'd say it over and over and over again. He lay down beside Rory and pulled him closer, and he snuggled up tight and gradually his little chest stopped hiccuping with sobs and he drifted into sleep.

James didn't. He lay there, emotionally drained and physically exhausted, and wondered when they'd ever get out of the dark tunnel that seemed to be going on for ever.

A light touch on his shoulder startled him, and he turned his head to find Kate looking down at him, her eyes shadowed.

'Are you OK?' she whispered, and he nodded.

'He's asleep. I'll come down.'

He got up off the bed, tucked Rory in and followed Kate down to the kitchen. There was a wonderful smell drifting from the hob, and she'd laid the table.

Like a normal family, he thought a trifle hysterically, and had to stop the runaway thought in its tracks.

'It's only spaghetti sauce that I had in the freezer, and I've got some fresh pasta. I'll cook it now, if you're hungry?'

'Starving,' he confessed. Dropping into a chair, he propped his chin on his hands and sighed. 'What a mess. The house, the car, and now this. When's it going to end, Kate?'

She poured boiling water into a pan, dropped in the pasta and sat down opposite him, sliding a glass of wine across the table to him. 'James, don't give up. You're getting there. It's just because it's Christmas. It's always hard on families in your situation, but it'll soon be next year, and things will pick up.'

'Will they? I need that job, Kate,' he told her, and he could hear the desperation in his voice, but he was powerless to do anything about it. 'I have to work. It's the only thing that keeps me sane and grounded, the only thing I seem to be able to do well.'

'That's rubbish!' she exclaimed. 'You're a wonderful father, James. I've seen you with your children, and you adore them, and they adore you. You're really close, and yet they're normal, well-balanced children.'

'Not according to my mother,' he said.

'Your mother's struggling, James. She's lost her husband, her sister's lost her husband, you've lost your wife—she's going through a bad time, and she's terrified she's going to make it worse by something that she does or doesn't do. She doesn't really think you should give them up, she's just worried for you all and can't see a way out.'

'She's not alone, but we'll get there, you're right. I just need to sort the kids out with some better arrangement.'

'What about asking Helen?' she suggested. 'Maybe she could have them to stay?'

He shook his head. 'I've tried that. She won't. Her husband doesn't mind her looking after other people's children during the day, but at night he draws the line, and I can understand that. It doesn't help me, but I can understand it. I think the only answer is a nanny, but I can't get one this close to Christmas—even if I had anywhere to house one. How's the pasta doing?'

'Oh!' She leapt up, drained it and sighed with relief. 'I think it's OK still. Sorry. Right—parmesan?'

He needed that job.

If ever a man needed a future to look forward to, that man was James.

He didn't make love to Kate that night, just sat with her on the sofa for an hour and then kissed her goodnight at her door. And she'd thought they'd moved beyond that. He hadn't worn his wedding ring since the night of the wedding party, and she'd foolishly allowed herself to attach some significance to it.

Stupid. Clearly there was no significance to it. Maybe he'd just lost it, but, whatever the reason, he wasn't with her tonight. She guessed he was too raw, and Rory's plea to Father Christmas must have brought thoughts of Beth back to the surface.

Damn. Well, she'd known in her heart he was still grieving for her, she'd known it wasn't for ever, but she still felt ludicrously lonely with the bed to herself. Still, that was her problem. Getting the job was his, and if there was a way she could make it work for him, then she had to try it, for all their sakes.

The following night she went over to see her mother while James was putting the children to bed and talking to his mother. 'How do you fancy a job?' she asked, and her mother laughed.

'I don't. Why?'

'I just need James to have reliable child care, and for that he needs a nanny. You must know someone. I wondered if you wanted to come up with a shortlist of people you'd trust.'

She laughed again. 'It would be a short list.'

'Please try.'

'OK. I will. Is this about the new consultant's post?'

Kate nodded. 'I can't put him forward for it until he's sorted, but he needs it so desperately. He's sad, and Rory—' She broke off, and her mother tipped her head on one side.

'Rory?'

So she told Sue about the letter, and her mother clicked her tongue sympathetically. 'Poor little mite. Of course, you could solve the problem at a stroke.'

'How?'

'By volunteering.'

'For what? To be his nanny?'

'No. To be his wife.'

She sat back abruptly. 'His— Mum, you're being ridiculous. He doesn't want another wife. He's still grieving for the first one.'

'Is he? When you came back from the wedding he didn't look to me like a man who was grieving for his wife.'

Damn. Her mother saw too much.

'It's just physical,' she said, looking down at the table and chasing a few grains of salt around with her fingertip. 'I know it's not going anywhere.'

'But you'd like it to.'

'I don't know,' she lied, because she couldn't bear to admit out loud just how much she loved them all, how much he'd fallen for a man and a family wrapped in grief, and how much her heart was breaking every day...

'I spoke to Tracy's boyfriend yesterday,' James said as they paused in a break in their clinic the following morning. 'He said he really missed her, but he just felt sick whenever he thought about it. I suggested he go along with her to see her counsellor, because he's part of her problem, really. If stress is triggering it, and breaking up with him is stressing her, it won't help her at all.'

'And?'

'He's going to talk to her. They're only very young, but they seem to care about each other quite genuinely. We'll have to wait and see. I've done what I can, and at least he's prepared to talk to her now.'

Kate smiled at him, her eyes warm, like caramel. Not toffee. Not any more. The sharp shards seemed to be gone, and the warmth gave him hope. 'Well done,' she said, and he felt a glow inside.

Crazy. She wasn't interested. She'd gone over to her parents' last night, and after his mother had gone he'd hoped she'd come through to see him, but she hadn't, and he'd ended up going to bed and reading and wishing he was with her.

Of course he could have tapped on the door himself, but since she'd told him on Monday that she couldn't recommend him for the job without reservation because of his child-care issues, she hadn't been near him. Well, not in that way.

And he missed her. Stupid.

And stupid, of course, for having suggested to her that she might not want to have such a close relationship with him. If he hadn't done that, then she might have come in last night, but maybe not. It put her in a difficult position, after all, if the hospital board was going to be asking her what she thought of him and they were involved to that extent in their personal lives.

Involved?

Was that really the word for the most amazing, astonishing, mind-blowing sex—no, scratch that, relationship—he'd ever had in his life? Hell. He'd loved Beth to bits, but they'd never had what he had with Kate. He'd never felt that he'd die if he couldn't hold her, that the day was colourless if he couldn't be with her, that the nights were endless…

'How did you get on with your mother?' she asked, bringing him slamming back down to earth, and he scrubbed a hand through his hair and shrugged.

'OK. We had a long talk, and she's not really happy.'

'But she will do the weekend?'

He nodded. 'Yes, she'll do the weekend. She did mention your parents as back-up—will they be there?'

'Yes, of course, and they won't mind at all. And if it all goes haywire, I'm sure Mum will step in.'

He felt a wave of relief, but it was short-lived. She couldn't failed to notice hers. She'd lost his father only four years before Beth had died, and he'd been so tied up with his new job and his new wife and his new house that he hadn't really been there for her.

And then she'd had to support him through his own grief, and now her sister was widowed and ill, and he was expecting her to drop everything and deal with a stroppy toddler and an active little boy so he could carry on with his life.

So what kind of a son did that make him?

Selfish and unthinking, he decided, and it didn't taste good.

He bought her a pamper day, as Kate had suggested, and some smellies, and then she took the children off so he could find them a few presents. He also wanted to get something for Kate, and then he saw a pretty little jumper very like her favourite. His favourite, too, and she'd said only the other day that it had a hole in it. This one might be just the thing to replace it.

He didn't even look at the price. He owed her so much that the price was irrelevant and, anyway, he found he was enjoying it. It was such a long time since shopping had been more than a chore, and he was getting into his stride. He found another jumper which he thought would suit his mother—Kate had said get her something pretty, so he did, and he picked up all sorts of little bits and pieces for the children—stockings to hang under the tree, and all manner of things to fill them, and a wooden jigsaw for Freya and a train set for Rory—not the mother he'd asked for, but there was nothing he could do about that, he thought bleakly, and then caught sight of Kate's dark head in the crowd and felt his heart squeeze.

If only…

'I'm shattered,' he said with a groan, unloading the car after he'd brought the children in and got them off to bed.

Kate laughed and eased her shoes off. 'Me, too. It's surprising how much more tiring it is when you've got to keep an eye on a toddler. I'd forgotten. It's a while since I've helped Mum with little ones. I think they had fun, though, don't you?'

'Yes, I'm sure they did, and it's all thanks to you. It was a great idea.'

He hung the bags full of presents in the under-stairs cupboard, out of reach, and turned back to her. 'Fancy a cup of tea?'

'I'd love one. I'm parched. I'll make it.'

She filled the kettle and put it on, and then glanced up at the window and saw him watching her reflection. The light wasn't good enough to read his expression, but there was a curious stillness about him. She turned round slowly and met his eyes.

'What's the matter?' she asked softly, and if she hadn't been watching him so carefully she would have missed the shrug.

'Nothing. I was just thinking how much difference you've made to our lives.'

'Oh, James.'

She didn't know why he'd kept his distance—because she'd said what she had about his child care being unreliable? Probably, and he'd seemed to imply that he wanted a little space between them, although he'd suggested in the end that they should keep work separate and carry on as they were, but they hadn't. Because of circumstances getting in the way, or because she'd destroyed something special between them?

She didn't know, but she couldn't let him stand there in the middle of the kitchen with that rather lost look in his eyes without giving him a hug.

She slid her arms round him, and after a second she felt his arms close around her and his head come down, his cheek resting against her hair.

'Thank you for tonight,' he murmured. 'It's really been fun. I wouldn't have thought of taking the children Christmas shopping if you hadn't suggested it, and they've really had a ball.'

He sighed, and she tipped her head back and stared into his eyes. 'What is it?'

'Oh, my mother. It occurred to me when you suggested I didn't think of her as a woman that I probably hadn't so much asked as told her she was helping me with the kids so I could get back to work. And I'd never asked her about her feelings or if she felt up to it. I just made her promise to help me, and I shouldn't have done.'

'So what are you going to do?'

'I don't know. Find an alternative, certainly, but what? Got any suggestions?'

'I might have. I asked Mum to think about it and see if she could come up with anyone.'

'And has she?'

'Not that she's mentioned yet, but when I asked her to draw up a shortlist, she said it would be.'

He chuckled, his eyes crinkling at the corners and softening the bleak expression they wore all too often. Then the crinkles faded, replaced by an unspoken question, and she went up on tiptoe and pressed her lips to his.

'Do you really want tea?' she said, and held her breath.

The corner of his mouth tugged down with irony. 'Tea?' he said softly. 'I don't think so. I think the only thing I really want is you.'

She stared up at him as his eyes darkened, wondering if

she was reading more into his words than she should. Yes. Of course she was. She was simply a diversion, something good to take the edge off his loneliness, a physical release that helped him deal with his emotional stress.

He didn't really want her. Not like that.

She stepped back and held out her hand. 'Ditto,' she said with a smile, and led him through the connecting door to her house.

He had two hours off at the end of Friday afternoon, and he collected Freya and his mother and took them to see Rory in his school nativity play. He was a shepherd, and when Freya saw him she shrieked and giggled and pointed, and James cuddled her on his lap and shushed her, but nobody minded.

And his mother really seemed to enjoy it.

He was looking at her through different eyes, he realised, and for the first time in ages, he gave her a hug as they came out of the hall and got their refreshments and waited for Rory to join them.

'That was such fun,' she said wistfully. 'I haven't been to a nativity play since you were tiny.'

'That's a long time ago.'

'It is. Decades.' She smiled up at him. 'Rory was lovely.'

He grinned, full of paternal pride. 'He was. He's a great little guy—and here he is. Hello, tiger.'

'Hi—hello, Grandma! Did you see me?'

'We all saw you—didn't you hear Freya calling you?'

He giggled. 'She's naughty.'

'No, she was just excited,' he said. 'Shall we go home, then? Where are your things?'

'Here,' he said, holding up a carrier bag stuffed with paintings and a shoebag with a sock hanging out of it.

James rescued the sock, took the carrier bag from him and led them out to the car. He had to drop them off, and then he was due back at work. He just hoped the weekend went without a hitch.

Sue still hadn't come up with any solutions, and his mother had agreed to cover for him on the understanding that Kate's parents would help her out if necessary, but before he could go back to work that evening he needed to take them home and get them settled and introduce his mother to Sue so she was reassured.

He couldn't believe it had never occurred to him that she'd be apprehensive, and he felt so guilty.

They'd have to have a long heart to heart at some point, but for now, he just gave her a hug as he left to go back to work. 'I'm really sorry I've put you in this position,' he said softly. 'I feel awful asking you to do it, but it's the last time, I promise. I'll find someone else.'

'Don't be silly,' she said, trying to sound brave and failing. 'We'll be all right. As you said, they aren't little hellions like you were.'

He grinned a little off-kilter. 'No. That would be a nightmare.'

She chuckled and pushed him towards the door. 'Go on, go to work. Sue's promised to give me a hand if I need it, and I'm sure I'll be all right.'

He hoped so, because the last thing he needed was any more screw-ups. He'd spent last night with Kate—or the early part of it, anyway—and it had been amazing. Again. Neither of them had mentioned work or children or anything remotely contentious, and it had been bliss. And now they were going to be working together all weekend, and he found he was looking forward to that, too.

OK, it was the weekend before Christmas, the height of the party season and prime time for accidents and hernias and intestinal disasters, but he loved it. He thrived on it, and the busier, the better.

And it was busy.

By the time he got back, Kate was in Theatre with a strangulated hernia in a man who'd tried to carry too much shopping in out of the car, and no sooner had he scrubbed to assist than he had to go down to A and E.

'What have you got for me?' he asked, and Tom looked at him and sighed.

'It would be Kate's team on take this weekend, wouldn't it?' he said under his breath.

'Why?'

'Because it's her ex-husband.'

He frowned. 'Jon? He always goes private, she said.'

'Not when his car's been involved in a collision and he's got suspected internal injuries,' Tom said drily.

'Well, I'll have to deal with him. Where is he?'

'In Resus. He's stable, but he's definitely in pain, so we're monitoring him closely. He's booked for CT shortly.'

'Any clues?'

Tom pursed his lips. 'Might be spleen. He was driving, and there's some evidence of a seat-belt injury across the upper left quadrant. That would be consistent with spleen, and I've just got a feeling about it. It certainly doesn't look like his aorta.'

'Good. I don't need that and I don't suppose he does. Have we got an ultrasound machine down here?'

'Yeah, there's one in Resus you can use. It's not brilliant. I couldn't see anything a few minutes ago, but if it's got worse it might show now.'

James went into Resus and found Jon Burgess restless, in pain and, if his guess was correct, a little frightened.

'Hi, Jon. I'm James—we met at the wedding. How are you doing?' he asked, finding a professional smile from somewhere.

'James? Kate's friend?'

'That's right. Tell me how you're feeling.'

'Sore. Really very sore, and it's getting worse.'

'Can you point to it?' he asked, turning back the blanket, and Jon indicated an area covered by a mottled bruise. 'OK. I want to do another ultrasound scan of the area. It may hurt a little when I press, but if it gets too much, just tell me.'

Jon grunted when he ran the ultrasound head over the bruise, but James had seen enough. There was a large mass behind the spleen, and he was convinced he had an encapsulated haemorrhage. And if the membrane tore...

'Jon, you're going to need urgent surgery,' he said, not bothering to beat about the bush. 'I think you've ruptured your spleen.'

'Are you sure about that? You know what you're looking for with that stupid machine? There were just a load of lines and blotches. A better one—'

'I'm sure,' he said. 'As sure as I can be—and, yes, I know what I'm looking for. I don't think there's any point in waiting for a CT scan, I'd rather get you up to Theatre now. Kate's just finishing off, so we won't keep you long.'

'I don't want Kate doing it!' he said hastily. 'I mean, I'm sure she's perfectly competent, but—'

'Kate won't be doing it,' he told him firmly. 'I will. I need you to sign a consent form, and then we'll get you straight up to Theatre.'

'I hope it'll be thoroughly sterilised! I don't want any

hospital superbugs,' he said, but then the seriousness of his situation began to dawn on him, and panic filled his eyes. 'Um—if I give you a number, could you ring someone for me? Her name's Julia.'

'Sure.'

He took the number, got the consent form signed and then went and broke the news to Kate.

'Jon?' she said, looking stunned. 'Oh, Lord. Is he all right?'

He grinned. 'Well, he's talking about superbugs, so I don't think he's that near the brink. It's his spleen—should be straightforward.' He handed her the number. 'Here. Can you ring this lady for him? I think it's your ex's latest conquest.'

She stared at it, surprise on her face. 'No, it's his mother. They haven't spoken for years, but she was at the wedding, of course. I'll call her. She's a darling. And—James?'

He met her eyes questioningly.

'Take care of him. Don't give him too big an incision. He'll hate the scar.'

Like he would have hated hers? He felt his mouth tighten. 'Of course I'll take care of him. He's a patient, first and foremost.' Even if he was cruel and insensitive and stupid and had made Kate feel bad about herself. And he'd do his best not to split him open from end to end, however tempting.

He went and scrubbed.

'Busy weekend?' Sue asked Kate on Saturday afternoon when she managed to slip home for a while.

'Dire. Jon's in. He had a car accident and ruptured his spleen. James operated while I phoned his mother and broke the news.'

'Good heavens. Is he all right?'

'Oh, yes. He's in a side room, complaining about the service and driving all the nurses mad, apparently. We're obviously giving him too much pain relief. I'll have to get James to reduce it.'

Her mother frowned at her. 'Kate, that's not funny.'

'Oh, Mum, lighten up. James has much too much integrity to do anything like that, and so have I. You should know that.'

'I just know what Jon did to you.'

'It was years ago,' she said, and realised that it was, and for the first time, it really felt like it. She yawned and stretched, and looked hopefully into the fridge. 'Is there any food I can raid?' she asked, and her mother moved the kettle off the Aga and headed for the larder.

'A bowl of Saturday soup, and some fruit cake?'

'Fantastic. And a cup of tea, and then I'll have to dash. I'm taking it in turns with James to come home, and he's got to tuck the children up for the night, so I mustn't make him late. How's his mother coping?'

'Marion? She's fine. We've had a wonderful day. We took the children for a walk to feed the ducks, and they joined us for lunch, and it was lovely. She's a nice woman. Very nice.'

'She is a nice woman. She just can't cope, and I find that really odd. I suppose I'm spoilt, because you can cope with anything.'

Sue smiled wryly. 'Oh, no, I can't. I nearly went to pieces when I saw you in hospital after that idiot kicked you.'

'But you didn't. That's the thing. And you never do.'

'Horses for courses. I can do children. Do you ever go to pieces when you're faced with a difficult operation?'

'No, because it wouldn't help.'

'So how would it help in a domestic situation?' she asked with her usual common sense, and Kate just laughed.

'OK, you win, we're all good at something. So what's Marion good at?'

'Playing with them. She's marvellous. She just lacks confidence, but today she really enjoyed herself. I don't think she's got a problem at all, you know, I think if she could get back her confidence she'd be in her element. She's just out of practice. I think you should back James for this job. It could be just what he needs. Well, apart from a wife, and you know what I think about that.'

The microwave pinged, and Kate rescued her soup, sat down at the table and didn't answer.

But that didn't mean she wasn't thinking about it, because she was, all the time. It was how to put the idea into his head that was the tricky bit...

They got through the weekend without any major dramas, and handed over their patients on Monday afternoon to another team. He and Kate had Tuesday and Christmas Day off, and Sue and Andrew were having the children for him with the family on Boxing Day, but Helen was having them on Christmas Eve, so he went straight over there and retrieved them as soon as he was finished, to give her a little time off.

'Can we have a Christmas tree?' Rory asked excitedly on the way home. 'Helen's got a tree. It's really nice.'

'I expect so. We haven't got any decorations, though.' None at all. He'd thrown them all out in a fit of despair last Christmas, when he'd been packing up the London house, and he hadn't got round to replacing them. Now, suddenly, he found he wanted to put up a tree and decorate it with his children. 'Let's go and ask Kate's mother where we should get everything from,' he said, and they went home and found Sue and Andrew in the farmyard, struggling with a huge spruce.

'Good grief—Andrew, let me give you a hand,' he said, and

Sue surrendered her end and took charge of the children while they struggled into the high-ceilinged hall and jammed it upright in a great big bucket of sand.

'I was going to ask you where we could get a tree,' he said a little faintly, 'but I don't think we need one that big!'

Sue laughed. 'I've put one in the barn already. I hope you don't mind, but with the others coming—well, we always put a tree in there, but I haven't decorated it. I thought the children might like to help you do that.'

He felt a lump in his throat. 'Thank you, that's really kind of you. I need to buy some decorations.'

'No, you don't, we've got hundreds,' Andrew said drily. 'Boxes full of them. I'll sort you some out.' He straightened up and stood back, looking at the tree with a critical eye, then nodded. 'Right—teatime?'

'What a good idea. Rory, would you like some apple cake? Freya? Or do you want a boiled egg?'

'Egg and cake,' Rory said, and James opened his mouth to protest, caught Sue's challenging smile and subsided.

Gratefully.

What a day.

Kate arrived back from finishing off her Christmas shopping just as James and the children were straggling back to the barn laden down with boxes.

Well, James was laden. Rory had a bag of what looked like fairy-lights, and Freya was carrying an armful of tinsel.

It was starting to trail, and as she walked towards them, a loop slipped down and Freya caught her foot in it and started to topple.

'Whoops!' she said, scooping up child and tinsel together, and Freya giggled and shoved the tinsel into her face.

'Pretty!' she said, and Kate grinned.

'You are, you're gorgeous.' She kissed her plump rosy cheek. She smelt of apple cake, and Kate realised her mother had been at work again.

'We're going to decorate the tree,' James said a little obviously, and then added, after a slight hesitation, 'Do you want to join us?'

She hesitated, but then Rory tugged at her sleeve. 'You have to, Kate. Please?'

She met James's eyes over the top of the tinsel and searched them for hidden messages, but there didn't seem to be any. He was just asking her if she wanted to join them. Nothing significant. Nothing earth-shattering or meaningful.

'Actually, I've got rather a lot to do,' she said, and then wondered if she'd imagined the withdrawal in his eyes, or if she was just trying to convince herself there was something there when there wasn't.

'I might join you later,' she added, hoping to see a return of that warmth, but it was gone, carefully veiled now, and he nodded.

'Do that—if you've got time. Come on, Rory. We've got a lot to do. Help Freya with the tinsel.'

So she put the toddler down, and she ran after her father and brother, and left Kate standing there alone.

Oh, well. It was her own fault. She could have said yes.

Kicking herself, she unloaded the car and tried not to look into the barn at James and the children unpacking all the decorations and exclaiming in delight.

She could have said yes.

So why hadn't she?

CHAPTER TEN

HE OUGHT to leave her alone.

He'd invited her in, and she'd declined. He couldn't bully her. It was up to her, and she'd said she was busy.

But the communicating door was calling to him from the corner of his eye, and he could hear her moving around.

Doing all the things she had to do. She was probably wrapping a mountain of presents—something he still had to do, if he ever got round to buying paper—and she wouldn't have time for him and his children. She'd probably got a tree of her own to decorate.

But it just seemed wrong, somehow, without her. As if there was someone missing—and, curiously, the someone wasn't Beth. Beth seemed like someone from another lifetime, and he supposed she was.

He thought about it, but decided he didn't feel guilty. Well, he did, about plenty of things, but not Beth. He just felt lonely, and if Kate was there, somehow it would be more fun for all of them.

He was at the door with his hand raised when there was a knock on it, and he pulled it open and gave her a wry smile. 'I was just coming to get you,' he said, and she smiled back and went up on tiptoe and kissed his cheek.

'I'm sorry. I just had some things I needed to do. How far have you got— Oh! It's looking lovely!'

'Not really. It's a bit sparse and a bit lopsided, and the lights aren't quite even, but, hey. We did it.'

She gave him an encouraging smile and headed towards the tree. 'You just need a few more little things on it. Oh—what's this?'

'I made it at school,' Rory told her. 'It's an angel.'

It was an angel, but it was a pretty scruffy angel, he thought. Kate, though, didn't seem to think any such thing.

She moved it to a more prominent position, rummaged in the box and came up with more red baubles and a fairy, and then after they'd put the baubles on in the gaps she made James stand on a chair and hold Freya up so she could put the fairy on the top.

'There!' she exclaimed, laughing. 'Now it's finished.' And she took Freya from him and swung her round, which gave him time to straighten the fairy before he got down and put the chair away.

And swallowed the lump in his throat.

Christmas was coming with the speed of an express train.

They spent part of Tuesday rounding up all their things and taking them through into her house, and changing the sheets ready for the family's arrival the next day, Christmas Eve.

And because she only had one spare room, that meant James would be sleeping with the children.

Still, she consoled herself, it was only for two or three nights. The family never stayed for long—not long enough, really, but this time she realised she'd be glad to see them go.

'Why are we moving into your house?' Rory asked as

they sat down for a drink and a biscuit when all the shuffling was done.

'Because all my brothers and sisters are coming to stay,' she explained. 'There are lots and lots of them, and some of them are married now and have children, so it's busy.'

'Why do you have so many lots?'

She laughed and ruffled his hair. 'Because my parents love children,' she answered honestly, without going into detail. 'You've met Dan and Rachel and little Sean, haven't you?' He nodded. 'They're just coming on Christmas Day. And there's my brother Michael and his wife, Louise—they won't stay over, either, but Angie and Joel and Patrick will be here with their other halves, and Patrick's got four children, and Angie's got two, and then there's Lucy, and I'm not sure about Barney. He might be coming, but he's a pilot so he may not be in England, even.'

'Good grief,' James said, looking stunned. 'Really that many? Where do they put them all?'

'Oh, that's just some of them. Some of them won't come, some will drop in, others just ring. Those are the main contenders, though. The hard-core family members who never miss it, come hell or high water. It's a lot of fun, but we all fit in somehow. I hate it when I'm on duty, but because I work locally, I can usually spend some time here, if not all of it. It's great.'

'That sounds so alien to me. I'm an only child, and Christmas—well, if you blinked, you missed it.'

'Poor you. That's awful.'

'I never thought of it like that. It was just how it was. Your mother must be exhausted by the time they go,' he said a little faintly.

She laughed. 'Actually, she misses them. She loves it.' She tipped her head on one side. 'So—are you all ready?'

'Ready?'

'You know—done the wrapping and so on. When are you seeing your mother?'

'This evening—so I suppose I ought to sort her things out,' he said, looking preoccupied. 'Um—I don't suppose you've got any wrapping paper?'

'Oh, I might have a little left,' she teased, and took it out of the dresser and handed it to him. 'Sticky tape?'

He just smiled, and she found a reel of tape and added it to the pile. 'Bows? Tags?'

He snorted. 'I think that's enough. A couple of tags, maybe. I'll get some later, when we go over there. It's only for her things. I'll do the rest later on, when the children are in bed.'

'Because it's ours?' Rory asked mischievously, and James tweaked his nose and grinned at him.

'Maybe.'

'We're having presents,' he chanted, and she was so relieved to see it, after the Father Christmas letter incident, that she almost joined in.

Then Rory said, 'Will we put them under your tree, or ours?' and she bit her lip.

'I don't have a tree,' she confessed, and James looked stunned.

'You don't? You must have a tree.'

'I haven't. I never bother. There's one next door, and one in the hall in the house, and one in the drawing room—why would I need a tree here, too?'

'Because it's Christmas!' Rory said, horrified. 'Kate, you must. Where will Father Christmas put your presents? Daddy, get her a tree!'

'I think I will,' he said, his face strangely disturbed. 'I'll go and do it now. Come on, kids. We're going tree shopping.'

Kate laughed and stood up. 'We don't go shopping. We grow them on the farm. We'll go and pick one. My uncle Bill will find us a nice one. Come on, then, if you insist. Let's go.'

They bundled up in coats, tramped up through the farm and found her uncle cutting trees in the field behind the Dutch barn.

'I thought Andrew had come and got a tree for your barn?' he said, so she explained.

'Oh. So the children need their own, do they?'

'No, Kate needs one,' Rory explained earnestly, and Bill nodded.

'Right. Well, I quite agree. Let's find a nice tree for Kate, and then you can go and help her decorate it.'

They came back from his mother's armed with presents and found Kate had put the lights on the tree but not the baubles, so they hung them, and then went and retrieved Rory's angel and hung it on the branch at the front, and put all the presents underneath, and then he chivvied the children through the bath and into bed.

They were so tired they fell asleep immediately, and he could easily have joined them.

'I'm shattered,' he said wearily, finding a smile for Kate when he went back down to the kitchen, and she gave him an answering smile and handed him a glass of wine.

'It's been a tough few days,' she said. 'I think we've earned this.'

'Too right,' he said, following her through to the sitting room and settling on her lovely, comfy sofa. 'Oh, bliss. Wake me up if I start snoring.'

She laughed. 'Certainly will. So how was your mother?'

He cracked an eye open, then sat up straighter. 'Curiously happy,' he admitted. 'I think she enjoyed the weekend, and she said she was looking forward to babysitting on Boxing Day night when she gets back from her sister's. Will we be back to normal by then, by the way, or will it still be crowded?'

'Oh, no, I think the barn will be back to normal. The house might not, but most people will have gone.'

He nodded. 'Good. That'll make it easier having her over.' He stretched out his legs and groaned. 'The tree looks nice, by the way.'

'It does. Thank you. I really wouldn't have bothered if you hadn't chivvied me, and I should have thought of the children. It's just that this side of the barn is usually adults, so we don't mind. There are enough trees about the place.'

He chuckled and reached his hand out, threading his fingers through hers. 'I could get used to this,' he said with a sigh. 'Sitting here with you in the evenings while the children are asleep upstairs. It'll be really odd when the boiler's fixed and we go home.'

She shifted slightly, turning towards him, and he moved his head so he could meet her eyes. 'What are you going to do about the consultancy?' she asked quietly.

He searched her eyes, but they were strangely unreadable. 'I don't know. Apply, I think, when the time comes. I thought I was going to have to do something else about child care, but my mother seems to have turned a corner—I don't know, your mother's given her so much confidence, and we're talking now and she realises how much I appreciate what she's doing—I hadn't really told her, and I think she was just overwhelmed. But if she's all right, and happy to do it long term, then I don't see why we can't manage—especially now her sister seems to be on the mend. And it doesn't matter if the kids get attached to her, because she's their grandmother, and they're supposed to.'

And then he thought about Kate, and how the children were getting attached to her, and to this place, and to her parents, and he felt a shiver of unease run over him. Would they be massively disrupted when they moved back to their own house again?

Would he?

Oh, God. He was letting himself get drawn into this fairy-tale life of hers, but it was just a mirage, and when the mist cleared he'd be alone again. If only he could find a way of convincing her to move back with him, but no one in their right mind would want to take on such a complicated family. Especially not someone orderly like Kate, who had a row of boxes she was systematically ticking.

There was no way they were one of her boxes, and no amount of wishful thinking would change that.

'I'm bushed,' he told her. 'I think I need to go to bed.'

'OK. Sleep well, I'll see you tomorrow,' she said, and leaning over, she touched her lips to his.

It was like a spark to tinder.

'Oh, Kate,' he groaned, and threading his hands through her hair, he plundered her eager, willing mouth, his body aching for hers, longing to find solace within it, the peace that came afterwards as they lay sprawled together in those few precious minutes before he returned to his own bed.

What would it be like to have the right to stay with her, to sleep with her, to wake with her?

No. She wasn't interested. She didn't want long term.

In your dreams.

His heart heavy, he eased away, brushing the lightest of kisses over her lips before getting to his feet and staring down at her. 'I'll see you in the morning. Sleep well,' he murmured, and headed for the stairs and solitude.

Christmas Eve at the hospital was chaos.

They had the usual flurry of minor surgical emergencies—two hernias, an appendix, a blocked gall bladder that they cleared using an endoscope and a stent to keep the duct patent, and otherwise they were discharging patients as fast as they reasonably could.

Including Jon, who was making excellent progress and couldn't get out quickly enough.

He wasn't alone. Everybody wanted to go home for Christmas, including the staff, and Kate was a firm believer in recovering in familiar surroundings and with familiar pathogens, instead of hospital bugs and noise and an unusual and busy routine.

So they discharged, and they did admin, and then the ward clerk handed her a handful of post.

'This is for you and Mr McEwan—cards and things.'

'Thank you,' she murmured, and went through to her office. James was just finishing off a discharge letter, and he looked up as she went in.

'Cards for you,' she said, handing him the envelopes, and he slit them open.

'Oh. This is from Jon. "Thank you for all your excellent care. I underestimated what you do. Please pass the enclosed on to the League of Friends. Many thanks." Wow. Big cheque.'

She stared at it and laughed. 'Well, that's a turn-up for the books. Who's the next one from?'

'Tracy,' he said with a grin. 'She's back with her boyfriend, and she's dyed her hair purple. There's a photo of her.'

He flipped it across the desk so she could see it, and then pulled the other card out of the envelope.

She was still looking at the photo of Tracy and her boyfriend, but there was something about his stillness that brought her eyes up from the photo to his face. 'James?'

'It's from Amanda Symes,' he said, his voice like gravel as he read it out. '"Steve died peacefully at home on Sunday. We were all with him. It was very calm and dignified. Thank you for all your support…"'

His voice cracked, and he dropped the card on the desk and pushed his chair back, then swore, quietly but comprehensively.

'Sorry. I was hoping they'd have Christmas together, but maybe it's better this way.' He stood up. 'Right, I've got things to do. I'll catch up with you later.'

She watched him go, his eyes shuttered, and if the phone hadn't been ringing and the ward staff hadn't been clamouring for her attention, she would have put her head down on her desk and howled.

'Happy Christmas!'

Kate prised open her eyes and found Rory standing by her bed, his eyes sparkling with excitement. 'Happy Christmas, sweetheart,' she said, and reaching out for him, she gave him a big hug. 'Where's your daddy?'

'Right here, with a cup of tea for you. I'm sorry about the noise. Happy Christmas.'

She laughed and levered herself up the bed. 'Happy Christmas yourself,' she said, taking the tea from him and drawing him down with her other hand to kiss his cheek, trying to ignore the fact that he was dressed only in a pair of pyjama bottoms hanging loosely on his lean hips. 'So where's Freya?'

'Asleep. It's only six, and the excitement of meeting all the other children last night seems to have worn her out. Not Rory, though. He's as bright as a button.'

'I've got presents under the tree,' he said, clambering up onto her bed and settling down at her feet. 'Lots of them. Are you going to get up?'

'In a minute, when I've had my tea,' she said with a laugh. 'Goodness, you're in a hurry. It's very early.'

'I know,' he said, looking crestfallen. 'Daddy says we have to be quiet because of all the others sleeping in the other house, but I expect they'll want their presents, too, so if we make lots of noise they'll know they can get up and then they'll be happy, too!'

James was rolling his eyes, and she stifled a chuckle. 'Just give me five minutes, Rory, OK? I need to drink my tea and wake up, and then I'll come down.'

'OK,' he said, sliding off the bed and grabbing James by the hand. 'Come on, Daddy, we can go and squash the presents and see if we can guess.'

'Hang on, I need a jumper on, I'm freezing. Now, shush, don't wake Freya.'

They went out, and she listened to Rory trying so hard to be quiet while he was fizzing inside, and smiled.

Oh, she couldn't stay there, lying in her bed while he was so excited. And Freya was stirring, so she pulled on her slipper socks and her dressing-gown, went through to the bedroom next door and lifted her out of the cot, gave her a cuddle and changed her nappy, then took her downstairs.

'Guess who I found?' she said, and Rory jumped up and ran over and gave her a big, slobbery kiss.

'Happy Christmas!' he said, bubbling over with excitement, and Freya wriggled out of her arms and ran over to James and swarmed up him with a huge smile.

'Ch'is'mas!' she said happily, and gave him one of her special baby kisses, and when he looked up at Kate, she could see the happiness in his eyes, and she couldn't help but be glad for him.

If she'd done nothing else, she'd given them this Christmas, and with a new year about to dawn, maybe he'd be able to move on.

It would be without her, she knew that, especially after seeing him yesterday when he'd opened Amanda's card. Beth was still too big a part of their lives, his heart still too raw, but maybe one day…

And then he patted the sofa beside him and invited her over, and her mother's words came back to her.

Of course, you could solve the problem at a stroke.

How?

By volunteering.

For what? To be his nanny?

No. To be his wife.

Could she be the wife he needed? The mother of his children?

Oh, please, God, yes, she thought. But she didn't think he was going to ask her, and she didn't have the courage to volunteer…

They opened their presents, and Kate's eyes filled when she unwrapped her sweater.

'Oh, James—it's like my favourite one! Oh, it's lovely—and it's real cashmere! Oh, you shouldn't.'

No. He probably shouldn't, but it was so pretty, and he loved her so much.

What?

'Go and try it on,' he said, choked, just to get her out of the room, but she shook her head.

'In a minute,' she said, and came over to him and kissed him. Properly. On the lips, in front of his children. 'Thank you.'

'My pleasure,' he said, trying to smile, but emotions were crashing through him and it was all he could do to breathe.

'Here—there's one for Freya,' she said, pulling a present out from under the tree, and gradually his lungs started to work again and his mind began to function and somehow he managed to get through the rest of the happy mayhem without falling apart.

How could he have been so stupid? She didn't want him. She was just being sweet to them all, but she had a life, a career, a grand master plan that didn't include him and his damaged little family, and he'd better remember that.

But then she handed him a present from her—a book on restoring Edwardian houses, and she'd signed it, 'With all my love, Kate.'

With all her love?

Really?

Or was it just a figure of speech?

Something was wrong.

He seemed—what? Distant? Preoccupied? Unhappy?

Missing Beth again, of course. Oh, stupid, stupid her, to imagine she could compete with a ghost.

'Right, everyone, let's get washed and dressed and go over to the house!' she said with what was surely too much enthusiasm, but the children scrambled to their feet and ran for the stairs, and she followed them up, James in her wake, and at the top he stopped her.

'So what happens now?' he asked.

'We normally go over to the house and meet up for coffee, then we head up the hill to the church for the family carol service. Then we all help with lunch, and after that we lie around eating nuts and chocolates and Turkish delight for as long as we can bear it, and then we have tea. It can be quite full on, so I don't know how much of it you want to be involved in.'

His eyes clouded, and he nodded. 'Well—perhaps we should amuse ourselves till lunch, then,' he said, and she realised it had sounded as if she didn't want them.

She gave a quick shake of her head in denial. 'James—I only meant you might find it all a bit much. I didn't want you feeling obliged to join in if you didn't want to. But you're *really* welcome. We want you here.'

'Do you?' he asked, his voice curiously brittle. 'Do you want me here?'

She couldn't lie, but the truth...

'Yes,' she said, giving him the truth in the end, because there was no other way to go. 'Yes, I do want you here. Very much.'

His mouth softened, and he smiled. 'Then we'll come over now, and we'll tough it out, and eat the nuts, and if the children haven't been sick we'll have tea, and then we'll come back here and I'll try to get them to sleep.'

The sweater was gorgeous on her.

It was a perfect fit, and it was as much as he could do to keep his hands to himself and not stroke it. He behaved, though, all through the noisy greetings and the kisses and the bustle and jostle of getting them organised for church, then in the church he was mercifully at one end of a pew with the children between him and Kate, and then at lunch she was seated opposite him next to her brother Michael, so it was easy.

But then later, when the noise had died down and the children were playing a little more sensibly and the adults were sprawled by the fire, he sat in a chair with Freya asleep on his lap and she came and sat down on the floor at his feet and leant against his legs, and he couldn't resist it any more. His hand found her shoulder and squeezed it, and she slid her hand up and caught his fingers and held them, right there in front of all her family.

And it would be so easy to imagine it could last for ever, that he could be here with them next Christmas and the Christmas after and the one after that...

Freya stirred, and he eased his hand away and looked down at Kate's enquiring, upturned face.

'All right?' she asked, and he nodded.

'I'm going to take her back to the barn and change her nappy,' he murmured.

'Want me to come?'

Did he? Was this the time to tell her that he couldn't do this any more, that he needed to get out of here and stop pretending that they belonged, stop playing Happy Families and get back to normal?

'I'm fine,' he said. 'You stay and enjoy your family. Could you keep an eye on Rory for me? We won't be long.'

'Of course.'

He took Freya over to the barn, changed her nappy and lay down with her, but she wouldn't settle again, so he braced himself and went back to the fray.

He was in the sitting room alone, with just the fairy-lights on, and she hesitated in the doorway.

'James?'

He looked up, but she couldn't read his expression in the dark. 'Hi. Is the party finally over?'

'Oh, they'll go on for hours,' she said with a little laugh, 'but Michael and Louise have gone home, so I thought I'd come and keep you company.'

'You don't have to do that.'

Oh, he was so wrong there. She absolutely had to do that. She'd missed him horribly. 'Would you rather be alone?'

'No. Of course not. I've been waiting up for you.'

She went in and perched on the end of the sofa and tried to read his eyes. 'Are you all right?'

'Yes, I'm fine,' he said quietly. 'It's just all a bit—you know. Happy Families.'

Her heart contracted. 'Oh, James. I'm sorry.'

'No, don't be,' he said, reaching for her hand and drawing her down beside him. 'It's been wonderful. The kids have had a brilliant time, and so have I. It's just—well, it would be too easy to get carried along by it, to imagine we're really part of it, but it isn't real, and we'll be going home soon. I mustn't let myself forget that.'

She wished she could read his eyes.

'The other night you said you could get used to it—sitting here with me with the children asleep upstairs,' she said, her heart pounding.

'I could,' he said softly. 'I so easily could. I have. And I'll miss you, when we go. Miss all of you, but you especially. I know you're not interested in us—I mean, why would you be? We're a strange little family, just about managing to keep our heads above water, with a house that needs so much doing to it that if I start now and work every weekend and evening for the next ten years it might almost be fit to live in.'

'Not if you can afford to pay someone to do it. You've got

the job, you know. I saw the clinical director yesterday. They want you, so your money problems are over.'

Her eyes had grown accustomed to the dark, and she saw his rueful smile. Saw it, and didn't really understand it.

'I've got it?' he murmured. 'They haven't even interviewed me yet.'

'Of course they have. And they've seen a few others. They'll want to talk to you formally, of course, but it's yours if you want it.' She felt a sudden fear that he was going to leave. 'You do want it, don't you?'

His laugh sounded bemused. 'Well, yes, of course I want it. It'll be fantastic—but it isn't really the nuts and bolts I was thinking about. Not the house, or the job. It's us.'

'Us?' she echoed, hardly able to breathe.

'Yes, us—if there is an "us". I'm hoping against hope that there is—that there will be. You see, I've just realised, in the last—what, twelve hours or so?—that I love you. And so when I go home without you...'

Her heart lurched. 'You love me?'

'Oh, yes, Kate,' he sighed. 'I love you. But it's OK if it's a problem to you. I won't make it difficult at work, but I thought you ought to know.'

'Oh, James.' She didn't know whether to laugh or cry, so she did both, a funny strangled little sob that could have been either.

'Kate, don't laugh.'

'I'm not. Not really. Only—it's not a problem to me, James, because I love you, too.'

'You love me?'

He sounded stunned, so she reached out a hand and cradled his jaw tenderly. 'Yes, James. I love you. I've told myself it's too early, you're still grieving for Beth, but I think, given time, we could have something good, something solid and decent and—'

'And the children?' he asked, his hand coming up to grip hers where it lay against his cheek. 'Do you love the children?'

'Oh, James,' she whispered unsteadily, tears filling her eyes. 'How could I not love the children? Of course I love the children.'

'This isn't just because of what Rory said? You know, the Father Christmas thing, about wanting a mummy for Christmas? Because I couldn't stand that, you being with us because you pitied us.'

'I don't pity you!' she said, shocked. 'Why would I pity you? OK, you've had a hell of a time, but you've got Rory and Freya, and you're all so close, you love each other so much, and they're yours. Your own family. That's so precious. I've wanted that so much,' she said wistfully.

His arm slid round her shoulders and he hugged her gently. 'I know. I could tell, from the way you talked about kids, from seeing you with mine. You're a natural mother, and it's a wicked waste that you haven't got your own children. You'd be wonderful with them.'

She gave a little huff of laughter. 'I thought, when I married Jon, that maybe I'd have all that, but he was...just wrong for me. So wrong.'

'And you think I could be right?'

'Absolutely right,' she said, hanging on to his hand as if she'd die without the contact. 'You're warm and generous and loving, you don't make judgements, you care about people— I love you, James. I didn't think I'd ever dare to love again, after Jon, but I can't help loving you, or your family. And you aren't a strange little family. You're just sad.'

His lips brushed hers. 'No. We were sad. We aren't sad now, because we've found you, and you've made such a difference to our lives that the idea of going back to our house and leaving you behind is unbearable.'

'Then don't. Stay here, with me while you do up your house. Or take me with you, and we'll live in a muddle. Or I've got another house we could live in, or we could sell both and live here and buy the other barn off my parents and convert it and live in that. I don't care, just so long as I'm with you.'

Kate, shut up! Let him speak. Let him think. Stop talking about nothing.

He laughed softly, and his lips brushed hers. 'I don't care, either. I love you so much,' he murmured. 'I realised it the other night, and I was gutted, because I didn't think there was any way you'd be interested in me. In us.'

'Oh, James, you idiot,' she chided softly, and he laughed again, a little oddly, and squeezed her hand.

'Yeah. I am, aren't I? A real fool. And sitting here in the dark waiting for you to come home, I seem to have turned into an optimistic fool,' he said, then, easing away from her, he stood up and walked towards the door.

'James?' she said, fear and confusion gripping her as he walked away, but he just put the lights on low so they could see each other and turned round and came back to her, kneeling down in front of her and taking her hand, that slightly crooked, uncertain smile a little unsteady.

'Marry me, Kate—if you really mean it, and you really love me in the way that I love you—that the sun won't shine and the night never ends if I'm not with you—then marry me. I put the past behind me, ages ago. I loved Beth, and there'll always be a special place for her in my heart, but in a way I let her go when she was diagnosed. And then I was so busy with the practical stuff that before I knew it, it didn't really hurt any more. It's the present that's been getting me down, but since I've met you everything's changed. It feels as if the sun's come out again, and all I can think about is the future—with you.'

He pressed her fingers to his lips. 'I love you. I need you. We need you. Be part of our family. Extend it—or not. Whatever you want, because I can't live without you, Kate. I need you, more than I need air. You're my heart, my soul. My life. My love.'

'Oh, James.'

His eyes were bright, the pale blue shimmering with emotion, and she leant forwards and touched her lips to his.

'Is that a yes? Please, tell me it's a yes.'

'Yes, my love,' she said. 'Yes, it's a yes. I'll marry you, because I need you, too—all three of you. And I can't live without you, either. But I have to warn you, I do want children of my own. And maybe other people's, too. I'm afraid I'm a bit like my mother.'

He smiled. 'A full house, every Christmas, till the end of our days?'

She laughed a little unevenly. 'Probably, so your lovely house may not be big enough for us for very long. Can you bear it?'

He drew her into his arms and hugged her tight. 'It sounds wonderful,' he said softly, and then lifting his head, he stared down into her eyes and smiled.

'Happy Christmas, my love,' he murmured, and kissed her…

THE ITALIAN SURGEON'S CHRISTMAS MIRACLE

BY
ALISON ROBERTS

Alison Roberts lives in Christchurch, New Zealand. She began her working career as a primary school teacher, but now juggles available working hours between writing and active duty as an ambulance officer. Throwing in a large dose of parenting, housework, gardening and pet-minding keeps life busy, and teenage daughter Becky is responsible for an increasing number of days spent on equestrian pursuits. Finding time for everything can be a challenge, but the rewards make the effort more than worthwhile.

CHAPTER ONE

THE silly season.

Aptly named.

And the sooner it was over the better, as far as Luke Harrington was concerned.

Chaos was gaining hold in the cardiology ward of St Elizabeth's Children's Hospital and the people who should be at least trying to keep a lid on things were clearly failing.

The noise level was well above normal, thanks to children already being hyped up by the approach of Christmas Day. There seemed to be a lot of giggling going on and the seasonal music had somehow followed him from the theatre suite. Gaudy decorations hung everywhere, including loops of fat silver tinsel on doorframes that threatened to garrotte anyone in his position of being over six feet in height.

A nurse passed him, a small child balanced on her hip, a huge white teddy bear under her other arm. The bear was wearing a Santa hat and the nurse was singing 'Jingle Bells'. The child was beating time with two small fists and a wide grin on her face. Luke smiled back.

'Hello, Bella. I'm coming to see you soon.'

'Three sleeps,' Bella informed him. 'Mummy says I'll be

home by then but even if I'm not, Father Christmas will know where to find me.'

'He sure will.' Bella's nurse had stopped singing. 'Let's get you back to bed, Trouble, so Mr *Harrington* will know where to find you.' The tone suggested that this nurse was well aware of the problems caused recently by his patients being anywhere but in their beds when Luke did his rounds.

The charge nurse, Margaret, had spotted his approach to the central nurses' station. She held out a clipboard.

'Can you sign, please, Luke? It's the telephone order you gave for increased analgesia for Daniel.'

Luke reached for a pen. 'Have the results come in on Baby Harris?'

'Yes. I've got them right here for you.' Margaret turned as swiftly as her substantial figure allowed, reaching for a manila folder on the cluttered desk.

Luke scrawled his name, looked up to wait for the folder but then found his attention diverted to the same place Margaret's had been. A large artificial Christmas tree had been positioned near the central desk. Cardboard boxes were scattered around its base. A nurse was kneeling beside one of the boxes and she had a group of children gathered around her. As she opened the box, the children grabbed decorations and that was what had attracted Margaret's notice.

'Not those ones, Ange.' She moved to pick up the box. 'I thought we'd got rid of these. We've got all the lovely new decorations for this year, remember?'

More boxes were opened to reveal decorations still wrapped in tissue paper. The box that was overflowing with rather sad-looking, bent, cardboard stars and chipped coloured balls was pushed into a corner behind Luke, near the rubbish bin. Margaret straightened and smiled at Luke's expression as he watched children gleefully shredding tissue paper and crowing delightedly over their discoveries.

'It's Christmas.' No one else would get away with the kind of motherly rebukes Margaret could deliver. 'We're allowed a little bit of mess.' She handed him the manila folder.

Luke said nothing. Margaret had been running this ward for ever. She knew as well as he did why tidiness was important. Right now it would be impossible to move a bed past this section of the corridor. The boxes were enough of an obstacle course for people, let alone, say, a crash trolley. Yes, it was highly unlikely that an emergency would occur in the next fifteen minutes but what if it did? Part of Luke's not inconsiderable skill as a surgeon came from being able to anticipate and prevent a broken link in a chain of response.

He placed the folder on the desk and opened it just as his pager sounded again. Automatically, he reached for the nearby phone.

'Harrington.'

'It's an outside call, Mr Harrington. From a Mr Battersby. He's been waiting a while. Shall I put it through?'

Luke was very tempted to say he didn't have time to take this call, but he thought better of it. It wasn't just the chaos of the run-up to Christmas that he wanted to be over. 'Put him on,' he said. 'Thank you.'

His solicitor obviously respected time constraints. He got straight to the point.

'Sorry to disturb you, Mr Harrington, but we have a problem.'

'Oh?' Luke tucked the phone between a shrugged shoulder and his ear as he opened the folder and fanned out the sheaf of test results with one hand.

'Have you, by any chance, had the opportunity to take a look at this house on Sullivan Avenue that you've inherited?'

Maybe the constraints weren't understood clearly enough.

'Time is a luxury in my line of business, Mr Battersby.' Luke frowned at the graph in front of him. Started at birth, continued by the GP and now being monitored by ward staff, charting the weight of a three-week-old boy who had been admitted two days ago in urgent need of major heart surgery.

'Oh, I understand that. But...'

A muscle in Luke's jaw bunched. As many of the staff at Lizzies were aware, '*but*' was one of his least favourite words. 'Find a solution, not an excuse' was a phrase he had to use all too often.

His tone was still patient, however. Calm and professional. What any member of the public might expect to hear from the head of the paediatric cardiothoracic surgical department.

'We've been through this, Mr Battersby,' he said. 'The house is derelict. It's sitting on a particularly valuable piece of real estate.' And central London real estate was always valuable. Especially this close to Regent's Park. Luke raised his gaze for a moment. If he walked past the Christmas tree into one of the inpatient rooms on that side of the ward, he could probably see the property from the height the second floor of the hospital provided.

Not that he would recognise the house. He hadn't seen it and he didn't intend to.

'Extremely valuable,' the solicitor concurred.

Luke ignored the murmur. 'As I told you last week, I want the house gone. Demolished.'

Wiped from the face of the earth.

'And I want it done immediately.' Luke allowed his determination to show. 'I want a clean piece of land to put on the market in the new year. Preferably the first of January.'

Good. The baby's weight was creeping up again, finally.

Having dropped to 1.6 kg due to an inability to feed, the underlying heart condition and a respiratory infection, it was now back to 2 kg. An acceptable point to go ahead with the surgery.

'We have a problem with that,' the annoying voice in his ear repeated. 'Particularly the time frame.'

'I'm not interested in problems.' Luke caught the phone with his hand, preparing to end the call. 'That's why I employ a firm with the kind of reputation Battersby, Battersby and Gosling has. You sort it.'

'It's not that simple.'

Nothing ever was. Luke was doing a quick mental rearrangement of his commitments. Which of tomorrow morning's cases could be shuffled? Some might well have to wait an extra day or two given the length of time this case would involve and nobody would be happy about that. Not that anyone was going to get out of the intensive care unit let alone get home for Christmas with surgery planned for tomorrow, but everybody wanted it over with and recuperation to look forward to. Christmas was a family celebration tiny Liam Harris might never be able to share if this surgery didn't happen very quickly.

'It's the tenants, you see…'

'What?' Theatre schedules slid to the back of Luke's mind. He tried to block out the increasing noise level from the excited children helping to decorate the tree. 'What do you mean, "tenants"? According to the information you sent me, there's been no income on this property since its owner died.'

'It's complicated. There's been an informal arrangement, apparently. Your father—'

Already tense muscles tightened another notch. Luke's jaw ached. 'Giovanni Moretti is no relative of mine.'

The name might be on his birth certificate but it had never been spoken. Or used. Part of his genetic make-up, admittedly, but it had been buried long ago as something to be ashamed of. Despised.

Italian.

Emotional.

The path to chaos and misery and broken lives.

All so far in the past even the reminder had been shocking, but Luke had been well brought up. Given strength of character like tempered steel. He knew not to go there. Not to even take a single step in that direction. He could almost see his grandmother's approving nod as he drew in a careful breath.

'Proceed with the demolition,' he ordered calmly. 'The tenants will simply have to find somewhere else to squat.'

'They can't.' Mr Battersby, senior, sounded a lot less frail than Luke knew him to be. Defiant, even.

'Excuse me?'

'There's children involved.' Reginald Battersby cleared his throat and his tone became slightly bemused. 'Rather a lot of them, actually. And they're in the care of a young woman who flatly refuses to leave the house before Christmas. She is somewhat…ah…passionate about it.'

Passion. Even the word was distasteful, let alone its implications. The fastest route to chaos. The ultimate in losing control.

'You don't have to deal with it yourself,' he told his solicitor. 'Turn it over to the police. Or Social Services. There are plenty of places for people like that.'

Irresponsible people who would think nothing of taking over a deserted house and living rent free.

'You might know this woman.'

Luke's huff of expelled breath was incredulous. 'I doubt that very much.'

'We've done some investigation. Her name's Amy Phillips. She works as a nurse in the cardiology ward of St Elizabeth's.'

Luke rubbed his temple with the middle finger of his free hand. The ache from his jaw was creeping upwards. He did not like this. Not that he'd heard of this nurse but this was a busy ward that dealt with patients from both the medical and surgical areas of cardiology. He couldn't possibly know the names of every junior staff member. It wasn't the fact that this Amy Phillips was employed here that was disturbing. It was the potential connection. A totally unexpected link from something he had no intention of touching in any form to… Luke raised his gaze again.

At first it was a suspicious scan of the area. Was that this Amy Phillips carrying the stepladder? Or the one with a pile of linen in her arms, heading towards the sluice room? The older woman, maybe, pushing a wheelchair who had just come into view at the end of the corridor. No. She had been here for years and years and her name definitely wasn't Amy. It was…something else.

The attempt to remember the name faded. All the noise and bustle became simply a muted background. The walls almost invisible. What Luke was aware of were in the beds behind the walls. Or in the playroom at the end of the corridor. Being carried by nurses who sang Christmas carols or held up to hook an angel to a high branch on a tree.

The *children*. Life was hard enough, wasn't it, without starting with the kinds of difficulties these sick children had to contend with. *They* were the reason he put so many unforgiving hours of his life into his work. It *was* his life, this place. His career. A stunningly successful one that changed the lives of many, many people.

Having it tainted by a shameful past was simply unthinkable.

'I don't give a damn who she is or where she works,' he said grimly. 'I want her gone and I want a demolition crew on site tomorrow. Deal with it.'

'It won't—'

'Yes, it will,' Luke contradicted. 'Money is not an object here. The proceeds from the sale of this property will be donated to an appropriate charity. Find an organisation who is prepared to take in these...*tenants* and I'll make sure they are a major beneficiary.'

'That might help,' Reginald Battersby conceded. He still sighed, however, as though the task was supremely distasteful. 'I'll see what I can do.'

The phone was still ringing.

Amy gave the large pot one more stir to make sure the meatballs weren't sticking at the bottom of the rich, tomato sauce they were simmering in.

'Hello?'

'Amy! It's me, Rosa.'

'Oh!' Amy made an excited face at two small boys who were lying on the flagged floor of this huge old kitchen. 'Angelo! Marco! It's your Mamma!'

Relaying the information so fast probably hadn't been wise. Now Amy had a six-year-old boy on either side, tugging at her arms, begging in voluble Italian for a turn on the phone. It made it a lot harder to hear what her older sister was saying.

'What was that? How's Nonna?'

'She hates being in the hospital.'

'How bad was it? The heart attack?'

'The procedure they did was successful, apparently. The arterio—plaster thing.'

'Angioplasty?'

'That's it! I knew *you* should have come with Mamma, not me. Neither of us have any real idea what they're talking about.'

'I couldn't go, you know that. Work's crazy and nobody's getting leave before Christmas. And there's trouble with the house. That horrible old lawyer was here again today. He's threatening to—'

The voices of her identical twin nephews became louder. '*Mamma!*' Angelo cried pitifully. '*Piacere, Zietta Amy—*'

'*No!*' Marco shoved his brother. '*Mi!*'

'Travelling with Mamma was a nightmare,' Rosa either hadn't heard or wasn't listening to Amy. 'She lost everything. Twice. Tickets, passport, luggage. I'm exhausted. And… I miss the boys.' She sounded close to tears. 'Are they okay?'

Her sister had enough to handle. A sick grandmother. A distraught mother. Being separated from her children so soon after being deserted by that no-good husband. It wouldn't be fair to share the fear that Amy wasn't going to be able to hold the fort here, even for a few days. That the walls of their world were crumbling at an alarmingly rapid rate.

'The boys are fine,' she said. 'Angels. Here, you talk to them for a minute. I need to check on Summer.'

Amy pushed the phone towards four small hands. 'Marco first,' she ordered. 'And don't hang up. I need to talk to Mamma again.' She spoke in Italian because it was their first language and more likely to be obeyed.

Another quick stir of the sauce made it spit and splatter onto the pitted surface of the ancient stove but Amy didn't have time to do more than wipe up one of the bigger spots with the corner of her apron. She crossed the room, taking just a moment to drop a kiss onto a bent golden head at the big, pine table.

'You're doing a fantastic job, Chantelle.' She spoke in English now, switching languages effortlessly. 'I really like your cutting out.'

'I need more colours.'

'I'll find some more old magazines. Did you find the glue?'

'Here. See?'

The jar of paste tipped and Amy hastily righted it. 'They'll be the best streamers any Christmas tree ever had. Weren't the others going to help you? Or are they doing their homework?'

'They're watching telly.'

'They'll have to get busy after dinner, then. Could you tell them it'll be ready soon?'

There was a somewhat battered old couch in the corner of this kitchen. It was covered with a mound of soft pillows at the end and lots of warm blankets, although the range did a wonderful job of heating this part of the old house. A small radiant heater was also on because the stone floor had an amazing ability to suck in heat.

An oxygen cylinder was tucked safely between the end of the couch and the wall. Tubing snaked towards nose prongs and the pale plastic accessory was made more obvious by how black the little face beneath it was.

Amy loved the feel of Summer's fuzzy hair. She stroked it again as she dropped to a crouch. 'How are you doing, sweetheart? Are you hungry?'

The small girl shook her head.

'Could you eat something? Some eggy soldiers, maybe?'

Another head shake but Summer was smiling her gorgeous smile. Enjoying the attention. Saving her limited breath for something worth saying.

'Soup? If I help you?'

The smile widened and Summer nodded.

'Chicken or tomato?'

'Chicken.' The word was a whisper. It was an effort to speak. An effort just to stay alive, really.

'Good girl.' Amy's fingers sought a pulse in the matchstick wrist as she kissed Summer's forehead. It was thready and too fast. As it always was. A quick glance at the regulator on the oxygen cylinder was a relief. The tank was still more than half-full and there was a new one in the bedroom upstairs. One less task to find time for. She gave her another kiss, this time concentrating on how the child's skin felt under her lips. Was it a little too warm? She took off one of the blankets.

'*Zietta Amy!*' Angelo called. '*Nonna* wants to talk to you.'

Amy took the phone, greeted her mother and then listened to a garbled version of how her grandmother was doing, how tiresome the journey had been with so many people traveling to be home for Christmas and how worried she was about all 'her' children.

'We're fine,' Amy said when she could get a word in edgeways.

'What are you feeding my *bambinos*?'

'Tonight it's spaghetti and meatballs.'

'And vegetables?'

'Yes.' Tomatoes counted as vegetables, didn't they?

'How's Summer?' There was a new note in her mother's voice that went beyond the expected anxiety. Summer was their special one. Every day had to be treasured.

Amy cast a glance back at the couch. Summer lay quietly, just watching. As she had been all day.

'She's happy. She wants chicken soup for dinner.'

'Give her an egg. There's more goodness in an egg. It's

her favourite. Mash up the egg and cut the crusts off the bread and—'

'Chicken soup is good, too, Mamma. That's what she wants tonight.' Amy walked towards the pantry as she spoke, to get the can of soup while she thought of it. The pantry was vast. A relic from the days when this old house had had kitchen staff with scullery maids who would have used the old tubs in here to scour pans. Many of the shelves had nothing more than dust on them. Amy needed to find time to get to a supermarket. She had to get to work so she could pay for the groceries.

'She's too tired to eat? Is that it?'

Amy's hesitation said too much. Marcella Phillips clicked her tongue in distress. '*Dio*, but I hate being away from her.'

'I know, Mamma.'

'She's my little angel. How long is she being lent to us? This Christmas has to be the best. She's in my prayers every day but—'

'She's on the list for a heart transplant. *That* would be the best Christmas present.'

Amy put the can of soup on the bench and opened a drawer to search for a can opener. The bolognese sauce was bubbling enthusiastically. Bright spots of sauce were landing some considerable distance from the pot. The large pan of water beside it was finally coming to the boil. Amy dribbled some olive oil into the water, taking an anxious glance at her watch as she added a handful of salt.

'I need to go, Mamma. It's dinner time and I have to get ready for—' Amy bit her lip but it was too late.

'Ready for what, Amy Elisabetta? You're not going to *work* tonight?'

'I have to, Mamma.' There was no point alarming her mother by telling her how empty their household account was.

She would discuss it endlessly with Rosa and that would only make things worse. Rosa's husband had left her penniless and this was the only home she had for now. The boys needed their mother at home for a little longer, not out working because she felt compelled to help support the family.

'You said you would get time off until Rosa and I got back. It's only a few days. Maybe tomorrow, even.'

'Zoe is coming to stay with the children.'

'Zoe? *Zoe?* She's a child herself!' The fact that her mother had switched from English to Italian was a sure sign that stress levels were zooming up.

'She's sixteen, Mamma. Responsible.' It was quite difficult to hold the phone and open a can of soup at the same time.

'*Pfff!*' The sound was eloquent. 'Responsible people do not keep putting holes in themselves.'

'You get Zoe to babysit yourself. You love Zoe.'

'Not at night. Never *all* night.'

'Lizzie's is only five minutes' walk away. Three if I run. I've talked to my charge nurse. If there's an emergency at home, they'll let me come back.'

If they were quiet, that was.

'It won't do. We'll have to come home.'

'But what about Nonna?'

'She's going to be allowed out of hospital. Maybe even tomorrow. We're going to bring her home with us.'

Amy's heart sank. Nonna was the absolute stereotype of an old Italian woman from a small village. Tiny, wrinkled and always shrouded in voluminous black clothing, she spoke not a word of English. She would hate London.

'Are you sure about this, Mamma?' she asked carefully.

'Of course I'm sure.'

'But—'

'But what? You have a problem with your *nonna* coming to live with us?' Amy recognised that tone of admonition. It was dangerous. 'You don't *love* your Nonna?'

'Of course I do.'

'She can have Vanni's room.'

Amy was silent. This was just getting worse. Uncle Vanni's room might not be available for very much longer. Something had to be said. But what?

Again, Marcella interpreted the silence. 'You think we'll lose the house? No, no, no! That isn't going to happen, *cara*. I know Vanni made a will. It's in the house somewhere. We just have to find it.'

'We've looked everywhere. His desk, the bank, every single box in the attic…'

'He was disorganised, my cousin. It will be somewhere we don't expect.'

The water was boiling now. Ready for the pasta. Chantelle was climbing down from her chair at the table, trailing a string of coloured paper loops for admiration. Angelo and Marco had vanished and happy shrieks were coming from the lounge where the television was.

'I *have* to go, Mamma,' Amy said firmly. 'Give Nonna a kiss for me. Call me tomorrow.'

'You keep looking. Try the dresser.'

'What dresser?'

'The one in the kitchen. With the recipe books and the old… What are they?' It was a sure sign of overwhelming stress when words failed Marcella. 'The letters to say the bills are paid?'

'Receipts.'

'*Sì*. There's a lot of receipts in there. Other papers, too, maybe.'

* * *

It was getting late by the time Luke Harrington had finished his ward round. Very late.

'What are you still doing here, Luke?'

'I could ask you the same thing, Margaret.'

The charge nurse laughed. 'I'm legit. I'm doing a long day so I don't finish till 9:00 p.m., after handover for the night shift. What's your excuse?'

'Johnny Smythe got admitted. Heart failure.'

'I heard that. He's having a bad run, isn't he? Even for a Down's syndrome child, he's getting more than his fair share.'

'They can't put off the surgery any longer. I'll have to try and fit him in in the next couple of days. Tomorrow, possibly.'

'Isn't wee Liam going to Theatre tomorrow?'

Luke slotted the case notes he'd been writing in back into the trolley. 'It's certainly shaping up to be a long day.' Another one. He rubbed the back of his neck, wondering why he felt more drained than usual. Ah...yes...

'Do you know a nurse called Amy Phillips?' he asked Margaret.

'Of course.' Margaret gave him a puzzled glance. 'Why do you ask?'

'Someone mentioned her name today, that's all. I couldn't place it.'

Margaret shook her head. 'Honestly, Luke. Sometimes I think you operate on a different planet. She was a theatre nurse for ages before she came onto the ward here.' Her look was resigned. 'It's no wonder you're still single if you don't even notice women as gorgeous as our Amy.'

Luke didn't discuss his personal life. So far, the hospital grapevine had been denied any juicy titbits regarding his background.

'Someone else clearly thought the same way,' he said dismissively. 'It sounded to me as though she has more children than she can manage.'

Margaret laughed. 'She has, at that. Her mother has, at any rate. She's a foster-parent. They're lucky children that end up in the Phillipses' house.'

Luke frowned. The squatters were fostering children? It didn't make sense. It was also disturbing. He had ordered the demolition of a house full of disadvantaged children?

'The latest addition was Summer Bell. Do you remember her? That dear little Somalian girl who was here a few months ago?' She gave Luke a wry smile. 'You're better at remembering patient names than staff members.'

'I operated on her twice. Of course I remember.' Luke was feeling faintly dizzy. He needed to sit down. Or escape. And it was high time he had something to eat. 'She's terminal,' he said quietly. 'Unless a transplant becomes available in time, and we both know how unlikely that is. She was...sadly... sent home to die.' A case that was not one of the success stories. Never a good idea to dwell on those.

'She had no home to go to,' Margaret said softly. 'Her foster-family couldn't face looking after a terminally ill child. Amy had fallen in love with her. So did Marcella.'

'Marcella?' The Italian name sent a chill down Luke's spine.

'Amy's mother.'

'She's...' Luke swallowed. 'She's Italian?'

'Marcella is. Amy is half-Italian. Marcella married an English policeman, of all things. He brought his family to London when Amy was about five.' Margaret was smiling. 'You wouldn't know she was half-English to look at her, mind you. She's dark and gorgeous and more than a bit fiery.'

Passionate.

It felt as if the walls were closing in. 'I have to go,' Luke decided aloud. His sudden movement clearly startled Margaret enough to need an explanation. 'Early start tomorrow.'

He needed some time alone. To say he was shaken would be an accurate description, except that Luke Harrington did not *get* shaken. The physical movement of striding through the familiar corridors of St Elizabeth's should have been enough to centre himself, but it wasn't.

Something had changed.

Tentacles were pulling at him. Threads of a connection he hadn't expected and most definitely didn't want. More than one of them, too. It felt like some kind of portal had opened and it was following him.

All thanks to an inheritance he wanted nothing to do with. A house he'd probably driven past a thousand times until he'd learned the significance of the address and had gone out of his way *not* to pass it on his way to and from the apartment.

He slid into the driver's seat of his sleek car and drove smoothly to the car-park exit. He had a lot to do tonight. He wanted to plan the major surgery on tiny Liam. He needed to think about the best way to tackle Johnny's oversized septal defect, as well.

He was *not* going to allow himself to be distracted. To feel guilty that he might be scattering a foster-family right before Christmas. They would be better off somewhere else. They were living in a substandard house, for heaven's sake. Practically derelict according to the independent surveyor's report on the dwelling he had received via Mr Battersby.

Missing slates on the roof, a chimney that had a dangerous lean, broken windows that hadn't been repaired properly. He could probably see how inappropriate it was from the outside if he took the time to drive past now that he knew the precise address he was looking for.

No. He didn't want to do that. He didn't want to go near the place.

Not in this lifetime.

There *were* a lot of papers in that hutch dresser. Amy was sitting in a sea of them. She'd only meant to have a quick look but somehow the table hadn't been cleared, the children were not in bed as they should have been and she was running out of time to shower and change into her uniform.

And now someone was pounding on her door.

It couldn't be Zoe, who knew to come in the back. In fact, why wasn't Zoe here yet?

'There's someone at the door, Amy.'

'I know, Chantelle. Oh, you're in your pyjamas. Good girl.'

'Shall I see who it is?'

'No.' It was dark and there shouldn't be anyone knocking at this time of the evening. Amy's heart rate picked up as she went into the shadowy space of the wide hallway. She had a nasty feeling it was going to be that elderly solicitor who'd been here earlier. Or worse. Maybe it was the police coming to evict them.

Standing on tiptoe, Amy peered through the spy hole. She rubbed at the tiny piece of glass, not believing what she was seeing. She peered harder. And then she opened the door, without putting the safety chain on first.

She knew she was probably gaping like a stranded fish but this was so weird!

'Mr *Harrington*,' she gasped. 'What are you doing here?'

CHAPTER TWO

HE WAS still angry with her!

Gorgeous looking, unapproachable, important men did not turn up on Amy's doorstep. Luke Harrington was so far out of her league that this was as disconcerting as it would have been to find a member of the royal family knocking on her door.

However unprofessional and unprecedented it might be, the only explanation Amy could come up with was that Mr Harrington had found out where she lived and had come to yell at her. On top of the worry about her family and yet another fruitless search for a document that represented safety for all of them, this was too much.

Amy almost burst into tears.

Like she had last week, when she had utterly failed to come up to the standards this surgeon expected from his staff.

Had he come to tell her not to bother showing up for work tonight? That he'd persuaded the principal nursing officer that Amy needed to be let go without even serving any notice?

It could be the final straw. Her family might soon have no income, as well as nowhere to live.

But why wasn't he saying anything?

He was staring at her. As though she had just walked into

his operating theatre stark naked or something. As though he couldn't believe what he was seeing and it was so far from being acceptable he couldn't decide what to do about it.

He hadn't expected her to be terrified of him!

Luke recognised her, of course. Sort of. Not that he'd ever seen her out of a uniform that usually included a surgical mask and hat, but those eyes were unique. Dark pools of the variety Luke instinctively avoided ever letting his gaze do more than rake past.

The kind of pools men with lesser control had difficulty not falling into.

He couldn't drag his gaze away this time, however. Because of the fear he could see there. Real fear. The kind he often saw in the eyes of children when they were facing a necessary but painful procedure.

The kind of expression that made you want to protect them. To comfort them and tell them everything was going to be all right. And what good would that do? Someone had to do the hard yards. To distance themselves enough to be able to do what had to be done to actually *make* everything all right.

Precisely what he'd come here to do. He had gone against his better judgement, having parked across the road just to confirm the opinion of that surveyor's report, by deciding to front up in person. To tell this Amy Phillips that this situation was not the end of the world. That he'd make sure that she—and the children—would find new accommodation in time for Christmas.

Better accommodation, dammit!

Luke drew in a deep breath. She'd asked him, quite reasonably, what he was doing there. With an effort, he dragged his gaze away from her eyes. Away from the tumble of dark hair with enough curl in it to make it shine from the dim light of the hallway behind her.

Like a halo.

Away from the way her soft woollen jumper and tight jeans clung to curves that a scrub suit or nurses' uniform had never revealed. Away from an apron that was smeared with red stains and had what looked like... Good grief, tomato skins glued to it? It was filthy!

Luke let his breath out with a rush that gave his words more force than he might have intended. The words themselves were not what he'd planned to say, either, but a wave of something like outrage was building. Were these disadvantaged children in a not simply substandard but *dirty* house?

'I'm here because this is *my* house,' he said.

She certainly hadn't been expecting that. He could see shock and then bewilderment on her face. The unconscious, small head shake that made the tumble of waves shiver and gleam.

And then her jaw dropped and her eyes—as impossible as that seemed—managed to get even larger. Darker. Lakes instead of pools now.

'Oh, my God!' she whispered. *'Harrington.'*

He waited. Curious to know what connection she was making. Maybe she hadn't expected this, but she was figuring out why it was happening.

'Harrington village...that was where Uncle Vanni's wife grew up.'

Uncle Vanni? Was this woman some kind of blood relative? A cousin? Or, worse, a half-sister, perhaps? The notion was distasteful.

Unacceptable.

'The owner of this house was your *uncle*?'

Another tiny head shake. 'Not really. He's...he was my mother's cousin. Or second cousin. A distant relative, really, but they grew up in the same village in Italy.'

She made a soft sound of inexpressible sadness. 'Everybody called him Uncle. He... You...'

Lakes were becoming pools again and Luke found himself transfixed, watching Amy Phillips focus.

'There was a story that Caroline came from an enormously wealthy family. They lived in some vast manor house. We never knew her surname but villages used to get named after the manor houses, didn't they? Harrington village. Harrington Manor.' Amy's chest rose as she took a steadying breath. 'You're a Harrington,' she said quietly. 'It's your family?'

Still, Luke remained silent, letting her join the dots herself. She ran her tongue over her lips as though they had become suddenly dry. It might be rude to stare, but Luke couldn't look away for the life of him.

'Of course it is,' Amy continued. 'You're a Harrington. We were told that the property would probably go to one of Uncle Vanni's wife's relatives if a more recent will couldn't be found.'

'It did.' Luke finally spoke. 'It came to me.'

'So you're a nephew or something?'

'I'm Giovanni Moretti's son.'

'No.' Amy released her breath in what sounded almost like a sigh of relief. 'There's been a mistake. Uncle Vanni's son is dead. He was killed in a terrible car accident. The same accident that killed his mother.'

'Amy?' A small voice was calling from inside the house. 'Can I hang my streamers on the tree?'

'Soon, hon. Put your dressing-gown and slippers on,

though. It's freezing in there. I haven't had time to light that fire.'

It *was* freezing. Why hadn't Luke noticed the goose-bumps on Amy's forearms where the sleeves of the jumper had been pushed up? Or the way she was wrapping her arms around herself now? And she was shivering.

It was all very well for him. Luke had his full-length, black cashmere coat over his suit, a warm scarf around his neck and soft, fur-lined leather gloves on his hands.

Not only was this Amy Phillips cold, she was letting icy air into a house that had children living in it.

'May I come in?' The request was reluctant but he didn't have to go any further than the front entranceway, did he? 'I would like to talk to you.'

But Amy was clearly more reluctant than he was. She actually had the nerve to start shutting the door on him.

'There's nothing to talk about,' she said. 'There *is* another will and we'll find it. Soon. You can't turn Uncle Vanni's children out into the streets. I won't let you.'

Luke caught the door just before it closed. He put his foot in the gap as insurance. He wasn't going to leave until he'd sorted this out. Imagine what people would think if this was the story that reached the hospital grapevine—that a paediatric surgeon had arrived in person to try and turn children out to live in cardboard boxes under a bridge somewhere.

To freeze to death in the coldest December anyone could remember. Too cold even to snow, which was disappointing everyone who was hoping for a white Christmas this year.

'What was his name?' he demanded.

'Uncle Vanni's son? His name was Luca.'

The word was said with an Italian pronunciation. It echoed. Touching some long-buried memory.

Luca...

How old had he been? Three? Old enough to remember his mother's voice?

Luca...

Amy was staring again. Realising the implication. Luke was simply the anglicised version of the name. He was telling the truth, but she wasn't about to accept it because it wasn't something she wanted to hear. Would showing her that long-faded scar that ran from his left temple to his hairline make any difference? Ironic that he should find himself in the position of *wanting* to prove he was Giovanni's son.

'Zietta Amy! Vieni! Rapidimente!'

The language made Luke flinch but, as always, it was more intelligible that he was comfortable with. Mind you, that kind of verbal alarm would transcend any language barriers.

'Che cosa succede?' Amy turned in alarm. *'Vengo!'*

She was going to see why she was being summoned so urgently. Luke found himself standing alone on the doorstep as Amy ran after a small boy with curly, dark hair. Down the hallway and through a door that seemed to have a wisp of smoke coming through it.

And then he could smell it. Something was burning! A fire had started in a house full of children.

With a strangled oath, Luke stepped inside and pushed the door closed behind him.

Amy stomped on the flaming remains of the paper streamer that had been inadvertently draped over the small heater, slipping through the grille to touch the bars.

'I was just showing it to Summer,' Chantelle wailed. 'I'm sorry, Amy.'

'It was a stupid streamer, anyway.' Fourteen-year-old

Robert was reacting to his fright by retreating into teenage surliness. 'Girls are *so* dumb!'

'I'm not dumb,' Chantelle sobbed, 'Am I, Amy?'

'No.' But Amy was more worried about the smoky air and how it could affect Summer's breathing. It was hard enough for her poor, malformed heart to get oxygen into her blood without having smoke added to the mix. Amy reached for the regulator on the cylinder.

'I'm going to turn up the flow for a bit, darling,' she told Summer. 'It might tickle your nose.'

Summer nodded. The alarm in her face had begun to fade as soon as Amy was in the room and she was now watching with interest as Marco stirred scraps of charred paper with his foot to draw shapes on the flagstones.

'Don't do that,' Amy chided. 'It's enough of a mess in here as it is. Could one of you please find the dustpan and brush in the scullery and we'll clean it up.' She looked up from adjusting the regulator to see how many of the children were in the kitchen and who would be first to respond to the request.

And then she froze.

Luke Harrington was standing in the doorway. Staring again. Silently. Looking absolutely...appalled.

And no wonder! It was all too easy to follow his line of vision and see things from his perspective. Amy could feel a hot flush of mortification bloom. If he hadn't already considered her to be incompetent after that disaster in the ward the other day, she was offering ample proof right now.

The kitchen was in utter chaos.

Robert and Andrew had still not begun their allocated task of dishwashing. Pots and plates smeared with tomato sauce and festooned with strings of spaghetti littered the bench. Bowls with spoons and puddles of melted ice cream had been pushed to one end of the table. The other end was crowded with ripped-up magazines, scissors, rolls of sticky tape and a pot of glue that had spilt, making a larger puddle that was now congealing around shreds of discarded paper.

The doors of the hutch dresser were open and it had been Amy who had created the piles of recipe books, ancient domestic paperwork, long out-of-date telephone directories and any number of other random finds including a set of ruined paintbrushes and several half-empty tins of varnish.

The room was hot and steamy and it smelt of cooking and smoke. It was dingy because one of the bare light bulbs that hung from the high ceiling was burnt out and Amy hadn't had a chance to haul in the ladder so she could replace it. The walls were covered with examples of children's artwork but most of the pictures hung at drunken angles because the tape was rendered useless when it became damp.

And there were children everywhere in various stages of undress. Chantelle had pyjamas on but, instead of a dressing-gown, she had pulled on a vast woollen jersey that had been a favourite of Uncle Vanni's. It hung down to her knees and her hands were hidden somewhere within the sleeves.

Twelve-year-old Kyra had a woollen beanie on her head, ug boots on her feet and a flannelette nightgown between the accessories. Standing together, the girls were the picture of children who looked like they had no one who cared about them.

The twins seemed oblivious to their visitor and marched about importantly. Marco had the dustpan and Angelo the hearthbrush, but they couldn't decide how to co-ordinate their efforts and were finding the task highly amusing.

Eleven-year-old Andrew was beside Robert. He elbowed the older boy, who obligingly scowled at Luke.

'Who are you?' he demanded, flushing as his voice cracked. 'And what are you doing here?'

Amy caught her breath. This was actually rather stunning. Robert had been passed from foster-home to foster-home in his short life, becoming progressively more 'difficult' and setting up a vicious cycle where the things that children needed most—an accepting, secure, *loving* environment that had boundaries—were getting further and further from his reach.

He'd come to the Phillips household six months ago, which was already a record for him, taken in as Marcella's way of coping with her grief at losing her beloved cousin and a signal that she intended to carry on what had become a passion for Vanni. Caring for 'lost' children. Being told that 'a man of the house' was needed had been startling for the teenaged Robert.

Right now—standing up to this stranger in their kitchen— it was possible he was reaching out to accept that position of responsibility. That he felt safe enough himself to feel the need to protect his 'family'.

Amy still hadn't let out her breath. Imagine if he learned why Luke was really here? That he had inherited this house and was planning to kick them all out? That the children might be separated and Robert could find himself back in a home where no one was prepared to accept him, let alone make him the man of the house.

She couldn't let it happen.

Catching Luke's gaze, Amy knew she was sending out a desperate plea.

'This is Mr Harrington,' she told Robert. 'He's Summer's doctor and he's just come to make sure she's all right.'

'Oh...' Robert straightened his shoulders and became visibly taller. 'That's OK, then.'

Amy could see Luke assessing the situation. Deciding whether or not to go along with her white lie.

Please, she begged silently. *Don't hurt these children. At least give me time to prepare them. To reassure them and find a solution.*

Luke's face was expressionless. He looked at Robert for what seemed like a long time and then turned slowly to meet Amy's gaze again, and she'd never been so acutely aware of this man's looks before.

Oh, he was gorgeous. Everybody knew that. Very tall, very dark. His features as carefully sculpted as the way he carried himself. A bit over the top, really—like that designer coat, probably French, that he was wearing so casually unbuttoned to reveal a pinstriped suit. There was a distinct aura of perfection about Luke Harrington. The way he looked. The way he worked. The standards he expected from everyone around him. Perfection. Control.

What on earth was she thinking, even hoping that he might back up something that was rather a lot less than the truth?

No wonder there was no hint of a smile on his face when he opened his mouth to respond. Amy's heart skipped a beat as it sank, waiting for the blow to fall.

'That's right,' Luke said gravely. He began to walk over the flagstones. Slowly. As though he was sleepwalking. His gaze still touching Amy's. 'How *is* Summer today?'

Tears of gratitude stung Amy's eyes and she hurriedly blinked them away. As Luke reached the couch and bent down, his face loomed closer and Amy could see what had not been apparent at a distance. He knew exactly what he was doing by not contradicting her.

He *understood*.

And it was enough for hope to be born.

Enough to make Amy's heart sing and her lips to curve into a smile that said exactly how important this was. He understood, so surely he would not be able to go ahead and hurt this family.

She was smiling at him.

As though he'd just given her the greatest gift anyone could ever receive.

It made her eyes sparkle and the warmth emanating from that smile seemed to enter every cell of Luke's body.

He felt…weird.

Powerful and generous and…and like he'd done something wonderful.

How ridiculous was that?

All he'd done had been to keep the real nature of this visit private from a bunch of children who should not be involved in business between adults.

It didn't mean that he was about to change his mind. No matter how gorgeous that smile was. Luke dragged his gaze away from Amy's face.

'Hey, Summer. It's been a while since I saw you.'

Automatically, he took the tiny wrist between his fingers to feel her pulse and watched the small chest to assess how much effort was going into breathing. Post-surgery, patients like Summer Bell returned to the care of a cardiologist so unless Luke made an effort, it was hard to keep up with how well they were doing.

And this little girl was not doing very well. Little Summer was the kind of case that could break your heart if you let it. Some months ago, Luke had done his best to make final corrections to the major congenital anomalies of her heart and the vessels that connected it to her lungs, but there was only so much that could be done. And in this case, it hadn't been enough.

If she stayed alive long enough, she would be a candidate for a heart transplant, but her condition was clearly deteriorating.

'Have you got a pulse oximeter?' Luke queried.

'No.'

'A stethoscope?'

Again, Amy shook her head and Luke tried to push aside his frustration. This was a house, not a hospital ward, after all. Summer was probably fortunate to have a qualified nurse caring for her.

Or she would be, if that qualified nurse wasn't running some kind of orphanage. Luke looked over his shoulder. The two small boys behind him were scuffling over their sweeping duties. Giggling. They were indistinguishable and, Luke had to admit, very cute. Curly and dark and energetic. Rather like the woman they had called, what had it been—*Zietta*? Aunty? He shifted his gaze to Amy who was watching him assess Summer, her eyes wide and anxious.

'How many children do you have living here?'

Amy blinked. She looked nervous, Luke decided. Was she thinking he was about to criticise her ability to care for a sick child because there were too many other demands on her attention?

He could see no reason to do so, so far. Summer was warm and comfortable and looked happy. She was receiving oxygen. Presumably being given all her medications or she would be a lot worse than she was. What more could anyone be doing?

'Right now?' Amy was responding. 'Seven.'

'And you're trying to care for them all? By yourself?'

Her chin lifted a fraction. She had taken his incredulous question as criticism rather than concern.

'Of course not,' she said. 'My mother is the official foster-parent. My sister also lives here. Marco and Angelo are her children. My nephews.'

'So where is your mother? And your sister?' He would have to speak to them all. Three Italian women who were not going to like what he had to say, God help him!

'Um…' Amy's gaze slid sideways. 'They're in Italy just at the moment.'

'*Bisnonna*'s sick,' Angelo piped up helpfully. 'She is a sick…' He looked at Amy questioningly. '*Cuore?*'

'Heart,' Amy supplied. 'She *has* a sick heart. It's my grandmother,' she explained to Luke. 'She's had an MI. My mother had to go to her and she needed my sister to travel with her. I couldn't leave because I have to work.'

Luke's eyebrows rose involuntarily.

'It's only for a day or so. They're going to bring Nonna back.'

Luke sucked in a breath. 'Here?'

'Yes,' Amy said firmly. 'Here. We're going to give her Uncle Vanni's room.'

Luke let his breath out slowly. So he was not only going to have to find suitable accommodation for a collection of children, including one who was terminally ill, he now had to throw an elderly, recuperating cardiac patient into the mix.

With a bemused shake of his head, he turned back to something much easier to deal with. Summer.

'Can I listen to you heart, chicken?' he asked. 'With my ear?'

Amy looked startled but Summer didn't seem to mind the unusual request and the twins were fascinated to see Luke bend his head to place his ear directly on Summer's bare, frail chest.

'What you doing?' Marco asked.

'I'm listening to Summer's heart. And her lungs.'

'Can I listen, too?'

'No.' It was Amy who spoke. 'I want you boys to go and get into the bath before it gets cold. Go now. Shoo!' she added as the twins shuffled reluctantly. 'I'll be up in a minute to make sure you've washed behind your ears.'

'Can we make it hot again?'

'Just a little bit. The big boys still haven't had their bath.'

The information that the hot-water supply in the house was less than ideal barely filtered into the back of Luke's mind thanks to his concentration. Even without the magnification a stethoscope would have provided, he could hear all he needed to reassure himself there was nothing major happening on top of the expected murmurs of abnormal blood flow through Summer's heart.

He lifted the blankets a moment later to check her ankles. There was no swelling to suggest that her heart failure was not under control but he still wasn't entirely happy and he knew he was frowning as he looked at Amy.

Her face was so…alive. She could talk without saying a word. Luke could see she understood his disquiet perfectly. That she also sensed something was brewing but, as yet, there was nothing to point out the direction any deterioration was taking. It was impressive that this nurse could share what was an instinctive warning bell. It was somewhat disturbing that they could communicate almost telepathically.

Amy probably found it equally disturbing. 'We're looking after her,' she said aloud. 'We all love Summer.' She stooped to kiss the child. 'I'm going get your medicine now, darling, and put you to bed. Zoe's coming to look after you and read you a story.'

'Zoe?'

'The babysitter. I'm on night shift tonight.'

Luke was shocked. 'You're going to work? Tonight?'

Her look was steady and Luke almost felt embarrassed. Yes, she could communicate very well non-verbally. Bills needed to be paid, the look said. Mouths needed to be fed. Not everybody had the luxury of being able to afford designer coats. Some people had no choice about having to work, no matter how difficult it might be.

'Robert's here, as well.' Amy motioned towards the lanky boy who was now washing dishes. 'He's fourteen and he's our man of the house.'

Luke could hear the pride in Amy's tone. He could see the way the corner of Robert's mouth twitched—as though he was suppressing a pleased smile. The teenager didn't turn towards them, however. Instead, he spoke gruffly to the younger boy beside him.

'Get those bowls off the table,' he ordered. 'They need doing, as well.'

'That's Andrew,' Amy told Luke. 'He's eleven.' She smiled at the boy. 'You're doing a great job, Andy. Thank you.'

The twins had disappeared, presumably into the bath, but the two girls were still at the table and Luke raised an eyebrow. Seeing as they had started introductions, they might as well finish.

'Chantelle's eight and Kyra's twelve,' Amy said co-operatively. 'They've both been living with us for nearly two years now.'

'Amy?' Chantelle had her hands full of paper loops. 'Can we put these on the tree now?'

Amy nodded. 'And then it's bed for you and homework for Kyra. I'm going to put Summer to bed now and get changed for work.'

'OK.' The girls headed through the door.

Luke suddenly felt as though he didn't belong there. He should get out of the way and let Amy sort out her unconventional household.

'I still need to talk to you,' he warned.

Surprisingly, Amy nodded. 'Give me a few minutes to get Summer to bed and the other children organised. Unless it can wait until tomorrow?'

'I don't think so.' Luke wanted to get it over with. He had no intention of coming back here tomorrow. Or any other day, for that matter.

Amy disconnected the tubing from the oxygen cylinder and gathered Summer into her arms. A few minutes later, the boys finished their task of clearing the bench and also left the kitchen. Luke found himself alone, the noise of activity and voices fading into the distance.

He scanned the room. The old range still had spots of burnt sauce all over it. The table was a mess and it looked as though somebody had had a tantrum with the contents of the hutch dresser. Why was it being emptied all over the floor like that? Had Amy been searching for something?

Like a will?

Was there another will that would have left the house to its current occupants? His information was that the only will ever recorded by Giovanni Moretti had been made shortly after his marriage to Caroline Harrington in which he had left all his worldly goods to his wife and any children they might be blessed with. His wife had died over thirty years ago, however, and he'd never bothered to locate his child.

It was quite possible he would be less than happy with what had eventuated.

Well, tough! If he wasn't getting what he wanted, it was exactly what he deserved. Even if he *had* made another will, Luke could contest it and no doubt win the case easily as the closest living relative.

Still...Luke felt uncomfortable. Movement seemed a good distraction and it could be useful. Already he could see things that made this house substandard, like the old cooker, the dripping taps, the bare light bulbs and the peeling paint on the ceiling. Was the rest of the house in even worse condition? A list of such inadequacies would strengthen his case that better accommodation would be more suitable for these people.

And with that in mind, Luke dismissed his aversion to being inside this house and set off to explore.

CHAPTER THREE

IT WAS worse than he had expected.

Or perhaps better, given that he was looking for ammunition with which to strengthen his position.

A large room next to the kitchen and scullery complex had a television in one corner. A fire burned merrily, safely covered by a wire screen, but the warmth and cleanliness of the room was easy to overlook.

Luke's attention was on several very old and mismatched couches that could well have been rescued from a rubbish dump, with their lumpy cushions and frayed fabrics. Battered toys lay scattered about, some of the lead-light windows had cracks covered with masking tape and, if he concentrated, he could feel a draft of icy air around his ankles.

The two older boys lay on the floor in front of the television with what looked like schoolwork around them. Robert noticed Luke entering the room and he could feel the challenging glare on his back as he walked over to a set of French doors. This was where the draft was coming from but Luke could see why the curtains had not been drawn. The ancient velvet would probably disintegrate under the pressure required to pull them into place.

Enough light escaped the room to illuminate a flagged terrace area and the shaggy edges of a large, dark garden. Luke knew it was a large garden because a plan of the property had been included with the paperwork his solicitor had sent him weeks ago now.

Large was not really the word for it, he thought, staring out at the smudged outlines of old trees. It was vast by London standards. With the house removed, it would be easy to build an entire apartment block on the site. With Regent's Park virtually across the road, it wasn't reasonable for anyone to sit on private parkland that supported only one dwelling. Financially, it was just plain stupid.

The observation he was still under from Robert made Luke vaguely uncomfortable but he was satisfied with the list of inadequacies he had noted in this room, so he acknowledged the boys with a nod and somewhat tight smile, leaving the room to cross the wide hallway where he entered what must have originally been a drawing room.

There were more leaded windows here and the fanlights had coloured glass in an intricate pattern. The ceiling in this room was very high and the plasterwork very ornate, but it failed to impress Luke. How could it when it was a pale imitation of the architectural splendour Harrington Manor had to offer and when its condition was so bad? The paint on this ceiling was peeling off in large flakes. Probably lead-based paint, Luke decided. Dangerous for children.

Such as the two girls who were sitting on a faded rug in front of a cavernous fireplace that contained some half-burnt logs and no doubt provided a whistling, icy draft. The girls didn't notice Luke enter the room because they were too intent on admiring their handiwork.

A tall but scraggly tree branch—possibly yew—was propped up in a plastic bucket that had a tartan ribbon tied around it. More of the tartan ribbon was tied in bows on the branch offshoots and it was now also draped with the strings of paper loops he'd seen Chantelle carrying.

'We need an angel,' he heard her say to Kyra. 'For the top.'

'Angels are expensive,' Kyra said doubtfully. 'There might not be enough money if we're all going to get a present.'

'We could make one.'

Kyra shook her head. 'That would be a really hard thing to make. We could make a star, though. A really big one and I think we've got some glitter.'

'Silver glitter?' Chantelle asked hopefully.

'No. I think it's blue. Or green. It's left over from that birthday card we made Robert.'

'Oh… That was blue. 'Cos he's a boy, remember?'

'Oh, yeah… That's right.'

Blue didn't seem to be acceptable. Luke watched as Chantelle wriggled closer to Kyra and the older girl put her arm around her shoulders.

'It's still beautiful,' Kyra said. 'And we're lucky. Some kids don't even get a tree.'

And some had so many beautiful new decorations, they had no use for a big box of older ones. Imagine how excited these girls would be if they had that whole box that had been left in the ward office. It wouldn't be hard to pick it up and leave it on the doorstep here.

The apparent brilliance of the idea was surprising. The strength of desire to follow it through was unsettling. What was he thinking? The cleaners had most likely taken the box away as rubbish by now and even if they hadn't, all he'd achieve would be to give the impression that he wanted these children to stay here and enjoy Christmas. He could make sure they got a much better tree somewhere else. In their new home. A real spruce tree that had gifts beneath it and an angel on the top.

The girls needed to be cuddled together for more than comfort. That fire would have to be well stoked for a long time to take the chill off this enormous room. He took note of a slightly damp smell, as well, as he slipped out.

A peal of childish laughter drifted down the sweep of the staircase at the end of the hallway, but fortunately Luke could think of no reason he needed to go upstairs. Except that he felt curiously disappointed. Although he had seen enough to fuel the argument he knew was looming, he decided to check out the last downstairs room. Perhaps the distinct feeling of discomfort at what he was doing here would be relieved if he found something more personal to the previous owner of this house.

Something that might rekindle the anger that had grown from the loneliness of being so different. Alone. Brought up isolated from parents or siblings. Unwanted to the extent that not even a spark of responsibility remained.

He hit the jackpot through the door that opened beneath the staircase. Having turned on the light and instantly sensing that this room's occupant had been absent for some time, Luke froze.

This was it. Away from an upstairs inhabited by numerous women and children, this had been a man's domain. The old brass bed had a maroon cover. A dark woollen dressing-gown hung on one of the brass knobs and a pair of well-used men's slippers lay beneath it. A maroon colour, like the bedspread, the woollen toes of the slippers were a little frayed and the sheepskin lining squashed into an off-white felt. They could have been anyone's slippers.

Except they weren't.

These slippers had been worn by Giovanni Moretti.

His father.

Luke's mouth was dry. He hadn't expected anything like this. He'd grown up knowing that his father was a monster. Responsible for his mother's death and too uncaring to think of his son. He had been an ogre until Luke had been old enough to start feeling angry. To start hating the man. Even then, he had always seemed larger than life. An enemy. A man powerful enough to ruin the lives of others.

But huge, powerful, evil men did not wear slippers like this.

They didn't collect homeless children and get called 'Uncle' by everyone, either. His father had owned this house and presumably lived in London since *he* had been five years old, and he'd never made contact. Never remembered a birthday or sent a letter. And yet he'd left him this house.

Why?

To underline the fact that he had existed—close by—and hadn't given a damn? To make sure Luke never forgot?

As if he could!

Luke could actually taste the bitterness that rose within him. Giovanni Moretti had cared about the children other people didn't want, but he hadn't cared about his own son.

He was right to hate this man. To dismiss his life—and this room—with no more than a cursory look.

A gaze that took in a plain dressing-table that had a brush and comb on its dusty surface and unframed photographs jammed into the frame around the large mirror. Snapshots of people. Dozens of them. Luke found his feet moving in much the same way as he'd been drawn towards Amy and Summer in the kitchen. Pulled by something he couldn't—or didn't want to—identify.

One photograph stood out from the rest. In pride of place maybe, at the top left-hand corner. Or maybe it looked different because it was older. Curled at the edges. The hairs on the back of Luke's neck prickled as he stepped closer, however. What, in God's name, was a photograph of himself doing in this man's room?

It wasn't him. Of course it wasn't. The explanation was genetic. This was a picture of his father taken more than thirty years ago when he had looked extraordinarily like Luke did now.

The gorgeous blonde woman in the photograph was just as easily recognisable. Caroline Harrington had been frozen in time and had always looked like this as far as Luke had known. Except there was a difference here. Compared to the studio portraits Grandmother had in plenty, this was just a candid shot. The focus wasn't perfect and the colours had faded. What was even more different was his mother's expression.

Sheer joy radiated from her face as she looked up at the man beside her.

Even the baby in her arms seemed to be laughing. Tiny fists punched the air in an exuberance of happiness. Luke had never seen a photograph of himself as a baby. For a long, long moment, he simply stood there. Staring.

Shocked.

Faintly, the sound of feet running down the stairs and Amy's voice filtered through the haze.

'I'll be back up in a minute,' Amy was calling. 'I just need to talk to Mr Harrington before he goes home.'

There was no time to try and analyse any of the odd, unsettling emotions Luke was experiencing. And there was no point, was there? It was all in the past and best forgotten. Destroying the evidence would make it all so much simpler.

Without really thinking about what he was doing, Luke tugged the photograph free of the mirror and slipped it into his coat pocket. He flicked the light off as he left the room and strode back towards the kitchen. The sooner he left this house the better.

All he had to do was make sure Amy understood that the same applied to her.

Amy wound a rubber band around the end of the sleek French plait taming her hair that she had accomplished before hauling the twins from the bath and getting them dry and into their pyjamas. She changed into the tunic top and trousers of her uniform as the boys scrambled into the bunk beds in the room they shared with Robert and Andrew. She laced comfortable shoes onto her feet as she sat on the end of the trundle bed in her room where Summer was now tucked up.

The bedroom oxygen cylinder was full and the coal fire stoked and screened. Summer was warm and already asleep. Amy kissed her, hating it that she had to leave to go to work.

'Zoe will be here any minute,' she whispered, more to reassure herself than anyone else. 'She's going to sleep in my bed so she'll be right here beside you.'

She kissed her again, and stroked her hair softly. One of these nights, Summer was going to go to sleep and simply not wake up.

Not tonight. Please... Not before Christmas!

Giving her uniform a final tug into place and letting the twins know she'd be back up to say good-night, Amy ran down the stairs. It was amazing how being clean and tidy and ready for work made her feel so much more in control.

Ready for anything.

Or almost anything. The empty kitchen took the wind out

of her sails momentarily. So did the odd expression on Mr Harrington's face when he appeared a few seconds later. Had he been snooping? Would that explain the curiously guilty flash she thought she saw in his eyes?

'This house is appalling,' Luke said without preamble, walking towards Amy. 'It's falling to pieces.' He stopped when he reached the kitchen table, resting a hand on the back of one of the chairs. 'It's neither a safe nor a healthy environment for anyone to live in. Particularly children. *Especially* a sick child. It's simply not fit for human habitation.'

'*We* love it.' Amy's heart sank at the wobble in her voice. She could do with a chair to hang onto herself. How had that confidence she'd brought downstairs with her evaporated so instantly?

Maybe there was a disadvantage to wearing her uniform, as well. The confidence might be part of her work frame of mind but work was a place where no one would dream of disputing the authority of someone like Luke Harrington.

Someone whose wrath was feared. You made sure children were where they were supposed to be when Mr Harrington was due for rounds. You picked up toys that could be tripped over. You made absolutely sure that any test results were available and you sympathised with the registrars and housemen who had to work to their utmost ability to win recognition from this perfectionist surgeon.

'You'll find something else is far more suitable,' Luke said firmly. 'A house that has adequate insulation and central oil-fired heating and plumbing that works, for instance.'

He was so confident. Standing there all dark and serious and so sure of himself. So far above Amy in any pecking order she could think of. It took courage to stand up to him.

'We can't afford to rent a house like that. Not big enough for all of us. Not in central London, that's for sure.'

'So move away from London, then. Surely a rural environment would be a better place to be running a...whatever the modern equivalent of an orphanage is?'

'A foster-home,' Amy responded quietly. 'And some of these children retain contact with their birth families. Kyra visits her mother every couple of weeks. She's hoping she can move home again one day. That contact would be lost if we moved away.'

Amy took a step closer. She had to make him see how important this was. Her voice rose but she was pleased to hear it gaining strength. 'We'd probably lose the children because Social Services tries to place them in a radius of their own homes for precisely that kind of reason. They need something familiar in their territory like a school. And besides...' Amy straightened her back and glared at Luke, outrage colouring her tone. 'This is my *home*. I came here to live when I was ten years old. When my dad died. Uncle Vanni was like a father to my sister and me. There's no way he would have wanted us to lose this house. There *is* another will. There *has* to be.'

'Arrangements are already in place,' Luke said with finality. 'The house is going to be demolished.'

'Over my dead body!' Amy snarled.

The surgeon was clearly taken aback by such blatant defiance. But then he simply turned away as though he couldn't see any point in continuing this discussion. He was avoiding eye contact. He didn't intend to be persuaded that any viewpoint other than his own might be legitimate.

'We're going to contest the will,' Amy added bravely. She stared at the vein on Luke's temple that had become suddenly more obvious. He had to be incredibly angry. Beside the vein, the tiny line of a scar ran from the side of his left eye upwards to disappear under the waves of dark hair. She'd never noticed that before, but why would she? The only times she had been this close to the surgeon had been when he'd been wearing a hat and mask.

'Have you any idea how horrendously expensive that would be?'

'We're getting legal aid.' Amy crossed her fingers behind her back. She *hoped* they were getting legal aid. 'And there's no way you can do anything about demolishing this house while we're still living in it and…and we're *not* moving.' She resisted the urge to add, *So there!*

That scar was disconcerting. The kind of scar that could be left from a long-ago injury. Clearly, her unexpected and unwelcome visitor was telling the truth but it begged the question of why Uncle Vanni had not known the truth.

Or had he?

Amy tilted her head just enough to be able to discern that scar again. Had Uncle Vanni been afraid of what might have been the result of an horrific head injury? Had the thought of trying to raise a disabled son alone been too much?

No. That didn't make sense because Uncle Vanni had devoted his life to helping other people's children. Including disabled children, like Summer. But, then, why had he stayed in London and not returned to his native country? Because he couldn't bring himself to get that far away from his son? It was confusing. Disturbing.

'My solicitor will be in touch. His name is Reginald Battersby.'

'I've met him.' Amy stepped sideways, trying to position herself between Luke and the door. She couldn't let him leave like this. Where had that ray of hope gone? He understood, didn't he? He'd protected the children by going along with her lie.

And what about that strange sensation she'd experienced when she had watched him listen to Summer's chest without the benefit of a stethoscope? To see his ear laid so gently on tiny, fragile ribs? The way his half-closed eyes had made the dark fan of his eyelashes and the shadowing of stubble on his jaw so much more noticeable. There had been more than hope in the curiously warm, fizzy sensation flooding Amy at that point. Trust had been mixed with hope, dammit!

What had changed while she had been upstairs? She couldn't have been that wrong, surely? What had she done to deserve having that newfound trust broken?

It wasn't fair.

More than that. It wasn't *right*.

'Why do you want to do this?' Amy demanded. 'What have you got against us?'

'Nothing. Until very recently I had no idea my…father was living here. Until today I had no idea who you were.'

That was a good way to fuel her anger. If he'd had no idea his father had lived here, it might explain why he'd never visited before, but she worked with this man, for heaven's sake. He'd bawled her out only days ago, but she hadn't been important enough for him to bother learning her name. Never mind what she'd seen with Summer. Luke Harrington was not a nice man.

Amy's control snapped. She was more than ready to go into battle to defend her family.

'It'll look good, won't it?' she said with deceptive sweetness. 'The photo in the papers with us all sitting in the street? Right before Christmas. In the *snow*. With Summer's oxygen cylinder. Millions of people will see that someone who's supposed to care about children doesn't really give a damn. Even about one of his own patients.'

Luke's face was grim. 'That isn't going to happen. Reginald is going to find suitable accommodation. For *all* of you.'

'In the same place? I doubt it. We stick together here,' Amy warned. 'And I also doubt that your Reginald has any idea about what's suitable. The man's as old as Methuselah. He probably thinks foster-children should be earning their keep sweeping chimneys.'

'Don't be ridiculous!'

But Amy was just warming up. 'And even if you don't give a damn about us, what have you got against this house? It's gorgeous! Early Victorian architecture that deserves to be preserved. A lot of people will be very upset when they learn it's going to be bulldozed. We'll probably get any number happy to chain themselves to the railings. The media will love that, too.'

'The house is falling down. It's not even safe!'

'It could be fixed.'

'It would cost a fortune.'

'From what I've heard, that's exactly what you've got sitting in the bank!'

Ooh, she'd stepped over the line now. Onto the kind of personal ground that hospital grapevines thrived on. Amy didn't need to see the dangerous glint in Luke's eyes to know that he would hate being the subject of gossip. She also had the distinct feeling she was going to regret this.

'What makes you think I'm planning to keep the proceeds from this property?' Luke snapped. 'Not that it's any of your damn business, but I intend to donate any profits to an appropriate charity.'

Amy's jaw dropped. He didn't need the money. He didn't want the house. He was planning to get rid of it and *give* the money away?

Why not just give the house away?

To *them*?

He had pulled his gloves and keys from a pocket of the black coat. He was ready to leave and he only had to step around Amy to reach the door. He began to do just that.

'W-wait,' she stammered. She needed to repair the damage she'd just done. To find a way to present their case calmly. To get down on her knees and beg if that was what it would take.

'What for?' The disgust in Luke's tone suggested that nothing Amy could say would be worth listening to.

'For...for...' For the children, Amy wanted to cry. For my mother and sister and grandmother. For *me*. But tears threatened to choke her words and she needed to think. To say something that would stop Luke walking out the door.

And in that tiny gap of time as she hesitated, a cold wind rushed into the room. There was a loud bang as the back door from the scullery to the garden slammed and then...

'Zoe!' Amy sucked in her breath at her babysitter's precipitous entrance.

The girl had obviously been running and now she stood there with her mouth opening and closing but no sound emerging as she tried to catch her breath. The anorak she was wearing had a ripped sleeve.

'Zoe?' This time Amy let her concern show. 'Is everything all right?'

'No!'

'What's wrong?'

'Bernie!'

'Bernie? As in your m―

'Yeah…' Zoe managed a ― a boyfriend any more. He's a― you're gonna get married?'

'Fiancé?'

'Yeah. He's gonna move in and he says ―

'What? Why?'

'He says he's just a smelly stray and he's too― costs too much to feed and he's…he's going to g― him!' Zoe burst into tears.

Amy gathered the girl into her arms. 'It's all right, *cara*,' she said, more than once because Zoe was crying too loudly to hear her. 'We'll sort it out.'

Turning her head, Amy could see that Luke had moved closer, reluctance and concern warring on his features. This girl was clearly in trouble. Possibly injured. As a doctor he had a duty to help.

As a man, he wanted nothing more than to turn and get out of this house.

Behind Luke, Amy could see the frightened faces of several children.

'It's OK,' she told them. 'Nothing for you guys to worry about.'

They continued staring.

'Kyra? It's time Chantelle was in bed and could you make sure the twins and Summer are OK? Give the boys a kiss for me. They're probably asleep by now.'

'But what's wrong with Zoe?'

Amy felt the girl shudder in her arms and a nose scraped painfully on her collar-bone as Zoe buried her face. No doubt this teenager was embarrassed to be seen like this by the younger children.

Not immediately, that was for sure. He could hardly walk out when this strange-looking girl was obviously in some sort of trouble with a soon-to-be stepfather. And what about that ripped jacket? How heavy handed was this Bernie character? Was it possible the confrontation had become physical? And who the hell was Monty? The girl's boyfriend? Brother?

She was just a kid. A weird-looking kid dressed completely in black, with jet-black hair that sported an electric pink streak and enough piercings to send a metal detector into overload. In the brief glimpse he'd already had, Luke had seen a ring through her lower lip, something in her nose and eyebrows and the ear that was currently visible had ornaments around its entire perimeter. Even through the tragus in the centre.

She was maybe sixteen years old? Young enough to be admitted to a paediatric ward in any case. Young enough to need protection. To deserve safety and assistance. If there was an angry man involved, he could hardly leave Amy and a bunch of vulnerable children to defend themselves, could he?

As fiercely as Amy had just demonstrated she was prepared to defend the people she cared about, she was just a slip of a woman herself. Delicate...physically, anyway. There was certainly nothing delicate about this woman's spirit.

The very thought of her having to defend herself physically was abhorrent. So much so that Luke had to take a deep breath to steady himself. He needed something else to focus on. Something real that couldn't stir imaginary and therefore useless emotional reactions.

'Can you get Zoe to sit down?' he suggested. 'We need to find out if she's been hurt.'

'I'm not *hurt*!' The girl pulled back from Amy's embrace. 'Bernie wouldn't hurt *me*.' Luke could see eyes that seemed disconcertingly pale thanks to thick black make-up that hadn't entirely run down the pale face. 'And I've hidden Monty so he can't do anything to him, either. Who're you?'

'This is Mr Harrington, Zoe,' Amy said. 'He's a surgeon at Lizzie's where I work.'

'What's he doing here?' Zoe's gaze flicked back to Amy. 'Is he your *boyfriend* now?'

'*No!*'

Did she have to sound quite that horrified? As though she wouldn't consider dating him if he were the last man on earth?

And why had Amy's face flushed so pink? Her eyes were so dark compared to the pale blue of Zoe's. Luke stared back at the two female faces. Dark eyes were *so* much more attractive, he found himself thinking and in that same moment he was horrified at himself.

Not because he considered Amy's eyes attractive but because something so shallow—so *emotional*—had actually distracted him so he wasn't thinking of anything else. Just the kind of mental behaviour he had conquered long ago.

What the hell was going on here?

'I'll explain later,' Amy told Zoe. 'Are you sure you're not hurt? Your jacket's all ripped…' She touched Zoe's cheek and Luke could swear he felt that touch himself.

So gentle. So full of genuine concern. It tugged at something deep within Luke. Something disturbingly poignant.

'I ripped the jacket on some wire in the shed. That's where I hid Monty.'

'It's too cold to leave him in there. You'll need to bring him inside.'

'He can come here?' Zoe's face brightened. 'You don't mind?'

'Of course not. We love Monty. We'll…adopt him.'

'What if Mum says you can't?'

'Do you think she would?'

'Nah. She'd be glad to get rid of him.' Zoe scrubbed at her nose and Luke winced at the thought of the metal spike in her nostril getting in the way. 'She wasn't that happy when I saved him from getting beaten up by those boys.'

'He's got a home here,' Amy said firmly. 'And you can visit whenever you want to. How much can it cost to feed one dog, after all?' With another squeeze of Zoe's shoulders and a discreet but anxious glance at her watch, Amy moved to the stove to pick up a kettle. 'Hot chocolate coming up,' she said cheerfully.

'I'll just go and get Monty,' Zoe said. 'And his blankets and stuff. Is that cool? I'll only be a few minutes.'

'Sure. But be as quick as you can. I can't be late for work.'

The cold-water tap over the old porcelain sink was turned on and a ghastly, shuddering noise filled the kitchen.

'Good grief,' Luke said. 'What is *that*?'

'Just air in the pipes,' Amy said offhandedly. 'It'll come

right in a tick.' Sure enough, the water spat and dribbled and then began to flow and the dreadful noise abated.

Luke opened his mouth and then shut it again. This was hardly the time to score further points about how inadequate this housing was. Not when Amy had just collected another inhabitant. Somehow it didn't surprise him that she would be prepared to lavish emotional energy on animals, as well as people. She was half-Italian, after all. Plenty of emotional energy to go around.

A heavy, unfamiliar feeling was gathering over Luke like dark clouds. He had known it would be a mistake to set foot in this house.

Amy seemed to be thinking hard, but Luke could read nothing in her expression when she glanced in his direction. She gave a slight nod just as the first tendril of steam escaped the spout of the kettle. Then she looked at her watch very deliberately.

'I absolutely have to go to work,' she said suddenly. 'I'll let Margaret know what's happening. She might be able to get a pool nurse in to cover and then I'd be able to come home.' Amy was speaking very fast, the words tumbling over each other. 'I've got my mobile. Could you please tell Zoe to text me if she needs me?'

'You can't leave!' Luke made the statement an order.

'I have to. I can't afford to lose my job.'

This was unacceptable. Luke stared at Amy. 'You're going to leave a house full of children? Unattended?'

'I'm not leaving them unattended,' Amy said calmly. 'You're here.'

'I'm not staying.'

'Why not? It's *your* house. And it's not for long. Zoe will be back in just a few minutes.' She sounded extraordinarily calm.

'I don't really see that you've got a choice, Mr Harrington. Sorry.'

She didn't *look* sorry. There was an expression curiously like satisfaction as Amy shrugged on a coat that hung behind the kitchen door, grabbed a bright red tote bag that stood beside the hutch dresser and practically ran from the house.

It all seemed to happen within seconds. Stunning! And now Luke knew what that strange, heavy feeling was.

Defeat. By stepping into this damned house he had stepped onto a battlefield and he had just lost the first skirmish. Something akin to admiration sneaked into the astonishment at the way he had just been manipulated.

Amy Phillips was certainly a force to be reckoned with.

There was no point continuing to stare at an empty doorway. Luke turned as the kettle began to whistle. He had to move to take it off the range and he was still standing there, lost in thought, when the back door opened again.

Zoe entered, holding a piece of rope. On the end of the rope was the biggest dog Luke had ever seen. Long, long legs and tufty hair and big sad brown eyes.

Luke stared. He couldn't help it. He knew he probably had an expression of extreme distaste on his face but he couldn't help that, either. He had a flash of sympathy for Bernie. This animal *was* too big and probably did smell and would, most likely, cost a fortune to feed.

'Don't worry,' Zoe told him scathingly. 'He probably doesn't like you, either.' She wrinkled her nose. 'I know who you are,' she informed him. 'And I *really* don't like you.'

'Oh?' Despite himself, Luke was curious. 'Why is that?'

'You made Amy cry.'

CHAPTER FOUR

THE route that cut through a corner of Regent's Park, crossed the busy main roads and then tracked past the ambulance entrance to Lizzie's emergency department had never been completed so fast.

Amy felt as if she was running for her life and her heart was still pounding so hard she had to slow down on the stairs up to the floor that housed the cardiology ward.

What had she done?

It had seemed like the perfect solution at the time. Of course the children couldn't be left without a responsible adult in attendance. Not when the babysitter was hardly more than a child herself and was currently distracted by her own problems.

Amy had taken a huge risk. She was banking on Luke Harrington's sense of duty being stronger than his desire to escape. She was also banking on nothing more than intuition, in the hope that she hadn't been wrong in sensing that he not only understood but was trustworthy.

She was forcing him to spend just a little more time in her household. Maybe enough time for him to think about what he intended to do and reflect on the effect it could have on the children he was—temporarily—responsible for.

But what if she was wrong?

What if he contacted Social Services or the police and reported a house full of abandoned children? A house that had sustained a small fire already that evening? Amy might arrive home to find they'd all been lifted from their beds and taken to places where they would be under more appropriate supervision.

She was good at texting as she moved. She fished her cellphone from the depths of her red bag.

'Zoe? U ok?'

'Al gud,' came the response. 'Talkin to G2.'

G2? Oh, *God!* Amy stopped on the landing between the first and second floors. She meant 'G squared'. Luke's nickname at Lizzie's. It stood for 'Grumpy Guts'. It hadn't occurred to Amy that the teenager would remember that, but there was nothing she could do about it now.

With a groan, Amy pushed up the last flight of stairs. She could only hope that Zoe wouldn't reveal her indiscretion to the head of Lizzie's cardiothoracic surgical unit.

'Do you know what they call you?' the girl said to Luke. '"G squared". It stands for "Grumpy Guts".'

'I beg your pardon?'

'Grumpy Guts,' Zoe repeated with relish. 'Nobody likes you. Not even Monty, and he likes everybody.'

Sure enough, the extraordinarily tall dog, who was now sitting on a patched old blanket, was giving Luke a steady glare that could only be described as menacing. If it started growling, Luke was out of there.

Zoe was watching him just as intently. Disconcertingly, only one eye was visible due to her strange, asymmetric fringe. 'Why don't you just go home?' she demanded.

Luke wasn't used to social interaction with teenagers and he had never been this close to one who looked quite like this. Was she a member of some cult? The absurdly immature response of '*This* is my home' occurred to Luke and he actually felt the corner of his mouth twitch. Instead, he shrugged off his coat, hung it over the back of a chair and sat down at the kitchen table.

'I'm not going anywhere,' he said calmly. 'I wouldn't dream of leaving a houseful of children with no adequate supervision.'

'Whaddya mean by that?'

'You're no older than the children you're supposed to be looking after.'

'I am so! I'm *sixteen*!' The single eye narrowed. 'Are you saying I'm stupid or something?'

Behind the aggressive response, Luke saw the fear that Zoe believed that might be true. Had somebody suggested it already or was this just the normal kind of low self-esteem teenagers could struggle with?

'Not at all.' Luke held her gaze. 'You've demonstrated you can cope very well. There's not many people that would rescue a wolf. Twice!'

Zoe was silent for a moment and then her mouth twisted into a grin that lit up her face. The delight was rapidly stifled, however.

'I still don't like you.'

Luke nodded. 'Because I made Amy cry.'

'Yeah.'

He frowned. 'I don't remember *seeing* her cry.'

''Course you didn't. She did it in the loo. She told me about it 'cos I was crying about something this chick at school said. Amy said it was good to cry but then you had to suck it up and get on with your life. You couldn't let mean things people said pull you down.'

'Mean things?' Luke was racking his memory. 'I don't say mean things to people.'

'You did. You told Amy she was stupid.'

'No.' The head shake was decisive. 'I would never say that.'

'You did!' Zoe insisted. 'It was in the middle of the night and this baby got real sick and it had to have a tube thing stuck into it and Amy was trying to help you and the baby was screaming and she tried to give it a cuddle and she touched the stupid tube and you yelled at her and told her she was stupid.'

Luke closed his eyes for a second. He remembered. About 3:00 a.m. last Thursday. He'd still been in the building due to emergency surgery on a child with major chest trauma from a car accident. An inpatient in the ward had run into trouble and needed a central line inserted. It had been a difficult enough procedure even getting local anaesthetic in place and then his nursing assistant had inadvertently brushed the sterile catheter with the sleeve of her gown.

'I didn't say she was stupid,' he said slowly. 'I think I said she was incompetent. That it had been a very clumsy thing to do.'

Zoe didn't answer. She was busy texting on her bright pink phone. Luke thought about the incident some more.

It had been a clumsy error and he'd been tired and concerned about the child he'd only just left in Intensive Care. And the nurse assisting him had been gowned and masked and gloved and…and he hadn't considered her feelings at all, had he?

The slip hadn't been a catastrophe. The trolley always had plenty of spare catheters and she had proved herself perfectly competent as she had silently continued to assist with the procedure. The knowledge that she had taken herself off afterwards to deal with the effects of his criticism came as something of a shock.

And 'Grumpy Guts'?

Yes, he avoided social interaction with his colleagues. And, yes, he expected others to try and meet the professional standards he set for himself, but he was always polite and fair and he gave praise whenever it was deserved.

He had made Amy cry.

Amy—who was brave enough to fight for her family. To comfort and protect anyone who was in trouble. Even a dog. Strong enough to go and do what she had to do even though she must have known it was a risk.

Had it not occurred to her that he could just call in some appropriate authority and have this household disbanded in one easy stroke?

Luke could still see the plea in those dark eyes when she had asked him not to reveal his real reason for being in the house. He remembered the smile and the way it had made him feel, and then he understood.

Amy was trusting him.

She may not like him any more than Zoe did but, for whatever reason, she had handed over the responsibility of something she cared about passionately. If he broke that trust, he could guarantee she would hate him for ever.

Luke didn't like that idea at all.

And it was only for an hour or two, wasn't it?

The ward was, mercifully, quiet.

Margaret was due to go home but she hadn't left yet. She was sitting in her office, gaping at Amy.

'Luke Harrington? In your house? *Babysitting?*'

'*His* house, apparently, and he wants to kick us all out onto the streets. Right before Christmas. Can you believe it?'

'No.' Margaret shook her head for emphasis. 'Why would he want to do something like that?'

'Because he's not a very nice man.'

'He's a lonely man,' Margaret said quietly. Her glance at Amy was a warning. 'Not that I'm one to gossip.'

'I know that.' Amy smiled at the senior nurse. 'And I'm sorry to dump on you, but I've got no one to turn to right now and I'm scared, you know? I can't let anything happen while Mamma and Rosa are away. These children are Mamma's life. They're part of our family.'

'I know.' Margaret leaned forward to pat Amy's hand. 'And I can help. Let's hope Personnel can come up with some cover for you tonight. If not, I'll stay on myself.'

'You can't do that. You'd be way over your hours.'

'Did you really leave Luke babysitting?'

'Kind of. I'm hoping he'll get a feel for the place and then realise how sad it would be to break up the family.'

Margaret's frown looked puzzled. 'I would have thought that would be the last thing Luke, of all people, would want to do.'

'Why do you say that?' And why had she described Luke Harrington as 'lonely'? The word was echoing in Amy's head.

Lonely people needed comforting.

They needed love.

'If I tell you something, will you promise it won't go any further?'

Amy nodded and Margaret lowered her voice. 'I grew up in Harrington Village,' she said.

'Oh-h-h!' Amy could feel her eyes widening. 'Where the

manor house is? And Mr Harrington's incredibly rich family?'

'You know about that?'

'I kind of guessed. It's why he's inherited the house. Uncle Vanni's wife was a Harrington. She died in a horrible car accident.'

'I heard that both Luke's parents were killed in a car crash.'

'It's obviously what they wanted people to think. Maybe Uncle Vanni wasn't considered good enough to be part of the Harrington clan.'

That was a possible explanation, wasn't it? That Uncle Vanni had said his son was dead because he'd been too mortified to confess he'd been deemed unacceptable?

Margaret was frowning. 'I don't know about that. What I do know is that my son went to school with Luke. He went to visit the manor house a few times. He said it was really scary.'

'Ghosts?' Amy was enthralled. She could picture a vast, old gloomy house with pictures of Luke's ancestors glowering down from within ornate gilt frames. A house that was hundreds of years older than the one she lived in and one that could have been the scene of feuds and scandals and possibly even murders….

But Margaret was shaking her head. 'Luke's grandmother.'

Amy blinked. OK, her nonna could be fierce and she had been known to poke an errant child with a knobbly finger or even her walking stick, but she was *family*. Family shouldn't be scary.

'She's a wonderful woman,' Margaret continued. 'She must be nearly ninety now but she's the guardian of just about every charitable trust in the district. I didn't exactly move in the same circles but I often saw her and she's the ultimate *lady*, you know what I mean?'

Amy thought of Luke. The way he chose his words and spoke so clearly. The way he dressed and his reputation as a surgeon with unparalleled skill and attention to detail.

Margaret lowered her voice to a whisper and there was a definite twinkle in her eyes. 'I wouldn't be the least bit surprised if Lady Harrington still wore corsets!'

Amy nodded slowly but her smile was distracted. She was beginning to understand. Luke had been brought up in an alien world and taught that everything had to be perfect. Lady Harrington wouldn't have considered there was space in that world for a foreigner. Especially an Italian with that reputation of volatility and exuberance the nationality carried.

Was it possible that Luke had been brought up to believe his father was dead? If that was the case, it would explain why no contact had ever been made. It would also mean that Luke would have been shocked to learn of his inheritance. Quite apart from a justified anger at a parent who had apparently chosen not to raise him, he was being left a dwelling in a state that was far from the perfection he'd been raised to expect.

No wonder his first reaction had been to consider demolishing it.

He'd never had a real family so he had no means to understand that it was what was within the walls of a dwelling that really mattered.

Maybe Luke was the one who was wearing a corset. An emotional one.

Amy got to her feet. 'I'm going to check on everybody on my list,' she announced. 'By the time I've done that, hopefully there'll be a pool nurse here and I can go home.'

She wanted to get home as soon as possible.

She knew how to fix this. There was a shining light at the

end of what had been shaping up to be a very dark tunnel. The shadowy shape still blocking that light was man-shaped but Amy wasn't the least bit deterred.

She could fix Luke Harrington, too, if he let her!

An hour had ticked past and Luke realised he'd missed his dinner, but he wasn't the least bit hungry.

He'd been sitting at the kitchen table since Zoe had disappeared to chivvy the older children to bed and to read a bedtime story to Chantelle. The big house was quiet and, uncharacteristically, Luke allowed himself to continue sitting in his somewhat dazed state. He hadn't noticed that Monty had slithered off his blanket at some point and was now under the table. It wasn't until he felt the weight of a large, black nose on the shiny leather of his shoe that he was aware of how close the giant dog had become.

He didn't want to antagonise the creature by shifting his toes. One chomp and that leather might not be enough protection. Zoe should be back shortly and the dog would be under control. Hopefully.

It was only partly due to Monty's breath on his ankle that Luke didn't feel alone. He didn't really need to hear the odd, muted bump or giggle from overhead, either, to remember how many occupants this house had. The feeling of their presence was everywhere.

Like a heartbeat.

Slow and steady. Different to when Amy had been in the house. She had an air of vibrancy that increased the beat. Gave it a few unexpected ectopics, even.

Luke found himself smiling unconsciously at the nice, cardiological analogy. Yes. The pulse of anything would increase and become a little erratic if Amy was around.

Especially when she was provoked. Her fierce words still rang in his ears.

Over my dead body!

A ridiculous thing to say. Over-emotional rubbish. Except that, at the time, he'd had the disturbing idea that she'd really meant it. She felt *that* strongly about it.

Had he—*would* he—ever feel that strongly about anything? Be prepared to lay his life on the line? To want something so badly that life would not be worth living without it?

Of course not!

But, curiously—and for the first time—Luke could feel envious of someone who did feel that way. Someone who could experience the euphoria of genuine passion. The notion was merely a flash, however. Easily pushed aside when recognised.

Passion denied rational thought. It involved lows, as well as highs. Misery that counterbalanced any happiness. An uncontrollable roller-coaster that Luke would never step onto because he was rational. He had to be. His career demanded it.

Why hadn't he used his rational intelligence and walked away from Amy's passionate outburst? He had certainly intended to. He knew there was no point talking to someone in that state and the only way forward was to create space until they calmed down.

She'd managed to get under his skin, though, hadn't she? Prodded some weak spot he hadn't known existed and he'd been sucked into responding. Worse, he'd lost it to the extent of revealing that he was planning to demolish this house out of spite and he didn't even intend to keep the proceeds.

Zoe would tell him it was a mean thing to do.

And, dammit! She would be right.

It wouldn't hurt to leave it for a few days, would it? Until after Christmas.

For Amy's sake.

Zoe eventually came back to the kitchen.

'Monty! Get back on your rug!' Zoe gave Luke a scathing glance as the dog wriggled backwards. 'You still here?'

'Apparently.'

'Robert said you were shouting at Amy before I got here.'

'I never shout. If anyone was raising their voice, that would have been Amy.' Luke frowned. How much had the other children overheard?

'Robert says you're gonna pull our house down.'

'*Your* house?'

Zoe flushed. 'Well, Monty lives here now and he's my dog.' Her voice rose defiantly. 'You know what one of my mum's boyfriends said to us once?'

'Um… No.'

'He had some stuff of Mum's he wanted to keep. Like CDs. *He* said "possession is nine tenths of the law".'

Luke sighed. 'The legal system doesn't see it quite like that, I'm afraid.'

Zoe snorted. 'I don't care. It worked for Wayne. He got to keep Mum's stuff. It'll work for us, too.' Her eye was an angry slit. 'You can sod off now. And when you're gone, we'll keep you out. You'll see.'

The confidence was impressive. Quite endearing, really, but misplaced. Zoe needed to learn to think things through.

'Maybe I won't go anywhere,' Luke suggested. 'I could just move in and then I'd have the nine tenths of the law. Ten tenths, if you consider that I'm legally the owner.'

'You can't do that!' Zoe gasped.

Luke raised an eyebrow. 'It doesn't seem a problem having extra people moving in around here, so why not? Uncle Vanni's room is empty.'

Zoe actually believed him.

How crazy was that? Luke had the weird notion that he'd fallen down a rabbit hole and landed in a parallel universe. That he could even pretend to be thinking of doing something that would give his grandmother cause to disown him was... Well, it was unthinkable.

Or it had been. Until now.

What was even worse was that there was something vaguely appealing about the absurd notion.

Zoe looked ready to cry again. Luke was about to reassure her when a small, pyjama-clad figure appeared in the doorway.

'Chantelle?' Zoe moved towards the younger girl. 'What's up, sweetie? I thought you were asleep.'

'I was.' Chantelle rubbed her eyes. 'Summer woke me up. She's making a funny noise.'

Luke's chair crashed over backwards due to the speed with which he got to his feet. Monty also rose and growled menacingly, but Luke ignored both events.

'Show me,' he demanded. 'Which is Summer's room?'

The 'funny noise' Summer was making was a distressed whimper on every outward breath. A tired sound, as though the effort was just too great.

Stepping into the room, Luke was instantly aware that it had the feel and even the smell of Amy. It was messy, with the clothes she had been wearing strewn over an unmade bed, but he barely registered a memory of how those jeans had clung to slim hips and how soft the woollen jumper had looked. The colours in the room were vibrant, with bright curtains and cushions. A faintly exotic scent that Luke couldn't place, along with the flickering light from a low-burning fire, brought the room to life.

It was an attractive, cosy space but even with the glowing coals the ambient temperature wasn't enough to account for the sheen of perspiration visible on Summer's dark skin.

He shook her shoulder gently. 'Summer? Wake up!'

The child didn't stir. Luke peeled the covers off the little girl and felt for her pulse. Her skin felt chilled and it took a moment to locate a pulse at all. When he did, Luke wasn't surprised to find it far too rapid and very weak. Her heart was failing and her blood oxygen levels were already too low to be compatible with consciousness.

'What's wrong with her?' Zoe asked from behind him.

'She's got a fever. Probably an infection of some kind.'

'Like a cold or something?'

'Yes.' It had come on very fast but Summer's immune system had already been compromised.

'Is she really sick?'

'Yes.' He couldn't be less than honest with Zoe. 'Could you call an ambulance, please? Tell them I'm here and I said it was urgent.'

Zoe hesitated in the doorway. 'She's not…going to *die*, is she?'

The tone was anguished. Something Margaret had said flashed into Luke's mind. Something about the children that ended up in the Phillips household being lucky.

No one else had wanted to care for this dying child but here she was clearly very much loved. Luke's own heart gave an odd squeeze.

'Not if I can help it,' he told Zoe sombrely. 'But we need to hurry.'

Robert took Zoe's place in the room a second later. He stared at Summer and then at Luke and his look was accusatory. 'I thought you were Summer's doctor.'

'I'm one of them.'

'So why can't you make her better, then?'

'It's not always possible to fix things, Robert.' He must know that, surely? If he was here in a foster-home, life had been a lot less than perfect so far for this boy.

'Well, it should be,' Robert muttered. 'It's not fair.'

He turned and walked away and Luke sighed. Of course it wasn't fair. Neither was it fair that he was made to feel so guilty. He did his best and he knew he did it better than most. He couldn't afford to feel guilty. A failure. And he wasn't, he knew that.

Luke also knew he was going to try harder than he ever had before for this particular little girl.

The benefit of the location being so close to St Elizabeth's made itself apparent in the speed with which the paramedics arrived.

'Are you going to be all right,' Luke asked Zoe, 'if I go to the hospital with Summer?'

'I'll look after her.' Robert had appeared again as Luke carried Summer to the waiting ambulance.

'Lock the doors,' Luke reminded them. 'And call the police if anything scary happens.'

'We'll call Amy,' Zoe said. As though that was all the back-up they could need.

'Text her now,' Luke said in parting. 'Let her know I'm bringing Summer in.'

Amy arrived in the emergency department of Lizzie's within ten minutes of the ambulance but already Summer was in the resuscitation area, hooked up to every monitor available and with an IV cannula taped into a vein on her arm.

Luke was there, bent over the unconscious child, a stethoscope in his ears.

'What's happened?' Amy tried to sound calm.

'She's in heart failure.' Luke straightened and nodded at the ED consultant. 'Fine crackles. Widespread. Bilateral. I think you're right. We've got an infection that's tipped her instantly into failure.'

'This is serious, isn't it?' Amy moved to the head of the bed, reaching out to touch Summer's forehead with a gentle stroke. She looked up and found Luke watching, his eyes dark. Intense.

She could read the answer to her query there, but she had already known that. She could also read a level of sympathy that came as a surprise. Again, she had the impression that Luke understood. More than he realised, perhaps. More than he would want to admit to, anyway. In response to his gesture, Amy moved to one side of the room.

'We're starting a dopamine infusion,' Luke told her, 'to combat the heart failure. We'll adjust her diuretics and add in spiranolactane. We'll also have a think about using an ACE inhibitor and beta blockade. We've taken bloods, of course, to try and isolate the precipitating infection, and we've already started her on antibiotics.'

'I should ring my mother. What time is it in Italy?' Amy looked at her watch, but then bit her lip. 'Maybe I should wait till morning. If I tell her now, she'll insist on heading home. Possibly with my grandmother in tow. That's not going to help anyone, is it?'

'What about consent?' Luke queried. 'We should talk about how you feel about mechanical support, like ECMO or a ventricular assist device.'

Amy stared at the surgeon. He was talking about extraordinary measures to keep Summer alive. ECMO delivered oxygen and removed carbon dioxide via catheters placed directly in a patient's heart and arteries. The ventricular device was only a little less invasive, with a device placed inside the heart to assist pumping. There were big risks associated with these therapies and they were only temporary. A lot of surgeons would argue there was little point in heroic attempts to keep Summer alive if it only delayed the inevitable.

Luke seemed to be reading her thoughts. 'It might buy some time,' he said quietly. 'I can't promise anything.'

But he looked as if he'd *like* to promise something, and Amy smiled. He might try to hide it but—underneath the armour—there was a man who really cared. Not someone who could throw a bunch of children out of their home.

'We should talk,' she agreed. 'As far as medical consent goes, I signed up as a carer for Summer along with my mother. I have the authority to sign any necessary consent forms.'

'What would you like me to do?'

'Whatever you can.' Amy's lip trembled. 'I know it's a lot to ask, but it would be so special if we can have Summer with us for Christmas.'

Luke gave a single nod, as though he had expected the response. He moved to talk to the ED staff.

'Let's get Summer up to the ICU.' He sought Amy's gaze as preparations were made. 'Are you coming?'

'Yes, of course.'

'We'll talk later, then, when we've got her settled and stable.'

A little over an hour later, Amy sat beside Summer's bed in the intensive care unit, holding her small hand.

'She's holding her own,' Luke decided, looking up from a printout of test results. 'Her arterial blood gas levels are as good as we could expect. Her blood pressure's up and her heart rate and temperature are down.' He frowned at Amy. 'You should get some rest. I spoke to the night supervisor and your shift in the ward is covered for the rest of the night.'

'I need to stay with Summer.'

'She's going to sleep for hours yet. And you know how good the staff are in here.'

Amy did know. She also knew that Summer was so used to being in hospital that she probably wouldn't even be frightened. But what if something happened?

'Nothing's going to happen,' Luke said. 'Not in the next few hours.'

How could he read her mind like that? Amy dragged her startled gaze from Luke's face back to Summer's. She looked as though she was sleeping peacefully now and those dreadful noises of respiratory distress had almost gone.

'You might be needed at home,' Luke added. He cleared his throat when Amy didn't respond immediately. 'I got the impression that some of the other children were very worried about Summer.'

'They'll be worried sick,' Amy agreed. 'I tried to text Zoe but she's not answering. Hopefully, they're all asleep, but still…' She glanced at her watch. 'Good grief, it's nearly 2:00 a.m.!'

'And I need to collect my car. I'll walk you home.'

No! a voice in Amy's head cried in alarm. A walk in the middle of the night, alone with Luke Harrington? How terrifying would that be?

The stumble of her heart felt like someone thumping her

from the inside. Wake up! it conveyed. What better opportunity could you have to talk to him?

To plead her case?

He had helped Summer, hadn't he? He was prepared to go to extraordinary lengths to keep their little girl alive.

Surely, surely he could be persuaded that Summer—and the other children—needed their home just as much?

'OK,' Amy said bravely. 'I'll grab my stuff from the ward and meet you outside ED in five minutes.'

CHAPTER FIVE

'You look like a dragon.'

'Pardon?' Was this going to be another insight into what the staff of Lizzie's considered a less than amenable personality? 'Oh...!' Luke breathed out again and noted the white pillow of his breath in the icy air.

Amy looked nervous. Was she expecting flames, as well?

'Where's your coat?' Amy was wrapping her own around her body more securely.

'Hanging over a chair in your kitchen.'

'But you can't walk home without one! You'll get hypothermia.'

'It's only a few minutes. I'll survive.'

Amy looked doubtful. 'We could call a taxi.'

'Could be a long wait. Besides, I could do with some fresh air and we need to talk.'

'Mmm.' He could see the way Amy sucked in a deeper breath. 'Right. About the house.' She set off as though keen to get it all over with.

Luke caught up within a couple of strides. 'Yes. Amongst other things.'

'Other things?' Amy latched on to a change of subject eagerly. 'Such as?'

'Summer.'

'Oh…' They turned to walk through the car park and Luke could see the top of Amy's head beside him, her dark hair hidden beneath a bright, rainbow woollen beanie. 'It's not looking good, is it?'

'No, I'm afraid not.'

'And she was well down the transplant list last time we heard.'

'I'll call the co-ordinating centre first thing tomorrow morning and see how she's placed at the moment.'

'Will you?' Amy's eyes shone as she looked up at him. 'Oh, thank you!'

Luke was getting that weird feeling again. Like he'd had when he'd gone along with that lie about why he had come to the house and Amy had smiled at him. The feeling of being powerful and generous even when he wasn't doing anything worthy of gratitude. It was less weird this time, though.

Pleasant, even.

'These lists can change dramatically. Sadly, a lot of children die while they're waiting.'

Amy sighed, her breath making a huff of vapour, the sadness of the sound chasing that pleasant sensation away. Luke wanted it back. She needed comfort of some kind but touching his companion in any way would not be appropriate so Luke stomped on the odd inclination to put an arm around her shoulders.

'Maybe Summer will be one of the lucky ones.'

'I hope so.' They waited at the side of the main road for a black cab to pass. 'It's awful to be wishing tragedy on another family, though.'

The taxi was gaily decorated with tinsel around the inside of its windows. Laughing passengers were wearing Santa hats.

'Especially at Christmas,' Amy added.

It was Luke's turn to sigh. 'It's just another day in the year, you know. The hype is out of all proportion if you ask me. I hate the way it becomes almost impossible to get things done.'

Like demolishing a house?

'And for what?' he added hurriedly, to drown out the uninvited voice. 'A commercial opportunity that's completely out of control.'

They were on Albany Street now, almost into the park, but Amy had slowed down. Virtually stopped. She looked horrified.

'But…but Christmas is *magic*!'

'You don't really believe that, do you?'

Stupid question. He could see she believed it. Her shining eyes and parted lips were illuminated by a streetlamp. She was practically *glowing*!

And…beautiful.

Amy Phillips was absolutely, stunningly…*beautiful*.

'Of course I do,' she said. 'It's the only time we all get to celebrate how important we are to each other. Oh, I know there's birthdays and Mother's Day and everything but Christmas is for whole families. For *everybody*! Neighbours and nurses and taxi drivers and…and even dogs.'

Luke was trying to get past the realisation of how stunning this woman was. How could he have never noticed before? He must have heard her voice with that tiny catch of exotic pronunciation even if he hadn't experienced the suggestion of huskiness that came with a subject she felt intense about. He must have seen that smile—the way it curled up at the edges and reached right into her eyes. Those *incredible* eyes! Had he been completely blind?

'Especially for the children,' Amy continued. 'It's magic

because they believe it's magic. The world is full of secrets and pretty decorations and special food and they get something to look forward to. To dream about.'

Unconsciously, Luke was shaking his head. Not all children. Not in the way Amy wanted to believe. Trapped deep inside himself was the echo of a four-year-old boy who had begged Father Christmas for a real family. One with a father and a mother and...*please*...a brother to play with.

'Ho, ho, ho,' Santa had chortled. He'd patted the little Luke on the back, firmly enough to encourage him to slide off his knee, and then he'd presented him with a lollipop.

A red one that was never eaten.

'I know...' Amy's expression had become anxious as she watched Luke's face. She started walking again and their feet crunched on frozen puddles on the path. Bare branches made an archway that drew them forward into the night. 'But it's like anything in life, isn't it? You can choose whether you focus on the good stuff or the bad stuff.' She smiled winningly up at Luke. 'What's that saying? Something like, "Life shouldn't be measured in how many breaths you take but by the moments that take your breath away"? Well, there's lots of those moments at Christmastime. *That's* what makes it magic.'

There was a plea in her face now. She wanted him to agree with her. It seemed terribly important that he should agree but Luke couldn't find a thing to say. He was having trouble catching his breath. Maybe it was one of those moments she was talking about but it had nothing to do with the time of the year and everything to do with Amy Phillips.

The path had the odd tree root sneaking along its edge and, because Amy's head was still tilted upwards as she appealed to Luke, she stumbled a little when her foot caught. Just enough to make it an automatic action on Luke's part to catch her arm and prevent her falling. She turned swiftly and, just as naturally, he caught her other arm and there she was—standing so close he could feel her warmth. Feel the almost desperate plea in her eyes.

She wanted something from him but Luke couldn't, for the life of him, concentrate enough to remember what it was.

Her closeness and the feel of her in his hands was mesmerising. In his experience, women who were in such close physical proximity and had a look on their faces even remotely like this wanted something he rarely had the time or inclination to bestow.

This time, however, he had no hesitation at all. It required no more thought than stealing that photograph had.

Luke bent his head and kissed Amy.

It was, absolutely, the last thing Amy had expected.

The conversation about Christmas had been the perfect lead in to presenting her case about the house but instead it had led to him intending to kiss her!

Here they were, on the outskirts of a huge, deserted, dark, frozen park in the middle of the night and Luke Harrington was going to kiss her!

Luke Harrington!

She should run. Physically and emotionally.

Life was way too complicated already.

Amy was poised to flee—every cell in her body charged with adrenaline—the choice between fight or flight made in the split second she saw the intention in Luke's eyes.

But then the distance between them closed and she could feel the warmth of his breath on the chilled skin of her face. She could *smell* him. A mix of potent masculinity and sheer power. She tried to run, at least mentally, but the instant Luke's lips touched hers, Amy tripped and fell headlong.

Into the kiss.

His lips felt cold and her own were more than half-numb but still this kiss felt like nothing she had experienced before.

It all happened so fast and Amy still had the sensation that she'd lost her balance and was falling, so she really had no choice but to reach out for something to hold on to. The solid chest in front of her was like a wall and her hands slid upwards, searching for an anchor. Luke's neck. Perfect.

So was the way his arms came around her body so securely. Safely. Counterbalancing the firm pressure from his mouth. With the fear of falling removed, Amy could relax just that fraction. Her lips parted just that fraction, as well, and the warmth of their breaths mingled and then there was *heat*.

Searing heat as Luke's tongue touched hers and Amy was falling all over again because the muscles in her legs were melting from that heat. Christmas decorations had nothing on the swirl of colours and sensations coursing through her entire body. Everything was melting, especially that core deep within her belly. The widespread, delicious tingle was changing shape, curling up at its edges and turning in on itself to make a hard knot of desire.

This wasn't simply a kiss.

It was an awakening.

A much less pleasant kind of awakening occurred when the kiss finally ran its course and they both stepped apart.

Luke looked as stunned as Amy felt and the chill of the night had increased dramatically. How long had they been standing, locked in each other's arms?

With a final, faintly shocked glance at each other, they continued walking. Silently.

Was Luke trying to absorb the startling effect of that kiss, as she was? She couldn't resist a tiny glance up at his face. If he hadn't believed in magic before, surely he was at least giving it some head room right now?

It was only a short distance from the tree beneath which they'd been kissing to the house on Sullivan Avenue, but if Luke had been as unaware as Amy of his feet actually touching the ground, he was giving no sign of it. When he eventually spoke, it was to express disbelief certainly, but the tone suggested anything but pleasure.

'Unbelievable!' The word was outraged.

The tension in the tall body beside Amy gave out vibrations that she responded to automatically. It was a rather similar sinking sensation to the one she'd experienced the other night, when she'd known she'd just touched a sterile object and brought a critical medical procedure to a screaming halt.

'What's wrong—?' Amy had to stop herself adding his name. It felt like it would be natural to call him Luke, but she couldn't, could she? And she could hardly call him Mr Harrington now. Not after he'd just kissed her so thoroughly!

Amy was following his line of vision even as the confused thoughts were jumbling in her mind. She could see his car. A gorgeous, low-slung, sporty model in an unusual shade of smoky blue.

Very low slung.

'Oh, no!' Amy breathed. Both the tyres she could see were as flat as pancakes.

Two brisk strides took Luke to the other side of his vehicle. 'Four flat tyres! This is deliberate vandalism,' he pronounced. His gaze snapped in two directions as he scanned the rest of the street. 'And mine seems to have been the only vehicle targeted.' He glared at Amy. 'I wonder why?'

'It does stand out,' she ventured. 'It's the only convertible and the colour is unusual.'

Luke said nothing and Amy squirmed inwardly. Oh, Robert, she thought in dismay. This was *so* not the way to express antagonism.

'Let's go inside, shall we?' Luke suggested dryly. 'I need to call a cab.'

He should have been as mad as hell about what had been done to his car.

Curiously, he actually experienced a flash of something that felt like gratitude for an excuse to follow Amy back into that house.

To stay close to her for just a little longer.

Luke was feeling slightly dizzy again. The way he had when Margaret had told him the house was full of children and Italian women. As though the very foundations of his world were being rocked.

And so they were.

It might have started when he'd recognised how attractive Amy was but the Richter scale had increased exponentially with that kiss.

Luke was feeling things right now that he had absolutely no experience with.

Intense, dangerous things.

They led to a place he'd never ventured into because he'd learned long ago that, if you were self-disciplined enough, you could keep yourself safe from that dangerous place.

Safe from nasty things. Boarding school had cemented

that lesson. And he'd already known that things that were *too* nice were also to be avoided. The hedonistic pleasures that were the stuff of irrational desires and behaviour. The benefits of a lifestyle that kept you safe from those places had been breathed in with the very air of his childhood.

Could he distract himself now?

Possibly.

Did he want to make any effort to do so?

No. Not just yet, anyway.

How could he, after *that* kiss? He was bewitched by a combination of the bizarre events that had unfolded since he'd left work for the day. It would wear off. Daylight would dispel the feeling of unreality. Even electric light might help.

Amy pulled off her woolly hat when they were inside the kitchen again. Wisps of dark hair escaped the plait and curled around her face, still picking up the inadequate light from the single bulb enough to gleam. Then she poked up the inside of the range, adding more fuel, and the fire tinged her face with a rosy glow.

Extra light wasn't helping. Luke's fingers were coming back to life now, stinging and burning at their tips. His lips had a similar tingling going on but he knew that wasn't from the recent, subzero environment. They were remembering that extraordinary kiss.

Wanting more.

'Sit down,' Amy invited. 'You must be totally frozen. I'll make some hot chocolate.' She put the kettle onto the stove and then moved to pick up another object as she walked towards Luke. 'Here's the phone. Why don't you call for a taxi while I just check on the children?'

She was back within a couple of minutes. 'They're all sound asleep,' she reported. 'Zoe's crashed in my bed so I'll use Uncle Vanni's room for the rest of the night.' She busied herself making a hot drink, spooning chocolate powder into mugs, wrapping a cloth around the handle of the kettle before pouring the boiling water and then opening a refrigerator to extract a carton of milk.

Ordinary movements but Luke found himself watching as though she was performing a magic show.

'Will the taxi be very long?' she asked.

'I haven't called them yet.'

She almost spilt the mugs of hot chocolate as she carried them to the table. She set them down carefully but the wobble in her voice gave away her nervous reaction.

'How come?'

'I want to talk to you.'

Amy sat down. She put her hands around her mug as though she needed the comfort of its warmth. She hung her head, pretending to inhale the rich aroma.

'The house,' she said finally.

Luke couldn't resist the opportunity. 'Amongst other things.'

Sure enough, her face lifted and he got a clear view of her eyes. The connection he was looking for caught instantly and, for a moment, Luke just went with it—torn between amazement and being appalled at the power he could sense.

Another dimension was there. Just waiting for him to step into it and to take that first step. All he needed to do was make physical contact. He could reach out and cover one of Amy's hands with his. Or stand up and pull her into his arms. Feel the...

'O-other things?' Amy's voice had a strangled quality.

With enormous difficulty, Luke broke the pull of the eye contact and stifled the first response that came to mind. The desire to talk about that kiss. About whether it had had the same kind of effect on her as it had done on him. About whether she would be interested in… *Hell*, he couldn't go *there*, could he?

Not with the obstacle of the intentions with which he had come to this house. He needed to ground himself. To remember why his life had intersected with Amy's in the first place.

'Tell me about your Uncle Vanni,' he commanded.

That should do it. He could listen to an account of his father's life. A happy life, no doubt, that had never included his own son. Involuntarily, Luke's gaze slid sideways—to where the flap of his coat hung around the back of the chair. To the pocket hiding that stolen article.

'Poor Uncle Vanni,' Amy said softly. 'He never recovered from losing the love of his life. *Both* of them, in fact.' Her gaze was accusing.

Luke could feel the hairs prickling on his neck again—the way they had when he'd seen that photograph. He was staring at a can of worms here and Amy had her hand on the lid, so to speak. Did he really want her to open it?

'What do you mean?' he asked, his voice harsh. 'Women?'

Amy shook her head. 'There was only ever one woman for Uncle Vanni. The other love of his life was his son. You.'

Luke couldn't meet her gaze. He didn't believe it. He couldn't afford to. It was doing more than rocking the foundations of his world. This had the potential to rip deep, dangerous crevasses in those foundations.

'Tell me,' he commanded gruffly. 'The story as you heard it.'

'OK.' Amy took a deep breath. 'Uncle Vanni fell madly in love with Caroline. He was working in a vineyard at the time, in northern Italy, and Caroline had been sent to this posh finishing school nearby. She was only eighteen and she had to go home but then she discovered she was pregnant and all hell broke loose.'

Luke found himself nodding slowly. He could imagine how that news would have gone down. His grandmother would have considered her daughter's life ruined.

'Caroline ran away,' Amy continued. 'Back to Italy. She married Uncle Vanni and they had a gorgeous baby and they were blissfully happy, even though they didn't have much money.'

They had certainly looked blissfully happy in that photograph.

'So what happened?'

'There was a dreadful accident. Their car was really old and the brakes failed on a mountain road. They were all badly injured. Caroline died just a few hours later and Uncle Vanni was evacuated to a big hospital in Milan. He was in Intensive Care for weeks and in the hospital for nearly six months. It was two years before he could work again and he had trouble with his back and feet for the rest of his life. Lived in slippers did Uncle Vanni.'

Luke pushed the image of those comfortable slippers from his mind. Then he cleared his throat.

'And...and the baby?'

'Caroline had her passport because they had been planning to cross the border at some point. They'd been married for three years or so by then but were going on their first real holiday. Anyway, the hospital and the police tracked down her family and her mother apparently arrived the next day. She arranged a medical escort and took both the baby and Caroline's body back to England.'

'And then?' Luke had to clench his fists to stop himself touching that scar beside his left eyebrow.

'It was months before Uncle Vanni was fit to travel but as soon as he could, he came to England to try and find his son.' Amy raised her eyes to Luke's and he could see the moisture shining in them. Could hear the catch in her voice that seemed to be attached by an invisible sting to his own heart. It tugged.

'Do you know, even more than thirty years later, Uncle Vanni couldn't talk about any of this without breaking down? He was in a really bad way when he got to this country. Broken in body and spirit. It took huge courage to go to Caroline's home and face her mother and when he did, he was told that his son's injuries had been too severe. Despite the best medical care the Harringtons could access, that little boy had died a week or so after they brought him back.'

Luke's mouth opened. He snapped it shut again. What could he say? Amy was clearly telling the truth as she knew it. What good would it do to tell her that his grandmother valued honesty above everything?

'He never went back to Italy. For a few years he just existed in London. He had a job as a school caretaker and he lived in a bedsit in some horrible high-rise. My mother found him when we came to live in London and he gradually became part of our family.' Amy took a deep breath and then gave her head a tiny shake. 'Anyway… My dad was a policeman and there was a job one night when these kids had to be taken into care. There was a big mix-up and Dad ended up bringing them home for the night. The youngest was a boy who was about three years old and he homed in on Uncle Vanni and climbed up on his knee. Looking back, I suspect that was the turning point but unfortunately things got worse before they got better.'

'How so?'

'My dad got killed on duty. Shot. I was nine. Mum was

going to pack us all up and move back to Italy, but she's never been very good at making decisions and then acting on them. She had to rely on Uncle Vanni and he finally started to come out of the depression he'd been struggling with for so long. And then he got the "great idea".'

'Which was?'

Amy stopped and took a sip of her drink and then continued. 'He decided that if his own son was lost to him, rather than waste the rest of his life, he'd spend it looking after children that other people didn't want. But he couldn't do it by himself. He needed my mother as part of the family to get approval to be a foster-parent himself. He found this house and persuaded her to stay at least for a while and that's where it all started. It's been my life ever since.'

'But your uncle's dead now.'

'My mother is just as passionate about these children as he was. When he was dying, she promised she would look after them as if they were her own. And they are, really. She loves them. We all love them.'

'So why didn't he do something about protecting them? Legally?'

'You mean, the will? I have my own theory about that.' Amy's smile was poignant.

'Which is?'

'Uncle Vanni was a wonderful man. He'd do anything for anyone, but he wasn't perfect by any means and he had a bad habit of convincing himself that he'd done things because he had intended to do them.' Amy stuck her tongue into her cheek as she pondered and Luke felt an odd twist in his gut as he watched.

'Like—he'd be given a chore like posting a letter or taking out the rubbish and he'd say he'd done it. And then, when he was asked if he'd done it, he'd sneak off and actually get it done before he got caught out. I was there once when he put his hand in his pocket and found a letter he'd forgotten to post and he winked at me, like it was our secret. The thing is, he was a hopeless liar. The real secret was that we all knew. Asking him if he'd done something was just a reminder but he would always say he'd done it because he didn't like to let anyone down and he always *intended* to do it.'

'So you think he intended to make a new will and didn't get around to it.'

Amy nodded. 'And nobody would have reminded him because anything to do with death was so upsetting for him. It would remind him of what he'd lost. Maybe that was the reason he couldn't bring himself to actually go and do it. Or maybe he just kept putting it off, telling himself there was plenty of time.'

'Only there wasn't.'

'No. It was so sudden. A massive stroke. They kept him on life support for a couple of days but then we had to let him go.'

Luke was silent. He was struggling with this. Clearly, Amy believed she was telling the truth. The story rang with the resonance of truth and he could sense that faded photograph hidden in his coat pocket. The evidence all around him supported Amy's account. And 'Uncle Vanni' had been a hopeless liar, so he must have believed he was telling the truth.

But if it *was* true, it went against everything Luke had been brought up to believe was true, and it threatened to cut deeply into the respect he had for the woman who'd raised him.

Things that had been so black and white—like the values he'd based his life on—were being held up for inspection and, instead of the solid foundation he'd believed them to be, they were shaky.

Flawed?

Luke didn't like that notion. It would mean that a part of himself was potentially just as flawed, and he wasn't ready to accept that.

He got slowly to his feet. 'I don't think I'll bother waiting for a taxi,' he said. 'I'll walk.'

'Is it far?'

Far enough to give him time to think, at least. Luke put his coat on. He picked up his scarf and gloves. 'I won't get cold this time.'

Amy went to the door with him. She seemed tired, which was hardly surprising given that it was after 3:00 a.m. now, but it was more than that. She was sad. Did she miss the father figure she'd had in her life?

At least she'd known him.

'You need to rest,' Luke told her.

They were close again. Too close. The temptation to kiss her again enveloped Luke with painful intensity.

'I will,' Amy said. 'I'll call Lizzie's first, though, and see how Summer's doing.'

'I'll check on her first thing. I'll be back at work by 6:00 a.m.'

'Maybe you should just stay here. You're not going to get much sleep after walking home.'

'I might go back to Lizzie's and use the on-call room.' The temptation was strangling Luke. He couldn't stay here and keep his hands off this woman.

But he had to pause, once more, as he stepped out into the night because the soft sound of Amy's voice was arresting.

'He did love you,' she said quietly. *'Luca.'*

There it was again. That name. That pronunciation. Pulling him…somewhere.

Somewhere he couldn't go because he had no idea how to get there.

And it was too disturbing.

'Did you really have no idea?' Amy asked.

'No.' Luke could hear the trace of bewilderment in his own voice. 'No idea at all.'

CHAPTER SIX

'CHRISTMAS shopping, was it?'

'Sorry?' Luke turned on the water and picked up the small brush to start scrubbing in. It was 6:30 a.m. and the question from his registrar was baffling.

'That huge carton I saw you coming out of the lift with. You looked as if it was something you were planning to hide.'

'Mmm.' Maybe he'd looked as furtive as he'd felt. Luke hoped he hadn't been observed earlier, down in the bowels of St Elizabeth's Hospital, following the directions of that cooperative cleaner to where the recycling and large items of rubbish were collected. 'Definitely Christmas stuff,' he said in a tone that would discourage any further questions.

'Great time of year, isn't it?' his registrar said cheerfully. 'Rather fun, hiding stuff and surprising people.'

'Mmm.' Luke paid careful attention to scrubbing beneath his nails. His registrar should know he wasn't one for idle chitchat right before surgery when his focus was on what lay ahead. He certainly didn't want to start thinking about that early morning mission because then he would start thinking about Amy. Wondering how he could present that box of decorations currently sitting in a corner of his office. Imagining the sparkle of pleasure he might see in her face.

And if he started to think about that, his mind would latch back on to what had kept him largely awake for the few hours he'd spent in the single bed the on-call room boasted. Back to that kiss. The way he had felt holding Amy in his arms. That spiral of desire—or was it actually *need*?—had to be firmly damped.

The bright lights of the operating theatre suite should be far more effective than daylight even in restoring reality, and Luke would welcome the return to normality. He could hasten it, by a nudge in the right direction.

'So you know what's on the agenda this morning? For baby Liam?'

'Three surgeries in one go, from what I could gather.'

'Pretty much. An arterial switch, VSD closure and repair of an aortic coarctation.'

His registrar whistled silently and any thoughts of Christmas shopping were clearly dispelled. They were in for a long, hard session in Theatre.

Preparations to put the infant onto the heart-lung bypass machine were painstaking and time-consuming, complicated by having to leave access to the arteries that needed repositioning. It was nearly 8:00 a.m. when the tiny heart was stopped with the cold, high-potassium solution that would also protect the heart muscle while it was not functioning.

Luke was already deep within the zone that would enable him to operate with no lessening of precision for many hours. Cutting tiny areas of miniature vessels and placing stitches he needed magnifying goggles to visualise accurately. Coating every suture line with fibrin glue.

Short breaks to flex muscles and counteract strain were taken, but for minimal periods of time only. Six hours on bypass were getting to the limits of what a baby could tolerate well and Luke intended finishing before then.

The session finished, as it had begun, with another complication. An abnormal rhythm persisted after the heart was restarted and did not respond well enough to the cocktail of drugs Luke ordered.

'We'll keep him ventilated and on sequential atrioventricular pacing,' he decided eventually. 'Let's get up to ICU.'

Had he bothered to think about it, Luke would have decided he was entirely grounded in reality again by the time he accompanied his patient to the highly specialised unit. The fact that nothing remotely unprofessional crossed his mind made it a non-issue.

So it was a huge shock to walk into the unit and see Amy sitting beside Summer's bed, holding the little girl's hand. Leaning forward to press a gentle kiss to her forehead.

To instantly remember his own experience of the touch of Amy's lips.

And—ever so slightly—to feel the ground shift beneath his feet once more.

'It's Christmas Eve tomorrow,' Amy was telling Summer. 'When all the boys and girls are asleep, Father Christmas will come and leave presents under the tree.'

'For…me?'

'Of course for you, darling.' Amy kissed Summer's forehead. 'I'll bring it in when I come to visit.'

She looked up, aware of the activity beyond the glass windows of Summer's cubicle, in time to see the surgical team come past with a tiny, post-operative patient that had to be baby Liam. It was no surprise that the baby's surgeon was still close by.

What *was* surprising enough to take Amy's breath away was the way her heart seemed to stop and her skin come alive so that every cell tingled. The way she felt a connection to this man that went far deeper than any she had the right to feel.

They had shared a kiss, that was all.

One kiss.

It was nonsense to feel as though so much more than their lips had touched. As though their souls had made contact. Maybe it was the result of over-thinking, which was a trait Amy was sure she had inherited or learned from her mother. The ability to endlessly replay and examine tiny snatches of life. To experience them again and again. To analyse them and consider every possible repercussion.

The way Amy had done only last night after Luke had gone. As she'd lain, wakeful, in Uncle Vanni's bed.

For a while she'd simply remembered—and missed—the person who'd been the most important man in her life for so many years. It had been a natural progression of her thoughts to realise that Uncle Vanni had, indirectly, been responsible for bringing a new man into her life.

Her mother would have probably proclaimed that it was meant to be and given thanks to some obscure saint.

Amy was fighting the same tiny voice in her own head that was saying the same thing. The one that was noting every reaction she had to Luke Harrington.

The one that was taunting her with the accusation that she was falling in love.

Amy had done her best to argue back.

Don't be ridiculous. He's from another planet.

He's a man, the voice whispered back. *You're a woman.*

He's rich. Incredibly rich. I wouldn't even know what spoon to use if he took me out to dinner.

But you want *him to take you out to dinner.*

No! It could never work.

Why not?

He's important. I'm...nobody.

Really?

Not according to the way he judges people. I'm nothing. Just a nurse. He couldn't even remember my name.

I'll bet he remembers it now. After that kiss.

Ah, yes... That kiss.

And the voice had an argument compelling enough to almost obliterate any arguments Amy's rational side could muster.

Remember what Margaret said? He's lonely.

It struck something nameless and deep and Amy suspected that's what the connection was all about. Yes, she and Luke came from totally different worlds and it might be far too great a challenge to understand and appreciate what was most important in each other's lives, but that could be part of the connection because Luke might not even realise how lonely he was.

He obviously hadn't had any idea his father had loved him and Amy wasn't sure that her heartfelt story last night had convinced him. He needed convincing if she was going to change his mind about the house.

He also needed—as everyone did—to be loved.

And that was something that Amy did have. Surely the ability to love transcended the barriers of status and wealth?

At some point during the remaining hours of darkness and internal conversation, an idea had been born.

A plan.

And while Amy's first objective in coming to Lizzie's this afternoon had been to spend some time with Summer, she had also been planning to see Luke. To talk to him. To offer up her plan.

There was an awful lot resting on his acceptance of that plan, so it was no wonder she was nervous. No wonder that her heart tripped and accelerated when she saw him. Not that it could explain why it was so hard to look away from him but the eye contact didn't last long enough to be an issue.

Luke was busy. She could see him supervising the transfer of the baby to the care of the unit staff. Consulting with the other specialists who came in. Making final adjustments to the life-support equipment and finally, taking a phone call.

When he caught her gaze on terminating the call, Amy had the horrible impression he had been aware of how often she had been looking in his direction. As though he had expected to make eye contact the second he had chosen to look *her* way.

Just as he expected her to respond to the subtle movement of his head that was an invitation to leave Summer's side and join him.

'Be back in a minute, sweetheart,' she murmured. The reassurance was more for herself than Summer, who seemed to be sound asleep again.

Could Luke feel that disturbance in the air that intensified with every step closer that she took? A feeling of...awareness was the only description she could come up with. She was *so* aware of everything about this man.

She'd seen in him in scrubs before, of course, but this was completely different because this time it was in the wake of having been kissed by him. She knew how hard the muscles beneath the ill-fitting cotton were. She could see a swirl of dark hair in the deep V-neck of the tunic top. She could almost feel the air being moved as he sucked in a breath. Amy focused on his hand, lying lightly on the high counter in front of the nurses' station. Long, elegant fingers drumming almost imperceptibly to denote, what? Impatience? Tension?

Maybe both, Amy decided, her gaze flicking up to note the faint shadows under his eyes and the way the muscles of his jaw were bunched.

'I called the transplant co-ordination centre first thing this morning,' he told Amy. 'I had to leave a message because it was too early, but they just called me back.'

Amy nodded. She couldn't read whether the news was hopeful or not in his expression. Instead, she got the curious impression that he was watching her just as carefully.

'Summer's at the top of the list.'

'Oh!' Amy caught her breath. And held it, knowing that Luke had something more to say. She could *see* it. Like a tiny flame in the depths of his dark eyes.

A ray of hope.

'There's a child,' Luke said quietly. 'In Scotland. Glasgow's Eastern Infirmary. She's been in a coma for three weeks now and the parents are ready to consider organ donation. The latest EEG showed some activity, however, so she doesn't yet meet the criteria for being a donor, but the activity has declined markedly since the last test. She's showing signs of multi-system failure but they're continuing life support in the hope that some good may come from it. They're going to repeat the EEG later today.'

Amy could feel tears prickling. 'The poor family! What a terrible ordeal for them.'

'Sounds like it might be a release in some ways,' Luke said steadily. 'This girl has severe intellectual and physical disabilities. She had a seizure and knocked her head hard enough to cause this coma.'

'Do you think...?'

'She sounds like an ideal match.' Luke nodded. 'Same blood group. Good size of heart. She's only a couple of years older than Summer. We'll just have to keep our fingers crossed that things come together. She could die from renal failure before her brain gives up. Or they may find the heart is not suitable when it's harvested. You know the kind of things that can get in the way.'

Amy nodded but she was thinking of the child's family. 'It would be so hard, wouldn't it? To have to send your child to Theatre when they were still on life support. Still breathing. If it was my child, I'd just want to hold it...' Amy had to sniff and blink rather hard. 'Sorry.'

Amy didn't need Luke staring at her to know that her emotive response was both unprofessional and unhelpful.

'Don't be,' was all he said, however. 'These situations are emotional for everyone concerned.'

With the possible exception of himself? He seemed perfectly calm. Totally professional. Sympathetic but detached.

One of the unit staff came out of the office.

'Your secretary just called, Mr Harrington. There's someone in your office who'd like to see you if you have a minute to spare.'

Luke glanced at the wall clock. 'Not really. We're due to start again in Theatre in twenty minutes and I need to see the parents.'

'It's your grandmother,' the clerk said.

'Oh...' The flicker of dark brows went up and then down and the frown made him look as though the surprise was not a pleasant one. 'In that case...' Luke gave Amy a somewhat curt nod. 'We'll talk later.'

She was being dismissed. Summer was forgotten for the

moment and there was no chance of an opportunity to present her plan. Or even to tell him that the tyre repair firm that he must have organised had been to deal with his car. It was frustrating enough to make Amy have to resist the impulse to follow Luke from the unit. She wanted time with him. Alone.

She also looked at the clock. If Luke was due in Theatre in twenty minutes and he wanted a few minutes to reassure his patient's parents, he would probably only allow five to ten minutes to talk to his visitor. If she timed it just right, Amy could catch him as he left his office and she could, at least, ask for an appointment to speak to him later.

They needed to talk about the house. He'd said so himself more than once and it hadn't happened yet. They had been sidetracked by those 'other things'.

Amy sat with Summer for a few more minutes. She was still sleeping peacefully. She caught the attention of Summer's nurse.

'If she wakes up, can you tell her I'll be back soon? I've just got a message to run.'

'Sure.'

Unaware of the determined expression on her face, Amy left the unit and headed towards Luke Harrington's office.

'Grandmother!' Luke shut the door of his office behind him. 'This is a surprise!'

'I was in the city for lunch.' Lady Prudence Harrington sat, ramrod straight, in the chair in front of his desk. She tilted her cheek for a customary greeting. 'With Reginald and Lucy Battersby and her brother.'

'At Barkers?' Automatically, Luke bent to brush a kiss to the papery cheek. Reginald's brother-in-law owned a department store that rivalled Harrod's.

'Of course.'

Luke didn't sit down. 'I haven't much time, I'm sorry. I'm due back in Theatre.'

'So I see.' The smile was tolerant. 'It's acceptable, is it? To be seen in public wearing pyjamas?'

'These are scrubs,' Luke said. 'You've seen surgeons on television.'

'I don't watch television. You know that, Luke.'

'Yes.' Luke had to resist looking at his office clock. 'Is something wrong? You never come to the hospital. You're not unwell in any way, are you?'

'Not at all. I'm as fit as a fiddle. As I said, I've just had lunch with the Battersbys and I had to come past on my way home so I got Henry to drop me off at the front door. A nice young woman at Reception told me where I could find your office. I think we need to have a talk, Luke.'

Luke raised an eyebrow. 'But I'm coming to see you tomorrow.'

There was a moment's silence and Luke noticed the way his grandmother was twisting the gloves she had taken off. It gave the impression the old woman was nervous. Surely not.

'Why didn't you tell me, Luke?' Prudence spoke in a very uncharacteristic rush. 'About that house?'

'Oh...' Luke leaned back against his desk, hooking up one leg, his eyes narrowing a little as he focused on his grandmother. 'Yes. The house. Giovanni Moretti's house.'

Amy's house.

'Reginald tells me it's being used as some kind of orphanage. That you're planning to demolish it. That you intend evicting these people immediately.'

Luke said nothing.

'That would be wrong, Luke. Especially at Christmastime.

Unless better accommodation can be found, of course. I think I can help. Lucy and I were talking about it and we decided—'

'Grandmother,' Luke interrupted. He kept his voice low. Calm and collected. There was no point in upsetting someone he respected and loved. His only family, in fact. And he had to give her the benefit of the doubt. Lying was dishonourable and it was not something the Harringtons ever did. 'Did my father ever try to find me?' he asked. 'Did he come to the village? To our house, even?'

'What makes you ask such a thing?'

'It's what his niece told me when I went to the house yesterday.'

Prudence went pale. Luke could see what little colour she had fading rapidly, and for a horrible moment he thought he was about to witness his grandmother collapsing.

'You went to the house? You spoke to a…a cousin?'

'Not exactly.' Amy was distantly related in some fashion but it wasn't that close. Not close enough to be any kind of obstacle.

An obstacle to what, precisely?

Luke had to shake the distracting thought away. 'You haven't answered my question.'

The soft, kid gloves were being strangled. 'You have to understand, Luke. It was a terribly difficult time.'

'He did come, didn't he?'

'Twice. The second time he came with a policeman, but he still had no right to trespass. Henry dealt with him.'

Henry. The devoted chauffeur and maintenance man who was married to Elaine, Harrington Manor's housekeeper. A man who would say or do anything his employer requested.

'And the first time? Was that when you told him I was dead?'

It was his grandmother's turn to be silent. To wait for what was clearly coming.

'You told me my father didn't care about me. That I meant nothing to him. That you were the only family I had or needed.'

'No.' Prudence shook her head. She looked suddenly much more than her eighty-seven years. She looked old and so frail Luke felt a twinge of guilt for confronting her. 'I never *said* that.'

'You let me believe it.'

'It was for your own sake. For all our sakes. Can't you see that, Luke?'

She kept using his name and it was starting to sound strangely formal. Cold, even.

Luca...

'It was wrong,' Luke said heavily. 'You denied me my father, but I was too young to remember him or know what I was missing. What was worse was denying a father his son.'

'It was for your own sake,' Prudence repeated. 'He would have taken you away, Luke. To live in poverty in a foreign country. Your education would have been inadequate at best. You wouldn't be the person you are today. I only wanted what was best for you. *You.* My grandson. The only person who is going to carry the Harrington name forward.'

A sensation akin to horror was crawling on Luke's skin. The enormity of what had been done, albeit with the best of intentions. A man's life had been cruelly damaged and— It was true, he might not have become who he was if things had been different.

'Are you not happy with the life you've had, Luke?' His grandmother was rallying now. Gathering her pride as she convinced herself, yet again, that she had done what had been only right and proper. 'You've had the best of everything. You're successful and important. I'm very, very proud of you.'

She was. She was also a strong, proud woman who had been fiercely independent since being widowed when her only child had been young. For the first time Luke had an inkling of how important *he* had been to her. The only link to a beloved husband and daughter. Without him in her life, she would now be a very lonely old woman, living virtually alone in an isolated mausoleum of a family home.

So very, very different to the kind of home and family Luke might have had with his father.

And Amy.

A messy, warm, volatile domestic mix.

Chaos versus order.

Crowds against solitude.

Making do instead of success.

The benefits of what he'd been given were obvious, so why did he feel so confused? Why did he feel the urge to grab his coat from the hook on the door, find that photograph and hold it under his grandmother's nose? He was dangerously close to doing something as unspeakable as shouting at her. Telling her she had done something wicked to both his father and himself.

Something that could never be undone.

And perhaps that was the key. If it couldn't be undone, what was the point in overreacting? And there was never any point in reacting to the extent that emotions overrode rational thinking. Luke pushed himself to his feet.

'I must go. We'll have to discuss this at another time.'

'As you wish.' If Prudence was disappointed in any way, she wasn't about to show it. She put a hand on the arm of her chair and started to rise slowly. With another twinge at how frail she seemed, Luke helped her to her feet. He picked up her handbag and the silver-tipped cane she used and then held open the office door.

'Are you all right? Do you need me to come down with you?'

'I shall manage perfectly well, Luke. As I always do. I believe you're needed elsewhere.'

That was true, but Luke walked as far as the lift with his grandmother. The doors opened as soon as he pushed the button and to his surprise a figure bustled forward. Luke had to catch his grandmother's arm to prevent a collision.

'Oh, I'm sorry!'

'Amy!'

'Oh…' Amy's eyes widened. She looked disconcerted. Then she looked at his companion. Prudence stared back.

'This is my grandmother, Amy. Lady Prudence Harrington. Grandmother, this is Amy Phillips, a nurse on my ward.'

'Indeed.' Prudence inclined her head graciously. 'Delighted to meet you, Miss Phillips.'

Amy smiled. 'You, too,' she said. Her eyes held a question as she looked back at Luke. 'You wouldn't have a minute, would you, Mr Harrington? There's something I really wanted to talk to you about.'

'One minute would definitely be the limit,' Luke said. He kissed his grandmother. 'We'll talk later.'

'Indeed,' Prudence agreed as the lift doors slid shut.

Amy was staring at the doors even after they'd shut, a puzzled frown on her face.

'Walk with me,' Luke invited. 'I really have to be in Theatre. We can talk on the way.'

'OK.' Amy gave a little skip as she caught up. Luke headed for the stairs that would take him to the theatre suite on the top floor. 'I have an idea,' she said a little breathlessly.

'Oh?'

'You're planning to get rid of my house and then sell the land and donate all the money to charity, yes?'

Luke stopped. That *had* been the plan. Funny how it seemed a rather long time ago that he'd made it.

'I know you think it's dreadful.' Amy's words tumbled out. 'Disorganised and messy and that maybe the children would be better off somewhere else, but I can prove that's not true.'

'Oh?' Luke was still trying to remember why it had seemed the best course of action.

'Give me a chance,' Amy begged. 'I can fix things in the house. Tidy everything up. Come and see what it's like when Mamma and Rosa are back and it's more...normal.'

He couldn't miss the flush on her cheeks or the way her gaze slid sideways. Whatever was normal for the Phillips household was hardly likely to seem normal for a Harrington.

'After Christmas?' Amy added hopefully.

Christmas!

Luke turned abruptly. 'Come with me,' he commanded.

He was heading back to his office.

Walking so fast Amy had trouble keeping up. She hadn't presented her plan very well, had she? It had been disconcerting, meeting his grandmother like that.

Prudence Harrington.

The old-fashioned given name was familiar but Amy couldn't locate the memory and it made her feel unfocused.

So did being in Luke's office. Especially when he closed the door behind them.

'There,' he said. 'It's for you.'

'What?' Amy could see a chair and a pair of gloves lying on the floor beside it, but surely he couldn't mean them? She looked up at the framed diplomas on the wall. A bookshelf stacked with glossy medical textbooks arranged according to height. Piles of journals that were probably filed by exact issue numbers. Plastic models of hearts. Everything in its place. Tidy and precise.

Apart from the large, battered cardboard carton in the corner, with a frond of tinsel poking through where the flaps had been closed over the top of the box.

'They were going to throw them out,' Luke was saying just behind her shoulder. 'I thought...'

He had rescued the old decorations from the ward. He was giving them to *her*.

For their Christmas tree.

For the children.

Amy turned slowly, to look up at the surgeon. This was the last thing she would have expected and she could see that it was out of character. Had he asked somebody for something that was considered rubbish?

Carried it himself, to his private office?

For *her*?

It was like a flash of lightning. A crack in the veneer of a man considered remote and unfeeling, and Amy could see clearly into that crack. She could see the lonely boy Margaret had told her about. She had met the cool woman, generations removed, who had raised him. She could see someone who didn't know what it was like to be really loved.

Cherished.

She wanted to hold him. To cherish him.

But all she could do was smile through her tears. 'Thank you.'

'You're welcome. Please, take them. I really have to go now.'

Except he didn't move.

'Would you...think about what I said? About my plan? I'll do *anything*...'

He was standing close again. Close enough to kiss her. And

he was staring at her mouth. Looking exactly like he had last night in the park. Like he wanted to kiss her. Like he wanted *her*.

'*Anything?*' His voice was husky.

The silent addition of 'Even *this*?' hung in the air as he bent his head to kiss her.

Oh, Lord, did he think she was offering herself? For the sake of saving her house?

She was offering herself, but not for that reason. Because he needed someone. He needed *her*.

And, yes, she would do anything for him.

Especially this.

Amy closed her eyes and gave herself up to the kiss, but it was a kiss barely begun when it was interrupted by a shocked voice.

'*Luke!*'

He stepped back as if Amy had bitten him. Confused, Amy turned to see his grandmother standing in the doorway of the office.

'I thought you were required in the operating theatre, Luke. Urgently.'

'I am.'

'I must have dropped my gloves. I came back.' Prudence gave Amy a look that made her want to check that her blouse was still buttoned and then sink into the floor and vanish.

And then, before she could finish cringing, she was alone. The gloves had been snatched up and given back to their owner and both Luke and his grandmother had gone.

Amy stood there, bemused. She touched her lips with her tongue and she could still taste Luke.

She looked at the box of decorations and she could still see the crack in that veneer. The glimpse into the soul of the man she loved.

But, most of all, she felt reprimanded. Prudence had informed her, with a single glance, of just how completely unsuitable she was. Unacceptable.

Prudence. More than being careful. More like being surrounded by an impenetrable wall. The woman had no soul.

Where on earth had she heard that?

From Uncle Vanni.

He'd said it. About Caroline's mother. Not to Amy, but she'd overheard and she'd known that she would not like this woman if she ever met her. Anyone that had made Uncle Vanni sound that miserable was not a nice person.

Luke was her grandson.

Harrington was the name he had chosen to use for the rest of his life.

It was getting a lot harder to hang on to the thought that Luke might not have known his father had been alive. That he might, in fact, have simply wished him to be dead.

And maybe that was why he really wanted to get rid of the house. How naïve had she been, thinking that she could offer to tidy it up and make everything all right?

Dazed, Amy eyed the box of decorations. She should leave it behind and pointedly refuse a gift from this man.

But that crumpled, messy box didn't belong in this pristine office any more than she did.

Amy picked it up.

And left.

CHAPTER SEVEN

THOSE brave enough to be out in temperatures well below zero, beneath a sky heavy with snow that wasn't ready to fall, turned their heads to watch the young woman, with long dark hair and an angry expression, stalking through the outskirts of Regent's Park with a large cardboard box in her arms.

Amy was oblivious to the stares.

And, yes, she was angry.

Confused.

Horrified, even.

The strength of the feelings she had for Luke were providing the confusion. How could she feel like this about a man who was prepared to destroy the house his own father had lived in? The only remaining link to the life he had built? To break up the only family Giovanni Moretti had retained and to pose a threat to the children who had become his father's life?

You'd have to really hate someone to be that vengeful.

Had he always hated his father? Why? Had Uncle Vanni known all along that it was hatred he had to get past? Had he stayed in London waiting until Luke was old enough to choose for himself whether he had anything to do with his father? Maybe Uncle Vanni had lived with the hope that something would change for all those years.

Lived with the background misery that he was being denied a relationship with his son. His only child. The thought made Amy angry. Very angry. And maybe Uncle Vanni *had* intended to give Luke his house and another will didn't exist. A final plea for forgiveness? With the largest token he could have presented to tell his son how much it had mattered?

Luke was prepared to take that token and hurl it into oblivion.

How on earth could she have fallen in love with someone capable of doing that?

'Zietta Amy!' The twins had been watching for her return from the drawing-room window and they flung the front door open. 'Is that a present? For *us*?'

'It's for all of you. Where's Zoe? And Robert and Andrew and the girls?'

They were all in the kitchen, which seemed overly warm as she'd come in from the outside. Amy peeled off her coat and draped it over a chair and tried not to think about Luke's coat hanging in exactly the same place. The children gathered to stare, wide-eyed, at the box, except for Robert, who stared at Amy.

'How's Summer doing?' he asked gruffly.

'She's much better. She's getting tired very quickly but she was awake and playing with her doll for a while. She's excited about Christmas.'

'Will she be coming home?' Chantelle asked. 'In time for Christmas?'

Amy had to shake her head. 'I don't think so, honey. She needs to be watched very carefully. We're all hoping she might get a new heart very soon but until then she might have to stay in the hospital.'

'*He's* supposed to fix her,' Robert muttered loudly.

'Who?' Chantelle and Kyra were edging closer to the mysterious box and the twins were climbing on chairs to see what was happening.

'G Squared,' Zoe supplied. 'Amy, I'm making baked beans on toast for tea. Is that OK?'

'Sounds good to me.' Beans were vegetables, weren't they?

'What's G Squared?' Chantelle queried.

'Gru—'

'She means Mr Harrington,' Amy interrupted hurriedly. 'Summer's doctor. Let's do some eggs to go on top of the beans,' she added to Zoe. 'Have we got eggs?'

'I'll have a look.' Zoe moved to the fridge and Monty sat up on his blanket, watching her hopefully.

Chantelle touched the box. 'Is that a puppy in there?'

Amy caught Zoe's gaze as her babysitter emerged from the fridge with a carton of eggs. Zoe grinned. 'You've got a puppy already. You might hurt Monty's feelings if you ask for another one.'

Monty obligingly pricked up his ears on hearing his name and did his best to look as appealing as a giant, scruffy dog could look. Marco and Angelo climbed down from their chairs to go and hug him.

Chantelle sighed philosophically and Robert and Kyra took advantage of everybody's attention being on their new pet to move in and fold back the flaps of the box.

'Oh!' Kyra gasped. *'Look!'*

'What? What?' Monty was forgotten as the younger children crowded close.

Kyra reached out to lift a loop of tinsel. 'It's decorations,' she said reverently. 'For our tree.'

'There's a heap of stuff.' Robert sounded impressed. 'Where's it come from?'

'They're old ones from the hospital.' Amy watched as the first of dozens of coloured balls and stars were lifted from the box. Nobody seemed to notice that the balls were a little dull and that some were chipped. Or that the shiny cardboard stars had bent corners. 'Actually, it was Mr Harrington that rescued them from being thrown out.'

Amy had no idea how difficult it might have been for Luke to find time in his busy schedule to do that but the fact that he had gone out of his way at all was amazing. And the way he had offered them to her with that oddly hopeful expression that begged for acceptance had been what had tipped the balance.

A moment that had been a pinpoint in time but one that Amy would always remember because that had been the moment she had fallen in love with Luke Harrington.

Head-over-heels stuff. A love as big as Africa. Bigger.

It didn't make any difference that it might be inappropriate. Or unwise. It had happened, it was as simple as that.

'Oh!' Chantelle was teetering on the edge of a chair to reach further into the box. 'Kyra! Look what I found!'

'I'll get it.' Kyra's arm was longer. 'You'll fall off in a minute.' She lifted something out of the box.

'It's an angel.' Chantelle's eyes were shining. 'For the top of our tree. Oh…it's just what I *always* wanted.'

He should be here, Amy thought suddenly. Luke should be here to see this. A magic moment. A child's pure joy. He should be seeing it because then he would understand how something so small and ordinary to most people could be so important to someone else.

To see the way the two girls hugged each other and how the older boys gathered up the decorations and led the way to their tree, with the twins babbling happily in Italian, the girls holding hands, Robert leading the way carrying the box, and Andrew keeping pace as his right-hand man. A disparate bunch of siblings, certainly, but right now—and for as long as they could remain living together—they were a family.

Amy was torn between wanting to help the children decorate the tree and needing to help Zoe get a meal on the table. She was saved having to make the choice by the telephone ringing and the relief of being able to connect with the missing members of this family.

'Rosa! How are you?'

'Totally exhausted but I've done it, Amy!'

'What?'

'I've managed to get tickets home. In time for Christmas. Almost.'

'Almost?'

'We fly in on Christmas morning. The plane lands at Heathrow really early…6:30 a.m. You wouldn't believe how difficult it's been and it's cost an absolute fortune. I don't know how much more the credit card will stand but we'll try and get presents for all the kids on our way home.'

'They'll be thrilled to see you. How's Nonna?'

'Getting stroppy. I think the doctors were only too pleased to sign a form to say she's fit to travel. Between her and Mamma, the staff have been pulling their hair out. How's Summer?'

'Holding her own, thank goodness.'

Amy told her sister about the faint possibility of a heart becoming available very soon. Inevitably, Luke's name was mentioned, more than once, but Amy resisted asking the question on the tip of her tongue.

'Where are my boys?' Rosa asked. 'Are they behaving?'

'They're wonderful. They're all decorating the tree in the drawing room right now. I'll get them for you in a tick.'

'What are they decorating the tree with?'

'There was a box of things that weren't needed in the ward. Shiny balls and stars and tinsel. Usual sort of stuff but there's an angel, too, for the top. You should have seen Chantelle's face. She's so happy!'

'I wish I was there. How did you score treasure like that?'

'They're old.'

'Doesn't sound as if the kids mind.'

'No. To tell the truth, Rosa, I didn't even know they were being thrown out. It was Mr Harrington that got them for us.'

'Mr Harrington? Summer's surgeon?'

'Yeah.'

'How amazing! He didn't seem like the kind of guy who'd do something like that when I met him last time Summer was in hospital.'

'No.'

'He must be nicer than he looks.' Rosa laughed. 'Not that there's anything wrong with the way he *looks*, from what I remember.' There was a heartbeat's silence. 'Ah! Is there something going on I should know about?'

Amy couldn't deny it, but she could change the subject and ask the question that was still hovering. The one that might allow a window of hope that she was wrong about Luke.

'Do you remember anything about Uncle Vanni's son?'

'Luca? Not really. He was only three when he was killed and our birthdays were on the same day so I was only three, too. Bit young to remember much.'

'You had the same birthday? I never knew that.'

'That was how they knew each other. Mamma and Caroline were in the hospital together and Luca and I were like twins for a year or two. There's lots of photos somewhere.'

There was only one Amy could think of. The one on Uncle Vanni's mirror with that chubby, laughing baby. She carried the cordless phone with her as she walked towards the room on impulse.

'So we weren't actually related to Uncle Vanni?' Why did the prospect of that being true make her feel better?

'No. But we adopted Uncle Vanni when we found him in London. He was so miserable. He needed a family and the rest, as they say, is history.'

Amy was in the room now. In front of the dresser. Staring at the gap at the top left-hand corner where that photograph had been. Remembering that flash of guilt she'd seen on Luke's face when he'd appeared in the kitchen, having been snooping around the house.

'Rosa?'

'*Sì?*'

'Did Uncle Vanni ever talk about Caroline's mother?'

'The Prude? Once. He swore me to secrecy and showed me a scrapbook Caroline had started making for Luca. It had her family history and pictures of the house and all sorts of things. It was like a cross between a photo album and a diary. She wrote in it. Mostly about how happy she was but there was a bit about how sad it would be to never see her mother again.'

'What happened to the scrapbook?'

'I have no idea. It was years and years ago and I'd forgotten all about it. Maybe it's still in the same place.'

'Which was?'

'Tucked under all the stuff in his bottom drawer.'

Amy opened the drawer while Rosa was still talking. 'You know, all Uncle Vanni had wanted for years was to visit the graves and put some flowers on them, but they were both buried in some private cemetery beside the family chapel.

Mamma persuaded him to try again and Dad even went with him in his policeman's uniform, but she wouldn't let them into the house and the butler or whoever he was said they would be prosecuted for trespass if they ever set foot on the property again. How horrible was that?'

'Pretty horrible.' Amy had found the leather-bound scrapbook exactly where Rosa had thought it might be. She carried it back to the kitchen. She had been five when they had moved to London, which made her older sister ten at the time. Luke had been the same age. Maybe Luke couldn't be held responsible for what had been said when he'd been five, but ten had been more than old enough to know about his father. To choose whether to have contact or not.

The hope that she might have been wrong died with a painful quiver.

Maybe Prudence had simply done what her grandson had wanted. It was easy enough to imagine a smaller version of Luke with his privileged life so precisely ordered. Had he been ashamed of the fact that his father was Italian? That he had been merely a vineyard worker? Even as an adult, he'd never come looking. Never given Giovanni a single chance.

Should she tell Rosa that her almost twin wasn't dead after all? That he now owned the house they were coming back to just in time for a Christmas celebration?

No. There would be time enough to say what had to be said later.

And Amy had a few things she wanted to say to Luke first. She also had something she intended to show him. She slipped the scrapbook into her red tote bag.

Six o'clock, but it seemed much later.

From the neon-lit interior of St Elizabeth's, it looked pitch-black outside. Luke could see the Christmas lights decorating the lampposts on the main road beyond the car park. He'd just come from the intensive care unit where baby Liam and his other surgical cases for the day were all doing as well as he could hope for. He'd checked on Summer, as well, and she was stable, but who knew how long that would last? Something could tip the balance at any time and send her into heart failure they had no hope of reversing. Or her heart might simply give up the struggle and stop.

Luke paused momentarily. He should put a call through to the Eastern Infirmary in Glasgow and find out what the results had been of the EEG they'd been planning to repeat on that child in the coma. Checking his answering-machine for a message first would be polite, however, so he changed direction to head for his office before going back up to the theatre suite's changing rooms to get out of his scrubs.

He was almost there. Just outside the on-call bedroom he'd used last night, in fact, when he saw a slight figure turn from his office door and stride towards him.

'There you are!'

Luke halted, taken aback by the anger he could hear in Amy's voice. What had he done? The last contact he'd had with this woman had been in his office earlier that afternoon. Rather close physical contact, and he hadn't been aware of any undercurrent of antagonism at the time.

Far from it!

Had Amy been as embarrassed as he had been when his grandmother had interrupted them? Was that what was upsetting her?

No. The commanding tone of the single word she spoke next put paid to that theory.

'Luca!'

He said nothing.

'Why?' Amy asked with deceptive softness. 'Why did you hate him so much? What did your father ever do to deserve that?'

'He was never a father to me.' Luke spoke just as quietly and he glanced swiftly around, but there was nobody to overhear. Nevertheless, this was a conversation that should be private. His office? The on-call room right beside them?

But Amy wasn't going anywhere. She planted her hands on her hips and glared up at him.

'And whose choice was that? You wouldn't let him be a father to you, would you? You refused to see him. Did he know that? Had he had to pretend to his family that you had died so he didn't have to admit to the shame of having a son who didn't want anything to do with him?'

'No! It wasn't like that. It was him who wanted nothing to do with me. Or so I thought. I grew up believing he didn't care.'

'Pfff!' The sound was outraged. 'It very nearly destroyed him, *Luca*!'

He wished she wouldn't say his name like that. He *wasn't* Luca. Hadn't been since before he could remember.

'He loved you. *So* much. As much as he loved your mother.' Amy sucked in a breath. 'Why did you steal the photograph?'

'I...ah...' God, she was mesmerising. Her face alight with the intensity of her emotions. Her eyes flashing sparks of fury.

'You destroyed it, didn't you?'

'No.'

'You're planning to. Just like you're planning to destroy his house.'

Luke couldn't deny it.

'You don't want to believe he loved you. That he would have died for you. That all he ever wanted was a chance to love you.'

'Listen to me,' Luke snarled. He put his hands on Amy's shoulders and turned her so that her back was against the wall. So she would have to look up and listen. 'I never knew he came looking for me. My grandmother thought she was protecting me. She told Giovanni his son had died. I grew up believing he didn't care and...yes, I hated him and that *was* the reason I wanted to get rid of the house, but now...'

'Now?'

'Now I'm not sure. I need time to figure out what to do. What it is I...want...' Luke's words trailed away. He'd got carried away with what he was saying. So carried away he'd actually forgotten it was possible that someone coming along the corridor could overhear and that his most private life could become a subject of gossip. Or observe him with his hands on a female colleague. Leaning towards her, for all the world as though he was about to kiss her.

Worst of all, he didn't give a damn.

Because he knew what he wanted. He was touching it and his hands were burning.

'Luca?' The word was a whisper and Amy's gaze clung to his. Her lips were slightly parted and the flush of anger sill tinged her cheeks. 'What *do* you want?'

Luke reached down beside Amy. To turn the handle of the door and push it open. He turned Amy's shoulder with his other hand and drew her into the privacy of the on-call bedroom.

'You,' he said, his voice raw. 'God help me, Amy. I want *you*.'

* * *

Amy was, quite literally, being swept off her feet.

Into a small room that Luke's presence filled with an overpowering force, even before he closed and locked the door behind them.

An outside window with curtains that were only half-drawn allowed light to filter in from the outside world. Just enough to give form to the force overpowering every one of Amy's other senses.

Not that she really needed to see Luke. She could feel him with every cell of her body. Smell his maleness and his arousal. Breathe him in along with the air she managed to snatch before his lips claimed hers with a hunger that could have been frightening.

Except it wasn't because her own hunger matched his. Her lips were parted before contact was made and her tongue tangled with Luke's before she gave in with a groan of need and allowed his to penetrate her mouth unhindered. The shaft of desire it sparked was so intense she groaned again, helping Luke as he rucked up her skirt, gripped her hips and pulled her against his hardness that the thin cotton of his scrub pants did nothing to restrict.

Thin layers of cotton and silk were the only barriers to the penetration her body was desperate for, and Amy couldn't wait. She slid her hands beneath Luke's tunic top to feel the smooth skin of his back and then her hands moved down and it was so easy to slip them beneath the elastic of the loose pants and delight in taking hold of buttocks that felt like silk-covered steel.

Luke echoed her own sounds of need and Amy's feet left the floor again as she was lifted and placed on the narrow bed. Not that she noticed the size of the bed. Or even the room. Luke filled the space. The room *was* Luke.

Her blouse lost at least one button and her bra was unfastened but not removed. Luke simply pushed it aside as his hands cupped her breasts. Then his lips and tongue replaced the brush of his fingers and Amy cried out softly as she felt the graze of his teeth against nipples that had never been this sensitive.

Clothes were a nuisance, bunched and clinging, but the luxury of getting naked was going to take too much time for either of them so they dragged them aside only as much as absolutely necessary and ignored the discomfort. They were unaware of it in the throes of physical passion, the likes of which Amy had certainly never experienced.

It was crazy. White-hot lust that carried her to the brink of insanity and then exploded. It wasn't until well after Luke had shuddered in her arms in the wake of his own climax and then slowly—heartbeat by heartbeat—relaxed against her that Amy could start thinking again.

Not that she wanted to think of anything other than the sensation of lying in Luke's arms like this. The patches of their skin that were naked still in contact. His breath, ragged against the side of her neck. His hands still holding her as though they never wanted to let her go. Her own arms were around him.

Holding *him*.

An embrace that was so tender it was heart-breaking.

She should say something, but what?

That was amazing?

I never knew sex could be that good?

I love you, Luca?

What would he say to that? That he wasn't Luca, he was Luke? A Harrington? That while the sex had certainly been good, this was a relationship that could never go any further?

Safer to remain silent and not risk hearing something that

could destroy what was still the most magic moment of Amy's life.

One that had, beyond any other, taken her breath away.

In the end, the transformation from Luca to Luke happened rapidly thanks to the strident sound of his pager coming from somewhere on the floor. Amy could feel the way reality came between them, breaking the connection. Making every muscle in Luke's body tense as he reached for the phone on the beside table.

'Harrington.'

He listened for less than a minute. 'I'm on my way,' he said.

He turned back to Amy. 'The EEG on the child in Glasgow was negative. The parents have signed donor-consent forms. Summer's heart's on the way.'

CHAPTER EIGHT

WHAT had he done?

For the next hour, Luke had no time to think about anything other than the logistics of bringing a donor heart to a dying child. Co-ordinating the harvest surgery in Glasgow, the helicopter that would rush it to London and his own part in the procedure—starting the surgery on Summer and getting her onto a heart-lung bypass machine, trimming and preparing the donor heart as soon as it arrived and then removing Summer's heart, matching the excision as exactly as possible to the same shape as the donor organ.

To create a perfect match.

This had to work because it would save Summer's life and…for the first time, Luke's motivation had a new edge. That he was doing this for Amy, as well as Summer, could not be dismissed as irrelevant.

It was a gift that would bring tears of joy to her eyes. An amazing gift that Luke was capable of bestowing, and Amy would love it.

Would she love *him* for giving it?

A respite in organisation came when everything was set up. The surgery would start in Glasgow and a phone line was being kept open, linking the theatres. When the donor heart was removed and pronounced viable, the clock would start ticking in London and Summer would move into Theatre and go under the anaesthetic. She was already in the anteroom and under mild sedation but the small girl did not seem at all frightened.

Why would she be?

She lay cuddled in Amy's arms and Luke knew exactly how that felt. How much was being given. And that was when the enormity of what had happened in the on-call room hit home.

Luke had never been cuddled. His grandmother loved him, he knew that, but she wasn't capable of being physically demonstrative. Maybe she never had been. Maybe that had contributed to his mother falling in love with someone who could show her how important that kind of comfort was. His own parents had certainly been comfortable with close contact. He could tell that from that photograph he had looked at many times since he had stolen it.

So he had known love through touch and then it had been wrenched from his life and he hadn't experienced it again.

Until now.

He wasn't a virgin. Far from it. But he'd never, ever felt threatened by sex.

Afraid.

Afraid he'd found something he'd been looking for his entire life because, having found it, he would have to live with the fear—no, the *knowledge*—that it could be wrenched away from him.

No. His heart told him he could trust Amy. With his life.

He could hear her reassuring Summer.

'Everything's fine, *cara*. It's going to be all right. I'm taking care of you. I'm taking care of everything.'

Everything?

What did that mean?

Oh... Yes...

Luke's brain dredged up what was ringing the alarm bell and his head had always won over anything his heart had to say. Good and bad. That's why he had learned to listen and follow what it said. Rational thinking over emotion. His head had something very different to his heart to say right now.

You can't trust it, it said. *Remember!*

Remember what?

Remember what she said.

What did she say?

She'd do anything to save that damned house. To keep it for her family. Anything! *And she just said it again, didn't she? She's taking care of everything.*

She might have meant the operation. The other children. Christmas.

No. She had sex with you because she wants something.

Me. She wants me the same way I want her.

No. She wants the house. That's all. Remember? She'd do *anything!*

It was true. He'd looked at her in his office and the desire to hold her and kiss her had been overwhelming, and she'd said she'd do anything and his body had screamed the question—*even this?*

And her eyes had given him the answer. *Yes.* Especially this.

She may have wanted it as much as he had, but had that been because she was prepared to do anything to save her home and he'd just gone along with it? His grandmother had been horrified that he was kissing Amy in his office. How shocked would she be to know he'd had sex with her in the on-call bedroom? Good grief, what if *that* hit the grapevine? His reputation would be ruined. Amy could blackmail him with that if she was so inclined. The thought sent a chill down his spine. He could not allow that to happen.

He could make sure it didn't. She could *have* the damned house. He'd hand it to her on a plate and see if that made a difference. He'd be able to tell. Her face. Those eyes—they were so incredibly expressive. If the house was all she'd wanted, he'd see satisfaction for payment of services rendered. Victory would be written there for him to read.

And if he saw something else?

There was no time to contemplate that scenario.

'The Eastern Infirmary's called through,' a nurse relayed. 'Heart's good. It's being chilled and packed now and the helicopter is standing by on the roof.'

'Code green, then.' Luke simply nodded at the anaesthetist, any personal thoughts banished instantly. 'You start while I'm scrubbing.'

He had to ignore the flash of fear in Amy's eyes. The way she used both her hands to stroke the child's face as she bent down for a final kiss.

'It's all right, *cara*,' she whispered. 'I'll be here when you wake up. Everything's going to be fine.'

The surgery was going to take hours. Rather than wait and pace outside Theatre, Amy chose to go home. While Zoe was happy to babysit and Robert proud to help, they were still both too young to have complete responsibility for the others, especially two lively six-year-old twins.

Part of Amy wanted nothing more than to stay and keep vigil and she was missing her mother and sister more right now than ever, but that was another reason to leave for a while. She needed to call them and tell them about this new, potentially miraculous development in Summer's life.

She would also need to answer the questions and give information that Marcella would demand to know even if she couldn't understand it. Amy rehearsed how she might explain the procedure in simple terms as she hurried home through the icy, dark evening, her mobile phone clutched in her hand in case her friend who worked in Recovery texted her with any news of progress in Theatre 3. Summer's theatre.

She took the time to reassure all the children and admire the newly decorated tree. Chantelle was beaming.

'Robert said we'd keep my paper streamers, as well, 'cos they're really cool.'

The look Robert exchanged with Amy was so full of adult comprehension and caring that she had to give him a hug. He stood there a bit stiffly and didn't return the affectionate gesture, but she could tell he liked it by how gruff his voice was.

'I'll get the twins to bed,' he said. 'Come on, you lot. It's getting late and it's Christmas Eve tomorrow. If you're not good, you won't get presents.'

'We're good,' Angelo insisted, chasing Marco to catch up with Robert. 'Aren't we, Roberto?'

'Sometimes,' he conceded. 'Come on. Scoot!'

The twins scooted. Amy put some fuel onto the drawing-room fire near the tree and tucked the guard securely into place. She patted Monty, who was lying on the hearth rug with Kyra, Chantelle and Andrew, and then she took another moment to admire the tree. She would have to remember to bank the fire again tomorrow night when she tiptoed in with the gifts currently in hiding under Uncle Vanni's bed. With the room warm and the tree looking so festive, Christmas morning was going to be something to look forward to.

Especially if they had good news about Summer to celebrate.

It was more than time to let Summer's official foster-mother know what was going on.

'How do they do it?' Marcella fretted. 'How can they do it in time? What happens when they take the old heart out? Is there just nothing there? An empty chest? *Dio mio*, but what happens to all the blood?'

'There's no blood,' Amy assured her. 'There's a special machine and all the blood goes through that. It gets oxygenated and goes to and from the rest of the body but leaves the heart out of the loop. There's special tubes—like a roadworks diversion.'

'So there *is* just an empty chest? *Oh*... Oh, my poor little angel! How do they do it, Amy? How do they put the new heart in exactly the right place?'

'It's actually quite straightforward,' Amy told her. 'Honestly! It takes ages because they have to stitch everything into place very carefully but it's a matter of joining up all the arteries and veins.'

It was too much information for Marcella. She needed to go and call on every saint she could think of to look after her 'angel'. Rosa wanted to know, however.

'So how do they join them? Like darning them on from the outside?'

'No. They cut the donor heart open and the first thing they do is stitch the pulmonary vein and arteries into place. They're the ones that take blood from the heart to the lungs and then back to the heart again. They have to join in the aorta which is the big vessel that takes blood to the rest of the body, and the big veins that bring the blood back to the heart again.'

'Isn't there a danger of things leaking?'

'The stitches are microscopic—that's why it takes so long. And they use a special glue stuff on the suture lines, as well. It's not likely that there'll be a leak but they have all sorts of special catheters in place afterwards and can measure exact pressures in the heart so they know if there is a problem and it's easy enough to go back in and fix it.'

'Does the new heart just start by itself? When it gets blood inside it?'

'Sometimes.'

'What do they do if it doesn't start by itself?'

'They have a special defibrillator that can be used right on the heart. Tiny little paddles that only give a very small shock.'

'How long will it take?'

'Hours. I'll call or text any news I get.'

'OK. You take care of yourself, too, Amy. Make sure you get some rest. Oh, Mamma wants to talk to you ag—'

The phone seemed to have been wrenched from her sister's hand. 'Amy? Will it work?' Marcella demanded tearfully. 'Will my little *angelo* get through this? I can't believe I'm not there to be beside her bed. To pray for her.'

'I know. I'm sorry, Mamma. I want you to be here, too, but this was a gift that couldn't wait and it might not happen again.'

'Why aren't *you* there?'

'I came home for a bit just to check everything was all right. And it is. Zoe's being a star and you won't believe how much Robert's grown up while you've been away. He really is the man of the house at the moment, Mamma. You'll be so proud of him.'

She could hear Rosa making soothing noises and then her sister took the phone back.

'It's OK, I'll look after her. Are you going back to the hospital now?'

'Very soon. I'll be there for her when she comes out of Theatre.'

'Will she wake up then?'

'No. I think they keep them well sedated for a day or two. On life support. Tell Mamma it's quite possible *she'll* be able to be with Summer when she does wake up.'

It was nearly dawn on Christmas Eve when Summer left the recovery area and was taken back to isolation in the intensive care unit, almost invisible in the midst of the bank of life-support machinery. She was on a ventilator, calibrated bottles hung from her bed for chest and urine drainage and tubes snaked into her skin in various places, allowing administration of drugs and monitoring of her blood pressures and oxygen levels. Electrodes were in place for continuous monitoring of the rhythm of her new heart.

Emergency gear cluttered trolleys. Equipment for suction, dressings, a pacemaker if it was needed and a defibrillator for a worst-case scenario of cardiac arrest. There were people everywhere. Gowned and masked in accordance with isolation protocols that would protect Summer from infection. Her cardiologist and her surgeon and his registrar. The ICU consultant and her registrars. Nurses and technicians.

And Amy, though not for long.

It was overwhelming. Both the level of care Summer would need for the next twenty-four hours or so and the fact that the procedure had been pronounced successful. Textbook perfect, in fact.

Summer had a new heart. It was quite possible she was going to live for a long time. Long enough to experience all the joys life could offer because she would be able to do all the things that normal, healthy children took for granted. To run and play. To go to school. To look forward to her birthdays and Christmases to come.

On top of the anxiety for the period of recovery, gratitude that a donor organ had become available and relief that the surgery had gone so well, Amy hadn't slept for more than twenty-four hours and had only had a restless few hours before that.

And, just to top that off, she had experienced the most emotional, intense love-making she had ever known, because she had been with the man she loved.

And would love, for the rest of her life.

It was all too much and if Amy didn't get home and sleep for a few hours, she would simply collapse. She had already rung Marcella and Rosa and given them the good news. She would tell the other children when they woke up, which hopefully wouldn't be for a little while. If she let Marco and Angelo climb into bed with her for a cuddle, she might get an extra hour's rest.

There would be time after that to thank Luke. It was far too soon to contemplate saying anything more. Hinting about how she felt, for example. She had done that with her body, in any case. Now she had to wait to see if the message was one that would be welcomed.

Until then, she couldn't afford to think any further ahead. She wouldn't begin to worry about the disparity of their backgrounds or the way they viewed life or the huge obstacle Luke's grandmother represented.

Thanking him was enough for now.

For what he'd done for Summer...and for her.

For simply being *him*.

Luke saw Amy leave.

He was deep in conversation with the other consultants,

talking about ventricular function and wedge pressures and when they could start thinking about weaning Summer from the ventilation, but he had sensed Amy's departure.

He tried to catch her gaze, to signal that he wanted to talk to her, but her focus was still on Summer as she slipped from the unit.

Things were well under control here. Luke had done his part and it had all gone extremely well. As close to a perfect procedure as anyone could have wished. Amy knew that. He'd seen the relief on her face when he'd pushed open the doors of the theatre, accompanying Summer to the recovery area, and had paused to tell Amy how happy he was with the way it had gone. He'd seen tears on her cheeks and had had to resist the strongest urge to brush them away himself. He couldn't, of course, not with a dozen colleagues so close and a child that needed intensive monitoring for hours yet.

The chance to share more than those few words hadn't come again but Luke hadn't pushed it. He wanted their next conversation to be private. No distractions, so he could see the effect of what he had to tell her.

That her Christmas gift would be the house. He would instruct Reginald Battersby to do whatever necessary to overrule his father's will and put the house into the ownership of the Phillips family.

He could catch her now, couldn't he? There was nothing more he could do here than watch and wait, to keep in close touch with the consultants now responsible for Summer and to keep himself available in the unlikely event of a complication that needed surgical intervention.

If he hurried, he could catch up with Amy. He'd have to grab his coat, which would look a little odd over his scrubs and white gumboots, but if he ran, he could probably close the distance before Amy reached the park. And how many people would be out and about this early on Christmas Eve?

Way too many people, it seemed. The traffic was heavy and everybody stared at the white gumboots beneath Luke's long, black coat. He hadn't bothered to grab his scarf or gloves and the first flurry of snow was finally starting to fall. His hands were frozen by the time he was striding rapidly though Regent's Park. Just short of running, so he didn't alarm too many people. He stuck his hands in his pockets and he could feel something he'd forgotten for the moment.

The photograph.

He pulled it out as he walked, shaking his head at how uncharacteristic a thing it had been to do—to steal this item.

Except, it was his, wasn't it—from a moral point of view?

The first, and only, inkling he'd had that he had been conceived and born with love. Surrounded by it when he had been too young to remember.

Possibly not too young. Did his soul remember? Was that why it recognised that what he'd found with Amy was so precious?

Something he couldn't afford to lose?

Luke increased his pace, which had unconsciously slowed as he'd looked at the photograph, but he'd been further behind Amy than he'd realised. She was about to leave the park and start down Sullivan Ave. She would be at her house in less than a minute.

The house she didn't know was really going to be hers.

'Amy!'

She turned, saw Luke and stopped dead in her tracks. Took in the white gumboots and the flash of pale blue scrubs that were showing with his coat flapping. He could see the way her face paled and her gloved hand touched her chest over her heart.

She thought he was chasing her to tell her something dreadful. That Summer had died?

'It's all right,' Luke called. 'I just need to talk to you.'

She was still afraid and Luke wanted to take her into his arms. As he closed the distance between them, he became aware of a loud sound behind him. A siren that was coming rapidly closer.

Just as he reached Amy, the fire engine passed them. So close it was automatic to grab Amy and pull her further onto the safety of the footpath. The siren was switched off but the beacons were still flashing. Snow was falling more thickly now and the dense grey white of the sky and snowflakes reflected the bright colours of the beacons, making them seem twice as bright. Twice as urgent.

The huge vehicle had stopped just down the street and another came around the corner, also silencing its siren the way they did when they reached their destination and no longer had to warn traffic to move. Both Luke and Amy watched as firemen in boots and helmets and fire-retardant clothing jumped from the vehicles. Luke let go of Amy's shoulders and somehow her hand slipped into his.

A fire hydrant was being opened and hoses unrolled—all in the space of seconds. Some of the firemen were wearing breathing apparatus, with masks on their faces and oxygen cylinders in packs on their backs.

'Oh, my God,' Amy said. 'Something must actually be on fire.'

They started moving, drawn towards the vehicles, as were other people who had started to gather on the footpath.

'It's close to our house,' Amy noted. A heartbeat later, she gasped. 'It *is* our house! Oh...*Luca!*'

He still had hold of her hand.

They both began to run.

CHAPTER NINE

'STAY out,' a fireman ordered. 'You can't go in there.'

'It's my house,' Amy shouted. 'There are *children* in there!'

'We'll get them out. Stay back!'

There was smoke pouring through a broken window in the drawing room but there was no sign of any flames or smoke from upstairs. A fireman lifted an axe to break open the front door.

'No!' The cry was one of despair. This looked like an execution. Her house was being sacrificed, which wouldn't have mattered a damn if it affected the safety of her children, but it wasn't necessary. 'Don't do that! Please. I've got a key.'

'Hurry up, then.'

Amy fumbled with the key. Luke was right beside her and he took it from her hand, slid it into the lock and pushed the door open.

Heat and smoke billowed out and Amy felt it scorch her throat. Her eyes stung and watered and she started coughing.

'Oi!' Someone sounded furious but she couldn't see through the smoke. Rough hands grabbed her arms and she was pulled backwards and then turned towards where an ambulance was backing towards the scene, its beacons flashing.

Amy craned her neck, blinking. The first rush of smoke

through the front door had lessened and it didn't look nearly as bad as it had. Hoses were being unrolled and carried into her house.

Where was Luke?

'Mad bastard,' she heard someone shout. 'We couldn't stop him.'

Amy's heart did a peculiar kind of somersault. Had Luke gone in there himself? Why? There were firemen here with safety equipment. Luke had to be risking his life to go inside the house. Had instinct overridden common sense? Was he doing it for *her* family?

For *her*?

'What?' Another man was wearing a fluorescent jerkin with the words 'Scene Commander' in bold, black letters. 'Get him out.'

The back doors of the ambulance were flung open. A paramedic urged Amy to climb the steps.

'Let's give you a bit of oxygen,' the young woman said. 'You've inhaled a good dose of smoke.'

But Amy shook her head. She just had an irritated throat, which was making her cough if she tried to take a deep breath. No big deal, and she wasn't going anywhere she couldn't see her front door. She didn't need to breathe deeply at the moment. She couldn't. Not until she saw everyone she loved coming out of that door safely.

Including Luca.

Especially Luca.

The first figures came through the smoke and then into the now thickly swirling snow. Bare feet and pyjamas. Robert was holding Kyra's hand and right behind him came a fireman with a twin under each arm. Marco and Angelo were shrieking with fright.

They all came towards Amy. A second ambulance was pulling up and there seemed to be people everywhere, holding blankets and oxygen cylinders.

'*Zietta*...Amy...' Marco was coughing and sobbing, holding his arms out.

'*Mi*! Me, too!' Angelo made an identical picture and already the distressed boys were shivering uncontrollably.

Amy found herself sitting on the back steps of the ambulance with a child clinging on each side. Blankets were wrapped over them all and paramedics fussed with oxygen masks and stethoscopes.

Robert was right beside the steps, refusing to climb into the second ambulance. Kyra was clinging to him, sharing his bright red woollen blanket, and they both needed to be close to Amy.

There was still no sign of Luke. Or Zoe or Andrew or Chantelle. Amy's heart pounded and then stopped for a beat as a new figure emerged. Another fireman, with Andrew in his arms. Andrew was also crying and held his arms out to Amy. Robert and Kyra wriggled closer and her view of the front door was completely obscured.

'Robert?' Amy tried to disentangle herself. 'Can you sit here? I need to find Chantelle and Zoe.'

And Luke.

'*No!*' the twins wailed. 'Don't go away, Zietta Amy!'

'I'll be right back,' Amy promised. 'You're safe now. Be brave for just a minute or two. Can you do that for me, darlings?'

Robert towered over the younger children. 'We can do that.' He coughed harshly. 'Can't we, guys?'

A chorus of assents, coughs and stifled sobs was what Amy left as she ran towards the people now coming out of the house.

Four people. Two firemen. One was carrying Chantelle and the other had his arm supporting Zoe. He peeled his mask from his face.

'The kid had locked herself in the bathroom,' he said. 'That bloke got her out.'

'She was...too scared...to open it.' Zoe had runnels of black eyeliner on her cheeks and looked a lot younger than her sixteen years. 'Amy...I'm so sorry.'

'It's not your fault,' Amy said firmly. 'And you're all safe, that's all that matters.'

Except they weren't all safe, were they?

Where was Luke?

The fireman was obviously thinking the same thing. He looked over his shoulder. 'He was supposed to follow us out. Where the hell has he gone now?'

Amy helped guide Chantelle towards the others. The twins had been persuaded to get into the shelter of the ambulance and they were both cocooned in red blankets. Wide-eyed, they stared out at the scene.

'Firemen!' Marco said, awed. 'And policemen!'

'And doctors,' Angelo added, looking at the uniform of the paramedic.

'There's flames,' Chantelle sobbed. 'Our Christmas tree is burning up.'

Could that have been what had caused the fire? All those paper streamers and an open fire not that far away and a rogue draft, maybe? But Amy had checked the fire carefully. The guard had been in place. The children all knew how important it was to be careful not to knock the guard.

Self-recrimination hovered but the extent of the damage was an unknown.

Nothing material mattered, anyway.

Where was Luke?

'*Where* is he?' Amy shouted at the scene commander. 'You have to find Luke. Mr Harrington. The man who went in first....'

'We'll find him. Go back to your children, lady. They need you.'

So does Luca, Amy thought desperately.

'For God's sake,' the man beside her growled. 'He risked his damn life for a *mutt*?'

'What?' Amy whirled back to face the house and there was Luke, stumbling a little with a fireman on either side of him, his arms full of a large, limp-looking dog.

'Monty!' Amy had completely forgotten about the newest member of their family. Luke's face was blackened by smoke and she could hear the harsh rasp of his breathing as he came closer.

'Monty!' Children poured from the back of both ambulances and crowded around as Luke laid the dog down gently.

Zoe was crying again. 'Is he dead?'

Luke shook his head. 'Too...much...smoke.'

'Same for you, mate. Here.' A paramedic slipped an oxygen mask over Luke's face.

'Monty needs one, too.' Robert's voice was deep. It had a new edge to it that Amy hadn't heard before. A commanding edge. The teenager eyed the paramedics' raised eyebrows. 'He's not just a dog, OK? He's one of us now.'

Luke had taken as deep a breath of the oxygen as he could. He coughed, took another breath and then slipped his mask off. He held it over Monty's huge black nose.

'Hey!' The paramedic sounded concerned. 'You need that more than the dog.'

But Luke shook his head and the paramedic shrugged. 'Guess I'll find another cylinder, then.'

'And a blanket?' Chantelle pleaded. 'It's awfully cold out here.'

A minute or two later the children were red blobs crouched beside Monty, who was also covered in a red blanket. Luke's breathing sounded almost normal again and to everyone's intense relief Monty was recovering. He tried to get up but Marco and Angelo were hugging him too tightly so he gave up and thumped his tail a couple of times instead.

'Thank goodness,' breathed Amy. She turned to thank Luke for saving the dog, but he was standing beside the scene commander.

'The kitchen seem's fine,' he was saying. 'A lot of smoke but nothing was burning. The dog was still trying to bark and warn everybody but he'd lost his voice and then he got another lungful of smoke and collapsed.'

There were people all around. The numbers and levels of activity had been steadily increasing but Amy hadn't noticed because she had been standing with an arm around both Chantelle and Kyra, watching for any sign of Monty's recovery.

'Fire's out!' A fireman was reporting to the scene commander now. 'Started in the main room, by the look of things, with a Christmas tree by the fire.'

'Is the house structurally damaged?' Luke asked.

'It will need to be properly assessed and that isn't likely to happen today. It's uninhabitable for the moment, that's for sure. Smoke and water creates one hell of a mess.'

'What about the occupants?'

He sounded so clinical, Amy thought with dismay. 'The occupants'? She was the woman he'd made love to so recently and these were all children that had already had more than their fair share of heartbreak in their lives.

'The police will deal with that side of things,' the scene commander told Luke. 'And Social Services. You don't need to worry about it.'

Paramedics were trying to herd Amy and the children back to the ambulances.

'We're taking you all to the hospital,' they said. 'You'll all need proper check-ups.'

Amy could hear Luke's pager sounding and saw him flip open his mobile phone. The thought that he might be being summoned because of some complication with Summer added a new level of anxiety. She broke away from the children and hurried towards Luke. Only days ago she wouldn't have dreamed of interrupting a telephone conversation he was having, but things had changed.

'Is that about Summer?'

He gave his head a curt shake. 'I'll be there as soon as I can. I'm five minutes away.' He snapped the phone shut.

'Is Summer all right?' Amy asked. 'I need to get back to her but I'll have to go with the others. They're taking them to hospital, hopefully Lizzie's, seeing as it's the closest, but—'

But Luke was looking down at himself rather than at Amy. The white gumboots were black and the scrub pants wet and filthy from the knees down. 'I'll have to get changed,' Luke said. 'I can't appear in ICU and talk to Liam's parents looking like this, can I?'

'Miss Phillips?' A policeman approached them. 'Can I talk to you, please? We need names and details for all the children involved here. And does this belong to you?'

It was Amy's red tote bag that she must have dropped ages ago when they had been running towards the house.

'Yes, it's mine.' She almost didn't want to claim it, knowing that her cellphone was in there. And that she was going to have to call her mother and tell her about this disaster.

'I have to go,' Luke said.

'Please…check on Summer? I'll be there as soon as I can.' Amy was being torn in too many directions and she was close to tears. She wanted to be with the children. To be with Summer.

To be with Luke.

'Of course,' he said.

'And…and thank you.'

'No need. Anyone would have done what I did.'

No, Amy thought, watching him stride away, dismissing a paramedic's renewed attention with a wave of his hand to indicate he needed no further attention. Not everyone would risk themselves to save other people's children, let alone their dog.

Even fewer people would brush off the chance to be seen as a hero. Or to get involved with the people that had been rescued.

Maybe Luke didn't want to be involved. With any of them.

Amy turned to look at the house. Her home. The front door stood open, snow swirling in to land in puddles in the hallway. Windows were blackened and broken and the reek of hot timber and sodden ash was everywhere. A policeman was putting tape across the gate to forbid entry.

She and the children were now officially homeless. Their clothing, toys and Christmas presents were being closed off from being claimed. Maybe those gifts had been destroyed. They were under Uncle Vanni's bed and his room was right beside the drawing room where the fire had started.

The engines of the ambulances were running and they were about to all be taken away. Amy would have to start answering questions about the children. Who they were and why they were in the house and why the level of supervision had clearly been inadequate.

Another child who needed her lay in the intensive care unit, fighting for her life, and the only other adult members of her family were still twenty-four hours away.

Amy had never felt more alone.

Luke had vanished through the crowd of onlookers, presumably intent on getting back to Lizzie's and his work as soon as possible. He hadn't looked as though he would have preferred to stay and help.

He had looked almost relieved.

And why not? He had got what he'd wanted all along, hadn't he?

The house was, at least partially, destroyed. The authorities were going to make sure that Amy and children couldn't return in the near future. It was possible that even minor structural damage from the fire would be enough to tip the balance and have the house condemned.

With dawning horror, Amy took in the implications.

It was the day before Christmas and she and her family were homeless.

CHAPTER TEN

'So where are you going to go? Have you got family in London?'

Amy tried to smile at the young constable because he was only trying to be helpful, but her ability to smile seemed to have deserted her. It just made her lips wobble.

'No,' she said. 'My mother and sister are in Italy until tomorrow. My only other family is my grandmother and they're bringing her back with them.'

'We'll have to get Social Services to organise placement for all the children, then.'

'No. Please, don't do that. We need to be together for Christmas. Isn't there any way at all we could go back to our house? If we stayed out of the damaged rooms?'

'You'll be shocked when you see how much damage gets done by thousands of gallons of water being sprayed everywhere. The place is saturated and the electricity and gas are shut off. There'll be no way of heating it and you'd all freeze.'

'What about getting our clothes? Christmas presents?'

'They're probably all wet. Stinking of smoke, anyway. Look, I'm really sorry but there's no way any of you will be going back to that house for the next few days.'

Maybe never, his expression said.

'So you've all got to go somewhere. You can't stay here.'

They couldn't. They'd already been in the emergency department of St Elizabeth's for hours. The children had all been given thorough physical check-ups. They'd been given lunch. They were all in clean, dry hospital pyjamas and still had the red ambulance blankets for extra warmth. Having been allocated a relatives' waiting room and provided with toys, books and DVDs, they had also been visited by Claire—a kind, middle-aged woman from Social Services.

Claire came into the office where Amy was talking to the police constable.

'They're all happy,' she told Amy. 'Except that Zoe wasn't too pleased at being collected by her mother. They wanted to know how Monty was getting on so I rang the vet. He's fine.'

'Oh, that's good news!'

'The clinic's not far from here and he can be collected any time. The children are also asking if they can visit Summer.'

'Not today.' Amy shook her head. She had been able to spend some time in the intensive care unit herself while the children were being assessed, and while Summer was doing brilliantly, she was still sedated and on a ventilator. It would be distressing for the other children to see her like that. Amy had wanted to find out when the life support would be deemed unnecessary but the ICU consultants were busy with a new arrival and Summer's surgeon had been nowhere to be seen.

'Did you get through to your mother and sister?'

Amy nodded this time. That conversation had been dreadful. Rosa had panicked about her sons and Marcella had cried with despair.

'Did they have any ideas about where you can all stay for a few days?'

Inspiration struck Amy. 'We'll go to a hotel,' she said.

'Can you afford that?'

'Yes.' It was a bill that wouldn't need to be paid until they left, wasn't it? Surely the house was insured.

'Have you checked availability? It's not a good time of year to be looking for last-minute accommodation. We do have foster-parents available.'

'We need to stay together,' Amy said stubbornly. 'We'll manage.'

'What about clothes? You'll need to go shopping. You'll need help with babysitting. There's meals to consider.' Claire was looking more and more doubtful. She also looked as though she was gearing herself up to do her duty, however unpleasant the repercussions might be.

'I know these children will be very upset if they're separated,' she began, 'but I really can't see any way around this.'

The office door opened as she spoke. Luke was back in his pinstriped suit. An authoritative figure that managed to take control before uttering a word.

'I need to talk to Amy for a moment. Excuse us, please.'

She looked dreadful.

As though this was the end of the world.

And, in a way, it was.

In an astonishingly short space of time Amy's world had disintegrated. Because of one family crisis, she had been left responsible for her home and the welfare of a large group of children. Now her home was damaged, possibly beyond repair, one of those children was critically ill and the others were in danger of being split up and having to spend Christmas in a foreign environment, away from anyone who knew and loved them.

Amy looked pale and worried but there was no air of being defeated, and Luke found that immensely admirable. There was no suggestion of accusation in her face, either, but Luke couldn't help a twinge of guilt, even though it had been purely coincidence that the disintegration of Amy's world had accelerated from the moment he had stepped into her life.

He had already decided not to evict the family prior to Christmas. At all, in fact. Not that he'd been able to tell Amy of his decision to hand over the house. It had hardly been the time when they'd seen that the house in question was on fire and the lives of its inhabitants in danger. And there hadn't been a chance since.

The system had enclosed them all. Luke had been juggling his patient commitments, monitoring Summer's condition and had had interviews with both the police and that woman from Social Services.

She had asked how much he knew about the Phillips family.

'Just how well are these children being cared for?'

'They have everything they need,' he had responded. 'Things are difficult at present with Amy's mother being away and the house might not be in perfect condition but these children are warm and well fed and…they're loved.'

'They do seem happy,' Claire had mused. 'And very close to each other. That oldest boy, Robert, is determined that they're going to stay together.'

'Have you spoken to Amy yet?'

'Not properly. I'll do that soon, when I've had a chance to decide what we need to do.'

Luke looked at the way Amy was standing tall in front of him now, her chin raised and determination lurking in anxious eyes, and he knew Claire would find her even more determined than Robert to keep the family together.

It reminded him of their first encounter. Had it really been only two days ago that she'd tried to shut the door in his face? She had demonstrated how fiercely she was prepared to fight for her family.

She'd do anything, she'd said.

Anything.

The word had been echoing in the back of Luke's mind with increasing intensity. His notion of gifting her the house and judging by her reaction whether her love-making had been as genuine as it had seemed was pointless now. The house was damaged and uninhabitable. Such a gift might even be seen as insulting.

So, amongst all the other duties that had kept him running, physically and mentally, for the last few hours, Luke had decided on another approach.

One that was out of character enough to be making him nervous.

Very nervous.

Not only was he going to listen to his heart properly for the first time in his life, he was going to act on what it told him even if it went against what was obviously more rational.

At least, he would, depending on the answer Amy provided to the question he was about to ask.

'You said you'd do anything to save your house, didn't you?'

'Yes.' Amy's smile was wry. 'It's a bit late now to put my plan into action, though, isn't it?'

It wasn't too late for *his* plan, though.

'When you said "anything"?' he asked softly. 'Did that include what happened last night?'

The play of emotions on Amy's face was so clear Luke could actually feel the emotions they represented. Her first reaction was confusion. What had happened last night of such significance? A frown of anxiety appeared. Summer's transplant? No. Amy couldn't see the connection between Summer's surgery and the house. What else had happened?

Amy's expression softened. Her eyes darkened and her lips parted and Luke could see—*feel*—the memory of their time together. A time that had no connection to anything else because it had been simply theirs.

That it had been difficult for Amy to make a connection was all the answer Luke really needed.

But, '*No,*' Amy whispered. 'No, no, no!'

Luke drew in a careful breath. 'Are you still prepared to do anything? To keep the children together and safe for Christmas?'

'Of course.' Amy looked puzzled now. Her gaze was fixed on him. She didn't understand. Their immediate future was about to be dictated by social authorities who had more clout than Luke did in such matters. How could he be in any position to suggest an alternative?

'What do you want me to do?'

Luke's smile was crooked. 'Trust me.'

It was the strangest meeting Amy had ever attended and it was just as well that input from her didn't appear to be required.

Dazed by the events and emotional turmoil of the last few days, she sat on a couch in the relatives' waiting room with the twins on her lap, a girl cuddled close on each side and two older boys flanking the arms of the couch like sentries, watching and listening while Claire asked the questions she should have asked Luke herself.

'What arrangements? What on earth are you planning to do with six children?'

'It's all in hand,' was all Luke seemed prepared to say. 'I'm taking full responsibility for this family.'

'Who did you say you were again?'

'Luke Harrington. Head of the cardiothoracic surgical department here at St Elizabeth's.'

'No.' Claire sounded faintly bewildered. 'That other name you said.'

'On my birth certificate? Luca Moretti.'

The way he said the name sent a curl of something very poignant through Amy. Had he noticed he'd said it with an Italian accent?

He'd been lost for a very long time, this man, and the thought made her heart squeeze tightly.

She loved him.

She trusted him.

More than Claire did, it seemed.

'I still don't understand. It all seems terribly complicated and rather irregular.'

'Let me make it easy for you.' The soothing note in Luke's voice had probably calmed many anxious parents in the past. 'My father—sadly deceased—owned the house Amy and the children live in. I inherited it. Because of that, I'm taking full responsibility for the inhabitants of that house.'

Was that the only reason he wanted to help? Some kind of guilt trip? Amy bit her lip to drive back weary tears and she cuddled the twins closer.

She trusted him. She needed to hang on to that.

Marco obligingly twisted in his half of her lap and wound his arms around her neck. 'I love you, Zietta Amy.'

'I love you, too,' she whispered back.

Luke was speaking more forcefully now. He was not about to allow a social worker to disrupt arrangements he had made. Whatever they were.

'I'll sign whatever forms are necessary. It's getting late and it's Christmas Eve. I'm sure we've both got better things to do than stand here debating this issue.'

Claire glanced at her watch and gave in with a sigh. 'Very well. But I must insist on knowing where you intend taking these children.'

Luke didn't look at Amy to seek her approval.

'Harrington Manor,' was all he said. 'In Harrington village. About an hour's drive from London.'

Claire made a final attempt at regaining some form of control. 'Amy? How do you feel about all this? Are you happy to go with Mr Harrington?'

The thought of being taken so far away from Summer was more than a worry. It was unacceptable. The thought of being in the same house as the old woman who had looked at Amy as though she wasn't fit to scrub her floors almost made her gasp with incredulity. It was impossible!

But small arms were tightening around her neck and the children were all staring at her. Questioning this new turn in their lives. Ready to stand by her and refuse to co-operate if she didn't think it was a good idea. Trusting her to keep them safe.

Amy stared at Luke. She had no choice here. She *had* to trust him.

He met her gaze without smiling and his eyes reiterated the words he had spoken in the corridor.

Trust me.

Amy turned back to Claire. 'Yes,' she said calmly. 'I'm happy. We'll all go to Harrington Manor.'

One step at a time, she reminded herself. All she could do

was to keep things together as much as possible for as long as possible.

And hope for a miracle.

It took two taxis to ferry them all to Harrington Manor.

Luke followed in his own car.

'I'll need to come back,' he explained as Amy prepared to climb into the first taxi where the twins and Chantelle were waiting. 'Summer's due to have her drains removed and we're thinking of lightening her sedation. She may be ready to come off the ventilator.'

Which meant she could wake up. Soon.

'I need to be there,' Amy said, 'when she wakes up.'

Luke nodded. 'You'll be able to come back. A car and chauffeur will be available. I thought you'd want to go with the children initially.'

A chauffeur? Not Luke? Why was he coming back with them now, then?

Did his grandmother not know they were coming? About to descend en masse on a home that both Uncle Vanni and her father had been threatened with prosecution for trespass if they tried to enter?

Oh…*Lord*!

Snow was falling more thickly and daylight was virtually gone by the time the small entourage finally escaped the city limits. Luke's car had taken some time to catch up with the taxis but the three vehicles were together as they left the motorway and turned onto more rural roads.

'Are we lost?' Chantelle asked.

'No way, darling.' The driver of the black cab was enjoying what would probably turn out to be his biggest fare ever. 'I've got GPS in this baby. No way we can get lost.'

'What's GPS?'

'It means we're being tracked from up in space,' Amy tried to explain. 'That little screen on the dashboard is telling our driver exactly where we are and where we need to go.'

'Space?' Marco sounded puzzled.

'*Spaziale*. Where the stars are.'

The children peered from the windows of the taxi but all they could see was the swirl of snowflakes in the headlights of the small line of cars.

'Will Father Christmas find us when it's snowing?' Chantelle asked. 'How will he know where we've gone?'

'Maybe he's got GPS these days, too.' The cab driver chuckled. Then he glanced in his rear-view mirror and saw the expression on the little girl's face. 'Hey, Santa comes from a very snowy place. It's no problem.'

Amy had something new to worry about now. The few presents tucked away for the children were lost. Shops might be open until late tonight but with the time it would take to travel back to the city and the time she needed to spend with Summer, how could she manage to fit any shopping in? How on earth could she do anything about giving these children any kind of Christmas surprises?

Would Luke's grandmother even have a tree?

The prospect began to appear unlikely. Huge iron gates swung open a short time later, presumably because Luke had a remote control in his car. Snow was piling up in drifts on either side of the long driveway and it was settling onto bare branches of the massive old trees that gave the impression of a guard of honour.

The house was enormous and dark and forbidding. Even Amy's taxi driver fell silent as they parked at the base of semicircular stone steps that had huge lions on pillars at each side.

Luke got out of his car and came to Amy's taxi.

'Stay here for just a minute or two,' he instructed. 'I'll be back.'

Amy cuddled the children close and tried to banish her sense of foreboding as the heavy front door opened and the house swallowed Luke.

If Luke had thought his grandmother nervous in his office yesterday, he had to consider her alarmed now. She was standing near the huge fire in the library. Beside a small table with spindly legs on which a decanter of sherry and small crystal glasses stood on a silver tray.

'Whatever's going on, Luke? What are all those taxis doing outside?'

'We have visitors.'

The housekeeper, Elaine, closely followed by her husband Henry, hurried through the door.

'Is everything all right, Lady Harrington?'

'That's what I'm trying to find out myself. Luke?'

'We have visitors, Grandmother. For Christmas.'

'I beg your pardon?'

'Henry said they look like children,' Elaine reported. 'He was watching from the garages.'

Henry looked at his feet. Luke looked at his grandmother just as steadily. 'They are children,' he said. 'There are six of them and they range in age from about six to fourteen.'

'Oh, *my*!' Elaine breathed.

'Are these the children I was trying to discuss with you yesterday, Luke? If so, I can make arrangements. They don't even need to get out of the cabs. Let me call Lucy and—'

'No. I will not allow that.'

His grandmother fluttered a hand, looking shocked.

'There was a fire this morning,' Luke continued. 'The house that is home to these children was extensively damaged. I have brought them here for a reason.'

Prudence sank onto the edge of an overstuffed couch. 'I don't understand.'

'Elaine?' Luke smiled at the housekeeper. 'Could you prepare some rooms, please? At least four, I would think.'

'But...' Elaine looked at her employer, but Prudence had closed her eyes. 'They're *children*...' The word was slightly awed.

'You're good with children, Elaine. Maybe you've still got that box of toys somewhere. You know, the ones they used to keep in the kitchens for me?'

A smile tugged at Elaine's mouth. 'I think I know where it is. Oh, my! Children. Here for Christmas.' She turned away. 'Henry? I'm going to need your help. Let's sort out some linen.'

Prudence opened her eyes and waited. Luke sat on the edge of the couch beside her.

'I know this is a shock,' he began. 'But things have happened in the last couple of days that have made me start to question my life.'

'This has something to do with that nurse, doesn't it? The one you were...ah...'

'Kissing,' Luke supplied. 'Her name is Amy and, yes, it has a lot to do with her, but that's beside the point just now. Look.' He fished in the his coat pocket and brought out a rather crumpled photograph. 'Look at this.'

'Oh!' Prudence put a hand to her throat and tears sprang instantly to her eyes. 'Caroline!'

'She was happy,' Luke said quietly. 'She loved my father and, by all accounts, he adored her. Maybe he wasn't suitable but my mother's death broke his heart. Losing his son was another tragedy as far as he was concerned and it was one that he didn't have to suffer.'

Prudence was silent.

'He *did* suffer,' Luke went on. 'And if I don't help his family and the children he loved, *they* will suffer, and that would be wrong.'

He picked up his grandmother's hand and held it. 'You are my family,' he said, 'and I haven't said this for far too many years but I love you. You did what you thought was right but you took something away from me. The chance to know my father. It's something that I think mattered a great deal.'

'I'm...sorry, Luke. I—'

'I know.' Luke leaned over to kiss her cheek. 'I'm going to bring the children in now. They're frightened and cold and hungry. Please, welcome them because this is also something that matters a great deal.' He stood up. 'We can't turn the clock back but we've got a chance here to do something right. Something honourable. Do it for me. Please?'

'I'll...try.' Prudence took a shaky breath and sat up a little straighter. 'Just for Christmas?'

'Just for Christmas,' Luke agreed.

One step at a time, he told himself as he went back to the waiting cars. For himself, as well, because he was stepping into alien territory here. An emotional landscape that had no map.

They trooped inside, silently.

They stood, silently, gazing at the biggest Christmas tree Amy had ever seen, positioned at the base of a stairway that curled gracefully up and then divided to form a U that swept past an uncountable number of doors.

A woman with grey hair in a bun, holding a pile of linen, beamed down at them before hurrying through one of the doors.

The tree was doing its best to reach the banisters of the U so it had to be at least twenty feet tall, and it was covered with thousands of white fairy lights in the form of tiny icicles that were twinkling on and off in sequence. A discreet few, gorgeously wrapped silver parcels lay at its base.

Luke ushered them on. 'Come into the library,' he commanded. 'My grandmother is waiting to meet you.'

Amy's misgivings made her heart thump alarmingly rapidly but she stepped forward, a twin attached to each hand. Robert, Kyra and Andrew were behind them but Chantelle, her face shining, skipped ahead. She came to an abrupt halt on entering the library, however, because standing in front of a roaring fire, with a forbiddingly remote expression on her face, was the woman who had dismissed Amy yesterday with no more than a passing glance.

Chantelle's mouth dropped open.

'Are you the *queen*?'

For a moment there was an odd silence and Chantelle gave Amy a look of trepidation.

'She *looks* like the queen,' she said in a small voice.

'*Che?*' Marco didn't understand.

'This is my grandmother,' Luke told the children. 'My *nonna*,' he added to Marco and Angelo. He smiled at Chantelle. 'But she does look a bit like the queen, doesn't she?'

Lady Prudence Harrington wasn't smiling but the tension in the room eased just a little. Amy kept her gaze on Luke, loving him so much for the way he hadn't let Chantelle feel she had said something stupid.

'Excuse me for a moment,' Luke said. He vanished through the door and the awkward silence fell again as Prudence stared at the wall of silent children.

'I forgot,' Luke announced as he came back through the door. 'He was asleep on the back seat of my car.'

'Monty!' the twins shrieked in delight.

'Luke!' The tone was as shocked as it had been yesterday when Prudence had caught her grandson kissing a nurse in his office. 'What in heaven's name are you thinking of, bringing a *dog* in here?'

'It's Monty.' Chantelle had been gazing at Lady Harrington as though still convinced she was in the presence of royalty. 'He's *our* dog now.'

'Dogs belong outside.' Prudence moved to push a button on the wall. 'I'm sorry, Luke, but this is too much. I need to call Henry.'

'Come with me.' Luke offered his grandmother his arm. 'We'll both talk to him. And Elaine. We need some hot food and drink for our visitors.'

They were left alone in the library for what seemed a very long time. Amy heard muted voices and more than one door closing. A telephone rang, the fire crackled and a grandfather clock at one end of a huge bookshelf ticked solemnly.

Then a man they hadn't seen before came in.

'I'm Henry,' he told them. 'I have a message for you, Miss Phillips. From Mr Harrington.'

'Call me Amy, please.'

Henry blinked. 'I'm not sure that's—'

'Spit it out, Henry.' The woman with the grey bun came bustling in. 'I'm Elaine,' she told Amy. 'The housekeeper. I've got your rooms ready if you'd like to come and see where you're all going to sleep?'

The children eyed her suspiciously.

'And then we'll all go down to the kitchens,' she added. 'Beryl is making dinner for you. And for— Oh, my! He's a big dog, isn't he?'

'That's Monty,' Chantelle said.

'Well, we'll find some dinner for Monty, too. And some nice old blankets. He could sleep in the scullery where it's all nice and warm from the coal range. If that's suitable?'

Robert gave a slow nod. He approved of Elaine. Amy could feel herself relaxing a little.

'What was the message?' she asked Henry.

'Oh, yes. Mr Harrington had to return to the hospital somewhat urgently. He said you'd be wanting to follow him and I'm at your disposal.'

'You've got another wee one who's sick at the moment, haven't you?' Elaine's face was creased with sympathy. 'Let me settle the others and get them fed and bathed and into bed.'

'That's too much work for you,' Amy protested. 'I'll stay and help.'

Elaine shook her head. 'It's been too long since this house heard the sound of children's voices. It'll be a treat.'

Amy was quite sure Lady Harrington didn't see it as a treat. It seemed rather pointed that she hadn't returned to the library.

Elaine seemed to be reading her thoughts. 'Lady Harrington sends her apologies,' she said, 'but she's not feeling very well and has had to retire to her room. She'll see you in the morning.'

Christmas morning.

'Whenever you're ready, miss,' Henry said kindly. 'And you're not to worry about your family that's coming, either. I'm to stay in the city tonight and meet them at the airport tomorrow. Mr Harrington said to tell you not to worry about anything.' Henry smiled. 'That everything's in hand.'

Things may have been taken out of her own hands but Amy felt curiously safe with the astonishing flow that was pulling them all along. It was as though someone was waving a wand to take care of everything that was worrying her.

A tiny seed of something as effervescent as excitement took hold inside her.

Miracles did happen sometimes, didn't they?

And what better time for a bit of magic than Christmas?

CHAPTER ELEVEN

SHE was asleep.

Tangled, dark hair framed a pale face that was cradled on one arm. The other arm still lay on the bed, fingers cupped around a much smaller hand.

Luke kept his voice low. 'How long has she been asleep?'

'Most of the night. She's woken every time I've done Summer's recordings but she's barely moved.'

Luke gave the latest set of recordings another satisfied glance. Then he turned his head to nod at someone else.

Henry ushered three women into the ICU, his fingers on his lips to warn them of the need to stay quiet and calm, and then he faded back into the corridor. One of the women was easily as old as Luke's grandmother. A small, slightly hunched figure leaning heavily on a walking stick and probably hampered by the long, black skirt she was wearing. The other two looked remarkably like Amy and Luke gave them a smile that came from the bottom of his heart.

'Only a few minutes,' he warned the new arrivals. 'There's only supposed to be one or two close relatives at a time.'

Amy's grandmother scowled at Luke rather ferociously but her mother was clearly struggling with tears. Hyperventilating as she tried to control herself. Luke put both his hands on her shoulders and gave them a reassuring squeeze.

'Summer's doing very, very well, Mrs Phillips. Be strong.' He smiled again. 'I wouldn't be at all surprised if she wakes up when she hears your voice.'

Amy woke up at the sound of her mother's voice. She lurched to her feet to be enveloped in a hug, first from Marcella and then a long, tight, relieved embrace from her older sister.

'Buon Natale, cara! Buon Natale!'

'You, too, Rosa,' Amy whispered back. *'Buon Natale!'*

Happy Christmas!

'Buon Natale, Nonna.' Amy helped her grandmother into the chair she had been sleeping in.

'Buon Natale, Mamma.'

But Marcella wasn't listening. Ignoring all the monitors, the IV lines, the beeping noises and everything else alarming, she was leaning over the bed, gently touching Summer's face, murmuring a constant stream of endearments.

'Oh!' Amy clutched her sister's hand and spoke in a hushed voice, not wanting to break the spell. 'Rosa, *look*! Summer's waking up.'

And she was.

Slowly. Peacefully. Surrounded by the voices and touch of the three women who were all mothers to her. Watched over by a benevolent small figure who sat, imperiously, in the armchair nodding and muttering approvingly at regular intervals.

Staff came and went unobtrusively, keeping a close watch on what was happening but not disturbing this special family moment.

Luke was there. He smiled at Amy. A smile that told her

he understood how special this was. That he understood how much this mattered.

Amy smiled back. Including him. Pulling him in to share the magic. Trying to find and reach through that crack she knew was there. To reach inside Luke—so he wouldn't feel lonely.

To let him know he never needed to feel lonely again.

The smile went on. And on.

It was no wonder Rosa noticed. She looked from Amy to Luke and back again. Then she stepped to where Luke was standing, well back from the end of Summer's bed.

'Does it hurt?' she queried. 'Where her chest was cut open for the operation?'

'Surprisingly little,' Luke responded. 'Pain from fractures comes from movement and there's very little movement of the sternum involved in breathing. Most children can be discharged from open-heart surgery with nothing more than paracetamol needed to relieve any discomfort. You'll be amazed at how soon Summer's up and about.'

Rosa had been listening carefully. Watching and assessing Luke just as carefully. She gave Amy a quick grin as she stepped back towards her sister.

'E un bell 'uomo, vero?'

Amy just raised her eyebrows. This was hardly the place to talk about how good-looking Luke was. Just as well he didn't speak Italian, wasn't it?

There was just a hint of a wink in Luke's expression as he nodded at Rosa while moving away, however.

'Grazie,' he murmured.

Nonna scowled disapprovingly. Rosa's jaw dropped and she flushed bright pink. Amy shut her eyes for a moment, took a deep breath and then walked after Luke, but he was now standing beside the ICU consultant so she could hardly apologise for her sister's inappropriate comment.

'Summer needs to rest,' the consultant reminded Amy. 'It's great if she has one or possibly two of you with her at all times, but we can't have this many here all day.'

'And it's Christmas,' Luke added. 'You'll all want some time with the other children, yes?'

Amy nodded.

'Henry's waiting. He'll take you back as soon as you're ready.'

'Rosa will want to see the twins,' Amy thought aloud. 'And Nonna will need a rest after travelling. I'll talk to Mamma. I can stay if she wants to see the others.'

Luke frowned, as though that plan wasn't the best. But then he simply nodded. 'Let me know,' he said, a little curtly. 'I have to go myself. I have a few things that need attention.' He turned back to the ICU consultant. 'I've got my mobile, of course,' he said, 'but I'd prefer not to be called unless it's an emergency.'

The consultant smiled. 'Of course. Enjoy your Christmas, Luke. Things are looking good here. You're happy with the lad you were working on last night?'

Luke nodded. 'Poor kid. Getting caught up in a gang fight and shot on Christmas Eve was a bit rough. He lost a lot of blood but I'm happy his cardiac function will remain normal. What we need to watch is…'

His voice faded into the background as Amy went back to her family. So Henry was taking them back to the manor and Luke had things that needed his attention. Was he not planning to go home for Christmas? Some of the shine of happiness from Summer's waking up and the reunion with her family faded.

Marcella elected to stay.

'I'll come and see the rest of my *bambina* later,' she said firmly. 'Right now, it's this little *angelo* that needs me the most.'

'We'll take Nonna with us, then,' Rosa said. 'Come on, Amy. I can't wait to see the boys.' She took her turn to kiss Summer. 'See you later, *tesora*.'

Summer smiled and gave an infinitesimal nod, but her gaze went straight back to Marcella.

'Mamma,' she whispered.

'I'm here, *carina*. I'm staying right beside you.'

'Chiesa!'

'It's a chapel, Nonna. A small church.' Amy hadn't seen the beautiful stone structure in the dark last night, but this morning, with its roof and the tops of surrounding gravestones softly blanketed by the deep snow, it was clearly visible amidst a forest of huge tree trunks.

Her grandmother crossed herself and nodded approvingly. *'Buona.'*

She approved of the Harrington family's faith. What would she say when she learned the Italian connection with a woman who lay buried in that small private cemetery? There was no way she would approve of a broken family. A father who had been deprived of his only child. Maybe it was just as well she spoke only her native language.

Rosa was still getting her head around the astonishing information Amy had shared—in English—during their journey from the city.

'It's so weird! Uncle Vanni's son? And you've been working with him for so long and we never knew. Who'd have thought?'

'He keeps his background very private.'

'I can see why.' Rosa was gaping as the manor house came into view. 'It's like something out of a fairy tale. If people knew how rich he was, he'd be beating women off with a stick.' She eyed her sister. 'He's not beating you off, from what I could see.'

'I'm not after his money,' Amy said sadly. 'If anything, I wish he didn't have a background like this. It makes things impossible. Wait till you meet his grandmother. She hates me so much she couldn't bear to stay in the same room as me last night.'

'Because you're in love with her grandson?'

'We haven't got that far. I think she hates me because I'm half-Italian. And because I'm connected with Uncle Vanni. I remind her of how she lost her daughter.'

They were parking in front of the house now. 'I saved that scrapbook,' she told Rosa. 'It might be the only thing of Uncle Vanni's that isn't lost in the fire. I'd been carrying it in my bag to show Luke and I'd forgotten all about it,'

Which had been hardly surprising because that had been when she'd been swept off her feet. Made love to with a passion that had driven all else from her mind. And from there she had been whirled into a series of unexpected and very sharp turns in her life.

'I left it outside Lady Harrington's bedroom door last night when I went back to be with Summer. I wonder if she's even looked at it?'

There was no sign of Lady Harrington when Elaine met them at the front door.

'We're all in the kitchen,' she told Amy, 'having our Christmas breakfast.'

Nonna seemed to be overcome by the sight of the Christmas tree in the foyer. Amy took her arm and urged her gently forward.

'It's just the Christmas tree, Nonna,' she said reassuringly. '*Albero di Natale*. Isn't it beautiful?'

Nonna made a clucking sound that said, very eloquently, that she disapproved of such opulence, but she followed Amy and Rosa willingly enough.

'I've made a room ready for your nanna,' Elaine said to Amy. 'She'll need to rest, I expect.'

'Soon,' Amy agreed.

'Where's Lady Harrington?' Rosa queried politely. 'I should introduce myself.'

Elaine looked embarrassed. 'I expect she'll be down soon.'

Christmas morning with six children in a house should have been seething with excitement, but the atmosphere in the huge, old kitchen was very solemn until Marco and Angelo spotted their mother.

'*Mamma!*' They scrambled from their seats at the table and launched themselves in Rosa's direction like small, human torpedoes.

Elaine laughed. The cook, Beryl, wiped her hands on her apron and grinned. Monty got up from his blanket in the corner to see what the fuss was all about. The other children, however, stayed at the table. They had plates of food in front of them. Slices of crusty bread and butter that looked homemade. Bacon and eggs and tiny sausages beside baked beans and mushrooms and potato cakes. The sort of food that was a special treat but they didn't seem to be eating much of it.

When the initial excitement of Rosa's arrival subsided, they all sent wary glances towards Nonna, who was now sitting at the far end of the table, and then went back to playing with their food.

'What's the matter?' Amy finally asked. 'Aren't you happy Summer's OK? You'll all be able to visit her in a day or two. Only one at a time, but I think she'll be home again before very long.'

That did it. Robert pushed his plate away, his fork clattering onto the china.

'We haven't *got* a home any more,' he said sullenly. 'It got burned, didn't it?'

'Not all of it. We'll fix things,' Amy promised.

'No, we won't. And even if we do, your Mr Harrington's going to take it away from us, so what's the point?'

Elaine exchanged a glance with Beryl. Raised eyebrows and quick head shakes indicated they knew nothing about this.

'And…' Quiet Andrew was looking as miserable as Robert. 'It's Christmas!'

Chantelle burst into tears. 'And we haven't got any presents,' she sobbed. 'Not even *one*!'

Amy sent a desperate glance towards Rosa, but her sister looked stricken. Maybe the credit card hadn't been robust enough to deal with any airport shopping.

'Hey!' Amy gathered Chantelle into her arms, taking her chair and smiling at the rest of the children. 'We've got each other, haven't we? We're all safe and we're all together. That's what *really* matters.' She waited until Robert raised his head and caught her gaze. 'Nobody is going to take our house away. Nobody.' She hugged Chantelle. 'And Summer got a present, didn't she? The best present she could ever get. A new heart.'

'So she's not going to die?' Robert's Adam's apple bobbed and his voice cracked and rose.

'She's got every chance of living now,' Amy said confidently. 'Much, much more than she had a couple of days ago.'

'And Monty's OK,' she went on, trying to put a positive spin on this strange Christmas Day. 'And he's like a present, too, isn't he? He can't live with Zoe and her mum any more so he's our pet.'

'Really?' Rosa reached past the twins to stroke the huge dog. 'Cool!'

Elaine put a steaming cup of tea in front of Nonna.

'Grazie,' the old woman said.

Elaine patted her hand. 'You're welcome, Nanna.'

Beryl filled the kettle again. 'Your Henry's coming back from putting the car away. He'll be wanting some breakfast.'

She didn't take the kettle away from beneath the tap, however. She was still intent on peering out the window.

'Mercy!' she said, as cold water flowed over the top of the kettle and then her hand. She abandoned the tea-making and peered from the window again. 'I don't believe this,' she muttered.

'What?' Elaine joined her at the sink. 'Oh, *my!*' She flapped a hand in a beckoning gesture. 'Children! You'd better come and see. Quick! Out the front.'

The excitement was contagious. A small stampede of children followed, Elaine with Rosa and twins bringing up the rear, closely followed by Monty who gave a single, loud woof as he bounded through the kitchen door.

Amy looked at Nonna but she was sipping her tea, apparently unperturbed.

'I'll stay with your granny,' Beryl offered. 'You go and see.'

Amy went.

CHAPTER TWELVE

BY THE time Amy reached the foyer, the front door was wide open and sparkling, cold air was pouring into the house.

The sound of bells could be heard, getting louder and louder.

Amy reached the door. The children were all standing on the top step, a semicircle of faces that all had open mouths and wide eyes.

And no wonder!

Coming down the long driveway, covered in tinsel, was a small lorry. The shop name 'Barkers' could be seen beneath loops of tinsel, painted in old-fashioned lettering on the side, but it was no ordinary shop employee that climbed down from the driver's seat.

He was wearing a red suit with white trim and he had ridiculously bushy eyebrows and a fluffy white beard that reached his chest.

'Ho, ho, ho,' he boomed. 'Merry Christmas!'

He winked at the adults. 'Sorry, I'm late. Lots of snow on the M1 last night.'

His gaze rested for just a fraction of a second on Amy.

Just long enough for her to know who was beneath the pillow stomach and bushy eyebrows.

Luca!

It was understandable that Rosa and the children didn't recognise him, but Elaine seemed just as taken in. Because doing something like this was so out of character for the Harrington grandson and heir?

The back door of the lorry was folding down, the recorded bells still jingling merrily.

'Come,' Father Christmas invited the children. 'Come and see what I've got.'

The children moved slowly down the steps. They stood in the driveway, staring into the back of the lorry, and the adults were not far behind.

'Oh, my!' Elaine breathed.

Amy blinked. And blinked again. The back of this lorry was full of brightly wrapped parcels. Hundreds of them, it seemed.

'I forgot my sack,' Father Christmas said. 'Can someone show me where the tree is and give me a hand to get them all inside?'

Robert stepped forward and spoke in a steady, deep voice. 'I can do that.'

The noise could have woken the dead.

Happy shouting. Laughter. Squeals of glee.

The gifts were amazing. Someone—possibly many people—had been given a list of those involved. Their ages and approximate sizes and the information that they had lost most of their belongings.

Many of the first packages contained clothes. Jeans and T-shirts and warm, fleecy jackets. Anoraks and gumboots in wonderful bright colours. Kyra's were pink with lime-green spots.

'Wow!' she said. 'These are *way* cool!'

Henry and Elaine and Beryl watched from the library door. Amy sat on the stairs, brushing tears form her cheeks on more than one occasion. Totally unable to wipe the smile from her face.

She was riveted by the scene. The generosity was overwhelming and the joy of the children heart-warming, but the real magic came from watching this Father Christmas. The joy *he* was getting, acting the part. Using Robert as his right-hand man.

'You're the chief elf!' he boomed in that astonishingly deep, unrecognisable voice. 'You get to find the next gift.'

Robert was scrupulously fair, making sure everyone had their turns.

It was Chantelle who pointed out when Robert was due for a gift. She tugged shyly at Santa's sleeve.

'It wouldn't be fair, would it? If the chief elf got left out?'

'You can be the deputy chief elf,' Luke told her. 'You get to find a present for Robert.'

'How did you know all our names?'

'I'm Father Christmas! I know everybody's names.'

Chantelle sighed happily. 'I love you, Santa.'

'I love you, too, chicken.'

Amy's joy overflowed and she gurgled with laughter. Father Christmas looked up and she knew *he* knew that she had recognised him. It was their secret and Amy could barely tear her gaze away from him as the gift distribution continued. She was waiting for each moment of connection.

Loving him more each time.

At one point she had to look up to blink away more tears and it was then that she saw the solitary figure standing to one side of the U at the top of the stairs, gripping the banister with one hand.

Lady Prudence Harrington looked dishevelled. She wore a dressing-gown and her hair was unbrushed. She didn't see Amy's shocked glance. She was too intent on watching her grandson and the children.

Amy saw something else, as well. Clutched beneath the old woman's arm was the leather-bound scrapbook of Caroline's. The knowledge that her gift had been accepted only added to the magic. Amy turned back to keep watching the seemingly endless stream of gifts.

There were toys galore. Lovely toys, like Lego for the twins and Meccano for Andrew. Robert had a telescope and books about astronomy. There were soft toy animals for Chantelle and a hair straightener and make-up for Kyra. There were even toys for Monty. A Frisbee and flinger. Rawhide treats and a huge, soft bed.

Rosa received perfume and chocolates and there was a beautiful mohair knee rug for Nonna. Parcels were put aside for Marcella and Summer. The massive pile of gifts was finally whittled down and the deputy elf tugged on Santa's sleeve again, this time with more urgency.

'But what about *Amy*?' she demanded. 'Where's *her* present?'

'Ah!' Luke's voice was still deep but it softened. 'I have a very special present for Amy. It's outside.'

Amy caught her breath. What could it be? Robert looked up from one of his books. 'Can we come and see it?'

Father Christmas shook his head. 'I'm afraid not.'

'Why not?' Chantelle asked. 'We *love* Amy.'

'I know, chicken. So do I.'

A sensation as though a bottle of champagne had been opened inside Amy sent its fizz right through her body. He loved her?

Chantelle seemed just as amazed. *'Really?'* But then she nodded. 'Because you love everybody, right?'

'Yes. But *especially* Amy.' He was looking directly at her and Amy couldn't breathe. Couldn't move.

'But why can't we see her present?' Robert took charge of the argument.

'It's not here.'

'You said it was outside!'

'Come,' Father Christmas ordered. 'You'll see what I mean.'

He disappeared into the back of the lorry and there was the sound of an engine roaring into life.

Amy had been able to move after all. She stood with everybody else on the steps and was just as astonished to see Father Christmas emerge, driving carefully down the ramp on a two-seated snowmobile. He did a slow turn and then parked in front of the steps. His gaze was on Amy and she could tell he was smiling beneath the bushy beard because of the way his eyes crinkled.

'Buon Natale,' Father Christmas said in perfect Italian. He patted the seat beside him. *'Vieni con me?'*

Of course Amy would go with him.

Anywhere.

A ride into a blindingly white Christmas day, on a modern sleigh, wrapped in a faux fur blanket with one of Luke's arms around her shoulders was too dreamlike to believe.

They went through a gate and up the long, gentle slope of a hill. At the top of the hill were some huge rocks, jumbled together like a pile of reject material from Stonehenge. A gap between two rocks formed an arch and it was beneath this that Luke parked.

He switched off the machine's motor so that all around them was that peculiar kind of silence a snow-clad landscape could produce, where the sounds of ordinary life were muffled and irrelevant.

'Look,' Luke pointed. 'That's Harrington village.'

Spread below them like a picture on a Christmas card was a church spire and a cluster of cottages. Amy could see the village green, a picturesque pub and a huddle of small shops. To one side of the village, buffered by woods and snow-covered fields, lay Harrington Manor. Smoke curled invitingly from more than one chimney. Somewhere in there were a group of children who were having the most exciting Christmas morning ever.

'Thank you, Luca,' she said softly. 'What you did this morning was amazing. I can't believe you've gone to so much trouble for us. You'd already done enough, you know—giving us a place to stay.'

'Enough? I've barely started.'

Amy caught her breath. Could he mean what she thought he might mean? What she could dream he might mean?

'Did you like it?' Luke held her gaze.

Amy couldn't smile because it was too big. 'It was a whole collection of those moments,' she said solemnly.

'The ones that take your breath away?'

'I felt as if I might never breathe again.'

Luke pulled his hat off, which got rid of the bushy eyebrows. Then he tugged his beard away and, looking like the man Amy had fallen in love with again, he placed a soft kiss on her lips. *'Buono,'* he murmured.

Amy pulled back so she could see his face properly. 'Since when did you start speaking Italian, Mr Harrington?'

In response he pulled her closer so that she was tucked into the circle of his arms. Cushioned on that ridiculous stomach. He kissed her hair but then raised his head to gaze at the scene below them.

'I grew up with this,' he told her. 'My heritage. I used to come up here when I was a boy and look down at everything. It all had my name on it. Harrington village. Harrington school. Even the Harrington Arms. It felt as if the whole world belonged to me and yet I felt…'

Amy twisted a little to look up. 'Lonely?'

'Yes. Not that I understood it then, but I knew something was missing. I thought it was because I was an orphan, except I knew I wasn't. I had a father who didn't want me.'

Not true, but he hadn't known that, had he? Amy slipped her arms over the top of Luke's and pressed so that he was holding her more tightly.

'I felt I deserved to be alone,' Luke said quietly. 'That there was something about me that meant I would always be alone.'

Amy had to swallow the lump in her throat. 'You're not alone, Luca. I'm here.'

'Yes.' He pressed his lips to her hair again and held her so closely it became another moment that took Amy's breath away. 'I don't want to let you go,' he confessed.

'I don't want you to let me go,' Amy responded. 'I love you, Luca Moretti.'

The sound Luke made was almost a groan. 'That's it,' he murmured. 'You turned my world inside out, Amy Phillips. Made me wonder who I actually was. You found the part of me that I knew was missing but could never identify. No…' His voice caught. 'You *are* the part of me that was missing.'

'The Italian half?'

Luke shook his head. 'Not entirely. It goes deeper than

that. Do you remember what you said to me that first night we talked? When I said I intended demolishing the house?'

Amy could feel her cheeks flush. 'I wasn't very polite, was I?'

'You said, "over my dead body" and I was shocked because you meant it. You were prepared to fight for what you were passionate about. To do anything.'

Amy was silent. Embarrassed. Had he really thought that was why she had gone to bed with him?

'I couldn't think of anything I could ever feel like that about,' Luke continued softly. 'Something I would be prepared to lay my life on the line for because life wouldn't be worth living without it. Until…' He drew in a long breath. 'Until I made love to you, Amy. Until I lay there in your arms and felt as though I would never feel lonely again. I know it's far too soon, but I love you. *Ti amo, Amy. Amore mio. Per sempre.* Is that "for ever"? My Italian is more than rusty.'

'I love you, too, Luca.' Amy blinked back her tears. 'It's not too soon and for ever sounds perfect to me, however you say it.'

'Are you sure?'

'I was sure the moment you gave me that box of old Christmas decorations.'

Luke kissed her again. Slowly. With infinite tenderness.

'And I was sure that first time you smiled at me.'

'When was that?'

'When I went along with that lie. When you said I'd come to the house to see how Summer was because I was her doctor. When you were protecting the other children.'

Amy grinned. 'You didn't act like you were in love with me.'

'I just hadn't realised it. I didn't understand what was happening to me. I do now.'

'I'm not sure I do.' Amy wrapped her arms around Luca's neck and brought her face close enough to kiss him. The tip of her nose touched his. 'But maybe I don't need to because it's magic. Christmas magic.'

'No.' His nose moved beneath hers as he shook his head. 'This magic is going to last a lifetime. So many Christmases you won't be able to count them, and every one of them will be magic.'

Amy could feel his breath on her lips and she closed her eyes as she waited for his kiss.

'Just like this,' she murmured.

'Always.'

Hours later. Many hours later, Luke was kissing Amy yet again. This time in the comfort of the glow the library fire was providing.

The house was almost as quiet as the hilltop had been because everyone else had long since gone to bed.

'This has been the most amazing day of my life,' Amy said, when she had a moment to catch her breath. 'Thank you.'

'What for?'

'For everything.' Amy started to count the reasons off on her fingers. 'For saving Summer and giving her a new chance of life. For bringing the children here. For that extraordinary pile of presents. For the Christmas dinner and having Mr Battersby here with those papers that gave the house to Mamma. For...*this*!' Amy held up her left hand.

Luke groaned. 'You're not supposed to be wearing that. It came out of a Christmas cracker, for heaven's sake. It's rubbish!'

It was. A lurid, square, pink stone stuck to a gaudy gold band, but Luke had offered it to her. In front of everybody, and it had been his choice to slip it onto the third finger of her left hand. Nobody had missed the significance of that gesture and the fabulous meal had become a celebration of far more than Christmas.

'I'm wearing it,' Amy said stubbornly.

'I'm replacing it, then,' Luke said firmly. 'With the real thing. As soon as the shops are open again. In fact, I'm sure Mr Barker wouldn't mind doing me one more small favour and I believe they have a wonderful selection of jewellery. I'll talk to him tomorrow.'

Amy sighed with contentment and gave herself up to another one of those kisses she would never, ever tire of. The clock in the corner was reminding them that the last minutes of this Christmas day might be ticking away but there still seemed to be plenty of magic in the air.

It was Luke who spoke when they reluctantly drew apart.

'It's me who should be thanking you,' he said.

'What for?'

'For giving my grandmother that scrapbook. I don't think she's ever going to put it down. She says she feels as if you've given her back part of her daughter. The happiest part.'

'Did you hear her say *"Buon Natale"* to Nonna?'

'Yes.' Luke smiled. 'Her accent was atrocious but it's a start, isn't it?' He held Amy close. 'You've changed everything for us, my love. Especially for me. I don't think I can ever tell you how grateful I am that I've found you. That, by some extraordinary miracle, you love me. It's too new. Too wonderful.'

'It's real,' Amy assured him. 'And this is my gift to you today, Luca. My love. My heart and soul. For ever.'

Luca's eyes were suspiciously bright. 'Then it's the same as my gift to you. *Buon Natale*, Amy.'

'*Buon Natale*, Luca.'

A sneaky peek at next month...

By Request
RELIVE THE ROMANCE WITH THE BEST OF THE BEST

My wish list for next month's titles...

3 stories in each book - only £5.99!

In stores from 18th November 2011:

☐ Christmas Kisses
  – Maggie Cox, Alison Roberts & Fiona Harper

☐ Pregnant with His Baby! – Kim Lawrence, Melanie Milburne & Laura Iding

In stores from 2nd December 2011:

☐ Billionaire Heirs – Tessa Radley

Available at WHSmith, Tesco, Asda, Eason, Amazon and Apple

Just can't wait?

Visit us Online

You can buy our books online a month before they hit the shops! **www.millsandboon.co.uk**

Book of the Month

MILLS & BOON

We love this book because...

Take one sweet-looking but tough-talking lawyer, add a supremely gorgeous hunk who's just inherited millions, then sit back and enjoy this sassy, flirty romance—finding love in NYC has *never* been so exciting!

On sale 2nd December

Visit us Online

Find out more at
www.millsandboon.co.uk/BOTM

1111/BOTM

Special Offers

Every month we put together collections and longer reads written by your favourite authors.

Here are some of next month's highlights— and don't miss our fabulous discount online!

On sale 18th November

On sale 18th November

On sale 18th November

Save 20%
on all Special Releases

Find out more at
www.millsandboon.co.uk/specialreleases

Visit us Online

 *Mills & Boon® Online*

Discover more romance at
www.millsandboon.co.uk

- 🌹 **FREE** online reads
- 🌹 **Books** up to one month before shops
- 🌹 **Browse our books** before you buy

...and much more!

For exclusive competitions and instant updates:

 Like us on **facebook.com/romancehq**

 Follow us on **twitter.com/millsandboonuk**

 Join us on **community.millsandboon.co.uk**

Visit us Online — Sign up for our FREE eNewsletter at **www.millsandboon.co.uk**